LATE CHECKOUT

Also by Carol J. Perry

LATE CHECKOUT

Carol J. Perry

KENSINGTON BOOKS
www.kensingtonbooks.com

KENSINGTON BOOKS are published by

Kensington Publishing Corp.
119 West 40th Street
New York, NY 10018

All Kensington titles, imprints, and distributed lines are available at special quantity discounts for bulk purchases for sales promotion, premiums, fund-raising, educational, or institutional use.

Special book excerpts or customized printings can also be created to fit specific needs. For details, write or phone the office of the Kensington Sales Manager: Attn.: Sales Department. Kensington Publishing Corp., 119 West 40th Street, New York, NY 10018. Phone: 1-800-221-2647.

Kensington and the K logo Reg. U.S. Pat. & TM Off.

First Printing: October 2019

ISBN-13: 978-1-4967-1462-6
ISBN-10: 1-4967-1462-8

ISBN-13: 978-1-4967-1463-3 (ebook)
ISBN-10: 1-4967-1463-6 (ebook)

10 9 8 7 6 5 4 3 2 1

Printed in the United States of America

For Dan, my husband and best friend

Author's Note

Sincere apologies to the Main Public Library
in my hometown of Salem, Massachusetts.
I have taken the liberty of completely
rearranging the interior of that fine historic
structure to suit my story.

For now we see through a glass darkly, but then face to face . . .

1 Corinthians, 13:12

Chapter 1

It was a cool, pretty October Friday morning in my home town of Salem, Massachusetts. My beautiful Laguna blue 2014 Chevrolet Stingray Corvette convertible was in the shop because some inconsiderate dope had run a shopping cart down one side of it, leaving a significant gouge in the passenger door. My aunt Ibby was in Boston at a librarians' convention, so her vintage but trustworthy Buick wasn't available either. My hours as a field reporter at WICH-TV had just been cut nearly in half because the station manager's wife's nephew had just graduated from broadcasting school and "needs some experience."

I'm Lee Barrett, nee Maralee Kowalski, thirty-three, red-haired, Salem born, orphaned early, married once, and widowed young. My aunt Isobel Russell and I share the fine old family home on Winter Street, along with our big yellow-striped gentleman cat, O'Ryan.

"Might as well walk to work," I grumbled to the cat, who watched with apparent interest as I pulled on cordovan boots over faded jeans, then tossed my NASCAR jacket over a white turtleneck shirt. "With the new schedule I don't have to get there until noon anyway." O'Ryan gave a sympathetic "Mmrrow," and followed me to my kitchen door and out into the front hall.

Aunt Ibby had surprised me with an apartment of my own on the third floor of the house when I returned from Florida a few years ago after the death of my race car driver husband, Johnny Barrett. Coming home to Salem had so far been a really good choice for me, and the field reporter job at WICH-TV had seemed like a dream come true.

"Listen, Ms. Barrett, this is only temporary," station manager Bruce Doan had said when he'd told me about my lowered occupational status. "The kid just needs a little television face time in local TV before he moves on. Meanwhile, your workload will be reduced, but you can still do your investigative reports on the late news once in a while." The "kid" in question was Buffy Doan's nephew, Howard Templeton. The reduction in income wasn't a problem. Between Johnny's insurance and the inheritance from my parents, I'm fine financially. Besides, Templeton seemed like a pleasant enough guy, but I was trying hard not to dislike him for disrupting my more or less orderly world. It was becoming a challenge.

I locked the kitchen door and started down the curvy, wide-banistered staircase to the first-floor foyer with O'Ryan padding along beside me. He paused at the arched entrance to Aunt Ibby's living room, peeked inside, then joined me at the front door. I patted his fuzzy head, wished him a nice day, unlocked the door, and stepped out onto our front steps facing Winter Street.

October days can be delightful in New England— some call it "Indian summer." This was such a day. Leaves had begun to turn to red and gold and the sky was an impossible shade of blue—think Maxfield Parrish paintings. My peevish mood began to melt away as I strolled along the edge of Salem Common, a pastoral oasis in the midst of a busy city. I waved across the wrought iron fence to Stasia, the pigeon lady who sat on her regular bench, surrounded by cooing birds. Across Washington Street, the tourist buses lined up in front of the Witch Museum while the massive statue of Roger Conant gazed down benignly upon us all. I could even smell the aroma of fresh, hot, buttery popcorn wafting from the same four-wheeled red-and-white wagon I remembered from my childhood.

Things aren't so bad, I told myself. *Howard Templeton will "move on" eventually. My car will be repaired in a day or so. I still have a job. I'm blessed to have my aunt who loves me, and Pete Mondello, the wonderful man in my life. Everything is going to be okay. . . .*

Those rose-colored glasses slipped off in a hurry when a horn tooted and the WICH-TV mobile van rolled past, a happily waving Templeton kid in the front seat and my favorite videographer, Francine Hunter, at the wheel. Great. That automatically left me riding around in the station's beat-up Volkswagen work van with Old Eddie for my driver. That's in case anything worth covering happened during my shift, and in case Scott Palmer—who wears about fourteen different hats around the station *including* occasional field reporter—didn't grab the call.

I turned onto Hawthorne Boulevard, kicked a crumpled-up candy wrapper aside (darned urban tumbleweed), trudged past the Nathaniel Hawthorne statue (old Nate, sitting up there, all famous and beloved), and headed for Derby Street, getting crabbier by the minute.

WICH-TV is housed in one of Derby Street's wonderful old waterfront brick buildings that hadn't been destroyed during the urban renewal madness of the 1950s. The front door opens onto the main lobby, where the brass-doored elevator still gleams and the black-and-white tiled floor is scrubbed daily. Before I went inside, I took a quick look into the adjacent harbor-side parking lot, checking to be sure Templeton hadn't glommed onto my parking space along with everything else. He hadn't.

Sometimes, in the interest of saving time, I use the metal stairway to the second-floor office suite, but being in no great hurry, I opted for "old clunky," trying not to focus on the brass panels. I have a thing about reflective surfaces. I'm what's called, in paranormal circles, a scryer. My best friend, River North, calls me a "gazer." River is a witch and one of the few people who know that sometimes when I look at a shiny object I see things that others can't see. Aunt Ibby knows all about my so-called "gift." My detective boyfriend, Pete, knows about it too, and struggles to understand it. That's all right. So do I.

I pressed the UP button. And waited.

The brass doors slid open and Scott Palmer stepped out. "Hi, Moon," he said. "Boy, am I glad to see you!" I've known Scott since I got my first job at WICH-TV. I was the last-minute replacement for late night show host and practicing witch, Ariel Constellation, who did psychic readings between old horror movies on a show called *Nightshades*. (Unfortunately, Ariel hadn't foreseen her own death and I was the one who'd found her body.) Anyway, I'd used the name Crystal Moon for that short-lived career and Scott sometimes still calls me Moon.

"Hi, yourself," I said. "When you're that happy to see me it usually means you want something."

"Yeah, well, I kinda do. Me and Old Eddie were all set to cover the golf tournament over at the Salem Country Club, when Doan decided he wants me spend my whole afternoon digging up background on some dead guy." He gave me the big smile and the long, innocent, deep-into-your-eyes look he's perfected. "How about it, Moon? You always liked that research stuff. Me? I'm all about action."

"I'd like to help, Scott," I said—because having been raised by a research librarian, I really *do* like that research stuff—"but my wheels are in the shop. I'm grounded. Stuck right here."

The smile faded for a fraction of a second, the eye thing didn't even flicker. "That's perfect. You can grab a company computer and do a fast workup on the guy."

"Who are we talking about anyway?" I asked. "Somebody famous?"

"I guess he was at one time. Name's Larry Laraby. Ring any bells?"

I frowned. The name was familiar. I snapped my fingers. "Sure. His picture is in the lobby. He worked here a long time ago."

"Right," Scott said. "Laraby was the station's first sports guy. Back in the sixties and seventies, I think. Anyway, will you do it? Old Eddie's waiting out front."

"Might as well, I guess," I said, "since you'll have the VW and Templeton has the mobile. By the way, why are we doing this?"

"The station's seventieth anniversary is coming up. Doan's planning some kind of special about the old-timers who worked here."

I thought about what I'd watched on WICH-TV when I was growing up. "I remember Katie the Clown. She used to do a kids' show in the morning."

"She's probably still around town somewhere. And did you watch Ranger Rob? He was on in the afternoon." A short laugh. "Hey, Phil Archer is still working here. He's pretty old. He might even remember Laraby." He gave me a quick salute and headed for the door. "Thanks, Moon. I owe you one."

The brass doors had closed by then, so I hit the UP button again. Scott was right about Phil Archer, the station's long-time news anchor. I remembered watching Phil on the evening news when I was a kid. Phil had since been moved to the noon news, so there was a good chance he'd still be in the building.

As the elevator clunked its slow way up to the second floor, I thought about a simple plan. Just a little something to fill my spare time until Howard Templeton "moved on."

Sometimes even the simplest little plan can turn serious.

Deadly serious.

Chapter 2

I pushed open the glass door to the office suite and wished a "good morning" to Rhonda, the station's way-smarter-than-she-looks receptionist.

"Hi, Lee." She pointed to the dry-erase schedule board behind her desk. "I don't have anything booked for you yet today. Mr. Doan said for you to just stand by in case anything turns up. By the way, Scott was just in here looking for you."

"Yep. Saw him downstairs. He needs some help on the Larry Laraby project. I can work on that, if it's okay."

"Don't see why not. I'll put you on the schedule." She scribbled my name in red marker under the heading "Anniversary show."

"Thanks. Is Phil Archer still here? I think I'll start with interviewing him."

"He's still down in the newsroom. I think he hates to leave this place."

"I know. It must seem like a second home to him, he's been here so long." I opened a green metal door and headed down the long narrow corridor leading to the newsroom. The glass-enclosed studio is by far the most impressive space in the building, with a floor-to-ceiling wall of monitors, banks of overhead lights, and a handsome curvy anchor desk backed by a panoramic photo of the Salem Common that changes with the seasons. The scene of the moment showed trees ablaze with fall colors. Even the offscreen positions manned by technical crew members, directors, and editorial staff looked attractive and comfortable. I spotted Phil Archer watching the BBC monitor. I checked to be sure the red on-the-air light was off and let myself into the studio.

Phil agreed right away to help with the Larry Laraby project. "I remember him well," he said. "Strange how he died, wasn't it?"

"Sorry," I said. "I'm starting from scratch here. I don't know the first thing about the man."

"No reason you would. It was a long time ago—in the seventies. I was a young intern here and Larry was sports reporter. A real V.I.P. in the New England sports world. He'd been with the station from the beginning and knew all the big stars, Larry Bird, Johnny Bucyk, Carl Yastrzemski, Bobby Orr."

"You said his death was . . . strange?"

"A lot of people thought so." He nodded. "Yes. A lot of people. Anyway, he'd retired from the station and was going all over the country managing a sports collectibles show. You know, baseball cards, autographed footballs, game jerseys. It was a big business." *I know that. I have a sizable collection of NASCAR memorabilia stashed in Aunt Ibby's basement.*

"What happened to him?" I asked.

He shrugged. "His wife found him dead one morning in their house. Found him in his library. He had a huge collection of sports books. I heard he was even planning on writing one himself. Anyway, there was poor Larry, dead on the floor with his books scattered all around him. He had one of those moving ladders that reach to top bookshelves. They said he must have fallen off of it. Broke his neck. They said that's what killed him."

"You didn't believe it?"

"No. But hey, that's just me. I probably shouldn't have said anything. Come on. I'll show you where the old videos are. That's a good place to start."

He was right. I viewed a couple of hours of Larry Laraby's videotaped sports shows, taking notes all the while. By three-thirty I felt that I had a pretty good over-all idea of what the man was like. Knowledgeable and passionate about sports. Good sense of humor. Happy at his work. *I would like to have known him.*

Aunt Ibby had planned to be home from Boston by four, so I phoned her to beg a ride home. "Of course I'll pick you up, Maralee," she said. "I have to stop at the library for a bit though. We have a new woman on the desk and I want to help her close. You don't mind coming in with me for a few minutes, do you?"

I laughed at that. "Did I ever mind going to the library?"

I clocked out with Rhonda, asked her to try to fix me up with a ride and camera for the next day's shift and—using the stairs instead of the elevator—hurried down to the lobby and out onto Derby Street to meet my aunt.

She pulled the Buick into the parking lot, stopping just behind the bench bearing a memorial plaque for Ariel Constellation. That bench was a gift from Ariel's coven. Our fine cat O'Ryan is, in a way, a gift from Ariel too. He was a regular feature on her late-night show, *Night-shades*. I inherited both the show *and* the cat. Some say O'Ryan was Ariel's "familiar." In Salem a witch's famil-iar is always much respected and often feared. He came to live with us and seems to be pleased with the arrange-ment. So are we.

I was interested in what my aunt would think about my plan for filling the idle hours my shortened work schedule had created. At least it would beat binge-watching back-to-back seasons of *The Bachelorette* or joining Stasia feeding pigeons on the Common. I began talking before I'd even closed the car door. "I have an idea."

"Good," she said. "Tell me about it."

"Since I have more time off than I want, and the library can always use volunteers, why don't I spend some half-days helping out there instead of wandering around feeling sorry for myself?"

"Oh, dear. Is *that* what you're doing? I think shelving books is a much better alternative."

"So you can use the help?"

"Absolutely. Give us as many hours as you can."

"Thank you. I'm thinking I can get some work done while I'm there on another assignment for the station that Scott Palmer kind of passed on to me." I told her about the Larry Laraby project.

"I remember him," she said. "Sports, right?"

"Uh-huh. Scott and I talked about some of the other old WICH-TV shows too. We remembered Katie the Clown and Ranger Rob."

"Of course. And you always loved watching Professor Mercury and his Magical Science Circus."

"Oh, he was amazing," I remembered, smiling, "and you used to let me mess up the kitchen doing experiments. There was a lot more local programing for kids back then, wasn't there? Maybe we could come up with an idea for a new kid show."

"Of course they have Nickelodeon and the Disney Channel now." She pulled the Buick into her reserved spot behind the library. "But I'll just bet we could come up with a good one if we put our heads together."

"Yep. We sure could." I pulled down the visor mirror to check my hair. Bad move. I saw the flashing lights and swirling colors that always precede a vision. My immediate instinct was to push the visor back up. Too late. The image filled the oblong space.

A row of books was lined up on a shelf. I squinted, leaning closer to the mirror. *What's that thing sticking out underneath?*

The vision obliged, as they sometimes do, with a zoom-lens kind of close-up. It was a shoe. A man's shiny black shoe. A man's shiny black shoe with a maroon ribbed dress sock on the foot wearing it.

Then the picture was gone and all there was in the mirror was a confused redhead.

Chapter 3

The whole mirror episode was over so quickly I was sure my aunt hadn't noticed that anything unusual had just happened.

"Come along, dear," Aunt Ibby said. "There'll be a little bit of paperwork for you to fill out."

"Coming." I slid out of the passenger seat and joined her, still thinking of the vision and remembering what Phil Archer had told me about Larry Laraby. "His wife found him on the floor," he'd said. "With books all around him."

I've learned that the visions can show things from the past, the present, and even the future. *Did I just see Larry Laraby's foot as he lay dead on the floor among his books?* I tried to shake the thought away.

We entered the old building via the side entrance, stepping aside as a parade of about fifteen chattering preteens tumbled through the door and out into the parking lot. "Musical story time," my aunt said. "Three-thirty to four-thirty. Middle school kids. Enthusiastic bunch."

I love the smell of the library. Every time I enter one I take a deep breath. This time was no different. I followed my aunt to the main desk, breathing in the lovely scents of paper and bindings and ink and floor polish and pencil shavings and new magazines and old paperbacks, all the while trying to focus on volunteer work instead of on a dead man's foot.

My aunt introduced me to the new librarian, Tyler Dickson. "This was Tyler's first full day working here alone," Aunt Ibby said as I shook the woman's hand. "I'm sure everything went smoothly?" It was a statement, phrased as a question.

Tyler smiled, flashing great dimples. "I had an absolutely wonderful day," she said. "I was never rushed—of course Friday is a slow day anyway—but everyone was so kind and understanding about my being new here. I'm going to love this job."

"I'm glad to hear it," Aunt Ibby said. "Maralee will be volunteering here part time so you'll soon get to know one another." Tyler gave a little wave, said, "Nice to meet you," and headed for the checkout desk while my aunt pulled a booklet and several sheets of paper from a file cabinet and handed them to me. "Just fill these out, Maralee, then tell me more about this project of Scott's we'll be working on."

"He's just looking for information on Larry Laraby, as far as I know. The other names, like Katie the Clown and Ranger Rob, just popped up in conversation. But Scott said that Mr. Doan is planning an anniversary celebration featuring the old-timers."

She caught on right away. "So you'd like to work on doing a kind of 'what ever happened to' piece for one of your investigative reports."

"Exactly." I pulled a pen from my purse and began filling out the volunteer application. Name, address, birth date, Social Security number, education, previous volunteer experience, references, skills, driver's license . . . I smiled as I wrote down Buffy Doan's name as a reference—why not? She was the main reason I was here. My previous volunteer experience included spending time along with Johnny visiting patients at VA hospitals. (A lot of those great guys and gals are NASCAR fans.) I've put in quite a few volunteer hours at animal shelters too, both in Salem and Florida, and I spent a summer once volunteering as property manager for the acting division of Salem's Tabitha Trumbull Academy of the Arts.

My aunt watched, obviously amused, as I carefully wrote down each answer. "You don't have to fuss with that, you know Maralee. You've got the job. I guarantee it."

I answered the last question—"How did you hear about this position?"—by writing my aunt's name, then signing, dating, and handing the pages to her. "Anything worth doing is worth doing well," I said, repeating one of her many favorite sayings. "Remember?" I returned the pen to my purse, along with the slim *Handbook for Library Volunteers*. "Okay. Where do I start?"

"First, you'll need an official ID," she said. "It's just a temporary one for now, but I'll order the real one for you right away." She pulled a round paper badge from her top drawer. It was marked "volunteer" and had a space for my name. She used a black marker, printed Maralee Barrett in neat block letters, removed the sticky back, and handed it to me. "Wear it proudly," she said as I positioned it on my turtleneck. "Now, shelving the returned books is always a good place to begin." She gestured toward a wheeled wire basket filled to overflowing with books. "I know you're familiar with the Dewey decimal system."

I am. Not too many home libraries are arranged according to Dewey, but ours is. The book on top of the pile was *Women in the Civil War,* so pushing the cart toward the 900s (history, geography), I began my first day as a library volunteer.

I fell into a sort of rhythm, wheeling the cart up and down the aisles, putting each book in its proper place. I found myself studying the bottom row of books in every aisle, as though I expected to see a foot sticking out from under a bookcase. Before long the wire cart was empty. I returned to the front desk, proud of myself for finishing so quickly.

My aunt had been busy too. She greeted me by waving a sheet of copy paper in my direction. "Maralee," she whispered, using her librarian voice. "See what I've found."

I hurried around the desk and stood behind her chair. "Look at this," she said. "I've located Ranger Rob for you. His real name is Robert Oberlin and he still lives in the area. Has a horse stable over in Rockport."

"That was fast." I peered at the paper. "Is that him?" I pointed to a blurred newspaper photo.

"That's what the caption says. Looks like he's put on a few pounds over the years, doesn't it?"

"That doesn't look like the skinny young cowboy with the fringed shirt and tight jeans I remember," I said. "Played a guitar too, didn't he?"

She nodded. "He did. And didn't he have a sidekick? Little guy? He wore a big white cowboy hat and had a handlebar mustache."

"Cactus," I said. "His name was Cactus. Maybe we can find him too. This could turn out to be fun."

"It could." She pointed to another cart full of books. "But right now, you have work to do."

"You're right." I grasped the handle, picked up the book on top of the pile—*Cats: Antics and Attitudes.* I smiled, thought of O'Ryan, and headed for the 590 shelves. The rest of the full cart was easy to shelve too and I discovered that even though I was "working," I didn't have to give this job my full attention. My mind raced as I considered various ways I might put together an investigative report on WICH-TV's old-time talent.

I'd reached the bottom of the cart and had only one item left. It was a notebook with handwritten lined pages.

It appeared to be a journal about gardening and bore no number on its spine or cover.

I returned to the desk and showed the notebook to my aunt. "Sorry," I said. "I couldn't figure this one out."

"No wonder. It doesn't belong there." She opened the slim book. "It's marked on the inside cover, see?" She pointed to the stairway behind her. "It goes up there. In the stacks. Better hurry. Stacks close in a few minutes. Tyler's already starting to check customers out."

I glanced at the clock. Children's room, reference area, and stacks always close fifteen minutes before the main desk does. I made a face. I don't like the stacks. Even when I was in high school and college, I never went up there alone. When I was around six, I wandered away from my aunt and climbed those stairs. "The stacks" refers to a book storage area, away from the general reading space. The bookcases up there aren't solid, wooden structures like the ones downstairs. There are no plants or teddy bears or autographed pictures of famous authors placed here and there to make it friendly. The unpainted metal shelves are on wheels so they can be moved around. I imagined that rats or snakes could crawl out from the space underneath the bottom shelves where those ugly black wheels were. It's been improved since I was six, with a few blonde wood chairs and tables and much better lighting, but back then it was dark and spooky and the narrow aisles with tall steel shelves towered over me. I was terrified until Aunt Ibby heard my cries and rescued me.

She recognized the pouty face. "Go along now. It belongs in a vertical file marked Salem Gardens. It's in the 580 section." She waved a dismissive hand. "Go along."

So, reluctantly, I did. I tucked the notebook under my arm and trudged toward the staircase. I glanced back to see if she was watching me. She was.

*Oh, get over yourself. You're a big girl. Paste on a
fake smile and climb right up there!*

Shoulders back, head up, eyes front, I ran up the stairs.
Looked for the numbers at the ends of the tall steel
shelves. *580-Plants*. I filed the notebook properly.

See? This isn't so bad.

And it wasn't. Right up until I passed the *790-Sports*
aisle on my way back to the stairs and saw the foot sticking out from under the bottom shelf right beside the
wheels. I very nearly screamed aloud, just as my lost,
frightened six-year-old-self had cried out all those years
ago. I clapped a hand over my mouth. This wasn't a vision in a car mirror. The foot was real. It wore a dark blue
athletic shoe and a grimy white sock. It was a small shoe.
Dear God, don't let it be an injured child. Very slowly,
deliberately, I forced myself to walk all the way to the
end of the aisle so that I could see the other side of that
long, dimly lighted row of shelves—so that I could see
the rest of whoever that foot belonged to.

Even before I saw the man—because surely it was a
man and not a child—I saw the jumble of books. The narrow aisle was strewn with them. Some lay open, their
pages crumpled, even torn. Some sprawled, tentlike, bent
leaves splayed out on the gray floor while ragged-edged
sheets of printed words, ripped from cast-aside volumes,
littered the confined space from end to end. I hardly
dared breathe.

Phil Archer's words rang once more in my mind. "There
was poor Larry," he'd said. "Dead on the floor, with his
books scattered all around him."

The man was spread-eagled, head propped at an unnatural angle against an old wooden card catalog file cabinet. His face was partly obscured by long gray hair and
one leg was hidden from the knee down by metal shelving. I didn't attempt to move any closer. He was obviously

dead. I backed away, rounding the corner to the aisle where the reproachful foot still protruded. I squeezed my eyes shut, feeling once again all of the horror, the fear, the need to escape from this dark scary place that six-year old-Maralee Kowalski had felt all those many years ago.

I found myself shaking, somehow sitting upright in one of the blonde wood study chairs as I tried to will Phil Archer's words away. *That was then. This is now. This isn't a vision. It isn't even the same shoe. That poor soul isn't Larry Laraby. Get out of here and call 911!*

Then, instinctively observing long-established library etiquette, I walked quickly, but quietly, down the stairs while calling 911 on my cell.

Chapter 4

My aunt, as always, remained calm as I whispered my startling message, including the fact that I'd already called 911. "I'm sure the man is dead," I stammered, trying hard to stay composed. "He's just lying there with his eyes open among all those books, not seeing anything." She nodded, and within what seemed like seconds, she'd blocked the stairway leading to the stacks with a velvet rope and a discreet "no admittance" sign.

By then I'd called Pete. He answered on the first ring. "Lee, I saw your name on the 911 call," he said. "What's going on over there? Dispatcher says there's someone on the floor unresponsive. EMTs and a couple of cruisers are on the way. I'm following because—well, because you're there. You okay?"

"Yes. Sure. I'm fine," I said, not at all sure that I really was. "There's a man on the floor up in the stacks. He looks dead. I didn't touch him. And there were books all over the place. We've blocked off the stairs. Is there anything else we should do before you get here? People are starting to check out. We close at five."

"About how many people are in there now?"

I looked around. "I'm at the front desk. The children's section and reference are already closed along with the stacks. I see eight library patrons, and of course there's Aunt Ibby and the new librarian Tyler Dickson and me. Oh, Dave Benson, the night security guard, just came in the front door. So there're a dozen of us in here right now."

"We're almost there," he said. "Ask your aunt to try to slow down the checkout process, will you? We'll want to ask questions. What are you doing there? Did you recognize the guy?"

"I was here signing up to volunteer my spare time," I said. I whispered Pete's request to my aunt and she moved over to the nearby checkout desk and spoke a few words to Tyler. "I didn't get close enough to recognize the—uh—the deceased," I told him. "Sorry."

"That's okay. We're pulling up out front. I'll be right in."

I heard the wail of sirens from outside. I knew that a 911 call like mine would result in the arrival of an assortment of first responders. EMTs, Salem fire department paramedics, and police officers would parade through the library and up the stairs to the stacks. If, and when, the victim turned out to be beyond help—which I was pretty sure would be the case this time—the EMTs and SFD people would soon leave and the medical examiner would be called. Then, if the death seemed to be an "unnatural" one, if it appeared that a crime had taken place, the police would take over and the CSI team would arrive with all of their technical expertise.

Actually, that was just about the way it all played out.

The EMTs were first through the door, followed by three uniformed officers, causing quite a commotion among the few library patrons, who until then had no idea that anything was amiss. One of the uniforms led the EMTs upstairs, while another stood next to my aunt and politely checked IDs, took contact information from each person, then escorted them, one by one, to the front door, locking it after each one exited the building. The third officer headed down the corridor toward the side door. Pete had arrived just behind the paramedics, watching as they followed the EMTs up the stairs. He spoke to the officer and my aunt briefly, paused at the checkout desk where Tyler had remained, then walked over to where I stood. I'd posted myself at the foot of the stairs, replacing the velvet rope as each group passed. I was so happy and relieved to see him that I almost cried.

Pete stood as close to me as he possibly could without tipping off everyone in the room that he and I shared a bed on a regular basis and I resisted an almost overwhelming urge to bury my face on his shoulder. He smelled even better than the library. "How're you holding up, babe?" he murmured. "Want to sit down and tell me what happened here?" He gestured to a nearby cluster of four matching armchairs.

I nodded. "I'm okay. It's been a bad day." I sat facing him as Dave Benson, the tall, white-haired nighttime guard took over the velvet rope duty.

Pete pulled a worn brown leather notebook and a stubby pencil from an inside pocket. "You told the 911 operator you'd found an unresponsive male on the floor," he prompted, using what I call his "cop voice."

"Unresponsive was her word, not mine," I said. "I didn't touch him. I'm sure I said something like 'he's not moving.'"

"Right. Go ahead. Describe what you saw."

"I was filing a returned book up in the stacks." I waved a hand in the general direction of "up." "On my way back I passed the sports section and saw a foot sticking out from under one of the tall steel shelving units they use up there."

"Sticking out?"

"Yeah. Like the person was on the floor on the opposite side with just one leg poked underneath. There are books lined up on both sides all the way up so there's no way to see into the next aisle. The shoe looked small. I was afraid a child might be hurt up there."

"So you walked around and looked?"

"Well, of course I did." Sometimes Pete's attention to every little detail can be exasperating, but that's the way cops work. "The shoe was near the end of a section that backs up to a wall. I walked to the entrance of the aisle and looked down to where he was lying on the floor."

"You mean the shoe with a foot in it?" He glanced up from the notebook. "Not just a shoe."

I sighed, nodded again. "That's when I saw the man and all the books on the floor."

"Books on the floor?" He put down his pencil. "Did you tell the 911 dispatcher that? About books on the floor?"

"I don't think so. But anyway there were—there are—books scattered around. Torn, messed up, thrown all over the aisle, pages ripped out. What a mess. I didn't touch anything," I said, trying to anticipate the next question.

The officer appeared at the head of the stairs. "Detective Mondello? You might want to come up here and take a look at this."

Pete stood. Frowned. Stuffed the notebook and pencil back into his pocket. "Books scattered around on the floor? Why didn't you say so?"

I frowned back. "I told you there were books all over the place."

"Sure! This is a library!" He hit those stairs at a dead run.

Chapter 5

My aunt and Tyler joined me and the three of us sat in a small, still circle, waiting to see what would happen next. Aunt Ibby broke the silence. "Maralee, do you know why Pete dashed upstairs like that?"

"Not exactly," I admitted. "It has to do with those books tossed around on the floor."

Her green eyes grew wide and Tyler actually gasped. "Books?" Aunt Ibby stood, facing the stairway. "*Our* books? On the floor? *Tossed*? Why didn't you say so?"

"Aunt Ibby, I'd just found a dead body. All I could think of was to call 911. I told you about the books as soon as I came down the stairs. I'm sure I did. I remember. I told you he was lying there among the books. Anyway, a few ripped-up books didn't seem so important at the moment."

"Of course he was among books. This is a library! You didn't say anything about *ripped-up* books! Actually *ripped up*? Our books? Good heavens, Maralee. Why didn't you say so?"

Tyler shook her head and twisted her hands. "Oh my God. Ripped books."

I was speaking to professional librarians—women who'll agonize for a full day over a turned down page corner. "I'm sorry I wasn't more specific." I knew I sounded snarky. "I thought reporting a death was more important. Will everybody please stop asking me why I didn't go into detail about a few old books?"

"*OLD* books? Exactly where were you in the stacks?" My aunt sat down. "What section?"

"The seven-nineties," I said, redundantly adding "sports."

Pete appeared at the top of the stairway, hesitated for a moment, then pulled the notebook and pencil from his pocket and started down the stairs. He wore his cop face.

"I have a few questions I need to ask you ladies," he said, pulling up the fourth chair in our little circle and sitting opposite me. "First, Ms. Russell. I presume there are video cameras placed throughout the library."

"Yes indeed," my aunt declared. "They cover most of this old building. Pete, how bad is it up there? I mean the books?"

"You can inventory as soon as we're finished." He scribbled in the notebook. "Multiple cameras," he mumbled, then looked up. "Where's the monitor?"

"It's right behind the high part of the main desk," Tyler said. "A quad split screen. Eight cameras I think."

"Eight cameras," Aunt Ibby agreed, counting them off on her fingers. "Front door, side door, main floor, children's, reference, parking lot, mezzanine, and stacks."

"Does the stacks camera show every aisle?" Pete wanted to know.

"Oh, no," Aunt Ibby said. "Just the seating area and the outer rows of shelves. It's the least used part of the library. The main floor camera shows us who goes up and down the stairs. That's always seemed good enough for our purposes."

"Until today." Tyler spoke softly. "I can show you

today's videos though. I'm pretty sure not many people went up there. Three or four, maybe."

"Well," Pete said, "one didn't come back down. I have to ask you to turn the videos over to us."

"Of course we will," Aunt Ibby promised.

The EMTs and the paramedics started down the stairs just as the officer at the door admitted the medical examiner. The folding stretcher the first responders had carried up to the stacks was still folded. I recognized the M.E. "Hello, Doc," I said.

"Ms. Barrett. Detective." Doc Egan and I have met several times—unfortunately in similar situations to this one. He acknowledged the others with a polite nod and hurried toward the stairs.

"Maralee, about how many books would you estimate have been damaged up there?" My aunt lifted her chin, eyes flicking upward.

I thought about that scene, trying to remember details. "I think most of them might just be soiled from being thrown around, you know? There are some bent pages though, and a few that are torn. I'm afraid there's at least one page that was all balled up." Aunt Ibby cringed slightly and Tyler looked stricken. "I'm sure the badly damaged ones can be replaced." I tried to sound encouraging. "We can easily fix the others up. I remember how you taught me, Aunt Ibby. Soft-tipped paintbrushes, art gum erasers, Absorene, air canisters." I had to smile at the memories of after-school book-cleaning sessions at this very library. "It could be fun."

"I'll see that the books are returned to you as soon as we finish our investigation, Ms. Russell," Pete said. "I promise we'll handle them carefully."

"I'm sure you will," she said. "Do you know what happened to the poor man, Pete? Was it a heart attack? I hope he didn't slip and fall. I hope it wasn't somehow our fault."

"We'll know more when the doctor finishes, but no. I don't believe the library was at fault here."

"Pete," I said, "the books thrown around mean something, don't they? Something important."

"They do, Lee. I guess there's no harm in telling you. We had a B and E a few weeks ago where the same thing happened. Books thrown around in the homeowner's study."

"Oh, dear," my aunt said. "Was anyone hurt there?"

"No. Fortunately no one was at home. There was a mess to clean up though. Just like here." Pete looked up as the officer once again opened the front door. "Oh-oh. Here's the crew from the coroner's office. Excuse me." He hurried to the entranceway where two jump-suited attendants maneuvered a wheeled gurney into the building. I recognized the coroner, although I hadn't seen him often enough to know him by name. *I guess that's a good thing.*

Pete spoke with the men briefly, then returned to where we sat. "Is there an elevator in the building?" he asked.

Aunt Ibby shook her head. "Regrettably, no. This is a designated historic building, you know. It was the mansion of one of Salem's early sea captains, so we're somewhat limited in structural changes we can make. We adhere to city and county codes, of course, and to the Americans with Disabilities Act. We've been able to install wheelchair ramps in the main areas, the mezzanine, and at the side door, but no. No elevator to the stacks. Staff delivers whatever the patron wants from up there if they're unable to manage the stairs."

"It's okay. We can bring him down on a stretcher. He's a small guy. We'll try to finish up here tonight so we won't have to close you down for the weekend."

I knew what that meant. "So this wasn't a natural death?"

Pete hesitated. "No. It wasn't. Ms. Russell, you may want to notify your superiors about what's going on. I expect we'll be here much of the night."

Aunt Ibby nodded and walked to the main desk with Tyler close behind her. I stalled until Pete moved back to where the coroner waited, then pulled my phone from my jeans pocket. If some poor guy had died in the stacks from a heart attack, that's sad, but it's not news. This was—and I wasn't about to hand it over to Howard Templeton. Or Scott Palmer either.

Chapter 6

A glance at the clock told me that Bruce Doan had probably left the office and headed home. It was nearly seven. I tapped in his personal number and rehearsed what I'd say about what was happening up in the stacks. If he agreed—and I was pretty sure he would—he'd send someone with a camera down here and I'd get to do a standup field report in front of the library.

He answered, sounding none too pleased about being called at home. "Yes, Ms. Barrett. What do you want?"

I used my library voice, speaking softly and slowly. "I'm at the Salem main library watching the coroner's crew carry a litter up to the stacks to pick up a body. There's a man up there who didn't die of natural causes. I need a cameraman."

His tone changed. "Gotcha. Francine will be there pronto."

I slipped the phone into my back pocket and picked up my NASCAR jacket from the back of a chair. Pete followed the coroner to the stairs and paused as he passed me. "See you later tonight?" he whispered.

"Yep. Whenever you're through here."

"Have you got a ride home?"

"I'll wait for Aunt Ibby. She'll have to stay here until one of the board members shows up, I guess." I hesitated, then continued. "Uh, Pete?"

"Yeah?" He looked impatiently toward the stairs.

"I called the station. I'm going outside for a little while. Francine's on her way."

He shook his head. "Not surprised. Tell the officer at the door I okayed your exit and return. See you later."

Sometimes our two jobs complement each other and sometimes they get all tangled up. We're learning to accept our professional differences with a lot less stress than we used to. He wasn't going to like my reporting on the dead man in the stacks, but he knows how important being first with breaking news is to me.

I stopped at the main desk to tell Aunt Ibby what I was doing. I knew *she* wasn't going to like the fact that this involved the library, but she knows that news is news wherever it happens. If I didn't break this story, someone else would. I gave the officer Pete's message. He looked back to where Pete still stood at the foot of the stairs. I saw Pete give him a "thumbs-up" signal, and the door swung open.

The county coroner's long black van waited at the curb, engine purring, a driver still at the wheel. As I walked down the library steps I saw the WICH-TV mobile pulling into the nearly empty parking lot, a smiling Francine waving to me.

I hurried around to the side of the building, following the mobile unit. Francine parked beside Aunt Ibby's Buick and was already unloading camera and mics from the side door by the time I caught up. "So what's going on?" She handed me a stick mic. "This okay? Would you rather have the lavalier? Doan just told me to get my fanny over here. What happened?"

I accepted the handheld mic. I like the way it looks on

screen. "There's a dead man up in the stacks," I explained, as I helped unload the portable video lighting kit. "They're working on bringing him down right now. No ID yet, but Pete says he didn't die of natural causes. The CSI team has arrived. That kind of proves it."

"Pete's here?" She closed and locked the van doors.

"Yeah. He came because I was the one who made the 911 call."

"You did?" We'd reached the front steps. "Want to do it here? On the steps?"

"I don't think so. What if they bring the body out and we're in the way?"

She smiled. "Doan would love that shot, but I guess you're right. How about you stand next to the big tree so the building is at an angle behind you. Everybody knows it's the library but we won't be zooming in on some poor dead guy. And you might want to take that off." She pointed to the "volunteer" sticker on my shirt.

"Oh, right. Thanks." I peeled it off, folding it into little squares, sticking it in my jeans pocket as I headed for the oak tree. "Let's hurry up before the other stations figure out what's going on. We'll get an eight o'clock teaser, then it'll probably be the lead on the eleven o'clock news."

"Maybe by then we'll know some more," Francine said.

"Maybe." I was doubtful. "The cops plan to be working in there until really late tonight. By tomorrow morning we might have something though."

We had lights and camera set up in minutes. Francine and I were a good team. I touched up my makeup and took my position in front of the tree. The library outdoor lights were on and the tall windows glowed from inside. The old building looked beautiful.

I did a quick mic test, then began. "Ladies and gentlemen, Lee Barrett here at Salem's main library on Essex

Street. Earlier this evening a man was discovered, unresponsive, in the library's upstairs stacks. He's been declared dead by the medical examiner. A member of the local police department has indicated that the unidentified man did not die of natural causes. The county coroner is in attendance. A library staff member reported that there was some damage to library property in the area where the man was discovered. The exact cause of death has not been determined. Stay tuned to WICH-TV for further updates on this breaking story as they become available. If you were in the vicinity of the Salem main library this afternoon and observed anything unusual, or if you have any information relating to this matter, please call the number at the bottom of your screen. I'm Lee Barrett reporting from the Salem main library for WICH-TV."

Francine signaled a wrap. "Sixty seconds on the button, Lee. Good job. I'll send this back to Marty at the station and remind her to scroll in the police department number."

"I hope we can get some more information by tomorrow," I said. "No name, no cause of death, and no suspects doesn't make for much of a story." We gathered up our equipment.

"Talked to your hot cop about it yet?"

"Not very much. We just talked about what I saw."

"Like what? What did you see?"

"I found the guy." We walked back in the direction of the mobile unit. "His foot was sticking out from under a bookcase."

"Sheesh. You have all the fun. I was covering the Manchester Dog Show with Templeton while you're over here hanging out with cops and the ME, the coroner and the corpse. Not fair."

I had to smile at Francine's idea of fun. We secured the mics, camera, and sound equipment in the back of the mobile. Francine looked around the parking lot. "Your car still in the shop? Want to ride back to the station with me? You can tell me all about finding the dead guy."

"Thanks, but no. Aunt Ibby is still here. She can't leave until one of the directors shows up. I didn't get a close look at the dead guy but I'll tell you about it tomorrow. And sorry to say, my car's not ready yet."

"Bummer. Well, let us know if anything interesting goes down here. I don't mind coming back." She climbed into the front seat, waved, and turned onto Essex Street. Seconds after she'd left, the library front door swung open. With a uniformed officer standing at each side, the wheeled gurney emerged, followed by the coroner and pushed by the jump-suited technicians onto the wide granite portico. The dark blue body bag looked oddly small on the long, white padded surface. Quickly, efficiently, the sad burden was transferred into the black van, the coroner took his place in the passenger seat, and the vehicle headed east on Essex Street into the darkness. I watched until the taillights were out of sight, then climbed the library steps once more.

I tapped on the glass panel and waited for an officer to let me in. One appeared, shaded his eyes, moved close to the glass, and peered at me. It wasn't the same cop who'd let me out, so returning took some back-and-forth. He asked me to show ID, which I couldn't do because my handbag was still inside. Finally, a not-too-happy-about-it Pete was called down from the stacks to identify me, and the door swung open.

"Sorry," I said.

"It's all right. I have a few questions I need to ask you." *Cop voice. Cop face too.* I halfway expected him to call me "ma'am." Pete took my arm and steered me toward the chairs where we'd talked earlier. Tyler and Aunt Ibby looked up as we passed. They got a curt nod from Pete and I managed a wave and a smile. *Big-time cop face.* I sat in the chair he indicated. He pulled another one close to mine. "Listen, Lee. It looks like the guy was recently killed. Like *very* recently. He was still warm when the EMTs checked for vitals. It seems possible that whoever caused his death either left minutes before you found him—or was still up there with you."

Chapter 7

It took a few seconds for what he'd just said to register. *A killer might have been there in the stacks. With me. Watching me.*

"I need you to think back to when you were up there. When you noticed the foot sticking out, when you went around the corner, when you first saw the man—the books. Try to remember. A sound? A smell?" He reached for my hands, cop face gone. "It's important, babe. I know you—sometimes—well, you see things, sense things other people might not." He rubbed my hands. "Your hands are freezing. I scared you, didn't I? I'm sorry. But can you think of anything you haven't told me? Any little thing?"

I closed my eyes and tried to focus on those moments. Some of it was kind of blurred. *Concentrate. You can do this. You're a reporter, for God's sake. You're trained to remember details.* The foot. The man. The books. The foot came first—not the one in the car mirror. Pete didn't even know about that one. Nobody did. I thought about the foot in the dark blue sneaker. Grimy socks. "There was an S on it," I said with my eyes still shut. "Skechers, maybe?"

"Good," Pete said. "What else?"

I thought about smells. The nice library smell was there, just a little different from the main floors. "Musty books," I said without opening my eyes. "Old book smell."

Pete didn't answer but I pictured him nodding his head.

Sounds. Was there a sound? I thought back to the moment I'd seen the man. Awkwardly sprawled. One leg partially hidden under the bookcase. Books all around him. But a sound? The normal library noises must have been there. A low hum of muted conversations. Outdoor noises when the front door was opened. A click. Was there a click? A light switch being turned on? The turn of a doorknob?

My eyes flew open. "A door, Pete. I heard a door open and close."

"A door nearby? Or downstairs?"

"Not really nearby. But not downstairs. It could have been the old exit door I guess."

"There's a door at the very back of the stacks," he said. "It's marked Emergency Exit. Is that what you mean?"

"I guess so. That's the only door up there. It's part of the old mansion. I think it leads down to where the original kitchen used to be. I'm not sure. Never used it."

"Good," he said again. "That's helpful. Anything else?"

I closed my eyes. Thought about those moments in the stacks. "No," I said. "Nothing else."

He let go of my hands and stood. "Thanks, babe. I'd better get back up there. We're bagging the books one at a time. Then the CSI team will take over. Tell your aunt we're all being careful."

"I will." I looked back toward the front door where two men I recognized as members of the library board had just been admitted. My aunt hurried to meet them.

"Looks as though Aunt Ibby and I will be able to leave soon," I said. "Library brass just arrived."

"I should be through here before midnight," he said. "Still okay with you if I come over? I'll bring ice cream."

"An offer I can't refuse," I said. Dave unhooked the velvet rope once again and Pete started up the stairs while I approached the main desk where my aunt and Tyler were in animated conversation with the two new arrivals.

One of the men pointed toward the top of the stairway, where a stern-faced uniformed officer stood in an almost military posture, while my aunt gestured toward the front door. The second gentleman had joined Tyler behind the checkout desk, where, with earnest expressions, they appeared to be viewing the security monitor beneath the high counter. I joined the group as unobtrusively as I could, with a polite nod of recognition directed toward the library board members.

Aunt Ibby smiled brightly in my direction, grasping my elbow and pulling me toward her. "My niece, Maralee Barrett, is our newest volunteer," she said. "It was she who discovered the poor soul—up there." She faced the staircase, tipping her head back, looking up. "A thoroughly disconcerting experience as you can imagine. I'm sure I speak for my niece and Ms. Dickson as well as for myself when I tell you how relieved we are that you gentlemen are here to represent the library's interests in this most unfortunate event."

The two nodded in unison. "We came the moment we received your call," said one, "and I've spoken with Police Chief Whaley. He's filled us in on what's happening here." The other man moved from behind the checkout counter and shook Aunt Ibby's hand. "Good job, as usual, Ms. Russell," he said. "The library is fortunate to have you on staff." He shook Tyler's hand and mine in turn, thanking us for our "clear-headedness" and "bravery." Within minutes, we'd been politely dismissed with the promise of phone calls from the board as soon as the time for the official reopening of the library was determined.

"I'll bet Pete will have most of the mess cleared up by morning," my aunt said as night security guard Dave—who was to remain on duty as usual—let the three of us out the side door onto the broad wooden platform, where a wheelchair ramp and a short flight of stairs led past the book drop to the parking lot.

"I agree," I said. "Pete's part of it may even be finished by midnight." We walked with Tyler to where her Volvo was parked near the back fence, waited until she was safely on her way, then climbed into the Buick. The visor over the passenger seat was still in the pulled-down position. I slammed it back into place so forcefully that I drew a puzzled glance from Aunt Ibby.

"Oops. That must have looked strange," I said. "Just before we went into the library I saw a . . . something . . . in that mirror. Didn't want to risk seeing it again—or another one. There hasn't been time to tell you about it until now."

"I'm listening."

"It was a foot—a foot wearing a shoe. It was sticking out from under a bookcase."

"Oh, my dear! Then you came inside and found the very same thing upstairs in the stacks!"

"Well, no. It wasn't the same at all. I mean it wasn't the same foot. The vision foot wore a shiny black shoe. The one in the stacks had a blue sneaker on it. The socks were different too."

"My goodness. That means . . ." She looked over at me. "What *does* that mean, Maralee?"

"I'm not sure," I said. "I can *never* be sure about these things. The visions can show the past, the present, or the future. Pete told me there was a recent local break-in where books were thrown around, so maybe somebody is still out there, looking for a certain book. No one was at home during that B&E, and apparently nothing was missing. What if whoever is looking for something doesn't find it? Does that mean there'll be another body found beside a bookcase? Hope not. I'm going with past though," I declared. "I think the mirror-foot belonged to Larry Laraby."

"Larry Laraby," my aunt repeated. "Of course. Have you talked to Pete about that case? It was before his time on the force, but maybe he's heard about it. Mr. Laraby was found under very similar circumstances—even though *his* death was an accident."

"Maybe it wasn't," I said, recalling Phil Archer's words. "Not everybody believed that accident story."

Chapter 8

Aunt Ibby didn't comment further on Larry Laraby's death and neither did I. We rode the rest of the way home in companionable silence. My thoughts, naturally, involved the shoes n shiny black one with a maroon ribbed sock and a blue athletic shoe with a none-too-clean white sock. There was a foot in each of them. Whose?

Pete would know the name of the dead man in the stacks soon, I was sure. But the shoe in the mirror remained a mystery. I figured my guess that it was Larry Laraby's shoe was a good one. At this point, it was the only possibility that made any sense. I'd tell Pete what I thought anyway, and see what he could come up with.

It was around ten o'clock when we arrived on Oliver Street. (Although our front door faces Winter Street, the garage opens onto the narrow one-way street behind the house.) My aunt activated the garage door opener and pulled inside, moving carefully to a stop when the yellow tennis ball suspended from the ceiling tapped the windshield. She locked the car, rolled the door down, and we stepped out the side door into the fenced yard. "Home again, home again, jiggity-jig," she recited from the old nursery rhyme, "and see who's come to meet us."

O'Ryan strolled toward us on the flagstone path, solar lamps lighting his way past the garden, illuminating his striped yellow coat. He greeted us with a tricky figure-eight maneuver involving one turn around my cordovan-booted right ankle and another around her kitten-heeled tan sandal-clad left one. We followed the cat, who darted into the house via his cat door while I used my key for a more traditional entrance. I clicked on the back-hall light while Aunt Ibby unlocked her kitchen door. O'Ryan had already used a cat entrance into that room as well, and waited impatiently for us, beside his empty red bowl.

"Will you join me for a bite of supper, Maralee?" she asked. "After I feed O'Ryan, of course. I made a lovely chicken à la king early this morning. Just have to heat it up. We'll have it on sour dough toast, all right? And I have some fresh raspberry turnovers for dessert."

"Chicken à la king on toast sounds wonderful," I said. "I'm hungry. But I'll skip dessert. Pete said he'd come over with ice cream after he gets through at the library."

"He must think they'll be finished quickly then." She poured dry cat food into O'Ryan's bowl. "That would mean we won't have to stay closed over the weekend."

"I guess it means Pete's part of it will be finished early anyway. The CSI team will still be there and you know how meticulous they are." I tossed my jacket over the back of a captain's chair, and set the round oak table with ivy-patterned Franciscan ware in anticipation of my favorite chicken dish. "Pete said to be sure to tell you that they're bagging each of the books individually and that they're being very careful."

"Dear boy. I know he'll take as good care of them as he possibly can." She donned a pink apron with "crazy cat lady" printed on it, poured the colorful chicken concoction into a copper sauce pan, and cut four slices from a loaf of homemade sourdough bread. "I like your idea of having a book-cleaning party when we get them back. Maybe I'll invite some young people from the Salem High Library Corps to help us."

"Good idea," I said, remembering how much I'd enjoyed being part of that careful cleaning process when I was a kid. "Pete asked about that emergency exit up in the stacks. I told him I thought it led to the mansion's original kitchen. Is that right? I've never used it."

"I should think not. You were frightened enough just being on that top floor, let alone climbing down that dank old staircase." She smiled. "Yes. It leads to the original first-floor kitchen and out into the little hall next to the side door. Nobody ever uses it except for the fire inspector. It has to be kept clear of obstructions in case it's ever needed for evacuation of that part of the building."

"Makes sense," I said, keeping an eye on the toaster where four slices of toast were about to pop up. I hadn't been kidding when I said I was hungry. The toaster popped as Aunt Ibby approached the table with a steaming tureen, and the house phone rang. She put the tureen on the table; I slathered butter onto perfectly browned toast and arranged the slices on our plates while she answered the wall-hung phone.

"This is she. Yes, Mr. Bagshaw. What seems to be the problem?" I recognized the name as one of the library board members I'd so recently met. My aunt frowned. "No sir. I most certainly did not. No. I'm positive of that. The last time? The fire inspector checked it a few weeks ago. You'll see the date noted on the library's online calendar. Very well. Thank you for informing me. Goodbye."

Hanging up the phone a bit abruptly, she sat in the captain's chair opposite mine. "Well, if that doesn't beat all," she said. "And you and I were just talking about that very thing!"

I assumed from the mention of the fire inspector that she and the board member had been discussing the stairway running between the stacks and the old kitchen. "What's going on?" I asked.

"Mr. Bagshaw wanted to know if the emergency door in the stacks was ever left unlocked. Imagine that! As though I'd allow such a thing to happen!"

"Of course you wouldn't," I said. My aunt was clearly offended by Mr. Bagshaw's suggestion.

"I'm sure nobody on *my* staff would allow it either." She ladled the hot, creamy green-pepper-and-pimento-accented chicken delicacy onto the toast with a little more force than necessary. "I think the night watchman checks it occasionally, but there's not been any kind of emergency use of the stairway since they used to have occasional fire drills back during the Vietnam era."

I glanced up at the kitchen clock while savoring my supper. "It's almost eleven," I said. "Pete should be along in an hour or so. He'll know more about what's going on. I'm quite sure I heard that door open and close just after I found the man in the stacks. I told Pete about it. There was no buzzer or bell or whatever is supposed to happen when it's opened."

"Oh my goodness, Maralee. If someone escaped through that door while you were there, that means . . ." Her voice trailed off.

"I know. There could have been a killer in the stacks at the same time I was. Creepy, huh?"

"It's not funny, Maralee," she scolded. "I wonder if any of the cameras caught whoever it was going in and out of the building—by whatever means they used."

"Well, there are cameras focused on both outside doors. They had to come and go through one or the other of them," I reasoned.

"True," she said. "Oh, Maralee. I just had another thought. What if whoever it is saw you coming up the stairs to the stacks? What if they know who you are, and what if they think maybe you saw them too?"

If they saw me, they know who I am. I was wearing a sticker with my name on it.

"I never thought of that," I said. "And I don't want to think about it." It seemed like a good time to change the subject. I didn't want to hear another word about a killer who might think I could identify him. Or her. "This may be the best chicken à la king ever." I reached for one more spoonful to cover the last bit of toast on my plate. "Just perfect," I said. "Can I have some of this bread to take upstairs for toast in the morning?"

"Of course. You say Pete's bringing ice cream for dessert? Want to take some raspberry turnovers up to your place to go with it?"

"I thought you'd never ask," I said with a faked smile, turning away from her and trying to cover the very slight nervous shaking of my hands as I carried the dishes to the sink.

Chapter 9

With dishwasher loaded, four turnovers waxed-paper wrapped, and the remainder of the loaf of sourdough bread in a brown paper lunch bag, I kissed my aunt good night and cut through the living room to the downstairs front hall. With the large yellow cat leading the way, I started up the handsome oak staircase to my third-floor apartment.

"Thanks for coming up with me, O'Ryan," I whispered, bending to pat his head before inserting my key into the lock. "I appreciate the company. Got a little case of the willies."

The cat looked up with sympathetic golden eyes. Okay, so maybe he had no idea about what I'd said. But O'Ryan's always seemed to have unerring instincts about human sadness, or loneliness, or fear. Aunt Ibby's thought about the killer knowing who I was had produced a rush of the latter. This time the cat ignored his special door and entered the kitchen beside me.

Anticipating Pete's arrival within the hour, I put the turnovers on a plate, loaded the Mr. Coffee with decaf, hung my jacket in the bedroom closet, grabbed a pair of leopard-print pajamas, and started down the hall to my bathroom.

There's nothing like a nice hot shower on a cool fall evening to relieve tension, so before long I felt the day's anxieties beginning to wash away. Worries about Howard Templeton taking my job gurgled down the drain. Memories of finding a body aren't so easy to purge, but the knowledge that professionals had taken over made it easier to accept. But thoughts about some unknown killer knowing who I am— maybe even where I am—especially while standing naked in a shower was way too reminiscent of a famous Hitchcock movie. I shut off the water, toweled off, tossed my clothes down the laundry chute, pulled on my pj's, and hurried back to my cheerful kitchen to wait for Pete.

I turned on the kitchen TV and caught the tail end of Buck Covington's late newscast. He ran my standup, reminding the audience of the importance of calling the number scrolling at the bottom of the screen if they'd observed any unusual activity in the vicinity of the main library. "If you see something, say something," he intoned, then using a happier voice, reminded viewers to "stay tuned for *Tarot Time with River North*."

O'Ryan always knows when Pete is about to arrive. He knows which door he'll use too. It was a few minutes after midnight and I was watching a commercial for Halloween party decorations when the cat raced down the hall to the living room and out into the back hall. I followed and stopped at the big bay window overlooking the backyard. Pete's Crown Vic pulled into the driveway, and I saw O'Ryan, in the golden glow of the solar lamps, run along the flagstone path to greet him. Pete, with a brown paper bag tucked under his arm, followed the cat to the back door. I felt myself relax then, almost as though I'd been holding my breath for hours.

I unlocked the living room door, stepped out into the

hall, and started down the twisty staircase, running into Pete's arms on the second-floor landing. He pulled me close, not speaking for a long moment.

"Hey," he whispered, "that's quite a welcome." He put his right hand under my chin and tipped my face up toward his. His kiss was gentle. "You okay?"

I shook my head. "Better. Now that you're here."

He put a finger to his lips. "Let's not wake your aunt." He put an arm around my waist, holding the paper bag with his other hand. He was right. The second-floor landing is just outside Aunt Ibby's bedroom. Together we tiptoed the rest of the way up to the third floor and through my open living room door. O'Ryan was already there, pretending to be asleep in his favorite zebra-patterned wing chair.

Pete closed the door, carefully locking it, kissed me again, then, smiling, backed away. "We'd better put this ice cream away before we melt it completely." I followed him down the short hall to the kitchen. He put the ice cream into the freezer while I turned on the coffee, muted the TV, and put our New Hampshire Speedway mugs and two Fiestaware bowls onto the Lucite kitchen table.

"I'm glad you're here," I said.

"Yeah. I could tell." He frowned. "You're frightened. Why?"

There was no point in pretending that I wasn't. Anyway, we've been together long enough that we don't play games. I told him what Aunt Ibby had said about the killer seeing me.

He nodded, his face serious. I knew right away that he'd thought of the same thing. "Here. Sit down, babe," he said. "We've got this under control. We've ID'd the body. He has a record and he has some shady associates. CSI has the library video and we'll have pictures by tomorrow morning of everybody who went in and out of the place."

I sat in one of the Lucite chairs and O'Ryan climbed up onto the windowsill behind me. "What was he after, Pete? Why all the books thrown around?"

"We don't know that yet," he said. "We're going to check with the homeowner who had the break-in I told you about. See if those folks knew the victim."

"That reminds me," I said. "Do you know about the Larry Laraby case? It was very similar to this one." I saw the beginning of a tiny smile playing around his lips. Pete always thinks it's funny when I say "case." He calls me Nancy Drew sometimes when I do it. This time I didn't care. I could tell by his expression that he didn't know about Larry Laraby's death. "I think this might be important," I told him. "It could help to explain the books."

I poured coffee into both of our mugs and he began serving the ice cream—half vanilla (his favorite) and half chocolate (mine). "The name—Larry Laraby—is familiar for some reason." He paused, ice cream scoop in mid-dip. "But I don't remember any Larry Laraby ever being associated with police business."

"He used to do sports on WICH-TV back in the day," I explained. "Aunt Ibby just barely remembers him. You've probably seen his picture hanging in the station lobby though."

"Right. That's probably where I've seen it. So what about him? What's his connection to what happened in the library today?"

I repeated what Phil Archer had told me about Laraby being found dead among books thrown all over the floor of his study. How they'd determined that he died from a broken neck because of a fall from a ladder.

Pete reached for a turnover. "Okay. The book mess is similar, but the man you found didn't die by accident."

"Phil doesn't think Laraby did either. He says he's not the only one who feels that way."

"I'll talk to Phil," Pete said. "You may be onto something. Did I ever tell you you'd make a good cop?"

"Thanks—but no thanks," I said. "Listen. Laraby was some kind of sports memorabilia expert, according to Phil. He used to run collectibles shows all over the country. Baseball cards and things like that. And Pete! I just remembered something. That man today—he was in the seven-ninety section in the stacks!"

"Seven-ninety?"

"Dewey decimal. Sports. Those books must have all been about sports. Right?"

"You're right. I bagged them all personally. Wore gloves and put each one in an evidence bag." There was a trace of excitement in Pete's voice. "I'll check tomorrow with the homeowner who had the break-in. Wonder if those books were seven-nineties?"

"Bet they were," I said. "Whose house was it anyway? I hope it wasn't around here."

"No. Don't worry about that. They live way over in North Salem. Big house on Dearborn Street. Nice older couple. Name of Stewart. Ring any bells?"

"I don't think so. Aunt Ibby might know them."

He smiled, reaching for a second turnover. "These are great. Did she make them?"

"Of course. You know I sure didn't." I looked up at the muted TV screen. River North, my best friend, looking gorgeous in hunter green velvet with a spray of miniature fall leaves woven into her single long black braid, smiled into the camera. The beautiful tarot cards were arranged in a pattern on the table before her.

Pete followed my glance. "Want to watch River?"

"Sure. The readings are always interesting, even when they're for somebody else."

"I guess so. I'm going to go grab a shower while you watch, okay?" He turned on the sound and picked up our ice cream bowls, putting them on the floor beside his chair. "Come on, O'Ryan. You can have last lick." Pete calls River's readings "hocus-pocus," and I'm pretty sure he puts my so-called "gift" into the same general category. O'Ryan tore like a furry yellow streak from the windowsill to the bowls on the floor and, purring loudly and appreciatively, finished every delicious drop.

I put our dishes in the sink, finished my coffee, nibbled on a raspberry turnover, and watched my friend as she held a card to the camera for a close-up shot. She'd recently begun selecting a card from her tarot deck each night and explaining for viewers a bit of the history and meaning of the beautiful illustration. On this night she'd chosen the Wheel of Fortune card from the Major Arcana. I pulled my chair a little closer to the screen. "This card is particularly interesting, I think," River said, "because of its many symbols." She pointed out the Sphinx at the top of the wheel and said that he represents wisdom, and that the serpent creeping down one side is Typhon, the Egyptian god of evil, and the jackal-headed being sliding up the opposite side is Hermes-Anubis, symbolizing intelligence. "Notice the four creatures at the corners of the card." She pointed to each one. I'd already noticed them. Each was shown reading a book. "They represent the four fixed signs of the Zodiac," she said. "See? Here's the bull for Taurus and the lion for Leo. There's the eagle for Scorpio and the angel for Aquarius."

Maybe it was just because I had so much on my mind due to all that had happened during the day, but that card looming up on the screen seemed to have a special meaning for me. River's words about fate and good fortune and unexpected arrivals simply floated away while I made up my own interpretation.

Wisdom and intelligence—that's the library. And the jackal thing? Look at his legs. One is in plain view and the other one is half hidden. It's pretty obvious what that means. And the evil snake—well, something evil is going on. That's for sure. It's the book-reading creatures that are the most important though. River sees the bull and the lion and the eagle and the angel as signs of the Zodiac. Uh-uh. I see the Chicago Bulls, the Detroit Lions, the Philadelphia Eagles, and the Los Angeles Angels. It's plain as day. It means seven-ninety. Sports. And more than likely it means those critters are all reading about sports collectibles.

I was still staring at the TV when Pete returned from his shower. The Wheel of Fortune card was no longer on the screen and River had moved on to the phone call segment of the show. I swiveled around in my chair. A handsome, well-built, shirtless man, fresh from the shower standing in your very own kitchen is a beautiful sight. My smile grew even broader when I realized that he was wearing flannel pajama pants patterned with a smirking snake clutching a baseball in his fangs. The Arizona Diamondbacks. So much for that serpent slithering up the side of the card! That was the clincher. River's card history that night was meant for me. No doubt.

"Want to watch the rest of the show in the bedroom?" he asked, reaching for my hand, pulling me to my feet.

"Good idea." I stood on tiptoe for the expected kiss. "But I don't need to see any more of the show. I got the message already."

Chapter 10

I awoke to the smell of coffee and the sound of country music. Both signaled the presence of Pete Mondello in the kitchen. While Mr. Coffee cycled Maxwell House Breakfast Blend and Alexa shuffled Carrie Underwood, I yawned, stretched, swung my legs over the side of the big warm bed, and sat up.

Pete and I are both "morning people," but in very different ways. The way Pete wakes up is what Aunt Ibby would call "bright-eyed and bushy-tailed." He's alert, ready for the day from the moment he opens his eyes, no matter how early it is. Not me. I need a little transition time. Time to snuggle under the cozy covers for a few more minutes, time to gather my thoughts, think about the day before and kind of visualize the day ahead. Yawning and stretching are good too. I always knew that but have perfected it since O'Ryan came to live with us. Cats are absolute experts at both.

I hadn't quite finished my thought-gathering and day-visualizing, but the coffee aroma called and I padded out into the kitchen. A glance at the Kit-Cat clock told me it was early enough for a fairly leisurely breakfast. I made a quick mental inventory of refrigerator and pantry. "I have some eggs," I said, "and some really good sour dough bread for toast. Fried egg sandwiches sound good?"

"Excellent," he said as he filled my coffee mug. I pulled a frying pan from a cabinet and put eggs and bread on the counter. My day-visualizing had begun to kick in and I knew that without doubt Bruce Doan would expect a follow-up to last night's one-minute standup. Hopefully one with some substance. Some facts.

"Pete," I said, while I put four thick slices of bread into the toaster and sprayed the frying pan with olive oil, "you mentioned that you had an ID on the victim. Will you tell me who he is? Doan is going to want something substantial today and I need to be first."

"Sure. The name will be released today anyway. He's Wee Willie Wallace. He was a minor league baseball player years ago. Got dropped by one of the farm teams for gambling. In Wee Willie's case it was for betting on his own games. Too bad. He was a fast little guy and a good hitter. He's got a record for some other stuff too. Used to live in Salem apparently. Been away from here for twenty years or so, far as we can tell."

I broke four eggs carefully into the pan without getting eggshells in with the eggs. I'm getting better at this cooking thing. "What kind of other stuff?" I asked.

"We're still checking sources. Had to do with horse racing. That's all I can say about that right now. Maybe later."

"Later the other stations will be onto this." I flipped the eggs, one at a time. Didn't break any yolks. "Can you at least tell me where to look? Some kind of time frame?"

Pete put two plates on the counter. I pushed the lever to lower the bread into the toaster. "Wee Willie may have worked as a trainer in New Hampshire at Rockingham before they closed in 2002," he said. "Papers up there might have mentioned him."

The egg sandwiches were darned near perfect, if I do say so myself. I pushed my luck a little bit more. "I gave you the idea about the Larry Laraby connection to all this," I said. "Want to hear about a vision I had yesterday that might be connected to him too?"

His "sure I do" was hesitant. Pete has come to accept my scrying abilities, but when they seem to overlap with his police investigations, he's still a little skittish when I talk about the things I see. Can't blame him for that.

I told him about the brief glimpse of the shoe I'd seen in the visor mirror of the Buick. "It was before I went up into the stacks. Before I saw Wee Willie. It was a completely different shoe."

"You think it was this Larry Laraby's foot? His shoe? His books?"

"I do."

"Can you describe it?"

I nodded, remembering. "Shiny black tie-shoe. Maroon dress socks, the kind with ribs in them."

"That definitely wasn't Wee Willie's foot. I wonder if anyone bothered to take any photos of Laraby's body. I'll check it out." He picked up our dishes. "Thanks for breakfast, babe. Gotta run."

"Will you tell me what you learn about the Laraby case?"

"It's only fair, Nancy." He grinned. "I'll tell you as much as I can about that *case*, and babe, please don't worry about somebody knowing you found Wee Willie. We've got your back. We'll have the guy in custody before you know it. Between the cameras in the library and dozens more up and down Essex Street he's practically a local movie star. Besides, we're pretty sure he was gone before you got there."

Just pretty sure?

Pete's words did make me feel safer though, and things always do seem to look better in the morning. We shared a fast kiss and Pete headed for the back door. O'Ryan followed, probably heading down to Aunt Ibby's kitchen, where the cuisine was undoubtedly better. I filled his red bowl with kibble in case he wanted a snack later and retrieved my laptop from the bedroom. Kit-Cat said it was only seven-fifteen. There'd be time to do a little online research on Wee Willie Wallace before I proposed to Bruce Doan that he assign me to the case. *Yeah, I said case again.*

I took a fast shower, dressed in jeans and sweatshirt, crossed my fingers, and called the dealership about the repair on my Corvette. "Yes, ma'am," came the welcome voice. "She's ready. Good as new. You can pick her up anytime."

Today is starting off a lot better than yesterday. With a positive attitude and more confident state of mind, I began to work.

Wee Willie even had a brief Wikipedia page. Pete was right about his baseball career. He'd had a tryout with the Red Sox and hadn't made the team but had found a home with an Alabama minor league team where he'd racked up some impressive statistics. After two years, though, his contract had been cancelled after his gambling habit was discovered, and he'd been banned from baseball. The article mentioned that he'd also worked with horses in various capacities and had spent some time in Hollywood during the eighties doing some stunt work in Westerns. Later, he'd been employed as a horse trainer at a New England racetrack, where he'd been found guilty of doping horses over a period of several years and had received a four-year prison sentence and a $100,000 fine.

Hmm. Bad little dude. I wondered what had brought him back to Salem. And why he'd ended up dead in a library, of all places. *And why I had to be the one who found him there!*

Pete had mentioned New Hampshire newspapers. I

knew Aunt Ibby had access to the library's database of newspapers on her computer. That would yield more information faster than I'd be able to get it on mine. I grabbed a notebook and headed down the front stairs.

My aunt is one of those "bright-eyed, bushy-tailed" morning people. I knew I'd find her at the kitchen table, dressed for the day, breakfast dishes washed and put away, the evening's dinner planned, something tasty already baking in the oven or simmering in the Crock-Pot, the *Boston Globe* and the *Salem News* open on the table and the *Globe* crossword nearly finished. In ink. O'Ryan met me at the foot of the stairs and together we entered her living room. "It's me, Aunt Ibby," I called from the doorway. "Got a minute?"

"Of course. Come on in. Coffee's on."

"Anything in the papers yet about—you know."

"Not yet. But the weekend papers are usually put to bed early. It'll be in tomorrow's for sure."

I helped myself to coffee (hazelnut) and sat opposite her. "Pete gave me the name of that poor guy we found in the stacks," I began, "and I need some help getting as much information as I can about him before everybody else gets the story."

She put down her pen, green eyes bright with interest. "Who is he?"

"Wee Willie Wallace. Sound familiar at all?"

"Vaguely. Something about horse racing maybe?"

"You're right." I told her what Pete had said about Willie working at Rockingham Park before he was arrested. "Maybe your database can find New Hampshire newspaper accounts about him faster than I can."

"Wouldn't be a bit surprised," she said. "Come on. Let's go."

Carrying my coffee, I followed her to her office. The large room had been what was called in the olden days a "sitting room," sort of an informal parlor. When I was a little kid it had been my playroom, with cutouts of Winnie-the-Pooh characters on the walls. Now it housed Aunt Ibby's impressive array of technical equipment.

Aunt Ibby sat at her long, curvy cherrywood desk and I pulled up a matching cherrywood chair beside her. Her computer was connected to three screens, which she could work on simultaneously. Her printer was huge. It looked like the ones behind the counter in the office supply store and it could print a full newspaper page. A smaller copier did smaller jobs. There was a fax machine, a light box, and a few items I didn't recognize, along with cherrywood file cabinets, both horizontal and vertical, along with a couple of comfortable chairs. A fireplace too.

"Do you have any dates in mind? Times when the man might have been working there—up in New Hampshire?" she asked.

"Pete said that Rockingham Park closed in 2002, so it would have been before then."

"I'll check for his name in the *Manchester Union-Leader* from 1992 to 2002 then." Her fingers flew over the keys. "Whoops. There he is. Popped right up. September 1999. Seems it was big news back then. He worked with a couple of vets. Used several different prescription drugs—and they got away with it for years." She sighed. "How sad. Look at this, Maralee. One of the horses fell and died on the track because of that horrible little man. Dreadful business. Shall I print this out for you?"

"Please," I said, quickly losing whatever sympathy I might have felt for the dead man in the stacks. I love horses. Used to ride when I was a kid. Western saddle. Barrel races mostly. "Wikipedia says he was sentenced to four years in prison. I wonder what he's been doing since he got out."

"I'll put his name in the national base. Might take a little longer. Of course, his name isn't actually Wee Willie. His name is William Anthony Wallace, it says here. A fairly common name, and there are probably a good many William Wallaces."

"I think you may be able to go to the library today," I said. "Maybe if you have time you can look into this further. Meanwhile, I'll take what we have and call Mr. Doan and see if I can do a quick update this morning."

"You go along then, dear. I'll keep digging. I suppose the police department will have to give out some kind of a press release pretty soon." She pulled up another screen. "For goodness sake. Did you know he was in the movies too?"

"Yes. Westerns. I hope he wasn't harming horses there."

"Dreadful man. Just dreadful." She made a "tsk-tsk" sound and focused once again on the multiple screens, which by then showed two newspaper pages and what appeared to be an old Hopalong Cassidy movie clip. "Look at this. It's a publicity shot from his days in Hollywood. And here's one of him in a baseball uniform. He seems to have had a number of talents. I'll print these out for you."

"Perfect." I watched the photos roll out of the printer and picked them up. I studied the studio portrait. The man was smiling, fair, with "Beach Boy" good looks. "Doesn't look much like he did last night," I said. "Of course he was much younger then. Can you send these over to the station? I'll go upstairs and call Mr. Doan. Thanks for helping. Don't know what I'd do without you."

No reply, just a smile and a brisk wave of her hand. The cat reached the front hall before I did and was halfway to the second floor by the time I started up the stairs. It was still early but before I reached the third-floor landing I called the station on the chance that Rhonda might be at her desk on Saturday. She was.

"Hi, Lee. What's up?"

"Mr. Doan in yet?"

"Yep. He's here. Got something?"

"I think so," I said. "Maybe I'll get a full day today."

"Good. We miss your smiling morning face around here."

I heard a quick buzz and the station manager answered with an abrupt "Bruce Doan."

"Lee Barrett," I said. "I have some more on that library death."

"Good. You coming in?"

"I just have to pick up my car and I'll be right along," I promised.

"Take a cab," he said. "I'll put you on the a.m. show with Phil Archer. Get your car later."

"Yessir."

I reversed direction and headed back down the stairs, undoubtedly confusing the cat, who was half in, half out of my kitchen cat door. "Aunt Ibby," I called before I'd even entered the living room. "Can you give me a ride to the station? Right away?"

"Certainly." She appeared in the office doorway. "I'll back the car out while you change that old shirt and put on some lipstick."

I looked down at the sweatshirt. "Ohmigosh!" I ran back up the stairs, raced across the kitchen, and threw my closet door open. The jeans I was wearing would be okay. I'd probably be sitting behind the news desk anyway. I yanked off the sweatshirt, tossed it onto the bed, pulled a pink silk blouse from a hanger, and inspected face and hair in the mirror attached to the top of my bureau. Hair too curly, but not bad. I shrugged into the blouse and buttoned it on the way to the bathroom. A quick fix with mascara and eyeliner, a brushful of blush, and some pink lip gloss would have to do for the moment and Rhonda could help with any necessary repairs when I got there. I grabbed a white cardigan, my purse, and the handful of notes and photos and took off running.

As good as her word, Aunt Ibby had the Buick warmed

up and the passenger door open when I reached the back gate—and she hadn't even asked what was going on! From my phone call to Doan to the moment I climbed into the Buick, less than fifteen minutes had passed. Phil Archer's morning news show began at nine. We made it to the station with twenty minutes to spare.

Chapter II

I had time to tap a few more notes into my tablet while Rhonda repaired my hasty makeup job. (She's a Mary Kay rep in addition to her regular job and has a bottom drawer full of sample products for emergencies.) Between what I'd observed in the library the previous night, plus what Pete had told me and the information I'd found online and Aunt Ibby's amazing cache of facts, I felt confident that I could scoop any of the competing morning news shows' reports on Wee Willie's demise.

The flattering studio photo of a much younger William Wallace was ready for the telecast and Phil had quickly searched the station's archives and pulled footage of Rockingham Park, Willie at some long-ago batting practice, and some of Francine's recent footage of the Salem Main Library. By nine o'clock, when Phil's theme music played and Wanda the Weather Girl was prettily posed in front of her green screen, no one would have guessed how quickly the whole production had been thrown together. I waited in a folding chair off camera for my cue to join Phil at the desk.

Phil did his usual morning intro, wishing the audience

a good day, referencing a few of the many Halloween-related celebrations going on around the city, then introducing Wanda, adorable in orange short-shorts, a lacy black peekaboo top designed to look like spider webs, and thigh-high black boots. As always, her thoroughly professional weather report belied her sexpot appearance.

I was scheduled to do my "breaking news" story immediately after the My Pillow commercial. While the sixty-second spot ran I gathered my notes and walked quickly to the news desk on its raised platform.

"Thanks for sending along the backup material and photos," Phil said. "Between what you've learned and all the stuff I dug up in the station archives, we'll be good to go for five, six minutes or even more. Marty McCarthy's in the control room, so you know it'll be smooth."

That was a relief. Marty is the best. "You think we can do five minutes? Even six?" I'd been thinking of about three. Five minutes doesn't sound like a long time until you try to fill it with your own voice making some sort of sense. But Phil seemed confident. *He must have found more material than I'd imagined.* "Wee Willie Wallace sure got around a lot, moving from job to job, didn't he?" I said.

Phil nodded. "Sure did. So did Wally Williams. Ready, Lee?" he pointed toward the cameraman, who'd started the backward countdown. "Three . . . two . . . one . . ."

"Who?" I stammered. But the green light was on. I smiled at the camera while Phil announced "Breaking news. Authorities have learned more about yesterday's fatality at the library. Here's our own Lee Barrett, WICH-TVs field reporter, to update us on this ongoing story. Tell us what's going on, Lee."

We hadn't had time to rehearse any of this. I watched a monitor carefully so I'd know which film, which photo, which material the viewers were seeing while I spoke. I had the pages my aunt had printed for me, along with my own notes on the tablet in my lap, hidden from the camera just in case I needed to refer to them. "Thanks, Phil. Good morning ladies and gentlemen," I began. "Yesterday evening seemed like a typical Friday at the Salem Main Library on Essex Street." The monitor showed a split screen, with me on one side (the pink blouse looked fine) and a still shot of the handsome old building in full sunlight on the other. "But it turned out to be anything but," I continued, watching, fascinated as the sunny scene morphed into a slow pan of two police cars with lights flashing, the coroner's vehicle, and the plainly marked CSI unit, all with the library, windows ablaze, in the background. I hadn't realized Francine had captured that one.

"A library volunteer, returning a volume to the upstairs stacks, made a chilling discovery," I continued. "The lifeless body of an elderly man lay sprawled in an aisle with books tossed in disarray all around him. The man has been identified as Wee Willie Wallace, one-time baseball player and sometime actor." Here Marty had inserted a video of Wee Willie sliding into home plate, giving the catcher a high five and grinning at the camera. "Wallace's baseball career was short-lived," I said, "cut short because of gambling on his own games. He did some stunt work in Hollywood Westerns." The studio portrait popped up, followed by a brief clip of a man who may have been Wee Willie on a horse. *So far, so good.* "Later, he had another brief career as a horse trainer at Rockingham Park in New Hampshire." Nice professional video of Rockingham Park, probably from an old advertisement back when they still had races there.

"So far the police have not revealed the cause of death," I said, "although a police spokesperson stated that the man did not die of natural causes." The screen once again showed Phil and me. A glance at the digital clock at the base of the monitor showed even with the generous use of the video clips, we'd not quite used up five minutes yet.

"Thanks, Lee," Phil Archer said. "We have a little more information about the man found dead at the library." His smile just then was not the usual professional anchorman smile. It was real and broad. "While checking the WICH-TV archives, I found an old kinescope of a sports program made in this very building back in the fifties. The interviewer is sports announcer Larry Laraby and the man being interviewed is the same man who was found dead last night in Salem's main library. I apologize for the quality but this recording was made before video film was introduced in 1956. Watch this, everybody!"

The picture filling the screen was black and white and grainy. The voices had a kind of gurgly sound but the words and faces were distinguishable. "Our guest tonight is Wee Willie Wallace," Larry Laraby said. "Willie had a shot at playing for the Sox, but what happened, Willie? You too short?"

Willie's answer sounded sincere, good natured. "More likely too young," he said. "They like my speed, but they say I need more practice. So down to the minors I go. It's okay. I'm only nineteen. Plenty of time." He leaned forward and handed something to the other man. "Look. I brought you a team-signed baseball for your collection."

The camera was back on Phil and me. "That's it, folks," Phil said. "The rest of the kinescope was pretty bad. They used to reuse them until they were useless. I just thought you'd like to see that Wee Willie Wallace, who died last night in the Salem Main Library, was once a small part of the WICH-TV family. Thank you, Lee Barrett, for your excellent report."

He went to hard break with back-to-back national car commercials. I picked up my papers and shook his hand. "The old TV sports show was the perfect ending for the piece," I said. "Thanks for taking the time to search it out." I checked my watch. We still had a couple of minutes before Phil had to resume the morning news. "Phil," I said, "you mentioned Larry Laraby when we spoke a few days ago. The scattered books around both bodies just can't be coincidence, can it?"

He paused, looking around the studio before answering. He covered his mic with one hand. "It doesn't seem so to me. That's one of the reasons I checked the archives to see if Wee Willie was connected to Laraby somehow. I wasn't even surprised to see that he was. I sort of remembered him being on that show several times but I didn't have time to search the old records any further." He looked at the clock. "Oh-oh. Back to work. Thanks again, Lee. Good job. Keep at it."

"I will," I promised, meaning it sincerely. "But Phil, who's Wally Williams?"

"That would be a good place to start." Broad wink. "Keep at it."

I had much more than a casual interest in this case and I had every intention of keeping at it. Not only had I found the body, but I was still pretty worried about the possibility that I'd been seen by the killer there in the stacks. What if the killer was worried too? About what *I* might have seen. Until Wee Willie's murderer was found, I figured that maybe I had good reason to be scared.

Chapter 12

I hung around the station for a while after my five minutes with Phil Archer. I waved hi to Marty as I passed the control room, then headed back upstairs to see if Rhonda had anything else scheduled for me before my usual afternoon check-in.

"Lookin' good, Lee," Rhonda said. "I never could understand that old rule about redheads not wearing pink."

"Me either," I said. "My red-haired aunt always told me it was an old wives' tale—started by jealous old wives. Is Mr. Doan around?"

"He is. Want me to buzz him?"

"Please. I have an idea about this Wee Willie Wallace and Larry Laraby connection."

"Larry Laraby's picture is in that rogue's gallery in the hall by the elevator, right? Old Eddie says he used to do sports here back in the day." She hit a button on her console. "Oh, Mr. Doan. You got a minute to see Lee Barrett? She's out here by my desk."

She nodded, then jerked a finger toward the manager's closed office door. "He says go right in. Good luck with your idea."

I knocked, and waited. "Come in, come in, don't dawdle."

I pushed the door open and greeted Bruce Doan. "Good morning, sir."

"Yeah. Good morning. Good follow-up. You got more for later?"

"Not yet," I admitted, "but I'm really getting interested in Larry Laraby and his connection with Wee Willie. I mean besides the fact that their deaths were kind of similar."

"The books on the floor," he said. "Yeah. Your cop boyfriend tell you about that?"

"No. Phil told me about the books they found around Larry Laraby's body even before Willie got—got whatever it was that killed him."

And I'm the one who told my cop boyfriend about it. "Did you know Laraby?"

"No. That was before my time here at the station. Buffy and I aren't natives like you, Ms. Barrett. When the station changed hands back in the early nineties, that's when they brought me in from Springfield. What about Laraby and Wee Willie? I didn't know the little guy had ever been on the station until I saw your piece this morning." He raised one hand in a small salute. "Not a bad job, by the way. Not bad at all."

"I'd like to take some time to search the archives. The way Phil did. I know the kinescopes are pretty rough, but I have to start somewhere."

"I suppose you want to be on the clock while you do it?"

I hadn't thought about that. Money isn't a problem for me. "I just like to have someplace specific to go in the morning," I told him honestly. "I miss clocking in and out."

"Okay. This is strictly in the investigative reporting and research category, okay? Just don't be horning in on Howard's field reporting gig. Got it?"

"Got it."

He shuffled some papers on his desk. "Well then, get moving. I'm not paying you to stand around. I'll expect at least one update a day on the dead guy in the library story in addition to a bang-up investigative piece on the Laraby connection to air in . . ." He looked at the calendar on the wall. "In two weeks. That should do it. And don't forget you're working on the anniversary show too. Have you rounded up any of the old-timers?"

"We found Ranger Rob. He's in Rockport, running a riding stable."

"Good start. Keep at it."

Why is everybody giving me the same advice? I guess I'll have to keep at it if I'm going to finish in two weeks. "Thanks, Mr. Doan," I said. "I'll check with Rhonda about getting into the archives."

No reply. I let myself out, gave Rhonda a thumbs-up and a smile. "I'll be right back," I told her. I was ready to get to work, but not before I got my beautiful car back. I called a cab, requesting my favorite driver, Jim Litka, and went outside to wait on Ariel's bench, facing the harbor.

Jim 's green and white cab pulled up beside me within minutes. He jumped out, ran around to open the passenger door. "Hi, Ms. Barrett. Back seat today, or up front with me?"

"Up front please." Jim's a wealth of information on practically any subject that has to do with Salem. I gave him the name of the Chevy dealership. "Going to pick up my car. Had a scrape down one side. Shopping cart."

He nodded understanding. "Yep. Darn lazy folks can't bother to put them into those little corrals." He shook his head. "Saw you the other night talking about Wee Willie getting offed in the library."

"Yep. Quite a night," I agreed. I never have to lead Jim to a topic. He just dives right in. "One of my other regular riders remembers him pretty well. Knew him when they both worked at your TV station. 'Course that was a long time ago. She's pretty old now."

Wee Willie worked *at the station?*

"No kidding. He worked there? I knew he was a guest on the sports show sometimes. Is that what she meant?"

"Oh, no. He worked there for a long time after he couldn't play baseball no more."

"Wee Willie did? You sure?"

"Sure I'm sure. Nice old lady like that wouldn't lie about it. She says he didn't use the name Wee Willie though. Kind of ashamed about booting the ball career, you know."

"Who is the nice old lady, anyway, Jim?" I asked. "Do you think she'd talk to me about when he worked there?"

"Probably. She lives over on Highland Avenue. She walks to the Market Basket over there every Monday to do her groceryin', then calls me to pick her up. Give me your card and I'll give it to her on Monday. She'll call you I'm sure. Quite a talker."

"What's her name?" I fished into my handbag for a card. I used the field reporter card. Didn't want to scare her away with the investigative reporter one.

"Her name's Agnes," he said. "But she used to be Katie the Clown."

Chapter 13

Jim Litka dropped me off at the dealership, where I was so happy to see my beautiful shiny Corvette it almost brought tears. I touched the side where the horrible scrape had been—ran my hand along the place, looking for imperfections. Perfect. I paid the bill, put the top down, and before long I was happily cruising along Route 114 with Lady Gaga's "Is That All Right" blasting from the ten-speaker audio system with bass box and subwoofers, heading back to the station.

Now I had one more piece to add to the puzzle, one more name to chase down in the WICH-TV archives. Katie the Clown, aka Agnes. I was sure Jim would give her my card and it was a good bet that she'd call me. But that couldn't happen until Monday and I was impatient. Maybe I could pull personnel files. There couldn't have been too many women named Agnes on the company payroll, even back then. Another name I'd look for was the name Phil Archer had mentioned. Wally Williams. Maybe Wee Willie had simply switched first and last names. William Wallace became Wallace Williams. Easy-peasy. I parked in my usual reserved space, regretfully put the top up, used the studio side door, and took the metal staircase up to the second floor.

Rhonda gave me directions to the archived materials and said she'd pull whatever old personnel files she could find. "I'm looking for Agnes somebody who performed a kids' show as Katie the Clown twenty-five, thirty years ago. I remember it from when I was little," I told her. "Besides Agnes I'm looking for William Wallace or Wallace Williams or both.

I started for the downstairs dataports, small rooms Mr. Doan had set aside for reporters to use for preparing scripts, making phone calls. I made good use of the tidy little hideaways. I reached the head of the metal stairs and turned back. "And Rhonda, if you don't mind, would you see what you've got on Robert Oberlin? He used to be Ranger Rob."

"Sure thing. I've seen videos down in the control room marked 'Ranger Rob Show.' You could pull some of those. If you want to take some home to watch them, I have to make out a card."

"Like a library card, huh?"

She smiled. "Something like that. You working on pulling together that anniversary show Doan wants to produce?"

I smiled back. "Something like that."

Once inside the dataport I pulled the notes from the morning's news show along with the printouts about Wee Willie Aunt Ibby had prepared for me. I checked the Wikipedia article about Wee Willie again, just to make sure I hadn't missed anything. Funny that it hadn't mentioned his working at WICH-TV. I know we're not very big as TV stations go, but we've been around a long time.

I tried Wallace Williams. Bingo. A photo accompanied the article, but the man in the picture didn't look much like the baseball player or the cowboy stunt man. He had jet black hair, a pointy beard, and a luxurious handle bar mustache. He'd apparently been an actor on the New England dinner theater circuit, usually playing villains, and had also played "character parts on a local television station in his home city, Salem, Massachusetts." The article didn't mention the parts he'd played. I calculated the dates and figured that the local acting must have happened before the racetrack mess. That would put it right around the late nineteen eighties. I printed out the article and the photo and added the pages to my growing collection.

My phone buzzed. Rhonda.

"There's a file cabinet down in the studio they use for a prop on the office set for the *Saturday Business Hour* show," she said. "Marty says it's still full of old files. She remembers seeing folders of show schedules in it. Take a look if you want to. I haven't found anything yet. Better hurry. Saturday Business guy is on from one to two."

That could be like finding gold! I gathered my paperwork again, locked up the dataport, and hurried upstairs to return the key. "Thanks for the tip," I told Rhonda. "I'm going right down there to look for . . . I don't know what."

She laughed. "Well, you'll know when you find it. Good luck."

Most of the studio was dark except for minimal lighting, indicating the aisles between sets in the long, black-walled room. She was right about the file cabinet. It was a dark green, vertical, metal, four drawer, plain-Jane piece of office furniture. Even in dim light it looked completely at home in the staged "office." There was also a bookcase, a desk, a fake plant, and a globe of the world. *I should have brought a flashlight.*

"You should have brought a flashlight," came a voice from the darkness. I shaded my eyes with one hand and looked around. A man walked toward me. I could only make out his silhouette. Couldn't see his face at all. It was too early for the Saturday Business guy. "Who is it?" My voice came out sort of squeaky. I tried again, with a lighter tone. "Who goes there?"

"It's me, Ms. Barrett. Howard Templeton. Hope I didn't scare you." He was only a few feet away from me by then, and he *had* brought a flashlight. One of those tiny little dollar store ones. I saw the pale circle of light moving along on the floor as he drew closer. "See? It's just me." He turned the beam upward, illuminating his face the way kids do at pajama parties when they want to frighten their friends. Worked for me.

"Jeez, Howard, don't do that! You look like some kind of a monster."

He quickly refocused the beam onto the floor. "Wow. I'm sorry, Ms. Barrett. You okay down here? Can I help you find something?"

"No, no. I'm good. Just doing a little historical research for the big anniversary celebration your uncle is planning."

"Here? Historical research?" He looked around the three-walled enclosure. "I thought the *Saturday Business Hour* was a fairly new show."

"It is." *Think fast. If he sees me open the file cabinet, he'll want to know what I'm looking for. He could talk Aunt Buffy into letting him in on my story.*

"I'm just checking out the different sets and props we already have. We'll need to create a really special set for the anniversary month shows." Quickly improvising, I reached over and tapped the globe. "I'm thinking we might borrow this. To show how TV has become a global influence since it began."

"Ah. Yes. I get it." He gave me a big smile. *If he ever does "move on" in this business, that smile will open doors for him.* "I'll keep my eyes open too, Ms. Barrett. If I see any good props around here I'll let you know." He began to back away. "Here, you take my flashlight. I'm going upstairs now."

"Thanks, Howard," I said, accepting the light. "And Howard? You have a beautiful smile. You should use it more often."

"Really? Thank you. I'll remember that."

Sure thing. I'll do anything I can do to help you "move on," kid. I gave the globe an affectionate spin. Using it on the anniversary show set wasn't a bad idea anyway. I made a mental note of it, looked around the room, then flashlight in hand, I approached the file cabinet. The oblong metal frames on the front of each of the top three file drawers held a blank card. No help there. The card on the bottom drawer read MISCELLANEOUS.

I aimed Howard's light toward the first drawer and pulled it open. Manila files—not the hanging kind—in alphabetical order displayed the names of the companies and individuals who'd bought time on the station decades ago. A brief scan of the file titles showed that a surprising number of them were familiar to me—businesses that had survived the years. The Hawthorne Hotel, of course, the North Shore Music Theatre, Salem Savings Bank, and Harbor Sweets were not only still here but were still advertising on WICH-TV! Some names were unfamiliar and some I'd heard Aunt Ibby mention. Almy's, Webber's, Empire Clothing, Fannie Farmer, Daniel Low's . . .

The scripts for the commercials were there too, neatly typed, complete with director's notes. I'd already switched hats from girl detective to program researcher. This file cabinet was going to be a nostalgia gold mine. *I may have to move into this make-believe office on weekdays!*

I could hardly wait to investigate the next drawer. This one looked like personnel. That's where I expected to strike the most nostalgia gold of all. It was packed with files—alphabetical, mostly manila, but a few in colored stock. I knew I should start at the beginning and look at each one in order. That's the way Aunt Ibby would do it. Not me. I went directly to the Ws. Wee Willie would be in there no matter which one of his names he'd used.

Actually, he was in there under three names—William Wallace, Wallace Williams, and Wee Willie Wallace. I pulled the Wee Willie one first. It was one of the files with the distinctive colored stock. His was green. The file contained his address, telephone number, and Social Security number. There were several publicity photos, including Willie at various stages and ages. There was a stapled-together stack of pay vouchers. I riffled through them quickly. They all seemed to be payments for appearances on the Larry Laraby sports program. Apparently, Wee Willie got paid $100 per appearance—probably really good pay for a few minutes' work back in the seventies. *I wonder what he did to earn it.*

William Wallace was next. Regular manila file folder. Here, once again, was the usual age, height, weight, and IRS and Massachusetts state tax–related information. This file held several stapled-together "style sheets"—the documents that describe in some detail the physical description, perceived personality traits, method of dress, and the like of a character an actor is or will be portraying. The sheet on top was a surprise. The heading read CACTUS. The subhead was "Ranger Rob's sidekick." There was an accompanying photo. Sure enough, it was the little guy with the handlebar mustache and the big white sombrero I remembered from childhood.

Wait a minute! I've seen that mustache before.

I pulled my stack of notes from the hobo bag. There it was. Right on top. Wallace Williams, actor on the dinner theater circuit. Not much resemblance to Ranger Rob's funny little sidekick, but the mustache matched.

Usually plays a villain.

The next page showed a photo of a small man looking like a dead ringer for the Boston Celtics mascot—a leprechaun. The heading on the accompanying sheet read "LUCKY LEPRECHAUN. Temporary guest on varied shows during the month of March."

Being short has its rewards.

The next one wasn't even unexpected. "ELF. Temporary guest on varied shows during the month of December." Next, not surprisingly, were EASTER BUNNY, TOM TURKEY, HALLOWEEN GHOST, and MARVEL the ROBOT.

That last name rang a special childhood bell. Marvel had been a favorite of mine. He'd been a regular with Professor Mercury and his Magical Science Circus. He'd often helped the Professor with experiments, and spoke with only a series of excited "beeps."

WICH-TV had kept William Wallace employed for most of the year, and had kept his true identity hidden with false hair, putty nose, and face-covering masks. The station manager back in those early days must have expected his employees to do more than one job. (Not unlike the current station manager.) I took a quick picture of each page with my phone.

The Wallace Williams file was the slimmest one of all. It contained some legal-looking documents. Nondisclosure and noncompete forms, signed by William Wallace, aka Wallace Williams. I photographed those too. Would I be able to find "Agnes" here with a meticulous search of names, or should I wait until Monday? I could wait. I moved on to the bottom drawer, wondering what it contained.

I'd just begun to pull the drawer open when the overhead lights went on. "Anybody down here?" came a voice.

Chapter 14

Damn. I recognized the voice. Scott Palmer. I pushed the drawer closed. Quietly.

"Oh, is that you, Moon?" He appeared at the end of the center aisle and walked toward me. "What are you doing all alone down here in the dark? You okay?"

"Just fine, Scott," I said. "No problem. Just doing a little scouting, looking for props for the station anniversary extravaganza." I stood with my back to the file cabinet.

"Oh yeah. Thanks for helping me out on that Larry Laraby thing. How'd it go?" He joined me in the faux-office.

"Well enough that I wound up with the whole project." I attempted a sigh. "Including the prop hunt." I gestured with my little flashlight, aiming the pale beam toward the globe. "The spinning globe will make a good background for the title shot, don't you think?"

Scott tilted his head to one side and fixed me with that wide-eyed stare he does so well.

Is he buying this?

After a moment he nodded. "Yeah. I like it. Denotes passage of time. Listen, if you need any help with this, let me know. It's the least I can do, since I kind of stuck you with it."

I darn near sighed again—this time with relief. I didn't want Scott horning in on my story. I wasn't about to let on that he'd handed me a connection to a recent murder, and maybe—just maybe—an old one too. "Thanks, Scott. If you see anything around here that connects to the station's past, let me know."

"Sure will. I know how Doan likes things that don't cost money."

"You've got that right. Well, so long."

He smiled, still standing there. "I think you can turn the little flashlight off now, Moon. The lights are on." Again, that damned stare. *Do I look nervous? Like I'm hiding something?*

I clicked the light off, slung the hobo bag over my shoulder and brushed past him, heading for the stairs. "Gotta go see if Rhonda has anything for me to do. Bye."

"Bye," he said. When I reached the metal door I sneaked a look back. He was still there. He wasn't looking at the file cabinet though. I decided to ask around to see if there was a key for it. If there was, I planned to keep it locked. A desk lamp would be a big help too. *I'll bet Rhonda can arrange that.* Mainly I planned to ask if I could use the set once in a while during the week when the station was on network feed—preferably when Scott was out of the building.

I climbed the stairs to the second floor and thanked Rhonda for the tip about the file cabinet. "Looks like there might be some useful stuff in there for the anniversary show. Know what? Some of the sponsors from back then are still with us."

"No kidding. Who?"

I rattled off the names of the few I'd noticed. "There are probably more than those."

"We should contact sales," she said. "They can probably get some extra ads from those old-timers."

"Good idea," I said. "By the way, can you get somebody from props to put one of those old green-shaded lamps on the desk? It would look right on that set."

Smiling, she scribbled a note on her desk pad. "And it would help you in your snooping, right?"

"You know me so well," I said. "And I want to thank Marty for the file cabinet tip too. Is she still in the building?"

Rhonda consulted her whiteboard. "She's shooting a promo for Pickering Wharf. She should be back in about half an hour. Want to hang out with me while you wait? You can help me address some postcard reminders about the Doans' big Halloween eve party. Guests were asked to dress as fictional characters. Seems Mrs. Doan e-mailed the invitations over a month ago and half the people she invited haven't RSVP'd yet. These are 'gentle reminder' notices with directions to the hotel. Doan thinks they should be hand addressed so the slugs won't ignore them like they did the first ones. You answered yours, didn't you?"

"Sure did. I don't ignore an e-mail from the boss's wife, no matter what it's about."

"Good. How's your handwriting?"

"Barely legible," I admitted.

"Good enough. Here you go." She handed me a stack of printed cards and a typed page of names and addresses. "Halloween eve's barely a week away so I'm supposed to get these in the mail today."

"These are nice," I said, inspecting the colorful cards, each one illustrated with storybook characters. "I don't remember the Doans celebrating Halloween eve with a party before this year."

"Yeah. It's mostly for young Howie. More than half of these go to his friends and family. They want him to feel at home here."

Hope he's not going to get too comfortable here.

"Does everyone who works here get one of these—even if we answered the first one?"

"I haven't read the whole list but it looks like most of us do. Except for River's show, the late news, and the station ID guy, the nighttime shows are always network programs anyway."

"We'd better hurry up and get these addressed then," I said. "So we can be sure to get ours." I pulled a chair up to the end of the purple Formica counter.

"I already wrote yours." She held up her pen. "The list is alphabetical and in two columns—the Doans' list is on the left and the Templetons' guests are on the right. I took the top half. You get M to Z."

I returned her pen-salute with my own Pentel, picked up my first card, and addressed it to the top name on my list—Marty McCarthy. Time passed quickly, with hardly any interruption. Rhonda answered a few phone calls, but most of the time we worked in comparative silence. Mr. Doan was away, so there was no noise from that quarter. I was surprised when the studio clock showed one-thirty and I was nearly halfway through my list.

"Want to stop and grab some lunch?" Rhonda asked.

"Good idea," I said. "I need to text Pete first though. To see if he's got anything new on the library thing. Mr. Doan says he wants daily updates."

I sent a brief plea. "Need update on library matter—Please?"

Rhonda and I headed across Derby Street to the Mercy Tavern. It's in the same spot as our old hangout, In a Pig's Eye, still convenient for all hands at WICH-TV and they still have great lunches. We'd just placed our orders, a Mercy burger for Rhonda, New England clam chowder for me, when my phone buzzed. It was Pete.

"Excuse me," I apologized. "Gotta take this."

"No problem."

"Hi, Pete," I said. "Thanks for getting back to me so fast. What've we got?"

"Cause of death and what was on the videos."

I fished in the hobo bag and grabbed my notebook, then realizing that I'd left my pen on Rhonda's desk. I made frantic writing motions. She handed me one of the bright red WICH-TV promotional pens. Good enough. "Shoot," I said. Then paused. "Is it okay if I report this?"

"Yep. Ready?"

"Shoot," I said again.

"Okay. William Wallace, aged approximately eighty, died of severe damage to the upper vertebrae in an area just below the brain stem. Death was probably instantaneous."

"How did it happen?"

"Don't know for sure yet, but it wasn't an accident."

"Murder?"

"That's a distinct possibility."

"An old man like that couldn't put up much of a fight I suppose. Got any suspects?"

"The old guy was in remarkably good shape for a man his age, according to the doc. Whoever did it must have sneaked up on him somehow. Anyway, the videos from the library cameras show us who entered and left the stacks on that day," he said. "The library staff is being asked today to identify those people they recognize. Then if there's anyone they don't know who went up into the stacks, those pictures will be released to the media. Maybe somebody in the audience can help us. Listen, babe, I'll try to see that WICH-TV gets first crack at those if I can."

"That'd be great, Pete. So the video might have the answer then."

"Yes, and no."

"What do you mean?"

"Well, we have good clear shots of everybody who went up those stairs all day—including you."

"That's helpful. And I suppose the ones of them coming down are better. You could see the faces."

"You're right about the ones that came down the stairs. Not everybody did."

"No, of course poor old Willie didn't."

"And one more. A man who came in the front door and went up the stairs apparently never came down. Besides that, a woman who left the library by the side door apparently never came inside at all." He shook his head. "Puzzler."

Our food had arrived by then and I nibbled on a Saltine cracker. "Okay then. Obviously, the man left somehow and the woman got in somehow. There has to be another entrance—or exit. A big building like that has more than two ways to get in and out."

"True. We're working on that. We're still examining those library tapes. Looking at the door in the old kitchen too."

"That's the only other way out I can think of. Besides, there's an alarm on the exit door in the stacks."

"I know. We're workin' on it, babe. Gotta go. Talk to you later."

I put the phone back into my purse. "That's totally weird."

"Spill it," Rhonda prodded. "I could tell from your end of the conversation something strange is going on. What's up?"

"As soon as we get back to work I have to do another report. They know what killed Wee Willie." I looked at my notes. "He suffered severe damage to his upper vertebrae near the brain stem."

"No kidding. Somebody must have twisted his head like a corkscrew to do that."

"How do you figure that?" I asked. Rhonda knows about an amazing number of topics.

She shrugged and took a bite of her burger. "Used to date a karate master in San Francisco. Thon. Cute as a bug. Anyway, he taught me about all kinds of ways to defend myself." Shrugged again. "Some of them were lethal." She leaned forward, elbows on the table. "But what was the impossible part?"

"The videos showed everybody who went up the main staircase to the stacks. It also showed everybody who came back down." I paused. "Except Willie, of course. He was dead. But another person who went up apparently didn't come down. A man. Besides that, there's a video of a woman leaving the building, but no picture of her ever coming in."

"That's impossible."

"I know. That's what I said."

"There has to be another way in and out then," she pointed out. "Aren't there videos?"

"There are videos of both the front and side doors and of the stairs to the stacks. Pictures of everybody who went in or out, up or down."

"Wow. A real locked room mystery." Her eyes sparkled. "Like in *Clue*. The colonel did it in the drawing room with a candlestick."

"Or in the library with a corkscrew." I signaled for the check.

Chapter 15

Back at the station I put my address list and invitations aside and scribbled some notes for my news break. I texted Old Eddie and Marty McCarthy. I'd need a camera and a location pretty quickly if I was going to have an update ready for the five o'clock news and a couple of teasers for station breaks every half hour. I was pretty sure Francine had the day off. Marty was busy building a new set for Wanda's cooking show, but Old Eddie was free for about an hour before he and Scott were due at a Salem-Beverly basketball game.

"That'll work, Eddie," I told him. "Let's set up in front of the library. That's where all the action has been so far."

"Okeydokey, Ms. Barrett," he said. "I'll pick you up out front in five minutes."

Rhonda did a fast makeup job for me, three minutes maybe. I grabbed my cardigan and notebook, said, "See ya later," to Rhonda, and headed downstairs. I was on the front steps when the VW pulled up. Old Eddie, always the gentleman, got out and held the passenger door for me. "Main library, right?"

"Right. Thanks for making time for this, Eddie."

"No problem. This is a real interesting assignment for me. I knew Willie, y'know."

That was a surprise. "I didn't know that. I just learned that he'd actually worked here at the station for quite a while on a sports show."

"Sure did. That Willie got around. I wasn't working here back then, but I used to bet some on the ponies, y'know. I knew him from when he worked up at Rockingham." Eddie gave me a kind of sheepish sidelong glance. "Used to give me tips on the races once in a while. He was a generous guy about some things. He had a lot of contacts in the sports world, you know? I heard once he brought both Bobby Orr and Larry Bird into the studio on the same day."

I figured that the gambling admission explained the sheepish look. Those races must have been the ones Willie had "fixed." I didn't comment on Eddie's gambling habit. "He apparently did some acting too," I said. "Hollywood Westerns and some local work."

He pulled the VW into the parking lot beside the library. "Yep. Saw him in a show once over in Beverly. Willie played a heck of a good vampire. Where do you want to set up, Ms. Barrett?"

I didn't see any police cars around. "Let's try the front steps."

Eddie opened the back door of the VW and handed me a stick mic. "Noticed you like these," he said, "and we got a new reflector too. Scotty says it makes the light softer on the face."

"I'm all for that," I said. "Let's get this done. You have a game to go to."

I picked a spot in front of the library doorway, while Eddie positioned the face-softening white circle to his satisfaction and set up his tripod. I read over my notes, took a peek at the previous night's script, and signaled the cameraman to begin filming.

"I'm Lee Barrett, reporting for WICH-TV from Salem's main library on Essex Street. Yesterday evening this historic old building was the scene of what some authorities are saying may be a murder. The body of William Wallace, eighty, was discovered by a library volunteer in the little-used upstairs section of the building known as the stacks. The elderly man had sustained significant damage to his upper vertebrae near the brain stem, sufficient to cause his death.

"Wallace, a one-time local baseball personality known as Wee Willie Wallace because of his short stature, had apparently been away from New England for more than two decades. He'd worked as a stuntman in some Hollywood Westerns and as an actor on stage. He'd also had an unfortunate stint as a trainer at the now defunct Rockingham Park racetrack in New Hampshire. He was convicted of doping horses and was sentenced to prison time. Longtime fans of WICH-TV might even remember Wallace as a frequent guest on a popular mid-century sports program called the 'Larry Laraby Show.'"

"Wee Willie Wallace's short stature was an asset on TV too. Here on WICH-TV, he played some familiar diminutive characters. Who remembers Cactus on the Ranger Rob show? Or the St. Patrick's Day leprechaun? Santa's elf? The Easter Bunny? Or my personal favorite, Marvel the Robot on Professor Mercury's Magical Science Circus?"

I saw Eddie's face register surprise and I imagined much of the viewing audience would be surprised too. I continued. "Police have no suspects in the matter, although security cameras installed within and outside the library have provided photographic records of all who entered the building and all who left it. Photo clips of the people library staff were unable to positively identify will be shown on this station. If you have any knowledge of unusual or suspicious activity of any kind in or nearby the library yesterday evening, please call the number at the bottom of your screen. This is Lee Barrett reporting from the Salem Main Library. WICH-TV will bring you updates on this developing story as they become available."

We shot a couple of ten-second leads for the teasers, Eddie sent the whole package over to Marty for editing, and we packed up our gear and arrived back at the station with time to spare. "Thanks Eddie," I said. "Good working with you."

"Same here, Ms. Barrett. I never knew that stuff about Willie being all those other little guys and he never told me about it. I remember all of 'em."

"I do too," I said. "So even if Willie wasn't such a good guy, he gave people some cute and funny characters to remember. I'm working on finding some of the others I remember watching on WICH-TV when I was a kid. Mr. Doan is planning an anniversary show. Do you remember Katie the Clown? And Professor Mercury?"

He beamed. "Sure do. My kids used to watch all those shows. Too bad the station doesn't do live programs like that anymore."

"Too expensive for small stations I guess," I said. "Actors and sets and all. Nobody does it these days except the big guys. Reality TV is a lot cheaper to produce. I'll see you later, Eddie. Enjoy the game."

"See you later, Ms. Barrett. Oh hey. Did you know Katie the Clown is still in Salem? Lives over on Highland Avenue. I see her once in a while at the grocery store."

"Do you know her last name, Eddie? All I know is Agnes."

"Sorry. I don't remember. I always heard that Agnes and Ranger Rob used to be an item though. He's got a horse barn over in Rockport. You could check with him."

"I will," I promised. "Funny how all the old employees stay linked together somehow, and they all seem to be connected to Wee Willie Wallace."

"Yep." Eddie closed the back door of the VW and climbed into the driver's seat. "Even me."

And now, me.

It was a little after three when I checked in with Marty. "Was the piece from the library okay? Was it long enough?" I asked. "Eddie used the new reflector. Did I look all right?"

She was about to attach a picture of a pumpkin pie to the wall of Wanda's kitchen set. "It was okay. Good, even. You looked fine. I padded it with a little footage of the robot—Marvel visiting kids at the hospital. Guess the tiny twerp wasn't all bad, huh?" She stood back to admire the pie portrait. "Did your cop boyfriend figure out yet who offed the little bastard?"

"Not yet. Did you know Willie too?" I knew Marty had been with the station for a very long time, but she wasn't as old as Old Eddie or Phil Archer. Still, I wouldn't have been surprised to hear that she had some connection to the dead man. *Everybody else around here seems to.*

"Nah. He was here before my time. Want to take a look at your spot and the thirty second promos?"

"Sure." She led the way to the control room. "Hey, is that good-looking security guard still working at the library?"

"You mean Dave?" I'd never thought about Dave's looks one way or the other. "Uh, yes. He's still there." I followed Marty into the small, equipment-filled room. "You know him?"

"I've run into him a few times. Wish I knew him better." She threw a few switches. "That thick white hair. Those bright blue eyes." She winked broadly. "Yes sir, that Dave Benson is quite a package." The monitor glowed and there I was in front of the library. "Here you go, Moon. See what you think."

Marty had done her usual good work—seamlessly

cleaned up the places where I'd flubbed a word or where a passing car messed up the sound. The Marvel Robot segment gave just the right balance to the piece. The teasers were good too. She'd used the introductory footage of me, then used bits from the longer report as a voice-over while she showed old photos of Willie and a few seconds of the police cars and coroner's van from the night I'd found the body.

"Great job as always, Marty," I said. "You make me look better than I really am."

"You've come a long way since *Nightshades*, kid," she said. "And tell Dave I was askin' for him."

I promised that I would. "Say, Marty. Rhonda says there are some Ranger Rob tapes in here. Can I borrow one or two?"

"Sure thing." She pointed to a shelf where a row of oblong plastic cases stood in a neat row. "Help yourself."

I selected two, each marked "Ranger Rob show," and tucked them into the fast-expanding hobo bag. "Do I need to sign for them?"

She waved a dismissive hand. "Nah. I know where you live."

I thanked her again and made my way through the long, black-walled studio and up the stairs to the second floor.

Chapter 16

I picked up where I'd left off on the card-addressing detail. Rhonda had finished her left-hand side and was already working on the Templeton list. "Howie's folks' list
looks like the society pages in the Sunday paper,"
Rhonda said. "Look at this." She held up her sheet. "An
ex-governor, a couple of old TV stars, a retired Hall of
Fame baseball player, and at least two Kennedys. Impressive."

"Yeah, well, look at mine," I said. "A retired Salem
bank vice president, the owner of the shop where Mr.
Doan buys his suits, and Marty McCarthy. So there!"

"Gotta admit it," she said, laughing. "You win."

We were still giggling when Mr. Doan pushed open
the glass door. "Glad to see happy employees," he said.
"How're we doing on getting our invitations in the mail?
Mrs. Doan wants to see those RSVPs coming in pronto!"

"We'll be finished by five o'clock, sir," Rhonda
promised, "and I'll drop them all off at the post office on
my way home."

I began to write faster, if not more legibly. Within
about fifteen minutes I'd finished the Doan half of my al-

phabetical sheet and moved over to the Templeton side, which held a longer list. I'd moved from Marlboro all the way to Merriweather when Mr. Doan emerged once again from his office. "Mrs. Doan just called me with a great idea for the party," he announced. "Going along with the Halloween theme, she thinks we need a magician. Guess who she suggested!"

Rhonda and I looked at each other. Blankly. "I give up," Rhonda said. "Who?"

"Here's where you come in, Ms. Barrett." He pointed to me. "Have you located Professor Mercury yet? For the anniversary show?"

"Not exactly," I said, which was a blatant overstatement. I hadn't the slightest idea whether the man was living or dead and I didn't even know his real name. "I've just begun searching the old WICH-TV personnel records."

"Well, speed it up, will you? Buffy thinks an old-time magician associated with the station would make a good impression on the guests."

"I'll get to work on it right away," I promised. "And if he's moved away or doesn't want to do it, I'm pretty sure we can get the Fabulous Fabio."

"The cake decorator?" Mr. Doan wasn't smiling.

"That's just his day job," I said. "He's really quite a good magician."

"Get Mercury." The office door closed firmly behind him.

"Okay," Rhonda said. "You two lost me back there at 'the Halloween theme.' Who are Professor Mercury and the Fabulous Fabio?"

"Professor Mercury had a kids' science magic show on the station back in the eighties and I have no idea where to find him. Fabio is a local part-time magician. In real life he's a baker at Pretty Party and I can get hold of him in two minutes."

"I guess I know which magician you're rooting for."

She picked up her pen and returned to her A-to-L Templeton guest list. "But I guess he's not Buffy's first choice."

"Guess not." *What Buffy wants, Buffy usually gets.* "Looks like I'll have to find Professor Mercury."

"Good luck with that. Write faster."

I did as she asked, but my mind was no longer focused on penmanship. I'd have to spend some serious time on the old files. *Maybe I can even take some home with me!*

I'd grab about half the personnel files from the old file cabinet, work on them at home, return them in the morning, and then take the other half. I'd probably have Agnes's name even before Jim Litka could give her my card and with any luck, by tomorrow night I'd get enough information on Professor Marvel to make Buffy Doan's Halloween wish come true. And first thing Monday morning I'd tackle the "Miscellaneous" drawer. I could hardly wait to get started.

I zipped through the Templeton names as though I was on automatic pilot, paying little attention to the "Who's Who" aspects of the upscale guest list. Rhonda still called out an impressive name every so often from her list and I made the appropriate *oh wow* responses. But my mind wasn't really engaged.

I'd already noticed that Wee Willie seemed to have some sort of connection to several past or present members of the WICH-TV staff. So far I knew he'd worked with Larry Laraby, Robert Oberlin, Agnes whatzername, Professor Mercury, and had a passing acquaintance with Old Eddie and Phil Archer. Was there a Mrs. Laraby somewhere in Salem? Some more staff or technical crew people who remembered Wee Willie? Or anything about him? I was especially looking forward to meeting Agnes, aka Katie the Clown. I was positive she'd be a wealth of information and as a former professional actress, she'd be a natural for a live interview.

Thank you, Scott Palmer, for handing this assignment

over to me so easily! It's going to be fun from here on in.
After all, when you start out by finding a dead body,
there's no place to go but up, right?

I scribbled my way through the list, made shorter by
the fact that my half of the letters contained the Qs, the
Xs, and the Zs and there were few last names beginning
with those. I reached the stamp-sticking part of the job
not long after Rhonda did, and as we put our stamped
postcards into neat piles, we finally had time for some
conversation.

I told her about how it was so interesting to me that
Wee Willie had, over the years, somehow touched so
many different people associated with the station—now
including me. "I think it may be important. But how am I
going to figure it all out and then how do I make enough
sense out of it to put it into a presentable report?"

She put down her roll of stamps, put her hand under her
chin, and got a faraway look in her eyes. She does that
when she's concentrating hard on something. I waited.

"Okay. I've got it." She resumed stamping. So did I.
"What you need is a flowchart. You know, one of those
charts with one name at the top in a little oblong box with
lines connecting it to other names in oblong boxes further
down on the paper. Then those names are connected by
lines to other names in little oblong boxes on the chart
until you can see how everybody is linked to the top
name and to each other." She gave a firm nod. "Yep.
That's all you need. A flowchart."

I visualized what she was talking about right away.
"You're right. I have to get a lot more information, and I
can fill in boxes as I go along. Thanks, Rhonda." I pointed
at the white schedule board behind her desk. "Maybe I'll
even get a whiteboard and some colored markers. I can
hardly wait to get home and get started."

"Hold your horses, girl. We've got a lot of postage
stamps to stick on before we can leave tonight. So keep

stickin'." They were "forever" stamps. I looked at my watch. *Maybe this is going to take forever!*

However, the stamp-sticking session gave me a chance to inspect each card for mistakes in addresses or illegible handwriting, considering that I hadn't been exactly focused on the project when I wrote them. They weren't in as bad shape as I thought they might be. Good thing there were extra cards though. I rewrote a couple that I'd messed up. I was all the way up to the Ws when what I'd written on one of them brought me to a complete stop. "Holy Halloween Party," I practically shouted. "Look at this." I held the card out so that she could read the name.

Mr. Wallace A. Williams.

She tilted her head to one side. "Who's he?"

"That's one of Wee Willie's names," I explained. "I'm beginning to visualize a bigger white board."

Chapter 17

"Must be a coincidence," Rhonda said. "Anyway, Wee Willie is dead."

"Wasn't dead when the Templetons made out their guest list," I pointed out. "I'm going to make a note of the address. Do you think that'd be okay?"

"The lists aren't marked 'confidential,'" she said. "Go ahead. Still, it's not a really unusual name. Why would high-society people like the Templetons have an old ex-con on their list? Must be some other Wallace Williams."

"You're probably right," I agreed. But I copied the name and address—a post office box—into my notebook just the same, then resumed my stamp-sticking. Rhonda and I finished with our designated cards at almost the same moment. She pointed to the gold starburst clock on the wall. It showed exactly four forty-five.

"Look," she said. "We got it done right on time. Couldn't have made it without you. Thanks, Lee. I'm outta here. Gotta get these to the post office." She swept the piles of cards into a large two-handled USPS plastic container. She tapped a button on her console. "Finished here, Mr. D. On my way to the post office. See you in the morning." She motioned for me to follow her. "Hurry up," she whispered, "before he thinks of something else for us to do for Buffy's Halloween bash."

I grabbed my purse and sweater and scooted along behind her into the hallway. She put the box on the floor and punched the elevator DOWN button "Take the stairs if you want to," she said. "I've got this thing." She tapped the plastic box with a toe.

"I'll ride with you," I said, grasping one of the box handles. "Here comes Old Clunky now." We waited for the brass cage to swing open and together we stepped inside.

"You know," she said, as we clunked and clanked our way down to the lobby, "I've been thinking about that Wallace Williams invitation."

"Me too. What about it?"

"Chances are, you know, that it's a coincidence. That the Templeton's Wallace Williams has nothing to do with your dead guy in the stacks."

"He's not *my* dead guy," I mumbled. "But what if it's not a coincidence?"

"Simple. Just ask young Howie Junior. He must know his parent's A-list friends."

I hadn't thought of that. "Maybe. I think I'll just do a little checking around first. You're probably right about it being a coincidence anyway. I don't want young Howie to think I'm curious about his family."

"But you are," she said as the elevator door slid open.

We each took a handle of the box and walked together across the black-and-white tiled lobby. "That's true," I admitted. "I'm curious lately about several people at this station. Maybe I'm just being nosy."

"I don't think so," she said. "I mean unless you're getting curious about me."

I walked with her to her car—a nice little white Kia Soul—and helped situate the box on the passenger seat.

"Not unless you've ever had some dealings with a short, baseball-playing, horse-doping, Hollywood-actor-type ex-con."

She raised her right hand and laughed. "Not my type. Honest! See you Monday?"

"See you Monday," I echoed and walked across the lot to where my sweet Vette glistened in the fading sunlight. I wondered if Aunt Ibby had been admitted back into the library yet. I sat for a moment in my car, admiring the beauty of the harbor at sundown and texted my aunt. "U home?"

It only took a moment for her to call me. "Hi," I said. "I was just wondering if you were home or if the police had let you go back to work."

"Yes. We're back! Just can't let anybody go up into the stacks yet. I think I'll work a little late tonight, dear. Are you all right for supper? Do you have plans with Pete?"

"I have some dinners in the freezer," I said, "and Pete's on duty all weekend. Guess it'll just be O'Ryan and me. We'll be fine."

"I know you will. Tyler and I will both work the Sunday shift too, one to five tomorrow afternoon." She sighed softly. "People have suddenly found a need to visit the library—I'm afraid it's due more to morbid curiosity than to intellectual pursuit."

"Probably," I agreed. "But some of those people will find out what a great library we have. They'll be back."

"I'm sure you're right." Her voice brightened. "I'll see you later this evening."

We said our goodbyes and I backed out of the lot. That frozen dinner option sounded pretty unappetizing. A nice rotisserie chicken and a prepared salad with blue cheese dressing sounded a whole lot better. I aimed the Vette for Shaw's and added a slice of cherry cheesecake to my mental shopping list.

By the time I left the grocery store with my chosen meal, plus one of Rachael Ray's newest kitty treats for O'Ryan, the sun had set. *Where did I park?* The parking lot was filled. Saturday night is food shopping night in many Salem homes. I pulled out my key remote, hit the unlock button, and watched for my headlights to flash.

Found it! I hurried across the lot toward the Bahama blue beauty, and put the bag onto the passenger seat. I walked around to the driver's side and noticed that the green Subaru Forester right beside mine was not empty. (Late model. Probably last year's. I'm pretty good at identifying cars. My years as a NASCAR wife taught me a lot.) The glow of a cigarette briefly illuminated the lower half of a man's face. A baseball cap hid his eyes. Was he looking at me? I couldn't tell. *So why is my heart pounding?*

I knew the answer to that. It was the idea I'd been trying to push out of my mind. *Did whoever killed Wee Willie up in the stacks see me? Does he think I saw him? Is he following me?*

I tried to force the bad thought away—thought instead about chicken and salad and cheesecake and that Aunt Ibby would be home soon and that it was silly to suspect every random person who looked the least bit suspicious.

There. Much better. I started the big engine, taking comfort in the powerful sound of it. I began to back up. Looked right. Looked left.

The man in the Subaru took a drag on his cigarette. It lit up his mouth and cheeks the creepy way that little flashlight had illuminated Howie's.

The man turned his head toward me and smiled.

Chapter 18

I backed out of the space much too fast and way too carelessly. *What if somebody is walking behind me? Or what if I tangle with a rogue shopping cart?* Neither happened, thank God, and I slowed to a proper pace before I'd reached the lot exit. But all the way home I kept checking the rearview mirrors.

This wasn't like me. Not at all. I was overreacting and I knew it. The idea that someone who thought I'd seen a crime being committed might be stalking me had brought with it a vivid and totally unrealistic point of view. Why shouldn't a man, sneaking a smoke while his wife shopped for groceries, look over at me and smile. Or more likely, look at my really cool car and smile.

By the time I'd reached Oliver Street and opened the garage door, my heart rate felt more normal. I'd hoped the Buick would be there but it wasn't. I rolled into my accustomed space, closed the garage door, and walked around to the passenger side and picked up my bag of groceries. The side door of our garage opens onto a flagstone path leading past the garden to the back steps of the

house. Solar lamps along the way gave a golden glow to
the low rows of herbs and fall blooms bordering the garden fence. Basil, mint, and rosemary were interspersed
with marigolds and zinnias. Within the fence though,
where hazy dark shadows had formed, the sunflowers
nodded round shaggy heads and waved skinny, leafy
arms in my direction. I walked a little faster.

O'Ryan, as always, knew I was coming and waited for
me on the top step. "I'm so happy to see you, big cat," I
told him as I unlocked the door. "Brought you a treat."

O'Ryan knows the word "treat," and acknowledged it
with a loud, purring, "Mrrripp." (It's entirely possible
that he may know *all* of our words.) We started up the two
flights of stairs to my apartment. Wait a minute! Did I re-
lock the door? I turned and rushed back down to check.
O'Ryan kept right on going. It was locked, of course. I gave
the knob a hard shake for good measure and hurried to
catch up with the cat.

O'Ryan was already inside when I unlocked and carefully relocked *that* door. He was curled up in his zebra-
print wing chair, pretending he'd fallen asleep waiting for
me. "Come on, you big fake," I said. "Time for our sup
per."

We walked together down the short hall past the bathroom to the kitchen, me clicking on light switches all the
way. O'Ryan jumped up onto the windowsill overlooking
the backyard while I put the groceries on the counter,
hung my hobo bag on the back of a Lucite chair, then
turned on the bedroom light and put my cardigan away.

I filled O'Ryan's bowl with "Paw Lickin' Chicken,"
then carved a couple of slices from the rotisserie bird for
myself, dumped dressing onto the colorful salad, and put
the cheesecake into the refrigerator for later. O'Ryan was
happily hunched over his bowl, and I'd just lifted a fork-
ful of cucumber with a lovely blob of blue cheese on it

when the cat suddenly streaked across the room, back to his windowsill perch. He pressed his face against the pane.

"What's going on, boy?" I pushed my chair back and stood behind him, leaning close to the window and peering into the darkness. "Is Aunt Ibby out there?" Kit-Cat clock indicated a few minutes before seven—just about the time I expected she'd be through at the library. "Aren't you going to go downstairs to welcome her home?"

O'Ryan turned his fuzzy head and looked at me, then jumped down from the sill and trotted down the hall to the living room, where I heard the cat door swing open. I stayed at the window, looking down to where the solar lights marked the flagstone path. I saw my aunt approaching the house and I smiled when she bent to pick some fresh herbs as she passed the garden. I couldn't see the back steps from where I stood, but imagined that O'Ryan would already be stationed there to welcome her home. I was about to return to my salad when a shadow appeared on the path, then a tall figure.

Someone is following her!

The fastest way to get downstairs was the front stairway. I bolted through my kitchen door and raced down the stairs, taking them two at a time. I dashed through her living room and into her kitchen. "Aunt Ibby," I cried, just as she opened the kitchen door. "Watch out! Someone is . . ."

"Good heavens, Maralee," she said. "Whatever is the matter? Come on in, Dave."

The security guard, carrying several cartons piled one on top of the other, ducked his head slightly as he came through the doorway, and placing the box on the counter, nodded in my direction. "Hi, Ms. Barrett. Everything okay?" O'Ryan looked from one to the other of us, then sat on his haunches in front of the refrigerator.

"Uh, hi, Dave. Sure. No problem. O'Ryan just tore out of my kitchen so fast I thought something might be wrong." The cat swiveled his head around, doing that cat-glaring thing in my direction. *Oh sure. Blame the cat, why don't you?* I almost heard the words.

"Dave was kind enough to follow me in his car," my aunt said, "and to carry this huge pile of old library cards, book donation records, and assorted other documents that have never been properly catalogued." She made a make-believe sad face. "Guess who volunteered to do the homework involved."

"I'll be glad to help if I can," I offered, hoping to derail any conversation about my near-panicked entrance, "if it's not too technical."

Her expression brightened. "Not technical at all. Just tedious."

"Well, if you girls are all set here, I guess I'll be getting back to the library." Dave moved toward the door. "Officer Costa was supposed to get off duty at seven."

"You go along then," my aunt said, "and here. Take some cookies with you. She reached into the Humpty-Dumpty cookie jar and put a dozen snickerdoodles into a plastic box. I walked with Dave to the back door, and watched as he hurried toward his car, then I closed and locked the door once again.

I locked the kitchen door behind me too, and opened the carton on the counter. "This looks like all different kinds of paper documents. What's in here?"

"Things that we've never found time to catalog properly." She sighed. "And there's not enough money in the budget to hire someone to do it."

I lifted a few of the papers at the top of one of the boxes and pulled out an old library card. "The date on this is 1979," I said. "What are you saving it for? It's just an old card."

"I know. Seems silly, but the directors don't like to get rid of anything until it's been copied or listed on a computer somehow. We just pick away at it when we have some spare time. Wait 'til you see the receipt books. Every time somebody donates books whoever is at the desk writes a paper receipt. People can take them off their taxes, you know."

I lifted a book of duplicate receipts from another box. "Like this? These plain old receipt books you buy at the office store?"

"Yep. That's just one. There must be hundreds of them in there. That's what makes it so heavy. We've always done it that way. For years. What's interesting about these is that the sports books on the floor where you found Wee Willie were mostly donated."

"Does Pete know about this?"

"It was his idea."

"I get it. If you go through these and match them up with the books Wee Willie was looking at up there in 790 you'll know where they came from—and maybe what the killer wanted. Do we have a list?"

"Pete e-mailed me the list. There are nineteen books on it. Want to help?" She arranged the boxes on the counter, largest to smallest.

Did the killer see me? Does he think I saw him?

"Sure. Let me run upstairs and put my dinner in the fridge. I left it on the table when I ran down here."

"Oh course. What was that all about anyway? You seemed quite excited." She frowned. "You must still be hungry. I'll fix something."

"Please don't bother," I said, not meaning it.

"No trouble at all," she said, knowing I didn't mean it. "I have homemade vegetable soup. Right from our garden."

"Thank you," I said. "I'll be right back." I climbed the front stairs once again and realized that I'd left the door to my kitchen wide open. *Not smart.* I hurried inside, closing it carefully behind me, covered all the components of my dinner with plastic wrap, put them into the refrigerator, and started back to my aunt's kitchen—and vegetable soup.

On the way down the front stairs I rehearsed the explanation for my bat-out-of-hell entrance to her kitchen earlier. Did I have good reason to be worried about the killer having seen me in the stacks? Or was I just being paranoid about the whole thing?

I sat at the round table—no room at the counter—with a steaming bowl of soup in front of me, New England pilot crackers and a glass of milk on the side. "I was looking out the window when you arrived home tonight and when I saw Dave following you—of course I didn't know it was Dave—I kind of freaked out."

"I see," she said.

"I've been thinking about what you said, about me maybe seeing the killer and him maybe seeing me."

"I see," she repeated. "You thought he might be following me?"

"I know. I'm being unreasonable. Pete says they'll have the guy in a day or so. He's surely going to show up on one or more of the cameras."

"I'm sure he's right. Trust Pete." She reached across the table and patted my hand. "Thank you for worrying about me though. Now enjoy your soup while I try to arrange these boxes in some sort of order."

So that's what I did. I enjoyed my soup and I trusted Pete and I hardly worried at all about the smiling man in the Subaru.

Chapter 19

With the receipt books—over two hundred of them—divided into two piles, and with a pad of paper and sharpened number two pencils in front of each of us, we began the search for sports books. Not as easy a task as it might seem. Not all of the receipts included book titles, although the ones that acknowledged quantities of books sometimes did. Most of the receipts had a "subject line" and those usually gave the category of the books involved. The titles, my aunt explained, would show up on an inventory list on or around the same date as the receipt. "Looks like lots of checking and cross-checking, doesn't it?" I asked.

"Afraid so." She sounded cheerful. She enjoys this kind of thing. "Almost all of the books in the stacks are hardcover editions. Most of the paperback ones usually go to the Friends of the Library book sales. Oh, look. Someone donated one on NASCAR drivers. Do you think your Johnny is in it?"

"Wouldn't be a bit surprised," I said. "Are we just going to put all the sports-related receipts in one place, then check those against the list Pete sent over?"

"Yes. I think that'd be best. Skip any fiction sports title though. Those wouldn't have been shelved in seven-ninety."

So we went through the receipts, one by one, struggling to decipher a variety of handwriting styles, pulling out any that seemed to refer to sports. While we worked, only pausing once for tea, I told her about Mrs. Doan's recent request that we find Professor Mercury for her Halloween party entertainment. "I've got a good lead on Katie the Clown, and you say you know where Ranger Rob is. I'm thinking that one or both of them will know where the professor is." I pulled a slip that said "Assorted sports books. Fifty-two pieces." I'd almost tossed it onto the pile when I looked at the name of the donor and did a Three Stooges–worthy double take. "Oh my God. Look." I held the receipt in front of her. "Look who it's made out to."

"Sharon Stewart," she read aloud. "It's dated a few months ago. Should the name mean something to me?"

"Stewart is the name of the family whose house was broken into recently. Books were scattered around there too. What do you bet these are some of the books that wound up on the library floor—along with Wee Willie?"

"I'll bet you're right. The names of the fifty-two books will be on the library inventory list. They get filed by date. I can pull it up on my computer. Want to put this job aside for now?"

I didn't bother to answer, just followed my aunt who was already halfway across the room on her way to her office.

She handed me the printout Pete had sent listing the books he'd taken from the stacks. I scooted one of the cherrywood chairs up as close as I could get to hers and watched as she logged into the library account. Her hands flew over the keyboard as she scrolled through myriad numbered categories. She landed on *inventory-donations*. "Okay. Here we go. What's the date on the receipt?"

Glad I'd thought to bring it with me, I read the date aloud and added "fifty-two books—sports related. Signed by Sharon Stewart."

"It'll be so much easier when we have actual copies of the receipts, by date and topic all in one online file," she said. "But this system is better than nothing. I'll read the titles aloud and you check them off if they're on Pete's list."

So that's what we did. The first few titles on the inventory list yielded no matches but then we hit two in a row. I checked off *A Day on the Bleachers* by Arnold Hana and *Ball Four* by Jim Bouton. That was enough to energize us. Before too long we'd found an even dozen books whose names appeared on both lists. That was all, but we knew it was enough to prove that there was a real connection between the B&E at the Stewart house in North Salem where nothing was stolen, and the murdered man in the library stacks.

"Do you want to call Pete about this, or shall I?" Aunt Ibby asked.

"You call him," I said. "This was your assignment and you did all the work. I'll listen in."

"I'll put it on speaker," she said. "Hello, Pete? Isobel Russell here. Maralee and I have done as you suggested. We've checked the donated books list with the list of the books you took with you and we've found a dozen matches."

"Good work, Ms. Russell. And fast, too. Would you fax the material over to me?"

"Of course, and Pete, we've learned a couple of new things you might find of interest."

"I'll just bet you have." I heard the smile in his voice. "What've the snoop sisters found this time?"

"Well, first of all . . ." My aunt ignored the "snoop sisters" designation. She's come to like the name. "At least a dozen of the books on your list were donated to the library by Sharon Stewart. Does that name ring a bell?"

"Sure does. The break-in on Dearborn Street. Good work, you two. Anything else?"

"I noticed that all of the books on your list were published between the fifties and the seventies—if that's important."

"It might very well be, Ms. Russell. Thank you. Good night—and good night to your sidekick too. Tell her I'll call her later."

"I will, and I'll fax all of this over to you right now."

Her conversation finished, she turned on the fax machine. "Did you get the significance of the publication dates?"

"Larry Laraby," I said. "The books were all published before he died. Wee Willie, Sharon Stewart, and Larry Laraby. I think maybe we have a three-way tie. I wonder if *all* of the books Sharon donated were around the same age."

"That won't be too hard to check," she said, those green eyes lighting up at the prospect of more snooping. "Once we can get back up into the stacks we'll do a thorough inventory of seven-ninety."

"If we're right, then Sharon Stewart is connected somehow to Larry Laraby. I'm going to need a bigger flowchart if this keeps up."

"A flowchart?"

I told her about Rhonda's idea of charting the various people involved and each one's connection to Wee Willie. "You'll be surprised when I tell you how many people I've found so far. Even the Templetons. Did I mention that they have a Wallace Williams on their guest list for the Halloween party?"

"It can't be *that* Wallace Williams, can it?" She turned off the fax machine and we started back to the kitchen. "Not at the Templeton's party."

"Probably not," I admitted, "but the way things have been linking up lately, I wouldn't be *too* surprised if it is. I'm wondering about Sharon Stewart too. Pete said the Stewarts are a nice older couple."

"Really? One of the women in my Zumba class lives on Dearborn Street. Maybe she knows them. I could text her." She looked at the kitchen clock. Nine-thirty. "I don't think it's too late." She didn't wait for me to agree, just pulled out her phone and those flying fingers tapped in a fast message.

"What did you ask her about them?" I wondered. "Just if she knows them?"

"That . . . and if she does, *what* does she know *about* them."

"You *are* a snoop!"

"I know. It's such fun. Decaf and snickerdoodles?" She gestured toward the coffeepot.

"Absolutely."

I'd just added French vanilla creamer to my coffee when my aunt's phone buzzed. "Hello, Hazel," she said. "Hope I didn't call too late." That was followed by a couple of "Uh-huhs," at least one "no kidding," and finally a "thanks so much, Hazel. See you in class." She turned to face me. "Guess you can put Sharon on your chart all right, but you'd better write her in as Sharon *Laraby* Stewart."

"Sharon Laraby Stewart," I repeated. "Larry Laraby's daughter. The books on the floor up in the stacks and the books on the floor at the Stewart's house and the books on the floor in Larry Laraby's study must be the same books. At least some of them."

"Must be," she agreed. "Want to call Pete?"

"I'll do it this time," I said, reaching for my phone. "I'll just text him three words."

She nodded. "Sharon Laraby Stewart."

"Right." I tapped in the text. "Now about those cookies . . ."

Chapter 20

Later, when I climbed the twisty back stairs to my apartment, it was with a feeling of achievement. My aunt and I had done a good job with our methodical approach to sorting out the question of the books in section seven-ninety of the stacks. The discovery of Sharon Stewart's link to Wee Willie was frosting on the cake. Never mind that Pete and the police would have figured it all out anyway. Just as I liked being first with breaking news, I liked being first with this.

O'Ryan had followed me upstairs and had already staked out his spot at the foot of my bed. He turned around three times, then, with eyes closed, plunked himself down on the cushy blue quilt. It was nearly time for the late news. Carrying my phone with me to the bathroom so I wouldn't miss Pete's call, I showered and donned Donald Duck–print pajamas, turned on the bedroom TV, and joined the cat on the bed. The station's popular night news anchor Buck Covington led with a story about estimated repairs on Boston's beautiful gold-domed Massachusetts State House, followed by an update on the murder in the library. Yes, they were calling it murder. Howard Templeton had scored a brief statement from the medical examiner's office verifying "foul play" in Wee Willie's death. Covington followed it up with a reedited version of my most recent standup in front of the library along with one of Marty's brilliantly constructed retrospectives of Wee Willie's life from sports hero to ex-con. I relaxed against the pillows. Good job all around.

River North's *Tarot Time* show would follow the news and I was still wide awake. I'd already seen the promos for the night's scary movie. During October River featured appropriately witchy topics and tonight's offering was *Practical Magic.* I remembered the 1995 hit starring Nicole Kidman and Sandra Bullock as witch sisters—I'd shown it myself on my *Nightshades* show. Good movie. I didn't mind watching it again, but I especially wanted to see River's tarot-card-of-the-day segment. Would it hold a message for me the way the Wheel of Fortune card had? I could hardly wait.

Sometimes Buck Covington stays around and makes a brief appearance on *Tarot Time.* Much of the audience has figured out that River and Buck are "an item" and they seem to look forward to Buck showing up on set to shuffle the deck of cards or to read the first commercial. River was ethereally gorgeous in silver and lavender with her trademark silver stars and moons woven into her hair. Buck, with his perfect movie-star features, was a fitting companion for her. Together they made one of those "beautiful couples" we never get tired of looking at, like David Beckham and Posh Spice or Prince Harry and Meghan.

River asked Buck to draw the special card for the night's extra explanation. He drew the King of Wands. I was somewhat familiar with the card. It's rarely shown up in any of the readings River has done for me, but I recognized it immediately when the camera moved in for a close-up. I'd always been fascinated, not so much by the kingly image, but by the little lizard that sits beside him.

"The King of Wands," River began, "wears exquisite royal robes and a long, flowing mantle. Lions and salamanders adorn the pillar behind him." *Salamanders, huh? They remind me of the little lizards I saw every day in Florida.* "The salamanders, including the live one in the foreground, signify fire," River continued. "Wands represent the scepter of the King and also can be read as the magician's wand of power. This particular magician's rod can conjure the elemental forces and use them for either spiritual or material gain." She tapped the card with her forefinger. "Sometimes this card can indicate an unexpected inheritance." She smiled. "Good news for somebody. But, be careful if the card is reversed." She spun the card so that the King was upside-down. "It might indicate a man with high principles who can sometimes be intolerant of others."

River replaced the King in the deck and Buck reshuffled the cards. He was getting very good at it, showing a bit of Vegas-like flair. River delivered a commercial for Harbor Sweets while Buck waved a reluctant goodbye and left the set. I tried to make the King of Wands message relate to me somehow the way the Wheel of Fortune card had, but other than the brief reference to a magician's wand—when I was looking for a magician for Buffy's party—there didn't seem to be anything at all in it for me.

Why should there be? It's just a TV show!

I plumped up the pillows and leaned back to watch the two witch sisters try to find a way around a curse that prevents them from finding everlasting love.

Everlasting love. Is there such a thing? I think so. Even though Johnny is gone, I don't think my love for him has to ever die. And my love for Pete? That's alive and well and growing, and that's a beautiful thing. I'd put the phone on the bedside table and I looked over at it, willing it to ring. I was excited about our Sharon Laraby Stewart discovery and wanted to hear what Pete had to say about this latest Wee Willie connection.

O'Ryan had left his foot-of-the-bed position where he was probably faking sleep anyway, and now rested on my lap, unblinking golden eyes focused on my face. Disconcerting. "Stop watching me," I told him. "Watch the movie. There's a cat in it." He did a little two-front-paw flex, which may be the cat equivalent of a shrug, and faced not the TV but the phone—which, of course, promptly rang.

"Hi, babe, sorry to call so late, but I promised."

"Not too late at all," I said. "O'Ryan and I are dying to hear what you've found out about the North Salem Stewarts and the Larry Laraby connection to what's going on."

"O'Ryan is interested too?" A smile was in his voice.

"Very. Sharon is Laraby's daughter. Is that right? And she had some of his old sports books, which she donated to the library? Is that what happened?"

He laughed. "Slow down, Nancy Drew. You're going too fast for me. Yes. Sharon Laraby is Larry Laraby's daughter. She did donate more than fifty books that *may have* belonged to her father to the library, but she'd only recently acquired them herself."

"Recently?" By this time O'Ryan had his head on my shoulder, listening intently. "But Larry died more than thirty years ago! Where have they been all this time?"

"Think about it. His widow, Annie Laraby, inherited his entire estate. She died in Florida two months ago, leaving everything to her two children. Sharon Stewart's half included the books."

"So the books—or rather whatever Wee Willie was looking for in the books—-was in Florida all this time?"

"Not exactly."

"Not exactly how?"

"Storage locker in Peabody. Books and other stuff have been neatly stored in air-conditioned comfort in a storage locker ever since Mrs. Laraby moved to Florida to live close to her oldest son in Palm Beach about six months after her husband died."

I've had some experience with storage lockers myself. The beautiful antique carousel horse who adorns my living room bay window was rescued from one. "Was Sharon paying for the storage all this time?"

"Nope. Mrs. Laraby's bank made the monthly payments and Sharon inherited that responsibility too. She chose to empty the locker and dispose of the contents herself."

"So somehow, Wee Willie and whoever killed him figured out where the books had gone."

"Apparently." *Do I hear cop voice creeping in? Is this all the information he's going to share?*

I pushed my luck. "Do we know yet what the heck they were looking for? Do we know if they found it?"

The smiley voice came back. "Where did that 'we' come from?"

"Come on, Pete. I'll bet you didn't know about Sharon being a Laraby until Aunt Ibby found out about her."

"Okay. You've got me. I called Mrs. Stewart as soon as I got your text. She filled us in on quite a few things. We've lined up a couple of people to talk to about what it might be that Willie was after. I can't name names though. You understand."

"Sure I do. Listen, this might not mean anything, but the guest list for Buffy Doan's Halloween party has a Wallace Williams on it. It's probably just a coincidence, but I wrote it down along with the address. Want it?"

"Sure. It's a fairly common name, but I'll check it out."

I retrieved my notebook and read off the name and

post office box. "So in exchange, how about one little hint—without naming names of course?"

"We plan to talk to some folks who worked with Laraby on his collectible shows." He spoke hesitantly. I understood the hesitation. He is, after all, really a police detective. And I am not, after all, really Nancy Drew. But he had given me the hint I was after. *Aunt Ibby and I will begin researching sports collectibles—and collectors—starting tomorrow!*

That flowchart just keeps growing.

Chapter 21

I don't usually work on Sundays, but with my shortened hours it seemed like a good option. I woke up in the morning with a mental to-do list buzzing around in my head. The job must come first, of course. Start rounding up those old-time WICH-TV performers for the station anniversary wingding. Next, the boss's wife's Halloween party. Find a magician for Buffy. Preferably Professor Mercury. If he's moved away or died, get the Fabulous Fabio instead. Next, and truly uppermost in my mind, tell Aunt Ibby about the sports collectible shows connections Pete had mentioned.

It promises to be an interesting day.

Maybe with a little luck, I'd even get to do a field report or two. I decided to grab coffee and a bite of something downstairs with Aunt Ibby while I caught her up on the Laraby situation. Then I'd head for the station and do as much as I could there about both celebrations—Halloween eve and the station anniversary. That way, I'd be available if anything good turned up that hadn't already been handed over to the Templeton heir. And what about the Templetons? Maybe I could do a little digging about their possible connection with Willie.

I showered, dried my hair, and dressed quickly in jeans and black turtleneck sweater. I tossed a denim jacket over my shoulders. Chose the big leather Jacki Easlick hobo bag again because it holds a ton of stuff and still looks great. Did eyes and lip gloss—if any TV face time was going to be involved during the day Rhonda could do the necessary makeup. Kit-Cat clock showed eight-thirty. "Come on, O'Ryan," I said, opening the door to the upstairs hall. "Pretty slim pickin's for breakfast here. Let's go downstairs."

O'Ryan didn't need a second invitation. Like a stripy yellow streak he zipped down two flights of stairs and disappeared into my aunt's living room before I'd even reached the second floor. Aunt Ibby welcomed us warmly as always. Because O'Ryan's early arrival had announced my imminent approach, she'd already filled my cup with coffee and placed a hot baking powder biscuit on a plate along with a tiny ramekin of homemade strawberry jam.

This day was off to a good start.

I didn't lose any time in catching my aunt up on the little bit—crumbs, really—of information Pete had been able to share. I knew that just the words "collectibles" and "collectible shows" would be enough to put her professional research librarian's mind into gear. I was sure that it wouldn't take long for her to start cooking up something worthwhile from those crumbs.

It took less time than I'd thought. I was still sipping my first cup of coffee and had just carefully pulled my biscuit apart into fluffy layers when she leaned back in her chair and smiled.

"Wee Willie," she said. "Remember the team-signed baseball?"

I searched my memory. "Uh, no."

"The kinescope of the Larry Laraby show that Phil Archer showed on your first interview. Wee Willie gave Laraby a team-signed ball. *For his collection.*"

"I see," I said, remembering the grainy film, and saw where she was going with this line of thinking. "Laraby was a sports memorabilia collector as well as a broadcaster—and later a collectibles show promoter!"

"Exactly. And if that film was from the early seventies, I'll bet that ball was worth something. Was his collection in that storage locker too?" Aunt Ibby wondered.

"Beats me," I said. "But now that you mention it, I wonder what else Wee Willie's big-name contacts signed for Larry's collection." I thought once again about the four book-reading symbols on the Wheel of Fortune tarot card, and repeated to my aunt Old Eddie's story of Wee Willie bringing real sports personalities right into the station.

"That's something else Phil Archer might know about," she said.

"Right. I'm going to ask him about the sports star personal appearances, and I'm going to find out what he knows about Wally Williams."

I didn't linger too long over breakfast, although it deserved more attention than I gave it. Aunt Ibby and Tyler were both going to work the Sunday shift, one to five o'clock. My aunt promised to research old newspaper ads and reviews of the collectibles shows Larry Laraby had hosted. I thought about the picture of the man in the station lobby and tried to picture him at one of his shows, surrounded by autographed baseballs and hockey sticks and brightly colored T-shirts and ball caps and crowds of memorabilia fans. But my mind kept returning to that sad foot in the black shoe I'd seen in the mirror.

By nine-thirty I'd backed the Vette out onto Oliver Street and headed for WICH-TV. If traffic was kind to me I'd be at the station in plenty of time to catch Phil doing his show prep for the noon news. The month of October in Salem attracts a lot of tourists and visiting witches, so we never know exactly what to expect on the roads. "Halloween Happenings" is more than a Chamber of Commerce catchphrase. There seems to be something happening relative to the witchy holiday in virtually every part of the city. Tour buses clogging narrow streets are the norm. I took the long way via Bridge Street, avoiding the Witch Museum and the Hawthorne Hotel and checked in with Rhonda at a little after ten. (Rhonda actually *likes* working Sundays. She gets time and a half, and Mr. Doan comes in late and leaves early.)

"Hey, I hope this doesn't bother you," she said, "but Chief Whaley just announced a presser about the library murder and I had to send Templeton over to the police station to cover it."

Is he getting time and a half too?

It did bother me just a little but I tried not to show it. "Well, that's exactly the kind of face time he needs, isn't it? What time is the presser?"

"They're trying for ten-thirty, but you know how skittish the chief is about these things. The man has terminal stage fright."

"At least they're never very long. The better Templeton handles this kind of report, the quicker he'll be 'movin' on' to bigger and better things."

She arched perfectly penciled eyebrows. "Guess that's one way to look at it. What's your plan for today?"

"I need to talk with Phil again. It's about the anniversary reunion thing. He still here?"

"Still here," she said. "I think he's in the downstairs studio. Something about a promo for the Witches' Ball. They're using River's set to shoot it."

"Makes sense," I said, thinking of the star-studded blue backdrop. "I'll just run on down there and try to grab Phil for a minute."

"The anniversary show, huh?" She cocked her head to one side and looked at me closely. "And maybe a little investigative reporting on the side?"

"Maybe," I admitted. "Just a little bit." I took the stairs down to the studio instead of the elevator. There was no red light glowing above the green metal door, so I let myself in. From the doorway I could see that the *Tarot Time* set was fully lighted. River's furniture had been replaced with three good-looking wing chairs and a long table with a centerpiece of fall flowers arranged in a black cauldron, flanked on either side by a pointed witch hat and a lighted pumpkin. A wispy cheesecloth ghost and a fluttering black bat animated by an offstage fan bounced above the set.

Marty was on camera and Phil sat in one chair facing an attractive woman I recognized as one of the major organizers of Salem's annual Halloween extravaganza— The Witches' Ball. The third chair was occupied by Christopher Rich. Chris is kind of a self-promoting genius, always available to anyone who'll let him talk about his shop, Christopher's Castle. I expected that he was there because the shop—which I admit is quite nice— carries a big selection of excellent costumes and jewelry. He undoubtedly does a good business with well-heeled ball-goers.

I tiptoed down the center aisle, pausing for a moment beside the *Saturday Business Hour* cubicle. *I need to find time today to get a peek at that miscellaneous file.* I slipped into a seat across the aisle from the set. Phil raised a hand in greeting. I waved back. Chris Rich noticed me too, and mouthed "Hello Lee." And made the "call me" motion with thumb and little finger forming a mock telephone. The man loves talking to anybody in the media—even those of us whose hours have been reduced.

I watched the group as they prepared to record the promo. Marty moved some props around, adjusted the sound mechanism, placed the teleprompter so that it was invisible to viewers, then pointed to Phil and the red light went on.

Phil introduced the guests first, then read from the prepared script on the teleprompter. "The chill winds of autumn whisper to witches and strangers alike who journey to Salem from around the globe to celebrate the season with the one and only Salem Witches' Halloween Ball!"

The chairwoman of the event described the grand ballroom and the laser light show, the free psychic readings and the ritual drummers' performance. She gave the costume theme of the ball, "Earth, Air, Water, Spirit, or other elements," and announced the thousand-dollar first prize for best costume, and another thousand for best group. Rich mentioned that he stocked costumes for fairies, elves, and other ethereal beings, and waxed poetic about the designer swag bags guests would receive and mentioned pentagram rings and crystals, also available at Christopher's Castle. "Don't forget," he added, "I carry a full line of magic tricks too. Mystify the guests at your own home celebration!"

Of course. I remember now. Chris carries all kinds of professional as well as amateur magicians' needs. I'll bet he might even know where Professor Mercury is! I'd definitely take him up on that "call me" suggestion. Phil asked a few more questions, advised viewers to make reservations soon, and gave the contact numbers. The haunting strains of "O Fortuna" from Carl Orff's *Carmina Burana* filled the studio as the phone and website numbers rolled. The red light clicked off and Phil and his guests rose from their chairs and shook hands all around.

With a dramatic bow, Chris Rich took the chairwoman's arm and escorted her toward the exit. Phil stopped to say a few words to Marty, who'd already begun putting River's set back together, then came across the aisle to where I sat. "Hello, Lee. Rhonda texted me that you had some questions about the anniversary show." He took the seat next to mine. "How can I help?"

"Couple of things," I said. "Do you remember Wee Willie Wallace working here?"

He frowned. "I remember him being on Larry Laraby's show occasionally."

"My aunt does too. Was Wee Willie the one who brought the big sports stars with him to the show?"

"Willie was the contact for most of the baseball guys," he said. "He knew a lot of the big-name players. Willie was kind of a novelty in the sport, you know? He was so darned small. Around five foot three or four, as I remember. The big men used to get a kick out of hanging out with him I guess."

"So he used to introduce them to Laraby and they'd appear on his show?"

"Sure. There weren't a lot of stations back in those days. The players liked the publicity and Laraby liked the ratings. He was good, Laraby was."

"Thanks Phil. I noticed that Willie gave Laraby a team-signed ball for his collection. With all the famous players coming by, I guess he got lots of souvenirs."

"Oh, yeah. But he didn't hold onto many of them. He used to place ads in the collectors' magazines and sell them. Baseballs, game shirts. I suppose he saved some of the loot for the collectibles shows he ran later. Ran those all over the country. Right up until he died." Phil's expression changed. He looked sad. "He was a popular guy. Everybody missed him. Big funeral."

"I'll bet. Say, Phil. What did you mean when you mentioned Wally Williams and told me it was a good place to start? I found out it was just one of Wee Willie's names," I explained, "but what was that supposed to be the start of?"

"You're a good reporter, Lee." He looked around and dropped his voice. "And a darned good investigator. I told you about how Larry Laraby died. I've always thought Wee Willie had something to do with it but I can't prove anything. I thought maybe if you got interested, maybe you could dig into it. Then, when Willie died the same way—well, almost the same . . ." He spread his hands in a helpless gesture. "Now I don't know what to think."

"For now, Phil, I'm working on the station's anniversary show," I said. "But Larry and Willie are part of that—so yes, you might say I'm interested. I'm trying to round up some of the other old-timers. Oops. Not that you're old . . ."

He laughed. "It's all right. Have you found Katie the Clown yet? Agnes Hooper? She still lives in Salem."

"Hooper," I repeated. "Thanks Phil. I was looking for her last name. And I know where to find Ranger Rob too. That leaves Professor Mercury. Know where he is? I loved that show."

"Sorry. No. I heard he left town years ago. Not much work here for kid show TV performers after the cable stations came. Disney and Nickelodeon and the cartoon channel."

"I know," I said. "Too expensive. I hope I can round them all up for the anniversary show though. It'll be kind of like one of those 'what ever happened to . . .' specials."

"We know what happened to Larry Laraby, and now Wee Willie, don't we?" Phil shook his head. "Let's hope the others have fared better."

"I wish I'd had a chance to talk to Chris Rich for a minute. He sells lots of props for magicians. I thought he might still have contact with Professor Mercury. But he seemed to be focused on the Witches' Ball organizer."

"Probably trying to score a couple of passes to the ball, I expect," Phil said. "Those tickets aren't cheap."

"I know. I scored free tickets once but never quite made it to the ball."

"I remember that night, Lee." Again, that pensive head shake. "A frightening memory for you."

"I try not to think about it." I looked at my watch and hurriedly changed the subject. "Almost ten-thirty. Time for the chief's presser. Templeton's covering it. I think I'll run upstairs and watch with Rhonda."

"Let me know if I can help with the anniversary," he said. "Good talking with you."

"Thanks, Phil. I pushed open the metal door and climbed the stairs to the upstairs lobby, thinking for the umpteenth time that between the stairs in the Winter Street house and the stairs in this building, I'd never need to join a step class.

Rhonda had spun her chair around and was already watching the monitor behind her desk. "Pull up a seat, Lee," she said. "Wish I'd remembered to bring popcorn. Let's see how the kid handles his first real breaking news standup."

"I hope he does okay." I moved one of the turquoise-upholstered chrome chairs closer to the screen. "He probably doesn't know the chief is just as nervous as he is."

"So far they're just showing the front of the police station." She squinted, moving closer to the monitor. "Look at that. They're using the big portable TV screen. They must have pictures. Didn't get any from us. I wonder what they've got. Hey, shouldn't Howie be doing some kind of voice-over or something while they wait for the chief to come out?"

"I would be," I said, silently willing Howard Templeton to *do* something, *say* something. "If there's anything Mr. Doan can't stand, it's dead air."

"You've got that right," she whispered. "Here he comes now." She motioned to the glass door. Bruce Doan had just stepped from the elevator.

"Come on, Howard!" I said aloud. As though he'd heard my urging, a smiling, confident-appearing Templeton looked into the camera, stick mic in hand. "Good morning, ladies and gentlemen. Howard Templeton here, for WICH-TV, reporting directly from the Salem police station, where we're awaiting the appearance of Chief Tom Whaley." Mr. Doan pushed the glass door open and stood behind me, facing the monitor as his youngest field reporter continued. "We expect an update on the ongoing investigation into the death of William Wallace—known to baseball fans as 'Wee Willie Wallace.' Mr. Wallace was found dead on Friday afternoon in the stacks at the city's main library building on Essex Street. The medical examiner's report cites severe damage to the upper vertebrae as the cause of death." Templeton's expression was appropriately earnest, his tone pleasantly modulated. He dropped his voice to golf-commentator-pitch as the camera focused on the chief, resplendent in full dress uniform, medals and all, emerging from the building and stepping before a bank of microphones arrayed in front of a lectern. "Here's the chief now," Templeton said, "let's listen in."

"Good morning, ladies and gentleman," the chief said. "Just a brief update on the matter of the death of William Wallace." He shuffled the notes on the lectern. "Mr. Wallace was found deceased this past Friday on an upper floor of the Salem main library. The coroner's office has determined that Mr. Wallace died from violent trauma to the upper body, not consistent with an accidental injury. The matter is being investigated as a suspicious death. Several security cameras in the vicinity of the library, both inside and outside of the building, have yielded footage of persons who may be of interest in this case." He motioned to the TV screen, which flickered to life.

"These people were filmed at, in, or nearby the library during the time we believe Mr. Wallace arrived on the second floor of the library, known as 'the stacks.' First, here's Mr. Wallace entering the front door of the library.

Next we see Mr. Wallace climbing the stairs to the stacks. Here he is on the second-floor area." The chief used a pointer, tapping the screen where the man, gray hair touching his shoulders, seemed to be reading the cards attached to the shelves, then disappearing around the corner of the front row of books.

"Next," the chief continued, "we have a series of still pictures showing four—so far unidentified—people. The time stamps on these photos indicate that these four people may possibly have had some contact with Mr. Wallace. If you are one of these people, please call the number at the bottom of your screen and identify yourself. If you recognize any of these people, please call that number."

A series of stills followed. No one I knew. There was a tall bearded man wearing a backpack; a teenager in a hoodie with a blonde girl in a mini skirt; an old woman carrying a satchel with a picture of a cat on it. There were several shots of the bearded man and the two young people. There was one of the old woman exiting from the side door that seemed to have been taken from somewhere behind the library, maybe from a security camera in a nearby building.

The camera returned to the chief. "Please note that *none* of these people are considered suspects in this investigation. We'd simply like to talk to them regarding anything they may have seen or heard while in the stacks area. That's all for now. Thank you." As usual, he managed to dodge most of the shouted questions from the assembled press, but replied to Templeton's "the dead man *is* Wee Willie Wallace, the ball player, is that right?"

"That's correct." The chief edged closer to the doorway. Someone else yelled, "Was there a weapon?"

"We have not found a weapon." He scooted inside the building.

The camera once again focused on Howard Templeton. "There you have it, folks," he said. "Chief Whaley has just confirmed what WICH-TV reported earlier. The deceased man is Wee Willie Wallace, a one-time baseball player, whose short career was plagued with scandals. Wallace was imprisoned for several years for allegedly doping horses at a New Hampshire racetrack. We'll show you those pictures again of the four people who may have seen or heard something." He repeated the telephone number the chief had given. "Also, ladies and gentlemen, the Friends of the Library organization has posted a one-thousand-dollar reward for information leading to the arrest and conviction of whoever killed Wee Willie."

The pictures rolled once more and Templeton signed off with a professional sounding "Howard Templeton here, reporting from the Salem Police Department for WICH-TV. Stay tuned for further updates on this breaking story."

"The kid did all right," Mr. Doan remarked. "Don't you think?"

"Not bad," I agreed. "He should be ready to move on in no time."

"No time," Rhonda echoed. "Some other station will be calling to grab him up real soon."

"That's what his Aunt Buffy thinks too." He looked at me. "By the way, Ms. Barrett, how're you coming on that magician for the party?"

"Got a good lead just today, sir," I said. "I'm on it. Don't worry. Mrs. Doan will have her magic show."

"Counting on you." He disappeared into his office.

"You got a lead on Professor Mercury?" Rhonda asked.

"Not exactly a lead," I admitted. "More of an idea. I think Chris Rich may know where the old magician is. Chris's shop has the best selection of professional magician supplies outside of Boston. If the professor is around here at all, Chris must know him."

"We keep calling him Professor Mercury. Haven't you found his real name yet?"

"Still haven't finished with those old files. When everyone clears out of the studio I'll go back to my snooping. I've got Katie the Clown's name—Agnes Hooper—she lives over on Highland Avenue, and I already knew that Ranger Rob is in Rockport."

"Not bad," she said. "You'd probably make a good cop."

"Yeah," I said. "So I've been told. Not interested."

"Hey, I fixed you up with that lamp you wanted. The Saturday guy loved it."

"I've got to listen to his show some day," I said. "Might learn something."

"I've learned a few things from him," Rhonda said, "and I have a degree in business administration."

"One of your degrees."

"Uh-huh." She turned down the sound on the monitor and picked up her copy of *People.* "Let me know when you find the old dude's name."

"I'll keep checking under miscellaneous."

She looked up from the magazine. "Hey, most of what everyone seems to know about this Wee Willie character seems to fit under that category, don't you think?"

I thought about that. From talented young athlete to disgraced has-been to horse-killing jail bird to dead old man in dirty socks, William Wallace's whole life had been unnecessarily, but pretty much totally, miscellaneous.

Chapter 22

The studio was silent and dim, but not completely dark, when I opened the metal door. I made my way down the center aisle. I could see why the *Saturday Business Hour* host liked the lamp. It was the perfect addition to the set, green shade and all. I clicked it on. This was going to make my work a lot easier. I pulled open the bottom file drawer and, on my knees, looked inside. Unlike the manila files with individually marked tabs I'd seen earlier, this drawer contained three wide accordion-type files, each one stuffed full.

I lifted the first one out, put it on the desk, pushed the drawer shut with my foot, and began snooping. It didn't take very long for the contents to become interesting. The file must have belonged to Larry Laraby. The first handful of papers I pulled out seemed to be letters from his fans. Mostly handwritten, on a variety of types of stationery, they all began with "Dear Larry." I read a few at random. They seemed to vary between letters from kids asking sports questions or inviting Larry to their games, to letters from women asking sports questions or suggesting "meeting somewhere to get acquainted," to letters from men asking sports questions or criticizing Larry's opinion of "their" team.

I replaced the file and pulled the second one out. This obviously concerned Larry's collectibles show business. There were contracts for the venues he'd rented all over the country. I was surprised at the scope of the Larry Laraby Sports Collectibles Shows. There were contracts too, signed by sports celebrities who'd made personal appearances at the events. Again, I only looked at a few but the ones I saw were a veritable "Who's Who" of sports stars. Most of the papers in this file, though, appeared to be records of signed items bought and sold by Laraby. Again I was surprised. The memorabilia Laraby dealt in often carried four-figure price tags, and sometimes five figures. *I had no idea autographs and baseball cards and balls and bats, hockey sticks and pucks, game-used footballs and stained jerseys could have such value!*

There was an address book in the file. It appeared to be a customer list with notations of items sought by each listed collector. I remembered that all this had happened before eBay and Craigslist. *I'd better take a closer look at all my NASCAR stuff. Maybe some of it's worth real money.* A stack of receipt books reminded me of the ones we'd just inventoried for the library. I rifled through a few. Why was I not surprised when the name William Wallace showed up numerous times on the carbon copies? Wee Willie had been a consistent provider of merchandise for Laraby for years. I put that file to one side for further examination later.

The third file was heavy. It contained two thick photo albums. I love looking at old photos. Always have. When I was a little girl I used to amuse myself for hours looking through the ones in the bookcase in Aunt Ibby's living room. No matter that I didn't know who the people were. The clothes, the automobiles, the houses and gardens and pets—I made up stories about them in my mind. I spread the first one open. It wasn't really old, like most of my aunt's were, with black-and-white photos pasted onto black paper pages with little black corner stickers holding them in place. These were mostly Kodachrome prints mounted under clear plastic. I recognized the hairstyles and clothing as maybe sixties and seventies. There were some that must have been taken in the WICH-TV building. There was a microphone bearing the station's call letters on a sports desk where the man I'd come to recognize as Larry smiled into the camera. A few had been taken outside the building, which didn't look a great deal different than it does now. There were many pages of Larry posing with men—mostly big, rugged guys—who I assumed must all be sports stars. I only recognized a few of the obvious ones, like O.J. Simpson and Pete Rose. I knew Richard Petty immediately, of course. There were a few photos of Larry with women athletes—even one with a petite Olga Korbut.

My phone vibrated and I read a text from Pete. "Sharon Stewart reported something missing."

I answered right away. "What?"

"Old framed photo of her dad."

"Call me when you can," I instructed. "Let's talk."

"Lunch? 12:30? Pick you up?"

"Ariel's bench. 12:30," I sent. Then, smiling, I returned to Larry Laraby's photo albums. About halfway through the first album, the backgrounds changed to what appeared to be the collectibles shows. Some of the shots that showed an entire hall were probably taken from a balcony or stairway above the sales floor. I whistled softly. There must have been over a hundred booths in each shot, and the

crowds of customers in the aisles indicated that ticket
sales alone must have yielded a hefty profit besides whatever big-ticket items Larry sold there. Most of the pictures showed vendors' booths, with a heavy emphasis on
baseball memorabilia. There were autograph signing tables too, with sports luminaries signing books, photos,
baseballs, and T-shirts (at twenty dollars a signature, according to the sign on the table).

I was so engrossed in my study of the photos, I didn't
realize that Marty had joined me in the little faux office.
"You look right natural there, Moon," she said. "Find
anything interesting in the file cabinet?"

"Oh, Marty. I didn't even hear you coming. Yes. Thanks
so much for letting me know about it." I turned the album
toward her. "See this? It's Larry Laraby's photo album.
Mostly covering his collectibles shows. He was quite the
showman. Here's a picture of a locked glass case with a
security guard standing beside it. The sign says, 'The
world's most expensive Baseball Card.' Look at all the
people lined up to see it."

"Must have been a Honus Wagner," Marty said, moving closer to the desk. "It'd be worth way more now than
it was back then. Couple of million, easy."

"Really?" I peered over the top of the album. "A baseball card?"

"Sure. Look it up."

"I will," I said, and typed "Honus Wagner" in the search
line on my tablet. A picture of a serious-faced man in a
Pittsburgh shirt led the article. After a moment I looked up
at Marty. "You're right. Wayne Gretzky bought a T206
Honus Wagner card for $451,000. It changed hands a few
times and sold in 2007 for $2.8 million dollars!"

She didn't appear to be listening. She continued to
stare at the photo.

"Marty? Two point eight million," I repeated.

She tapped the photo. "It's him, isn't it?"

I looked at the photo. "Who?"

"The security guard. It's Dave. Good-lookin' Dave from the library. Only younger."

And of course, it was.

Chapter 23

I took a quick picture of the Laraby photo, returned the albums to the miscellaneous drawer, turned off the lamp, and left to meet Pete. My mental flowchart was a mess. Maybe the name in the top spot should be Larry Laraby. Maybe everybody in my complicated scenario was connected to *him* and maybe Wee Willie was just one of the crowd. *Is there a connection between Dave guarding Laraby's valuable baseball card and Dave guarding the library where Wee Willie died?* My brain was in a blender, whirring around and around and going nowhere.

I opened the door at the back of the studio and stepped out into bright October sunshine. It was such a pretty day that spending the whole afternoon sitting on Ariel's bench, gazing out over at the sailboat-dotted deep blue water of Salem harbor was an attractive option.

Definitely not happening.

Pete is usually one of those exactly-on-the-button people when it comes to being on time. I still had a few minutes before twelve-thirty. I pulled the tablet from my purse and looked again at the photo of the "world's most expensive baseball card" display. I zoomed in on the security guard's face. No doubt. It was a much younger Dave. I enlarged the big glass box too, trying to see what was inside. No luck there. I was turning the tablet from side to side (as though that was going to make a difference) when Pete drove up behind the bench and gave a friendly toot of the horn.

I climbed into the Crown Vic and leaned across the console for the expected kiss. I wasn't disappointed. "Hi, babe," he said. "Burgers and a ride to the Willows?"

"One of my favorite lunch dates," I said. "What's all this about a picture being missing from the Stewarts' house? Does she think it was taken when their house was broken into?"

He nodded and headed for the closest Burger King. "Yes. She was dusting a bookshelf this morning and realized that the picture wasn't in the spot where it'd been for a long time."

"Seems odd it would take this long to notice it," I said.

"She says there are several framed photos in an arrangement on that shelf. The missing one is one of those old five-inch-square color prints in a five-by-five frame from the Dollar Store."

"Exactly what's it a picture of?"

"It's a candid shot of her dad. Taken in his study. He was holding a book in his right hand. And he was smoking a cigar."

"Did Sharon remember what book it was?"

"No. I knew you'd ask that question though."

"Too Nancy Drew-ish?"

"No. It's a good question, considering this case seems to be all about books." We pulled into the drive-through. Cheeseburger, fries, and vanilla shake for him. Hamburger with extra pickles and a diet Pepsi for me. "Why would a burglar pass up some really nice items in that house, mess up a room by tossing books around, and only take a snapshot in a cheap frame?"

We turned back onto Derby Street heading for the Salem Willows Park. The Willows is a popular destination for tourists and natives alike from May through September, with rows of sidewalk food stands, amusement park rides, and arcades, as well as beaches, boat rides, and ocean views. We love it there in the summer, but sometimes it's even better in October when most everything is closed up. We like to park under some ancient willow trees near the beach and enjoy the special quiet beauty of the place when the crowds are gone.

"Speaking of pictures," I said, when we'd unwrapped our sandwiches, "I found a whole album full of Larry Laraby's photos—mostly of the collectibles shows he ran. They were really big events. You won't believe who Marty spotted in one of the pictures."

"Who?"

"Dave Benson."

He frowned. "Dave, the security guard at the library?"

"I'm sure it's him. Much younger, but it's him." I pulled out the tablet and handed it to Pete. "Maybe he's *always* worked as a security guard. Do you think that's possible?"

Pete examined the picture, much the way I had. "Not in this case," he said. "We ran a check on all of the library staff—nothing in depth, you know, but a general background. Dave Benson was in the military for almost thirty years. Special Forces. He's worked at the library part time ever since he retired."

I sipped my Pepsi. "Maybe he's always liked being in uniform then," I said. "Marty finds him very attractive."

"No kidding?" He smiled. "Could I get a look at that album? Maybe there'll be a duplicate of the picture that's missing from the Stewarts' house."

"Could be, I suppose, but I'm pretty sure those five-inch prints came from an inexpensive kind of candid camera.

The ones in the album I've seen so far look like professional work."

"You're probably right. I think my sister Marie had one of those cameras when we were kids. I know my mom has those little square prints in scrapbooks."

"But Pete, there are two of those albums. I've just begun looking at the first one. Lots more pictures to look at," I promised. "I'll get permission to bring them home—research for the anniversary show, you know. We can look through all of them. Who knows who else we might find in there besides Dave?"

"I'm guessing our friend Wee Willie will show up for sure." He handed back my tablet.

"He was a big part of Laraby's sports show career," I said. "No reason he wouldn't be part of the collectibles shows too. I can hardly wait to get back to those albums."

"Do you want to skip the after-lunch-walk-along-the-beach?"

"Certainly not!" I said, meaning it. "That's the best part. Walking off the calories, breathing good salt air, and just hanging out together for a little while."

Pete agreed with my reasoning. He stuffed our napkins and straws and cups and burger wrappers into the Burger King bag and deposited it in a nearby round-topped trash can, took my hand, and we walked the short distance to Dead Horse Beach. (Yes, that's always been the name of it. Guess nobody ever thought of dressing up the name to impress the tourists. That's Salem.)

It's a nice little beach, quiet and breezy. There were only a few other people there and a couple of friendly dogs.

"So you say it looks as though Dave was working security at one of the Laraby shows?" A golden retriever dropped a green ball at Pete's feet and looked up expectantly. Pete obliged and threw the ball. "Sharon—Mrs.

Stewart—says that he promoted those shows all over the country. She thinks his shows, much more than his TV career, brought her father the most satisfaction."

"I'm guessing they brought him the most money too," I said. "From the pictures I've seen so far, they were held in huge halls, with hundreds of vendors."

"I think you're right about that. Mrs. Laraby, Sharon's mother, lived very nicely. Big house here in Salem and another one in Florida."

"Did the mother's house ever get broken into? Books on the floor and all?"

"The house Larry died in was the only books-on-the-floor experience Mrs. Laraby had that we know of. They sold that house right after his death."

"Don't blame them for that. Bad memories."

The golden returned with the green ball. Pete obliged again. "The new house is in a gated community. Plenty of around-the-clock security."

"Maybe Dave worked there too," I suggested, only halfway seriously.

"I'll check it," Pete said, all the way seriously. "I wonder exactly what card was in that glass box he was guarding at the collectibles show. The world's most expensive baseball card."

"Marty thinks it was a Honus Wagner," I said, trying to sound as though I'd known about the Pittsburgh player all along.

"Could very well be," he said. "A few years back Ken Kendrick paid two point eight million for one."

"Ken Kendrick?"

"Yeah," he said. "You know. Kendrick. He owns the Arizona Diamondbacks."

"Oh, that Kendrick. Sure." *The Arizona Diamondbacks. Like the snake on Pete's pajama bottoms. Like the slithering snake on the Wheel of Fortune card.*

One more ball toss for the golden and Pete and I headed

back to his car. "That was nice," he said. "The lunch and the beach and the dog too. Someday, I'd like to have a dog just like that one."

"I can see you with a dog like that," I told him. "Suits you."

He smiled. "Like O'Ryan suits you."

"I guess he does," I said. "I know Aunt Ibby and I love him a lot."

"He's not just a regular ordinary cat." Pete held the passenger door open for me. "There's something really special about him."

"That's for sure," I said. *You have no idea how special he is. Maybe someday . . .*

We headed back to the station, taking the long way, making this lunch date last as long as we could. He pulled up behind Ariel's bench. A woman sat there reading, a sleeping toddler in the stroller in front of her. I opened my door and stepped out. "I'll see about getting permission to take Laraby's albums home with me," I said, speaking softly so I wouldn't wake the baby. "For researching the anniversary show."

"I'll call you," he whispered, making the thumb and little finger phone sign, just the way Christopher Rich had done.

I need to call Christopher Rich! Better yet, I'll go over to his shop and see what he knows about the old magician.

I waved in the direction of Pete's departing car, smiled at the reading woman, tapped my employee code into the security pad, and opened the metal door to the studio. There was still no activity in the long, dark room as I returned to the *Saturday Business Hour* set. I clicked on my green lamp—I thought of it as mine—and knelt on the floor, pulling the miscellaneous drawer open. I reached for the third accordion file, lifting it to the desktop.

I called the station number, adding Rhonda's extension code. "Rhonda, I'm downstairs. Is Mr. Doan still in? I'd like to take one of these files home with me and I need to find out if that's okay."

"He's here. If it's about the anniversary show I'm pretty sure it's okay. Hang on. I'll put you through."

Mr. Doan is one of those men who always answers the phone as though he's either angry or in a big rush about something. I got the "big rush" tone. "Doan here. What do you want, Ms. Barrett?"

"I've been going through some old files, Mr. Doan. I've found some good pictures of Larry Laraby that were taken here at the station. All professional quality. There are two albums full—pretty much covering his whole career. I wonder if I can take them home and pick a dozen or so of the best ones. Good clear still shots for the anniversary show."

"Sounds good, Barrett. Go for it."

I said "Thanks," but he'd already hung up. *That was easy.* I hefted the two albums and decided to put one under each arm and put them into my car right away in case the boss changed his mind. I slung my hobo bag over one shoulder, picked up the albums, and headed back outdoors. I tucked the albums into the trunk of the Vette, walked around to the front of the building and took the elevator to the second floor. I wanted to tell Rhonda what I planned to do with what was left of the afternoon.

"So you're going over to see Chris Rich?" she asked, when I'd told her my latest plan for finding the missing Professor Mercury. "Maybe Chris knows his real name."

"His real name must be in the records here somewhere," I said. "I just haven't taken enough time to search for it. I'm not worried about it. I'm just assuming that Katie—Agnes—will know it anyway. She or Ranger Rob are the easiest to contact. Anyway, if he's still using magic tricks somewhere around Salem, Chris will have the info I need."

"Good luck. See you tomorrow."

"Right. But if they need a good field reporter before then, I'm not far away."

"Gotcha."

The sun was getting low in the sky and there was a chill in the air. October is beautiful in New England, but it's full of reminders that winter isn't far away. I climbed into the Vette and headed for Christopher's Castle. When I'd talked to Rhonda I'd sounded pretty confident that I'd find the fascinating magician of my childhood easily. Or not. I smiled as I turned into the lot behind Chris's shop. If this was a Nancy Drew book I'd call it *The Case of the Missing Magician.*

The shop looked busy. There were several customers milling around, leaning over jewelry display cases, checking out costume racks, experimenting with sample magic tricks displayed on a long table. Chris greeted me with a big grin and an enthusiastic "Lee! My favorite girl reporter! What brings you to my castle this fine day?"

"I'm on a special assignment," I said, knowing he'd like hearing that. "I'm trying to locate a certain magician, and who better to help me than you?"

The grin grew wider. "How can I help, dear Lee? I know them all. The great ones and the beginners. Did I ever tell you about the time the amazing David Copperfield stopped in here? I have a photo of us together."

"Yes, Chris," I said. "I remember seeing that picture." *How can anyone miss it? It's sixteen-by-twenty in a fancy gold frame right behind the counter.* "The man I want to interview was kind of semi-famous locally years ago. Do you remember Professor Mercury? He did a wonderful kids' show combining magic with science."

"Indeed, I remember the gentleman. Used to be a good

customer. Always looking for the latest, the newest, the best. He still comes in every once in a while."

"Do you know his real name? Do you know where he is now?" I held my breath and crossed my fingers behind my back.

"His real name? Certainly. It's Jerome Mercury. Jerry for short."

"You're kidding. His last name is really Mercury?"

"Sure. There are lots of them. Remember Freddie Mercury? Played with Queen? The rock group?"

"Oh, yeah. 'Bohemian Rhapsody.' But do you know where he is now? Jerry Mercury, not Freddie."

Chris put one finger under his chin and hit a pensive pose. "Hmmm. Last time I saw Jerry was a couple of months ago. He bought a new see-through card trick. He does a lot of kids' parties." Chris shook his head. "Seems like a come-down for him. He could have been one of the big ones."

"Does he still live in Salem?"

"I don't know. Could be. He just walked in off the street like anybody else."

"That's okay." I was disappointed but still hopeful. "If he's doing kids' parties he probably advertises somewhere. Local papers or online. Does he still call himself 'Professor'?"

"I think so. Wait a minute!" He stabbed the air with his forefinger. "He gave me a business card. I stuck it in the cash register." He hurried behind the counter and punched a combination of numbers. The drawer slid open and Chris removed the card. "Here you go." He handed it to me. It featured a colorful drawing of a typical cartoon magician—a dark-haired man with a curving mustache, piercing eyes, white gloves. Instead of the traditional top hat though, he wore a metallic gold crown and his magic wand had gold lightning flashes shooting from it. *The Magic King!* was printed in bold purple letters. Bullet points proclaimed: Mystify your friends!—Children's Parties—Office Parties—Charity Events—Church Picnics—Holiday Celebrations. A website address was given at the bottom. No phone number.

So here he is. The King of Wands.

"May I keep it?" I held up the card.

"Sure. He leaves one every time he comes in."

"Thanks, Chris," I said. "If you happen to see him or hear from him any time soon, will you give him my number?" I handed him one of my field reporter cards. "I have a job for him. Actually two. A private party and a TV appearance."

Chris's eyes danced with interest. "Anything there for me? You know I'm good on TV and I love parties. Did you mean Buffy Doan's Storybook Halloween eve bash? I've already RSVP'd for that one. I'm going as Heath cliff. I'll be fabulous. Did you like that interview we did this morning?"

"Very much," I said. "Really professional. I'll certainly keep you in mind. We're working on an anniversary show for the station's seventieth birthday, you know."

"Stay in touch," he said. "You always know where you can find me."

I wished him a good evening, tucked the Magic King's card into my purse, and left the store. I walked toward my car, trying to recall exactly what River had said about the King of Wands. Something about spiritual and material gain. The possibility of an inheritance. I wondered what else that card might tell me. I'd call River for sure. Meanwhile I'd check out the website on Professor Mercury's card. At least he was still alive, somewhere within commuting distance of Salem, and still performing magic.

The thought made me happy.

I headed for Winter Street with the feeling of a good day's work accomplished. I had Larry Laraby's photo albums safely locked in my trunk. I'd learned Katie the

Clown's real name and by tomorrow she'd have the card I'd given to Jim Litka. I felt sure she'd call me. Maybe Aunt Ibby and I would take a ride to Rockport tomorrow morning and surprise Ranger Rob with an invitation to appear on the anniversary show—and while we were there, we might find out a little more about where he fit on my so-far-imaginary flowchart.

Chapter 24

The first thing I did when I reached home was check out Professor Mercury's website. Disappointment was immediate. A cartoon guy with hammer and boards appeared, with the dreaded "Site under construction. Check back later" message. Bummer. My aunt was just as pleased as I was though, with the information I *had* gained, and was particularly interested in the photo albums. So was Pete. I'd only been home for an hour or so when he called. "Did you bring those albums home?" he wanted to know, "and if you did can I invite myself over to take a look at them?"

"Yes, and yes. Aunt Ibby and I are ordering pizza. Want to join us?"

"Pizza sounds perfect," he said. "Shall I pick it up? I'll be out of here in about fifteen minutes."

"Sure. I'll text the order in to the Pizza Pirate and tell them you'll pick it up at around seven-thirty. Work for you?"

"Yep. You need soda or anything else?"

"Nope. We're good," I said. "We won't open the albums until you get here. So hurry up."

He laughed. "You know I will."

I told my aunt that Pete wanted to be part of the Larry Laraby photo study group.

"Oh, I'm glad he's coming over, Maralee," she said. "Better order extra pizza."

"I will. Pete sounded really excited about seeing the albums. I'll bet he's looking for something in particular in them."

"Let's snoop it out of him then," my aunt said in a serious tone.

"You sound absolutely devious," I told her.

"I know. Isn't it fun?" The green eyes twinkled and her smile was mischievous. "Let's put the albums on the kitchen table. It's round so it'll be easy for us all to see them. We'll eat our pizza at the counter. That way we won't be getting cheese and sauce on the evidence."

"Evidence? Of what?"

She shrugged. "I don't know. That's what we're snooping for."

"You're incorrigible," I said as I texted the Pizza Pirate. "One cheese and pepperoni and one extra cheese okay with you?"

"Perfect," she said, and began setting out plates and glasses. I placed the two albums in the center of the round oak table, and spaced the four captain's chairs evenly around it. My aunt thoughtfully placed a couple of magnifying glasses beside the albums. O'Ryan sniffed each chair, chose the one closest to the back door for himself, and sat on the braided chair mat in an expectant pose.

I made a quick trip up to my apartment, checked my hair, added a spritz of Flowerbomb, changed my old gray T-shirt for a white silk blouse, and then went back downstairs to wait for Pete—and pizza.

"Did I tell you Professor Mercury's last name is really Mercury?" I asked my aunt.

"No kidding. Like Freddie Mercury?"

"Right." I said. "From Queen. Now I'm beginning to wonder if maybe he's really a professor."

"I wouldn't be one bit surprised. He certainly showed a vast knowledge of science on his TV show, and he had the ability to make it understandable even to small children. What a gift!"

I nodded, fondly remembering those childhood science experiments in this same kitchen. "Chris Rich has seen him fairly recently and thinks he must still live somewhere in the area. Chris says he's doing mostly kids' parties lately." I pulled out the card and showed it to her. "I checked out his website but it's apparently 'under construction.' I'll keep trying. I think he might like a chance to be on TV again, if only for an anniversary special."

She studied the card and handed it back to me. "The professor always seemed to have a lovely rapport with children. Perhaps he's enjoying his new career."

I hoped she was right. "Chris Rich spoke of it as a 'come down,' but I like your theory better." O'Ryan's ears perked up and he leaped from his chair, heading for the door. "That'll be Pete," I said. "And pizza. His arms will be full. I'll let him in."

I followed O'Ryan into the back hall, passed the laundry room, and unlocked the back door. He'd already zipped through his own door and met Pete halfway down the solar-lighted flagstone walk. The two walked together toward me and again I had that good feeling of a day's work well done. I stepped outside to meet them and reached up for the expected kiss. Kiss delivered, I held the door open for Pete and waited for O'Ryan to follow him inside. The cat had paused at the edge of the garden fence, looking back over his shoulder to the street. I followed his gaze, shading my eyes against the glow from the little path-lamps and the glare from the streetlight across from the garage. I saw nothing unusual. "Come, kitty," I called. "Pepperoni inside." He hesitated, then with a loud purr trotted up the steps and into the house.

I stood there in the open doorway for a moment. *What had O'Ryan seen—or heard?*

Was there someone standing in the deep shadows under the trees? Had the green Subaru with the smiling man at the wheel driven by? Nonsense. I shook away the bad thoughts. The cat had been distracted by a moth or a toad or a cricket or a dog barking in the distance. I closed the door and joined my loved ones in the cozy kitchen.

The pizza boxes had been opened, the pies transferred to "proper" serving plates. (Upstairs in my kitchen, they stay in their boxes.) Chilled cans of Pepsi and a bottle of chardonnay were lined up on the counter next to plates and glasses. "Smells great in here, doesn't it?" Pete said. "They ought to make pizza-scented candles."

"Let's eat it while it's hot," Aunt Ibby suggested. "Then we can get to work on those albums."

So that's what we did. The pizza was dispatched in short order—right down to the last slice of pepperoni, which O'Ryan claimed. We carried our drinks to the kitchen table and opened the first album. I passed it to Pete because I'd already looked through about a third of the pages. Aunt Ibby slowly inched her chair closer to his left. Following her lead, I slid mine over to his right. Before long we three were all crowded together, while O'Ryan stared across at us from the opposite side of the round table.

I caught myself holding my breath when Pete picked up the biggest magnifying glass, held it in front of him and leaned closer to the open page. Aunt Ibby leaned forward too. O'Ryan put both front paws on the edge of the table and focused golden eyes on Pete.

I could see from where I sat that he was inspecting a studio photo. It was one of the oldest ones—the ones with the call letters on the microphone. What had he seen in it that I hadn't seen? He made no comment, put the magnifying glass down and turned his attention to the next page. I let my breath out, Aunt Ibby leaned back in her chair, but O'Ryan retained his table's-edge position. *Okay, so what does the cat see that I didn't?*

Pete turned a few more pages without comment, then paused on a page that showed several photos of Laraby and Wee Willie. "I asked around about Larry Laraby," Pete said. "About his TV show, I mean. My dad remembers him. Had nothing but good to say about him. He said Laraby was a real 'sports newsman,' not a 'sports commentator,' like so many are today." Pete smiled. "Dad says Laraby would say the score was 5 to 3. Period. Not 'the score was 5 to 3 because the Sox pitcher blew the game in the seventh.' A real straight shooter."

"He seemed to have plenty of friends," Aunt Ibby said. "Including some famous athletes. She pointed across Pete's chest to a picture of Laraby standing beside a fireplace with a woman my aunt immediately identified as tennis great Billie Jean King.

Pete moved the album closer to me. "Did you notice this one?" he asked, tapping one of the photos taken at a collectibles show. He picked up the magnifying glass but didn't use it.

"I saw it," I said, "but I didn't notice anything special about it."

He handed me the magnifying glass. "Look again. On the counter just to the right of Laraby." I picked up the glass and did as he'd asked.

"You mean the book?" I focused on an open book, lying face down on a display counter beside a row of baseballs, each one neatly encased in a round plastic holder. It was as though a reader—in this case, Larry Laraby—had been reading a book between serving customers and had left it facedown, open, to mark his place. In our house, this was almost as bad as bending corners. "That's what bookmarks are for," my aunt had always scolded when I'd been careless enough to make that mistake. "He was reading on the job," I said.

"And he was disrespectful of his book," my aunt chimed it. "Do you know what that does to the book's delicate spine?"

"I was looking at the title," Pete said, a tiny note of impatience in his voice. "It's one of the titles that was on the list of books Mrs. Stewart donated to the library."

I looked more closely and read the title aloud. "*The Boys of Summer* by Roger Kahn. It's a baseball book lying upside down on a sports collectibles show table." That struck me as quite logical. "Is it interesting to you because Mrs. Stewart is missing a picture of her father holding a book?"

"That's part of it," he said. "But it's more interesting because so far, we haven't located that particular book."

'That *is* interesting. And I should have remembered that title from the list of donated books. I guess you've checked the rest of the books in the stacks?"

He nodded. "Uh-huh. Not there."

"So maybe," my aunt put in, "that book—" she pointed at the photo—"is the one the killer is looking for."

"And maybe has found." My words came out in an almost-whisper. "Is that what you think, Pete? That Wee Willie might have found that book in the stacks and then got killed because of it?"

"I don't think that at all," Pete said, cop voice engaged. "I'm simply gathering facts. Evidence from several places suggests that *someone* is interested in books about sports. We have here a picture of Larry Laraby holding a book about sports. Another photo, which a relative claims is missing, also shows Larry Laraby holding a book that may or may not be about sports. A library book about sports is also missing that may or may not be the one in this photo." Once again he indicated the picture of Laraby at one of his collectibles shows. "None of these facts lead to conclusions about deaths, one of which may or may not be murder."

"See?" I said. "That's why I could never be a cop. My imagination runs away with me every time."

"It's all in the training," he said. "Let's look at some more pictures."

We worked our way through the first album, with Pete flagging a few more pictures including several of the "most valuable baseball card in the world." All of those photos showed a stern-faced young Dave Benson guarding the display.

"I can hardly wait to see what Dave has to say about it," Aunt Ibby said. "I have a feeling that he's always liked the way he looks in uniform."

"Well," I said, looking at a side shot of the tall young man. "He *does* wear it well. Pete, do you suppose that's a real gun in his holster?"

"Looks real to me," Pete said. "If I had a genuine Honus Wagner, I know I'd want it well guarded."

"Dave's not armed when he's on duty at the library," Aunt Ibby said. "But in light of what's been going on there lately, maybe he should be."

"I don't think so, Ms. Russell." *Calm cop voice.* "What happened in the stacks is what we call an 'isolated incident.' It's highly unlikely that library patrons are in any sort of danger. No need for firearms there."

"I'm sure you're right." She returned her attention to the open album. "Probably no one at the Larry Laraby collectibles shows was in danger either. Seems to me the armed cop and the glass case were clever props to gain publicity for the shows—and for Laraby himself."

"Of course they were," I said. "Looks like Larry Laraby was quite a showman. I wish he was still around to help me with the anniversary show."

"You making progress with that?" Once again Pete used the magnifying glass, examining a photo of Laraby shaking hands with Danny Ainge. He looked at me, the glass still in front of him, making his eye enormous. "Rounded up those old-timers you were looking for?"

"What big eyes you have, Grandmother," I said, pressing his hand down so that his eye returned to normal size. "I'm working on it." I turned to face my aunt. "Aunt Ibby," I said, "want to take a ride over to Rockport tomorrow morning? I want to try to sign up Ranger Rob for the show."

"Yes," she said. "We can do that."

"With luck, maybe by tomorrow afternoon I'll hear from the other two."

"I'll bet you will, Maralee. Don't worry. This will all come together neatly after a while." My aunt's voice was soothing.

"I sure hope it will," Pete said. "Not just for the anniversary show, but for the little matter of somebody very quietly committing a murder in a library."

Aunt Ibby looked up from the album. "Oh Pete, did I mention that there was a musical event going on in the children's media center? Whoever did it had some cover from music—including kids on percussion instruments—coming from just below the stacks."

"Right," I said. "I remember there were kids leaving the musical story time from the side entrance when we got there."

"Noisy kids," Aunt Ibby said. "Enthusiastic noise, but noise nevertheless."

"I know about the class," Pete said. "But it would account for why nobody we've talked to heard any books falling on the floor."

"Are you—is the department any closer to finding this person, Pete? Haven't the security videos told you anything?"

"Well, the two teenagers—the boy in the hoodie and the girl in the short skirt—came forward right away and identified themselves. Out-of-town kids here for the Halloween festivities. Sounds like they went up to the stacks to sneak a little make-out session but they heard somebody else up there so they came right down."

I knew I was pushing him when I knew I should be patient. "Do you know how somebody could have disabled the alarm on the emergency door?" My voice sounded high pitched. Panicked. I tried to level it off. "I'm sorry," I said. "It's just that I'm really frightened."

"You're still afraid the killer might know who you are? That he might think you could identify him?" Aunt Ibby asked. "What about that, Pete? *Should* Maralee be afraid?"

The albums were still open on the table but we'd all stopped looking at them. O'Ryan's ears perked up again, and he focused narrowed eyes on Pete. Aunt Ibby and I both looked at him too. Pete sat quietly, looking down at his folded hands.

A long moment passed. Pete leaned forward, shoulders slumped. "I don't know for sure yet. I *believe* she's perfectly safe. From the time Lee called 911 until we arrived at the library no one else left the building by either exit. There was no one on the staircase or in the old kitchen where the emergency exit stairs end. We think it's extremely doubtful that Lee and the perp were in the stacks at the same time." He took my hand in his. "As for the emergency door alarm, it may be faulty. Apparently it hasn't been tested for over a month."

"But Wee Willie was *recently* dead, according to Doc Egan," I said, still pushing. "Does that mean *minutes*?"

"It can mean minutes," Pete said, still holding my hand. "In this case though, it's probably in the range of up to fifteen minutes before you found him. We still have no one leaving the library—who isn't accounted for—during the time frame we've been able to establish."

His words began to sink in. He was right. I was most likely perfectly safe. The perp had killed Willie, then scooted through that emergency door with a faulty alarm on it, and somehow left the building without being detected. It's a big building and not all of it is library space.

Imaginary light bulb illuminated.

"Pete, in a big old building like that, there must be more than two ways in and out, is that true?" I asked— voice restored to normal pitch and without a trace of panic. "You must have figured out by now how a person could get outside without using either the front or side door."

"I always said you'd make a good cop." He squeezed my hand, winked, but didn't elaborate.

Chapter 25

We didn't have a lot more time to study the albums, and Pete didn't say any more about a different route for the killer to get out of the library. He had to leave for a late hockey practice with his Police Athletic League team, but promised to come over again the next evening to go over the pictures more thoroughly. O'Ryan accompanied Pete back outside and followed him all the way to his car, while I stood in the doorway, watching until the lights of the Crown Vic disappeared down Oliver Street. The cat hurried back, passed me in the hall, and returned to my aunt's kitchen. I hesitated before closing the back door, once again peering into the shadows, listening to the nighttime sounds. Pete's assurance of my safety had made me feel a little better, but I still had a trace of that nagging feeling of something like fear. I closed and locked the door and followed O'Ryan's lead.

Aunt Ibby had cleared the table of the albums and glassware, slipping the albums onto her cookbook shelf, and I could hear the friendly sound of Mr. Coffee brewing a fresh pot. She'd put a pair of ironstone mugs on the table. "Well then, Maralee," she said. "What do you think about the possibility that someone figured out how to leave the library without being detected?"

"I think that's what happened," I said flatly. "You know the place a lot better than I do. How could it be done?"

"There are several ways." She spoke slowly. "None of them would be easy, and whoever it was would have had extraordinary knowledge of the layout of the building, along with keys to several interior and exterior doors. Of course, the emergency door from the stacks is always unlocked, but it has a loud alarm signal. The stairway from the stacks leads down to the old kitchen. The door there has a lock that allows a person to leave, but doesn't open from the other side. When you leave that room, the door locks behind you."

"The classic 'locked room mystery,'" I said, "à la Agatha Christie."

"That's it," she said, pouring coffee into our mugs. "Want regular creamer or pumpkin flavored?"

"Pumpkin," I said. "Pumpkin-flavored coffee is one of the joys of fall."

"Don't care much for it myself," she said. "I buy it just for you. I guess I'm a traditionalist."

"Pete is too," I said, "but like you, he does so many things just to please me."

"He loves you."

"I know he does. But do you think he said he thinks I'm perfectly safe just to make me feel better?"

"No. If he didn't believe it, he wouldn't say it. Why do you ask that? Do *you* have some reason to believe you *are* in danger? Something you haven't shared with him?"

Do I? Do I have a reason?

I dumped the yummy creamer into the coffee and thought about it. "Not really," I admitted. I told her about the smiling man and the way O'Ryan had behaved in the yard. "I guess I'm getting spooked by shadows."

"It's understandable," she said. "Finding the dead man

must have been terrifying, especially since you were afraid of the stacks in the first place. And O'Ryan is a cat. He chases shadows because he's naturally curious."

"You're right. As usual. Shall we go ahead and plan to visit Ranger Rob in the morning?" I changed the subject as I do so often when I don't want to think about something unpleasant. "It's been a long time since I've been to a riding stable. I used to love being around the horses."

"I remember," she said. "We'll go early. Hopefully, Katie the Clown will get the message from your taxi driver friend tomorrow and call you. Then we can concentrate on finding Mercury."

"We still need to find out about Dave's connection to Larry Laraby. There's obviously something there."

"Do you want me to ask him about it when I see him at the library tomorrow?" she asked. "Then you can concentrate on the old actors. Save time, you know. And I'll pull up a copy of *The Boys of Summer* while I'm at it. Maybe there's a clue of some kind in the book itself." She looked happily hopeful.

"Does Dave have keys to everything?" I asked. "I mean to all those interior rooms?"

"I suppose so," she said. "Someone on the board of directors has a set I'm sure, and the fire department does too. The keys are on a big round ring. There are ten or twelve of them, all different sizes and shapes. Mostly old ones. Some are quite pretty."

"You've seen them?" I asked.

"Just my own set but I believe they're all alike."

That was a jaw-dropping statement. "You have a set?"

"Not my personal property, of course." She gave a modest flap of one hand. "They belong to the library. But I've been entrusted with them, yes."

"No kidding. Do you ever use them?"

"Actually, I've never had occasion to use any of the old ones. I keep the one to the side door with my own keys in case the key pad malfunctions for some reason. Never has, though." She gave a little shrug. "I'm glad I don't have to carry the rest of them around. They weigh a ton."

"I can imagine," I said. "Where are they?"

"In my bottom desk drawer at the library," she said. "Where they belong."

That didn't sound right. "Is the drawer locked?"

"Of course. I carry the key to that with me too." She picked up our coffee mugs and carried them to the sink while I put the pumpkin creamer into the refrigerator. "I'm sure the board members must have given the police a full set of the keys."

"I'm sure they did," I agreed. "That must be why Pete hinted that the killer had found a different way out of the library after using the emergency door. I guess I'll go along upstairs now and try to catch a bit of River's show. One more thing I'm going to try to fit into tomorrow's schedule—I need to make an appointment with River about the tarot."

"Really? Are you going to ask her to read the cards for you?"

"Not exactly," I said. "I need her professional interpretation of *my* reading of *one* particular card. The Wheel of Fortune."

She spread her hands apart. "Doesn't mean a thing to me. I'm afraid all I know about the tarot is that the cards are sometimes uncommonly beautiful, and that sometimes River is able to learn remarkable things just from looking at them."

"That's true. She does. It's a mystery to me too, but I've come to rely on her advice more often than I ever dreamed I would."

"You'd better go along then. You surely have a full plate for tomorrow."

O'Ryan looked up expectantly at the words "full plate."

"We're not talking about food, big boy," I told him. "Come on upstairs with me. We're going to watch River." That produced one of those deep, throaty purrs he does so well. He loves River. He trotted happily to and through the living room to the front hall. I followed.

By the time I'd climbed up the two flights, O'Ryan was already sprawled out along the kitchen windowsill, eyes fixed on the dark TV screen. "Okay," I said. "I'll turn it on for you while I change into my pj's. You can catch the end of Buck Covington's late news. I'll be right back." I turned on the television, already tuned to WICH-TV, and headed down the short hall to the bathroom.

I returned to the kitchen, showered, shampooed, and towel dried, face moisturized, wearing almost new tailored navy blue satin pajamas, which I love because the top has pockets where they belong, one on each side instead of the usual one stitched awkwardly over the left breast. Covington was just winding up his show with a shortened clip of Howard Templeton's coverage of Chief Whaley's press conference.

O'Ryan saw me coming and raced for the bedroom. He likes to be first. I straightened up the kitchen, wiped down the counter, made sure the kitchen door was locked. I turned off the overhead light, turned off the TV, and checked the lock on the window. It opens onto a fire escape and although I sometimes leave it open during the day when the weather is fine, I almost always lock it at night. I paused there, looking down into the yard where all was quiet—just as it should be.

O'Ryan was already lying at the foot of the bed, front paws curled inward, eyes wide open, clearly waiting for me to turn on the bedroom TV. I obliged. River's theme music played while I plumped up my pillows and slipped under the covers. There was a mouthwatering commercial for a special Halloween chocolate assortment from Stowaway Sweets, Marblehead's premier candy shop, followed by a short trailer promoting the night's feature movie. It was *I Married a Witch,* the 1942 black-and-white classic starring Veronica Lake and Frederic March, one of my all-time favorite witch movies. I remembered showing it on *Nightshades* at about this same time in October a few years back.

I snuggled contentedly into the covers and patted the spot beside me, inviting O'Ryan to join me at the head of the bed, thinking that if I only had a box of those chocolates, this would be a perfect TV experience—my favorite pajamas, my best friend's show, a great old movie, and a fine cat companion.

I wondered if River would do one of her one-card explanations—and if she did, whether I'd feel as though I could do my own interpretation. I had oddly mixed feelings about that. If she didn't do it I'd feel a kind of relief. If she did though, I'd feel excitement—the kind of anticipatory flutter I always get on a roller coaster just before the big downward plunge, the thrill of knowing I'm going to be safely scared.

River wore an electric-blue halter-top gown, the gauzy fabric shot with bright silver threads. Once again she wore silver stars and moons woven into her dark hair, which tonight flowed loose over her shoulders. An absolute vision. If Buck was in the studio, he'd probably drop the whole deck of cards if he tried that fancy shuffle just then. "Welcome, friends of the night," she said as soon as the strains of *Danse Macabre* had faded away. "We're going directly to phone calls." She frowned slightly and turned her head toward the far corner where the control booth is. She touched her left ear, where I knew a tiny device kept her connected to the producer.

"My staff tells me there's a call waiting that seems to be urgent," she said. "Hello caller, your first name and birth-date please?"

The answering voice was hesitant, faint, and certainly youthful. "I'm—uh—my name is Pamela. My birthday is April first and I'm eleven and a half."

"You're up very late, Pamela," River said. "Do your parents know you're calling me?"

Uh-oh. Doan has a policy about taking calls from kids after ten p.m. on weekdays unless there's a major sports event going on.

The child sniffled and the voice broke. "No. But I sneak and watch you sometimes and I'm supposed to tell an adult if I see something, say something, and I can't tell my mom or she'll kill me and"—more sniffling—"and besides you know Mr. Buck Covington and if you tell him what I saw he'll put it on the news or something and the library lady won't know I skipped and my mom won't kill me." Pause. More sniffling. "Okay?"

I'd been smiling at River's dilemma right up until young Pamela uttered the word "library." I sat bolt up-right, displacing the cat, grabbed my phone from the nightstand, and texted Pete. "River's show NOW."

"Buck is right here in the studio, honey," River said. "I'm going to let you talk to him while I take the next caller. You hold on." She made a motioning signal stage right.

Good job, girl. Cover your own butt with Doan and make sure the kid's message gets through. River faced the camera, smiling brightly, and welcomed the next caller. "Hello, caller. Your first name and birthdate please?"

My phone rang. It was Pete. "What's going on? Why am I supposed to watch River?"

"There was a child caller who says she saw something in the library, Pete. River just handed the call off to Buck.

He's in the studio. Sounds to me as if the little girl skipped the library musical class somehow and saw something that frightened her. She wanted to tell an adult so she called River."

"Thanks, babe. I hope Covington can keep her on the line. I'm on my way to the station. Talk to you later."

Chapter 26

After I'd talked to Pete I tried to stay focused on River's show, watching her carefully to see if she showed any sign that anything was wrong. Buck Covington appeared after the second commercial, anchorman-handsome and as composed as possible considering his proximity to the ravishing River. He shuffled the tarot deck flawlessly and showed no sign of anxiety resulting from his conversation with Pamela.

O'Ryan had returned to his position beside me, watching River as carefully as I did. She did a reading for a woman who confided that she was anticipating moving to another state and needed to know if that was a good idea. She read for another who had met a new man and needed some guidance in that direction. She introduced the movie and I began to relax a little as lightning struck the tree where the spirits had been imprisoned and lovely Veronica Lake assumed human form once again.

Come on, Pete. Call me. I'm worried about the child. Did she see the killer? More importantly, did the killer see her?

I jumped, startled, when the phone rang. I muted the TV control and answered the phone.

"Pete? Did you talk to Buck? Did you find out what Pamela saw?"

"Yes. To all of it. Fortunately Buck recorded the conversation with Pamela, so we've got a good idea of what she saw. The producer has Pamela's cell number and location of course."

"Can you tell me what she said?"

"I'll give you a fast rundown of it. Can't release the recording." He sounded apologetic, as though he truly wanted to share it.

"That's okay. I understand."

"Here's the gist of it then. The kid, Pamela, went to the library with a bunch of other kids from her school. Seems she's tall for her age and some of the boys were teasing her. Made her cry." He paused. "Kids can be so damned mean. Anyway, she was at the rear of the group when they went in the side door. She saw a door that was partly open and ducked through it, planning to dry her eyes and join the group when she felt better."

I could see it in my mind. "That's the door to the old kitchen. It shouldn't be open."

"I know. She closed it behind her. She says the room was full of boxes and stuff and some old office furniture."

"That sounds about right. I've never been in there myself," I said.

"She was starting to feel a little better. Figured her eyes looked okay and was about to go and join the others for the music thing." Another pause. "She heard somebody coming. She was scared so she ducked behind a pile of boxes."

I realized I was holding my breath. "She saw who it was?"

"She did. She says she saw a man with black pants and a black jacket and some kind of shoes she called 'booties.'"

"That means really low-cut boots. I have some."

"Oh, I didn't know that." He continued. "The guy has short curly gray hair and he was wearing gloves and he had some kind of a big bag like a backpack except it wasn't on his back. He was carrying it."

"The poor child must have been terrified."

"She was. She says she closed her eyes and scooched down as far as she could and listened for him to leave. But he stayed in there for a long time, she says, and she heard noises but she didn't dare to look to see what he was doing. After a while, she heard the door open. She could hear the music from inside the library. Then she heard the door shut. She waited for a while longer before she came out. She was afraid to stay out there alone so she decided to sneak inside and join the others."

"And she never told anybody until she called River?"

"Right. She was afraid she'd get in trouble for ducking out of the group. She missed most of the music class. But when she saw the news about the murder on Buck's show she decided she'd better tell a grown-up. Like River."

"Good kid. Do you think there's any chance that the man saw her?"

There was no hesitation in Pete's reply. "Very unlikely. She was well concealed and he apparently went on with whatever he was doing in there without making a move toward the area where she was hiding."

I wished he'd sounded that sure about whether or not the man had seen *me,* but I didn't press that issue. "Did the person she described show up on the surveillance tapes yet?"

"No, and that's a problem." I could visualize his frowning cop face. "We have no pictures of anyone that fits Pamela's description of the man either entering or leaving the building. Nobody."

There was a long pause and I figured that Pete had told me everything he felt comfortable about sharing. "Well, thanks for calling me, Pete. I was really worried about the little girl. Is it okay if I tell River what you said?"

"I'm sure Buck will play the recording for her. Probably already has—while the movie was playing."

"True. But I'd like her to know you're not worried about little Pamela being seen while she was hiding," I said. "Okay?"

"Sure. I've already told Buck this is all confidential, of course—and I know I don't have to tell you that."

"I'm sure no one at the station would say anything that might put that child in danger," I said, "but thanks for keeping me up to speed on all this. Love you."

"Love you too," he said. "I'll call you tomorrow."

I put the phone back on the nightstand and turned the TV back on. Veronica Lake was about to wreck Frederic March's romance with Susan Hayward. That's one of the best parts but I found my attention wandering. *How could the man Pamela saw in the old kitchen have come in and out of the building without being caught by any of the surveillance cameras?* It was turning out to be a true "locked room" mystery. What would Hercule Poirot do? (I figured this one was above Nancy Drew's pay grade.)

O'Ryan had moved back to his foot-of-the-bed position and seemed to be concentrating on the movie—or possibly waiting for River to reappear. I was wide awake with mind racing. When that happens I usually just get up and do something productive. Wash dishes? Apply a facial mask? Neither idea appealed.

I padded into the kitchen, opened a diet Pepsi, and pulled a handful of the papers I'd been collecting all day from the hobo bag. I studied the scribbled notes I'd made about putting together a flowchart connecting the various people who seemed to be somehow associated with the dead William Wallace—or Wallace Williams. Did this new character, the gray-haired man in black wearing gloves and booties fit in? If so, how did he *get* in? And what should I call him?

I decided on "Curly."

Back to the "locked room" idea. Obviously, Curly had entered and left the library somehow. Pete had confirmed that there were other entrances to the old building. All locked and deadbolted. All had been examined and found to be secure. Aunt Ibby had a full set of keys in a locked drawer at the library. Dave might have a set too. That led to the conclusion that Curly might somehow have had access to keys to an exterior door. *Or not!* What about windows? Had they checked all of the ground-floor windows? Surely they had.

The Clue game crossed my mind once again. Did Miss White do it in the observatory with a knife? Did Miss Peacock do it on the patio with a bat? Then I thought about Rhonda's old boyfriend who'd taught her self-defense.

Did Curly do it in the library with a karate chop?

More confused than I'd been when I started this train of thought, I chugged the Pepsi, stuffed all the papers back into the hobo bag, joined O'Ryan on the bed, and watched River's show to the very end.

Chapter 27

Aunt Ibby had decided to get an early start on our quest to locate Ranger Rob and Agnes Hooper. I wanted to be back by noon, just in case anything along the line of field reporting turned up for me at the station. Since we'd be going to a riding stable I decided on jeans, checked shirt, denim vest, and the same pair of Frye Western boots I'd had since high school. (Keep them polished and conditioned and they last forever.) I briefly considered rescuing my raggedy old cowboy hat from the second-floor bedroom, but quickly decided it would be too much.

My aunt and I shared a quick breakfast of banana nut muffins, orange juice, and coffee. I tried the Professor Mercury website address again. Again, no luck.

I backed the Vette out of the garage and we were on our way down Route 128 toward Rockport by seven a.m. I tucked my phone in the breast pocket of the vest, volume turned up, not wanting to miss the hoped-for call from Katie the Clown.

Just turning into the wooded road leading to the Double R Riding Stable brought back a nostalgia rush of sweet memories of a typical young teenaged girl's fierce love of horses. I'd loved every single thing about those days from the riding competitions to mucking out the stalls. I still have a box of blue ribbons and, of course, the boots and that beat-up old hat.

We rounded the last bend and pulled up beside a show ring. A young woman led a plump gray pony around and around in the circle, an excited small boy in the saddle. Several other cheering little kids awaited their turns. Aunt Ibby and I approached a long barn with double doors open so that the row of stalls was visible. I could smell the hay and the horses and that incomparable good barn smell. *Yes, even including the poop.*

I parked in a space marked "Visitor" and we two walked up the slightly angled wooden ramp and through those inviting double doors. A palomino with chocolate eyes gave us a curious look and craned his neck from the first stall. I stroked the soft muzzle and called out "Hello? Anybody here?"

"Be right with you," came an answer from one of the other stalls. It had been a lot of years since I'd heard that voice, but I recognized it immediately. Ranger Rob still had what Bruce Doan referred to as "a good set of pipes." The stall door swung open after a brief moment and the tall man walked toward us. "Can I help you ladies?"

"Hello," I said. "I'm Lee Barrett. WICH-TV. You're Robert Oberlin, aren't you? Ranger Rob?" I stuck out my hand. He hesitated for a second, looked down at his own hand, and apparently decided that despite whatever he'd been doing horse-wise, it was sanitary enough for a handshake. His grip was firm and his smile was as warm and toothpaste-ad perfect as ever.

"Howdy, Lee Barrett," he said. "I'm guessin' you were one of my little buckaroo fans from the old days. Well, I'm a fan of yours now. Good job on that sad business over at the library."

"Thanks," I said, still a little starstruck even though my tall, lean, childhood cowboy-crush was now on the seriously portly side. I introduced my aunt and Robert Oberlin wiped his hand on his shirt before he grasped hers. "Howdy, Ms. Russell," he said. "Welcome to the Double R. Now what brings you folks here on this fine fall day?"

I explained briefly about the upcoming seventieth anniversary of WICH-TV, and how Mr. Doan had asked me to contact the big-name TV personalities from those early days. "So naturally, you were at the top of my list," I said truthfully. "We're hoping you'll agree to do a few appearances during the anniversary week."

"I'm pretty sure I can manage to fit that into my schedule." The smile broadened. "Even though I can't fit into my Ranger Rob outfit anymore. Just tell us when and where to show up. I'll be there. You rounded up any of the others yet? Agnes or Jerry?"

"Not yet," I admitted. "I'm hoping to hear from Agnes sometime today though. Haven't been able to locate the professor. Any idea where he might be working his magic these days?"

"Saw him a few months back at my grandson's birthday party," he said. "Hasn't lost his touch one bit. The kids loved him. He gave me his card. I could look for it in the office." He waved toward a small building behind the barn. "Must have a phone number on it I should think." I figured it would probably be the same card Chris had given to me, but I told him I'd appreciate having a look at it.

"You ride?" he asked, looking down at my boots.

"Used to," I said. "Not for a long time though."

"She was very good at it too," my aunt put in. "Had her own horse. A sweet Appaloosa named Smoothie. No reason she couldn't take the time to come over here to ride once in a while."

I looked at her in surprise. Smoothie had been my best friend and companion and playmate from fifth grade right up until I went to college. It about broke my heart when we donated him to the Horses for the Handicapped Foundation. It helped some that I knew how much he'd mean to the disabled people who'd love him too.

Rob said he had some fine horses to rent and that there were miles of good trails nearby. Even a couple of spots where horses were allowed on the beach. It was tempting. "I'll think about it," I said. "But right now I'm concentrating on that anniversary program."

"Do you remember Larry Laraby, Mr. Oberlin?" my aunt asked. "Were you at the station when he was the sports reporter?"

"I remember him." Rob began walking toward the double doors. "Never knew him well. He was about to retire when the Ranger Rob show began. I got to know him a little when he started the collectibles shows. Did a few odd jobs for him." He pointed to the Double R Stables sign over the door "See that? I kind of borrowed part of the name from the show. Remember the Triple R Ranch? It stood for Ranger Rob Ranch."

"You must have known Wee Willie Wallace then," my aunt persisted. She was asking the questions I should be asking. I took the cue.

"I've been doing a little research and it turns out that Wee Willie played quite a few parts in those old shows. Like being your sidekick, Cactus."

He looked down toward my boots again. "Yep. Cactus. Funny little guy, wasn't he? Listen Ms. Barrett, Lee. May I call you Lee?" He didn't wait for an answer. "Listen, you just come on over any day except Saturdays—that's when all the kids show up. Any day and you take yourself a nice ride on Prince Valiant here." He gave the palomino an affectionate rub on the nose. "No charge. And you just let me know about the anniversary thing. I'll be there with bells on. You bet. Well, gotta go pick up some feed. Good talking to you." He backed away.

"If you have one more minute to spare, Rob," I asked, "could I have a peek at that business card you mentioned? My boss is expecting me to deliver all three stars. Professor Mercury, Katie the Clown, and Ranger Rob."

"Tell you what." He approached an F-150 King Ranch Supercrew Ford. Late model. Probably 2017. "I don't recall exactly where it is," he called over his shoulder. "I'll find it though. You bet. I'll call you. Gotta go." He climbed into the cab of that big, beautiful silver truck and started the powerful engine.

My aunt and I looked at each other as the Ford disappeared down the long driveway. We returned to the Vette and, with a wave to the pony riders, left the Double R Stables. She spoke first. "What do you suppose he's hiding?"

Chapter 28

Before long we were once again on Route 128, heading back to Salem, Aunt Ibby at the wheel, me furiously scribbling notes on index cards. "Don't you think there's something about Robert Oberlin that's just not quite right?" My aunt pressed for an answer. I knew what she meant.

"It wasn't anything he said, exactly." I searched for the right words. "I mean, it was more what he didn't say. Does that make sense?"

"He was dodging some simple questions," she said, "and he was all of a sudden in a big hurry to get away from us."

"It almost seems as if he knew Larry Laraby better than he let on," I said, wondering if she felt as uncomfortable about doubting the motives of my once-time cowboy hero as I did. "But maybe he was just in a hurry to pick up feed. Running a business like that isn't easy."

"True." She nodded. "But he didn't want to talk about knowing Wee Willie either, and Willie as Cactus was his sidekick for years on that show."

"Not unusual," I said. "Some people who work together every day don't like each other much." I thought about my contentious relationship with Scott Palmer, and so far I wasn't too crazy about Howard Templeton either. "Professionals don't let it affect the job."

She smiled. "You're probably right. I'm just a nosy old woman—taking this snooping into police business much too seriously."

We dropped that subject and chatted about her plan for inviting the young people from the Salem High Library Corps to help clean up the books that had been on the floor. "There actually wasn't much damage to most of them," she admitted, "but it'll be good practice for the kids anyway."

It was only about ten o'clock when we reached the Beverly Bridge and crossed into Salem. We were suddenly in a slow-moving line of cars. "Oh-oh," I said. "I'd almost forgotten how impossible driving here can be in October. The closer we get to Halloween, the crazier it gets."

"I should have remembered," my aunt said. "Today is the Great Pumpkin Walk. The streets will be jammed."

There was no way to get to our garage on Oliver Street without going past the Witch Museum, which would be one of the important destinations in the annual event. "Oh well," I said. "We may as well relax and enjoy watching the people in costumes. It's going to be a long, slow ride. When we get home let's lock up the cars. We'd better plan on walking wherever we go for the rest of the month."

It was a few minutes before eleven when we finally reached home. I hurried upstairs to change into something more appropriate in case I might have an opportunity to do some actual reporting. *I don't know how the mobile unit will be able to get around, but I'd better be ready just in case.*

Shedding the denim and Western boots and opting for dark brown midi and beige kitten heels, I checked my phone for a message from Agnes. Nothing. I tucked the phone into a pocket (I love dresses with pockets) and, slinging the hobo bag over my shoulder, I started down Winter Street and crossed the common, where good-natured costumed revelers were already jamming the walkways, climbing onto the bandstand, and crowding around the food vendors' wagons. I crossed Essex Street where a harried traffic cop coped as well as possible with the surging mass of people. And it wasn't even noon yet! Johnny and I had been to New Orleans during Mardi Gras a couple of times and Salem at Halloween is very similar. Crazy—but so very cool.

Derby Street was almost as people-packed as the downtown areas. I ran up the steps to the WICH-TV building's glass front door and stepped gratefully into the lobby. I crossed the black-and-white tiled floor, trying not to step on the cracks, and pushed the UP button on the elevator.

On the second floor I was greeted by a relieved Rhonda. "Boy, am I glad to see you. Templeton just phoned in that he's stuck in a big traffic jam. He can't get here and Doan wants somebody to cover the Pumpkin Walk live, Pronto! Local color and all that. Phil's noon news has already started. Francine's glommed onto a four-seater golf cart somehow. She's in the parking lot ready to go. You'll just ride through the crowd—Francine driving, Marty filming, you reporting. Here." She shoved a typed sheet of paper into my hand. "Show prep. Get going. Good luck." She pointed to the door that leads to the studio. "I'll tell Phil you three are on your way and to stand by for live feed."

I ran for the green door when Rhonda called out again. "I almost forgot. Some guy named Jerry came by. He said you were trying to contact him."

Jerry? As in Jerome Mercury?

"Where did he go?"

"He's in Doan's office. I'll tell him you'll be back in about half an hour. Now beat it!"

I did as I was told. "First things first," as Aunt Ibby always says. We'd take a little golf cart ride through the throngs of pumpkin walkers—whatever that meant— then I'd meet the elusive Jerry Mercury. The magical Professor Mercury of my childhood. *If that's actually who's waiting for me in Mr. Doan's office.*

As Rhonda had promised, Francine and Marty sat in the golf cart parked close to the studio back door. It was a cute one, with a pink-and-white-striped awning. I climbed into the back seat, greeted the two, and pulled the show prep sheet from my bag. I studied Rhonda's notes. Apparently the Pumpkin Walk has to do with all things pumpkin. Pumpkin displays, pumpkin-related food items, giant pumpkins, a pumpkin-carving contest. Francine had started our vehicle and we moved toward Derby Street where happy pumpkin walkers merrily interfered with traffic. I personally could not understand the humble pumpkin inspiring all this excitement, but as I said, Salem is crazy in October.

We stuck close to the sidewalk, facing oncoming cars. Folks had begun to notice the large WICH-TV signs on either side of the cart and made way for us, smiling, waving, mugging for the camera. Marty focused on me and pointed. Go ahead, Moon," she said. "Five. Four. Three. Two. One."

"Welcome to the Great Salem Pumpkin Walk," I said. "I'm Lee Barrett, reporting from Derby Street and heading by golf cart toward downtown Salem. You'll notice that many of the walkers are holding maps." Several of the people closest to us waved colorful sheets. "The maps are available at the Witch House. There are lots of local businesses starred. According to the rules, if you pick up ten special stickers from participating businesses, you'll win a prize!" This brought cheers. "And you folks at home, it's not too late to join the pumpkin walkers." Marty slowly panned the camera over the crowd while I consulted Rhonda's notes again. "You can park at the MBTA station and join the parade where many of the sponsoring businesses offer cider and donuts, pumpkin-flavored coffee, and even a haunted house experience." I was beginning to understand the pumpkin people. The whole thing was just plain fun. I stuck my mic out of the cart and talked to costumed kids running along beside us. I talked with a couple of locals, a few from other states and one visitor from Ireland. Marty held up five fingers and gave me the cutoff sign. "Lee Barrett here reporting from the Great Salem Pumpkin Walk. There's still time to join these folks, all celebrating the city's Haunted Happenings, enjoying tasty pumpkin treats, and winning great prizes."

"Good job," Francine said. "Now to figure out the easiest way to get back to the station." We'd only traveled a little more than a mile, but between the slow-moving traffic and the jostling crowd, it wasn't easy to reverse direction. Francine is an experienced driver, even in a pink-and-white golf cart, but when we arrived back at the station the noon news was over and we'd been away the better part of an hour. *Is Professor Mercury still waiting for me?*

I knew my hair was messed up from the outdoor ride. "Is there a visor mirror in this thing?" I looked around the canvas edges of the topper. Is it silly to want to look good when meeting a childhood idol? I don't think so. I fumbled around in my bag and pulled out a comb."

"Nope. Sorry," Francine said.

"I've got one. Here you go." Marty handed me a round

gold compact. Aunt Ibby has a similar one, with compressed powder and a little white disk thing for applying it on one side and a mirror on the other. I popped it open and squinted at the tiny round mirror—moved it around a little so I could see my unruly mop of curls. "Aargh," I said. "I should have worn a hat." I moved it down to eye level once again. But it wasn't my own eyes I saw looking back at me. The eyes in the mirror were golden. Cat's eyes. O'Ryan's eyes. And there hadn't even been a hint of the flashing lights or swirling colors that usually precede a vision. There'd been no warning. *Maybe it's just a small mirror thing.*

We pulled into an open space on the parking lot. The cat in the mirror disappeared. I handed the compact back to Marty and she and I tumbled out and headed for the studio door while Francine arranged for the return of the golf cart to whomever she'd sweet-talked into lending it to us. Marty went right to work on adding more Halloween décor—flying bats and jumping spiders—to River's set while I stopped off at the studio dressing room to make repairs on my hair and makeup before meeting Jerry Mercury—if he was still there—and to wonder what my wise cat was doing in Marty's gold compact.

Jerry Mercury was indeed still there. During the time he and Mr. Doan had spent together it appeared that they'd become fast friends. Rhonda said they'd been in the manager's office together ever since Professor Mercury had arrived at WICH-TV, asking to see me. I gave my hair one last pat and knocked on the station manager's door.

"Come in," Bruce Doan called. "Here she is. Jerry and I just watched your pumpkin thing. Not bad for short notice. Not bad at all."

"Hello," I said. "Took longer than I thought to get back here. What a crowd out there!"

Professor Mercury stood as I approached. Amazingly, he looked almost the same as he had all those years ago when he taught me and thousands of other kids how to build an awesome volcano or to make a tornado in a box. (That one took first place in the sixth-grade science fair.)

He wasn't wearing his magician's hat or his purple cape, of course, but even in jeans with white shirt, open at the neck, he was a commanding presence. He was average height, slim build, tanned complexion. There was a hint of gray at the temples of the slicked-back black hair.

"Ms. Barrett, meet Jerry Mercury," Mr. Doan said. "Jerry, Lee Barrett is one of our field reporters. You've probably seen her on the news."

Mercury extended his right hand. "I rarely have time to watch the news," he said, "but it's sincerely a pleasure to meet you, Ms. Barrett." I shook his hand and realized that it was his eyes—those magician's eyes—that gave the illusion of power.

"How do you do," I said as my mind flashed back to another pair of eyes—the golden cat's eyes in Marty's little round mirror.

"Jerry here has agreed to be a part of our anniversary celebration," Mr. Doan beamed—a rare sight—"and not only that—he's going to perform at Buffy's Halloween party!"

"Fantastic," I said, glancing around the office, wondering if I should sit. Jerry Mercury looked as though he was about to resume his seat, but he remained standing too.

"Oh, have a seat, Ms. Barrett." Bruce Doan waved in the direction of a purple club chair. "Jerry has been regaling me with tales about the old days here at WICH-TV. Back then there were lots of shows originating right here in this building. Not so much dependence on network, you know?"

"I remember," I said. "I was a big fan of Professor Mercury and Katie the Clown and Ranger Rob." I looked directly at Jerry Mercury. "Do you ever see the others? Rob and Agnes?"

He shook his head, those hypnotic eyes downcast. "Not as much as I'd like. I ran into Rob not too long ago—at a kid's birthday party—but I do see Agnes once in a while. She does the children's party circuit too. Still fits into her clown costume. Cute as ever."

Interesting. I didn't know that.

Bruce Doan looked back and forth between the magician and me. "I think our audience is going to love seeing the old gang together again. Maybe we'll find some of the old scripts. Do a real reunion bit."

I decided to push the nostalgia envelope a little bit. "It'll be hard to duplicate without Cactus and Marvel though, won't it?"

Doan looked confused. "Who?"

"Sidekicks," I reminded him.

"Oh yeah, I remember. You mentioned them in your report on the dead man in the library." A sad head shake. "Did you people know back then this Wee Willie guy was such a snake?"

"I didn't," Jerry said. "Rob never liked him, though. And Agnes loved everybody. Probably still does."

I felt the phone in my pocket vibrate. *It's probably Agnes. Shall I answer it? Right here in the boss's office?* Curiosity won out over good manners. I reached for it.

"Would you excuse me? I'm expecting an important call," I said. I stood and moved toward the closed office door. "I'll be right back." The frown on Bruce Doan's face was unmistakable. The professor's expression didn't change. I ducked out into the reception area and pulled the door shut behind me.

Rhonda looked up, surprised. "Everything okay?"

I gave her a smile and a thumbs-up and spoke into the phone. "Hello. This is Lee Barrett."

"Hello. This is Agnes Hooper. Jim Litka said you've been looking for me. Why?"

It wasn't the sweet, happy, Katie the Clown voice I remembered and she didn't sound much like somebody who loves everybody.

Chapter 29

"Oh, Ms. Hooper," I said. "I'm so glad you called. This is Lee Barrett. WICH-TV."

"I know that. That's what it says on your card. What do you want?" *This is sweet little funny Katie the Clown?*

Might as well plunge right in, I decided. No small talk required here. "We're planning a celebration of the station's seventieth anniversary," I said. "We'd like to invite you, as well as some of the other folks who've worked here over the years, to help us celebrate. Union scale, of course."

"Oh. Really?"

I detected an immediate change in tone. "Of course," I said. "It was the talented people like you who built WICH-TV. We haven't forgotten it."

"Oh my goodness. I thought it was some kind of scam. You know, like you've won a trip or something when they just want you to change your cable service or buy their stuff. People are always trying to sell me things I don't want. They're on my phone. The internet. Tags hung on the front doorknob." She giggled. "I should have

known Jim Litka wouldn't be part of anything like that!
So do you want Katie the Clown? Or Princess Waterfall
Raindrop? I was also Mrs. Santa Claus at Christmas and
Witchy-Poo at Halloween, you know." *No, I did not know
that.* Another giggle. "I was even a lady gorilla once but
the costume was so itchy it gave me hives and I refused to
wear it again."

"I had no idea!" I admitted. "I was a faithful fan, and I
never guessed that you were all those people. I'll bet
most of our audience didn't know it either." I was already
planning a big on-camera reveal. "It'll really be fun to let
them in on the secret."

"It will, won't it? You said some of the others are
going to be there? Rob and Jerry?"

"Yes to both names."

"It'll be good to get together," she said. "They both
played more than one character too. We all wore many
hats in those days."

We do too, in these days. Only not in costume. "That
surprises me. Who was Ranger Rob, besides himself?"

"Let's see." Short pause. "Well, for one, Rob was Officer Tom when I did the safety features on my show." I remembered gruff-voiced Officer Tom. He had a pale
complexion and a blond crew cut. Glasses too, and a kind
of big nose. Used to scare us kids into following the rules.
"Fooled you on that one, I bet. Didn't look at all like the
tanned, dark-haired, handsome cowboy, did he?"

"Sure didn't."

"It's remarkable what makeup and wigs and nose putty
can do, isn't it?" she asked. "We all got good at it. And of
course, we had amazing costumes. I guess most of the
budget went for costumes back then. It was cheaper than
hiring a bunch of extra people I suppose."

I hope Mr. Doan doesn't get any ideas from this!

I glanced at the gold sunburst clock. *Maybe I'd better*

get back to the boss's office. "Can I get together with you soon, Ms. Hooper, to firm up the plans for your appearance? I want to go and tell Mr. Doan the good news about your coming to help with the anniversary celebration."

She agreed and gave me her number. "Call me Agnes," she said, "or Katie, if you want to." I thanked her, called her Agnes, tapped the number into memory, made a couple of quick notations on index cards, and hurried back to the manager's office, wishing I'd had time to find out what extra hats Professor Mercury had worn.

I tapped on the door gently, then pushed it open. Both men looked up. "Sorry to run out like that," I said, "but you'll both be pleased to hear that Agnes Hooper, aka Katie the Clown, will be delighted to join us for the anniversary celebration!"

"Good news." Bruce Doan leaned back in his chair. "Glad to hear it. Can you think of any of the other old-timers we should invite, Jerry?"

Jerry Mercury didn't look too pleased with that "old-timer" tag, but murmured, "Not offhand." Momentary pause. "Of course Wee Willie Wallace would have been a colorful addition to the group. Too bad about that. Say, maybe we can find another short person to wear the robot suit. Marvel never spoke and the audience wouldn't know the difference."

"True. What do you think about that, Ms. Barrett?"

"Quite a few people already know that Willie was Marvel," I said. "I've mentioned it a couple of times in my reports and I'm sure the Boston stations have too. I think it's best that we keep it real." Mercury didn't look pleased about that either.

"I agree," Doan said. "Keep it real. Anyway, I'm sure the robot costume is long gone."

Jerry Mercury stood up. "You're probably right. Anyway, I've taken up enough of your time." He reached across the desk and the men shook hands. He gave a polite nod in my direction. "Ms. Barrett. A pleasure to meet you. Look forward to working with you on the anniversary show."

"My pleasure," I said, returning the polite nod. "If you'll leave your number with Rhonda at the reception desk, we'll stay in touch."

"There's a contact link on my website," he said. "Rhonda has my card."

"Your site was down earlier," I said. "I'll check with Rhonda."

Still no phone. No address for the mysterious Professor Mercury. He pulled the office door open, then turned back, facing me, those hypnotic eyes locking onto mine. "See you soon," he said, and closed the door.

"Nice fellow," Mr. Doan declared. "Smart, too. He knows a lot about the television business. I'm almost tempted to hire him to help around here full time."

"I understand that he keeps pretty busy with the kids' party magic shows he does," I said, hoping the idea of hiring Jerry Mercury was just a passing thought and not a serious consideration. Call me silly. I just didn't like to think about having those magician's eyes on me every day.

"Yeah, you're probably right." He shuffled a few papers on his desk. "Well, I'm sure you have better things to do than hang around in here." He gave a dismissive jerk of his head toward the door. "See if Rhonda has anything for you this afternoon. Howie has some kind of car trouble."

"Yessir," I stood and moved toward the door, thinking maybe Howie should plan on either hiring a golf cart or leaving for work very early in the morning—before the tourists were awake. I checked with Rhonda and together we consulted the white board for possible assignments—

preferably within walking distance. "I'm lucky. I live just across the common. Easy walk," I told her. "How's your commute working out?"

"Easy," she said. "One of Wanda's boyfriends has a three-bedroom time-share right on the boulevard. Me and Marty and Wanda are bunking there until Halloween is over."

"Good deal," I said. "Look. There's an easy one." I pointed to the board. "A Halloween costume pet parade at PetSmart. We can put portable equipment in Marty's shopping cart and walk to it." (Marty had some years ago acquired a vintage shopping cart from a now-defunct A&P store. Now spray-painted red and bearing a WICH-TV logo, it had turned out to be a most useful piece of equipment and—pleasing to the boss—it didn't cost anything.)

"Oh, I wish I could come with you for that one. I love seeing animals in costumes—especially the puppies and kittens." Rhonda laughed. "I'll bet O'Ryan wouldn't wear one though, would he?"

"I wouldn't dare to even suggest it," I said. "Much too undignified."

"I know. Listen, if you plan to be on camera this afternoon you could use a little more makeup. I'll meet you in the ladies room in about two minutes. Okay?"

I knew she was right. I generally refrained from using the confined space of the reception area's cramped pink-and-lavender restroom with its purple plastic toilet seat in favor of the larger, less flamboyant facility in the downstairs studio. I pulled the pink door closed behind me and inspected my face in the star-shaped mirror. That was a mistake. This time, though, at least the flashing lights and swirling colors appeared before the vision. *Maybe the instant pictures only happen on small reflective surfaces. Like visors and compacts.*

It was O'Ryan again. This time the picture showed the whole cat, not just eyes. He was sitting on what looked like an old-fashioned trunk. There were metal bands across the curved top of the thing, and an oblong plate with a big keyhole in it. It looked vaguely familiar. A few pieces of fabric trailed from the edges of the lid, as though it had been slammed down in a hurry.

Okay, cat. What the heck are you trying to show me? This makes no sense at all.

"You ready in there?" Rhonda tapped at the door. The cat disappeared and the confused redhead looked back at me.

"All ready," I said. "And you're right. I definitely need more makeup."

I sat down on the purple seat lid and tried to relax as she worked her Mary Kay magic. "I called Francine," she said. "She and Marty are loading up the shopping cart. They'll meet you in the downstairs studio as soon as you're ready. The pet parade starts at two o'clock. You've got about twenty minutes to get there and get set up."

Within a few minutes, hair brushed and makeup refreshed, I joined the other two. They were seated on River's couch, the shopping cart, plainly marked with the WICH-TV logo on both sides, parked in the center aisle between sets. Marty had added some orange and black streamers to it, and had apparently liberated one of River's spiders too. "Hope I didn't take too long." I sneaked a peek into the *Saturday Business Hour* cubicle and wondered how much more information waited to be discovered in that old file cabinet. *One thing at a time,* I told myself. "Let's go look at the adorable pets," I said. "I didn't see anything else on the schedule that's within walking distance and the crowds seem to be getting bigger."

"Let's roll. The cart looks really cute, Marty." Francine pushed the contraption toward the outer door.

"Just getting in the spirit," Marty deadpanned. "Let's get this show on the road."

We actually made very good time getting through the

pumpkin partiers to the pet shop. Rhonda had been so right about the incredible cuteness of animals in costumes, and I could tell that Francine was loving it. The manager of the store showed us which animals might not mind being picked up. Marty turned out to be our own personal "pet whisperer," and easily coaxed a spotted pup dressed as a butterfly to hold a pose while Francine manned the camera. She retied a baby bonnet on a sweet gray tabby kitten, handed her to me, and wiggled her fingers, causing the kitty-baby to look, wide-eyed and adorable, directly into Francine's close-up lens. So it went. A poodle as an unlikely giraffe, a dachshund clearly embarrassed in hula skirt and lei, a fluffy white kitten in pink-and-gray mouse ears. The models were all rescue animals and I gave a heartfelt pitch for adopting these wonderful creatures. I was sorely tempted to take the black kitten dressed as Batman home with me, but resisted. *Maybe someday. Not now.*

We shot a good twenty minutes worth of video. We said our reluctant goodbyes to the animals and trundled our equipment back out onto the sidewalk. Marty promised to edit it down to a few two-minute segments for use every day until Halloween. "You can record a couple of quick voice-overs about adopting fur-babies when we get back to the station, okay Moon?"

"Sure. No problem." Francine shot some more footage of the crowds along Essex Street, focusing on some clever, some beautiful, some scary costumes. I thought about what Agnes had said about the actors and show hosts at WICH-TV in the old days donning costumes and stage makeup to play two or three or maybe more different parts. These days Doan just had everybody do as many jobs as they could—wigs and fake noses or not.

Chapter 30

Back at the station I watched over Marty's shoulder as she skillfully edited the seeming miles of footage Francine had shot. Like magic, she produced four different two-minute pieces showing the very cutest animals, the very most adorable poses, and the very most original costumes. I used almost the same hastily prepared script for each one and within an hour I was ready to follow the pumpkin path homeward.

The late afternoon sun cast a pretty glow on Winter Street and as soon as I approached our front door I saw O'Ryan at the long side window, nose against the glass, waiting to greet me. It makes me happy every time. I unlocked the door, paused for the expected deep-throated purr and wrap around the ankles welcome, picked up the beautiful and uncostumed cat, and started up the stairs.

I was halfway up the first flight when Aunt Ibby appeared in the foyer. "I'm glad you're home Maralee," she said. "Can you spare a minute?"

"Of course." I put O'Ryan down and retraced my steps, following my aunt across her living room and into the kitchen, the cat scampering ahead of us.

"What's up?" I asked. "Is anything wrong?"

"Oh, no. I'm fine," she said. "Here. Sit down. I was about to have a nice glass of sherry. Join me?"

I sat on one of the counter stools and O'Ryan opted for a nearby cushioned captain's chair. "Sure. Why not?"

She filled two wineglasses and sat opposite me. "I've been thinking," she said, "about Robert Oberlin."

I sipped the wine. "Thinking what?"

"Thinking that Rob had a pretty good motive for Willie's murder."

"Rob? How? Why?"

"The horses," she said. "Did you see how gently he stroked Prince Valiant, how he slipped him a sugar cube? He loves them."

"Well, sure he does." I agreed. "He runs a stable. It's a lot of work. Hard, messy, dirty work. Nobody would do it if they *didn't* love horses."

"Wee Willie didn't love horses," she pointed out. "Wee Willie abused them—apparently for a long time before he was caught. One of them even died. Right on the track." She shook her head and put her wineglass down hard enough so that some of the liquid splashed onto the counter. "Horrible. He was a horrible person, Maralee. And he did it for money. Ranger Rob must have been heartbroken. And furious."

"I'm sure he was. I'm furious too, and I just learned about it." I took a paper napkin from a diner-type chrome dispenser and wiped up the spilled wine. "But Rob wasn't in the library the day Willie died. We know who was in there and who wasn't."

"Yes. Well, I need to think it out a little more. But at least it's a credible theory, don't you agree?" She leaned forward, clearly back in snoop sisters mode, earlier resolutions to let the police handle it forgotten.

"It has to be more than credible," I said, knowing that

I hadn't been out of snoop sisters mode myself for even a minute since this whole thing started. "It has to be possible—or at least plausible. Wee Willie's murder is like an Agatha Christie locked-room mystery. Like a game of Clue. Nobody could have gone in or out of the library that the surveillance camera didn't catch."

"Nonsense," she sputtered. "Of course they *could* have! Just because nobody has used any other way to get into the building for many years, doesn't mean it's impossible."

That was a surprise. "There's another entrance?"

"Sure. Windows. And an old boarded-up cellar door too."

"I'm sure the police have checked those," I said. "Haven't they?"

"Yes. They have. I asked Dave about it and he says the police went around and checked all the windows on the first floor. Locked tight. Every single one."

"There's a cellar door?"

"Boarded up years ago." Her voice was firm. "They checked it. Dave went with them. He said it's completely covered by bushes out back. He's positive no one has touched that old bulkhead in decades."

"The bushes out there are always so neatly trimmed," I recalled. "I had no idea there even *was* a cellar door."

"I know," she said. "The city does a beautiful job on the groundskeeping. Always has."

"Okay then." I took a hefty sip of sherry. "How did Rob Oberlin get up into the stacks, kill Willie, and get out again without anyone seeing him?"

"Hmmm." She topped off both of our glasses. "Maybe we'll have to leave *that* part up to the police. But I'm quite sure it *could* be done. How was *your* day?"

I told her about our golf-cart ride through the Great Pumpkin Walk. "It was live on the morning news," I said. "Did you see any of it?"

"Sorry no. I had to take the long way around to get to the library without bumping into the Pumpkin Walk crowd," she said, "so I left early. Sounds like fun though."

"Not as much fun as our other assignment. Marty and Francine and I covered a costumed pet show. It was so cute. They'll be using clips from it right up until Halloween, so you'll see it for sure. Adorable puppies and kitties. I was almost tempted to bring home a companion for O'Ryan."

The cat in question suddenly halted his fairly intensive whisker grooming project and with ears straight up, shook his head from side to side. "Mmrrapp," he said, stuck his pink tongue out, and turned his back on us.

"Good thing you resisted *that* temptation," my aunt said.

"I knew right away it wasn't a good idea." I hurried to cover up such a serious lapse in judgment. "We already have the best cat in Salem." I watched O'Ryan's ears. Still straight up. He was listening. I realized he'd forgiven me though when after a few seconds of sulking he faced us again and resumed work on those luxuriant whiskers. "Speaking of O'Ryan," I continued, relieved, "I saw him today in kind of a mini-vision in Marty's little compact mirror."

"What was he doing?" she asked.

"Nothing, really," I said. "At least not right then. All I saw of him in the compact was his eyes. Later on, in the ladies room mirror, I saw the whole cat."

"Was he doing anything then?"

"He was sitting on top of a trunk. An old-fashioned-looking one." I described the metal bands, the big keyhole in the lock plate. "There was something familiar about it but I can't quite place it. Ring any bells for you?"

"It sounds a bit like the old trunk that was up in our attic for years. A nineteen-twenty-five Louis Vuitton. A fine piece of luggage. Your great-grandmother Forbes used it on her first trip to Europe."

I snapped my fingers. "Of course. I remember now. It burned up in the attic fire." I shuddered slightly at the memory. The fire that had consumed much of the top floor of our house had very nearly taken Aunt Ibby and me and O'Ryan with it.

"That's right," she said. "Some of the vintage clothes in that grand old trunk became the wardrobe you used when you were Crystal Moon." *So we're back to costumes again.*

Explaining the connection between a vision-cat on a trunk, the costumes I'd once worn on the defunct *Nightshades* program, the many costumes the assorted players may have worn on long-gone kiddie shows, and the mystery of the death of one of those players was just too complicated. I didn't even attempt it. Instead I returned to the more current question of how a killer could have entered the library, murdered Wee Willie Wallace with little or no noise, and left the building without calling attention to himself—or herself.

"I keep thinking of possible ways for a person to enter and leave within the time frame the police have established," I said. "We can see Willie climb the stairs to the stacks. A few others go up and come down. We know what time I found the—uh—found Willie." I finished my sherry. "How can this be? Everybody who'd been in the stacks left the building somehow—except for Willie, of course."

My aunt didn't answer right away, but looked at me thoughtfully. "This is not going to be an easy case to solve," she declared. "Not one bit easy. But between us all—you and me and Pete and the Salem police department—I do believe we'll figure it out."

O'Ryan, having finished the whisker grooming, was busily washing his underside. Pausing, he said, "Meeah."

"Yes, of course. You too," my aunt said perfectly seriously.

I stood and picked up my hobo bag. "I have a bag full of stuff I've been collecting. Time to go upstairs and try to make sense of it all. Thanks for the wine and for helping me remember where I'd seen the trunk before. Not that it makes any sense yet." I walked around the counter and gave her a kiss on the cheek. "Coming, O'Ryan?" He hunkered down in the captain's chair and closed his eyes. Apparently, I hadn't been entirely forgiven yet for that "companion cat" remark.

I thought about Aunt Ibby's new theory on my way upstairs. I didn't find it credible that Rob Oberlin could have killed Wee Willie. I was more interested in learning that there was a cellar door behind the library. Dave had referred to it as a "bulkhead." To me, that meant the same kind of cellar entrance we have. A slanted wooden trapdoor arrangement that leads to steps down to an actual cellar door. I used to use ours in the winter as a ski slope for my Barbies. The one at the library is so well disguised by tall, neatly trimmed hedges that I never even knew it was there. I was sure that Pete had already inspected it, inside and out. I arrived at the third floor even more confused than I'd been before I'd started up the stairs.

I unlocked my kitchen door and clicked on the overhead light. Slinging the hobo bag over the back of a Lucite chair, I checked the contents of the refrigerator. Most of the plastic-wrapped portions of yesterday's dinner still looked edible—except maybe the salad, which looked a little soggy. The cheesecake was blessedly intact. An appropriate adage came to mind. *Life is uncertain. Eat dessert first.* So, shamelessly, I did just that. There was part of a loaf of bread in the cabinet, so I made a sandwich from the slices of chicken, and the less wilted parts of the salad. I'd used paper plates, so cleanup was minimal.

I spread the contents of the leather bag across the tabletop. Most of the relevant material—some relating to the upcoming anniversary celebration and some to the recent murder at the library, and some perhaps to both—was scribbled on index cards. There were a few brochures there too—a few pamphlets on riding lessons and organized trail rides from Rob's stable along with some flyers I'd picked up at the pet store about adopting shelter pets.

I'd begun sorting the index cards into piles. Jerry Mercury. Agnes Hooper. Rob Oberlin. Some overlapped and I had to create some new ones. Aunt Ibby's theory about Oberlin killing Willie, for instance, and Dave's description of the library cellar door (complete with a sketch of my impression of same). Another card gave the description of that Louis Vuitton trunk with more of my decidedly amateur artwork. I didn't write anything about the vision. I didn't need a card to remind myself of that one—or any of them—ever.

I was about to start a pile of cards for Dave when O'Ryan came racing through the cat door. He ran straight for the house phone and sat, staring at it. Of course, it rang. *How does he do that?* Not too many people have that number. Caller ID said River North.

"Hello. River?"

"It's me. Surprise! I've got the night off. Doan decided at the last minute to run a network Halloween special. Buck has to work doing lead-in and commercials so I'm free for the evening. You?"

I looked at the array of cardboard and paper on the table and weighed my decision. Work on the anniversary program? Try to make sense out of the bits and pieces of information I had about the murder? Spend a little time with my best friend? O'Ryan had remained close to the phone, nodding his head in cat-approval.

"Sure." I said, "This is Pete's old-timers' hockey night. Want to come over?"

"Absolutely. I've got a bottle of wine. You got food?"

"Nope. We can order out," I said. "You bringing the cards?"

"Silly question. Of course. Looks like the pumpkin thing is about over. I'll be there in twenty minutes."

"Call me when you get here and I'll run down and unlock the back door," I said.

I knew River wouldn't be ready to go to sleep until the wee hours. I'd worked that midnight-to-three shift myself. It throws the biological clock completely off. This was going to require coffee. Not decaf—the real stuff. I loaded Mr. Coffee and cleared the table, carefully rubber-banding each stack of cards along with the brochures and stashing them in my top bureau drawer.

River's call came in less than twenty minutes. O'Ryan started down the twisty staircase ahead of me and beat it outside through the cat exit before I'd even finished the unlocking and unbolting routine. I waited until I heard her car pull into the driveway, then opened the door. O'Ryan was already waiting for her at the edge of the flagstone walk. He greeted her with the usual figure-eights around both ankles, and although I was too far away to hear it, I knew he was purring loudly.

River's spending-the-evening-with-a-girlfriend look was a lot different than her on-camera-glamorous-TV-star look. Scrubbed clean of makeup, River's complexion is absolutely flawless. Her long black hair was pulled into a shiny ponytail and she wore a yellow-and-white-checked minidress with a pale green cardigan and white sneakers. The fans of *Tarot Time* would never have recognized her. With a black-and-white-checked Vans backpack dangling from one shoulder, she looked like a college kid heading for a late class. She hurried up the path with O'Ryan leading the way.

"Great to have a night off," she said, handing me a brown paper bag with the neck of a wine bottle sticking out of the top. "White zin. Want to order Chinese or pizza to go with it?"

"Either one is fine with me. You may be drinking the wine alone though. I've already had a glass or two with my aunt." I gave her a hug. "It's so good to see you. Come on up." I locked the door behind her and O'Ryan scampered ahead of us as we climbed the twisty staircase. We entered the living room and River did her usual routine of standing in the middle of the room, turning around slowly, checking the surroundings for the proper feng shui. Sometimes she adjusts a picture or moves a plant but this time everything passed the inspection. "The plants in the bay window are glorious. They're happy that you haven't used drapes to block out the sun. Good healing energy." She pointed to my most recent acquisition, a wonderful shabby-chic bentwood bench. "The old wooden bench in the east area of the room is perfect for balance. You're getting good at this."

"Thanks," I said, not mentioning that the east end of the room was the only place the bench seemed to fit. Just above it is a framed black-and-white photo of my mother and Aunt Ibby sitting on that same bench when they were teenagers. Those are a couple of my most prized possessions.

River and I moved on down the hall to the kitchen. I put the wine in the refrigerator and River hung her backpack on a chair back. I picked up the house phone receiver. "Which'll it be? Chinese or pizza?" O'Ryan leaned against River's foot, gave her ankle a pink-tongued lick and a beseeching "mrow."

"Guess he votes for pizza. There's no pepperoni on moo goo gai pan." River doesn't eat pepperoni and she's learned to understand cat language very well. I texted the Pizza Pirate accordingly. Our large pizza—pepperoni on one side only and extra cheese all over—would arrive in twenty minutes. "I brought the cards," she said. "You don't usually ask for them so what's up? Is anything wrong?" She'd already pulled the deck from her back-pack and placed the Queen of Wands in the center of the table. That's the card she always uses to represent me. The woman sits on a throne, has red hair and hazel eyes, and there's a cat in the foreground. River motioned for me to sit opposite her. "Okay. What's going on?"

"I need to talk to you about a reading you've already done," I told her. "It was the Wheel of Fortune one. It meant something to me. It was as if that reading was actually *for* me."

She put the deck face down on the table. "Tell me about it while we wait for the pizza guy."

I looked at Kit-Cat clock. "This may turn out to be a long story. Come downstairs with me. Pizza guy always delivers to the Winter Street door and I like to be there so the doorbell won't disturb Aunt Ibby."

The three of us, River, O'Ryan, and I, walked down the wide staircase to the foyer. The cat stationed himself at the long window on the right side of the door while River and I sat together on the hall tree seat. I avoided looking at the mirror. "When you read that card, the Wheel of Fortune, I'd just been researching a man named Larry Laraby." I told her about Laraby's sports show at WICH-TV, and how he'd managed successful sports collectibles shows right up until he'd died in his home—surrounded by books on the floor.

"Uh-oh," she said. "That's almost like the way the dead man in the library was found, isn't it?"

"That's right, and I'm sure my research on Laraby explains why my interpretation of the cards is so different from yours. Of course I don't know the first thing about *actually* reading cards, but I'd like to know if you think my thoughts mean anything."

"Every thought means something. Let's see, I talked

about the Sphinx, the Typhon, Hermes, and the four fixed signs of the Zodiac. Right?"

"Right," I said, "and to tell you the truth I barely even *heard* what you said about each one. Especially the Zodiac part."

She frowned. "Taurus, Leo, Scorpio, and Aquarius. What else could it be?"

I couldn't help smiling at her confusion. "Uh, how about the Chicago Bulls, the Detroit Lions, the Philadelphia Eagles, and the Los Angeles Angels?"

"Sports. I've never thought of it that way. Actually, there's nothing wrong with your reading at all. You know, I get a call once in a while from one of those Fantasy Football people. If the Wheel of Fortune card ever turns up for one of them I think I'll use your method."

"So, it does make some sort of sense?" Before she could answer O'Ryan tapped at the window with one paw, signaling the arrival of Pizza Pirate and dinner. I stood, still avoiding looking at the mirror, unlocked the front door, paid for the pizza, added the tip, and we three headed back upstairs. I wondered what River would think about my versions of the Sphinx, the snake, and the jackal-headed thing.

Once back in the kitchen I glanced at the Lucite table with the lone Queen of Wands card in the center. I plopped the pizza box onto the counter, opened the cover, and put two paper plates and a plastic wineglass and a can of Pepsi beside it. "Help yourself," I said, finding the corkscrew in the junk drawer, retrieving the wine from the refrigerator, and opening the bottle. "Tonight we'll recycle instead of washing dishes."

We pulled up two stools as O'Ryan positioned himself between us. River reached for the un-pepperonied side and took a slice, while I took one from the other side and shared a round, spicy little delicacy with the waiting cat.

(I know. I know. It's not exactly good for him, but we don't do it often.)

"Okay then." She poured the wine. "What about the rest of the Wheel of Fortune?"

Between bites and sips I managed to give her an abbreviated version of the evil snake, the half-hidden leg on the jackal thing, and the wise Sphinx-library. She listened silently, nodding occasionally, smiling at my Arizona Diamondbacks analogy.

When we'd finished our dinners, put the leftovers in the refrigerator, cleared away our paper and plastic debris, and turned on Mr. Coffee, we returned to the kitchen table with the waiting tarot card at its center.

River bowed her head. "May the powers of the stars above and the earth below bless this place and this time and this woman and me who are with you." She shuffled the deck and extended it toward me. Silently, I cut it into three piles and River began to lay the cards on the table in the familiar pattern.

The first card she turned up was the Knight of Cups—a knight wearing armor, riding a pretty horse, and holding a cup. River saw a man with light brown hair and hazel eyes. She said he might be bringing a message, an invitation. I saw the young Ranger Rob, astride Prince Valiant, and wondered what his message might be. Next she showed me the Page of Pentacles—"a man with black hair with respect for learning and new ideas," she said. I saw Professor Mercury, no doubt about it. The entire reading went that way. The Six of Cups showed a little boy offering a girl a cup filled with flowers. "Enjoyment coming from the past," River said. "Happy childhood memories." I agreed and saw the girl as little Maralee Kowalski, and I knew the memories were of my childhood heroes and heroines. The remaining cards prompted messages like "handling two situations at once," and "mathematical gifts" and "hidden influences," the kind of words that can mean anything—or nothing. The last card she turned over was the Five of Cups. That one shows a tall man, wrapped in a black cloak. "He's wearing the black cloak of despair," River said. "See the three spilled cups of wine? You may find sorrow in a place where you expected pleasure." She tapped the card. "Does that make sense? Mean anything special to you?"

"Yes," I said. "The library has always been a source of pleasure to me. Finding Wee Willie's body has changed that—maybe forever. That makes me sad."

"Don't be sad, Lee," she said. "See the two cups left to be picked up? And the little cottage beyond the river in the distance? The river is the stream of the subconscious. There is a sense of loss for you, but there's something good left for you to discover."

"Thank you," I said. "And I'm glad there's a river. Makes me think of you." I poured the coffee. "Let's talk about you now. And Buck."

She colored a little and smiled a shy little smile. "Things seem to be going well in that department," she said. "Buck doesn't say much, you know? But we get along really well and my audience seems to like it when he's on the show to shuffle the cards."

Buck is such eye candy they'd watch if he was sound asleep. Aloud I said, "He's getting to be quite the expert at that. Like a Las Vegas professional."

"He's been practicing. He bought a CD on how to do it from Chris Rich's shop." She gathered up her tarot cards and returned them to their silk-padded box.

"No kidding? I was just at Christopher's Castle myself—trying to locate Professor Mercury for the anniversary show. Thought Chris might have kept in touch with him."

"Had he?"

"Not exactly. He gave me Jerry Mercury's business card with nothing much except a website on it," I said, "but I found him. Or else he found me. Anyway, want to know where?"

"Sure. I give up. Where?"

"Today in Mr. Doan's office. He's agreed to take part in the anniversary celebration and he's even going to do his magician act at the Halloween soiree Buffy is throwing for Howard Templeton."

"It sounds like fun, but Buck and I both have to work that night. So I suppose Mercury is connected somehow to the sports collectibles show guy? Larry Laraby?"

"Well, they both worked at the station at around the same time," I said. "Why do you ask?"

"Howie's daddy is a big sports memorabilia collector," she said. "Didn't you know that? Howie told Buck that Howie Senior paid a couple thousand dollars recently for a Pete Rose rookie card."

"That's very interesting. I don't know what it means," I admitted, "but it's interesting. *Another box to fill in on my imaginary flowchart?* Thanks so much for coming over tonight, River. I really needed to talk to somebody about the Wheel of Fortune card. There's another thing I'd like to ask you about."

"Shoot."

"I've had a few visions lately."

"Bad ones?" There was real concern in her voice.

"Not really. The most recent one was O'Ryan sitting on top of an antique trunk we used to have." The cat looked up at the sound of his name.

"Just sitting on it? Where is the trunk? Do you recognize it?"

"It burned up in the attic fire," I said. "So it doesn't exist anymore."

River leaned back in her chair and held both hands up in mock horror. "We've had an encounter before with something that should have burned up in that fire! This isn't another one of those is it?"

I knew what she meant. That experience had terrified both of us. I promised her that there'd been nothing unearthly or mystical about Grandmother Forbes's luggage. "It was just an ordinary old trunk full of ordinary old clothes," I assured her, "but why is O'Ryan sitting on it? What is he trying to tell me?"

We both looked at the cat, who'd hopped up onto his favorite windowsill, facing outside, roundly ignoring us. "I remember that it's not unusual for your visions to take a while to make sense, Lee," she said. "This one will reveal itself. Just be patient. My tarot readings take a while to manifest too, you know. Maybe your answer is in one of those two cups that didn't spill."

Chapter 31

River stayed until nearly eleven o'clock. We finished the pot of coffee, along with a sleeve of Girl Scout cookies I found in the Red Riding Hood cookie jar. There was no more discussion about visions or murder. Just girl talk—about clothes and boyfriends, office gossip—like was Wanda still dating that guy who used to be a Chippendale dancer? Later O'Ryan and I accompanied my friend to her car, wished her a good night, and walked back together along the lighted path to the house. After she'd left I heard another car drive past. Slowly. A green Subaru? I resisted the urge to look.

Once upstairs, O'Ryan headed straight for the bedroom. I followed and changed into comfy cotton pj's. O'Ryan did his usual turnaround trick and plopped down at the foot of the bed. Not quite ready for sleep yet, I padded back to the kitchen, pulled three fresh index cards and a pen from my bag, and put them on the table where the tarot cards had been. On one card I wrote, "Howard Templeton Sr. is a collector of sports memorabilia. (Pete Rose rookie card—$2000?)" I stared at it for a moment, then put it face down on the table and picked up another. On the second card I wrote, "O'Ryan on an old trunk." I don't always record my visions—don't have to. They're pretty unforgettable—but this one made even less sense than most of them.

Why was O'Ryan sitting on a trunk that had burned up in the attic fire years ago? There'd been nothing of value in it—just old "too good to throw away" clothes that had belonged to various long-ago relatives. I put that card on top of the first one. *Guess I could ask O'Ryan what it means.* I looked toward the bedroom, decided against waking him, then laughed at myself for thinking the cat would seriously answer my question.

I'd just picked up the third blank index card and looked at it, deciding whether any of River's tarot reading needed to be recorded, when my phone buzzed. Pete? I don't usually expect to hear from him on old-timers' hockey game night.

"Hi, Pete," I said. "How was your game?"

"Good. We won. Listen, babe, do you think your aunt might still be awake?"

"I'm pretty sure she's not," I said. "All her lights are out. Why? Is anything wrong?"

"No. Nothing's wrong exactly. I stopped by the police station on my way home and a question about the library security cameras has come up."

"Is it something urgent? Should I wake her?"

"No. It'll keep. Just something weird on the tapes."

"Weird?" Reporter brain kicked in. "How so? Is it anything I can help with?"

"I don't think so. Did Ms. Russell ever mention something being wrong with the time stamps on the cameras? Or the cameras themselves?"

"She's never mentioned it to me. Why? What happened?"

"Well, I told you about the bearded guy who comes into the library through the front door, goes into the kids' section, and up the stairs to the stacks."

"Yes?"

"We're sure now he never came down the stairs. We've checked every bit of video from the security cameras. So how did he get out?"

"You don't think he could have used the emergency exit?"

"Forensics says the alarm is still fully armed. Nobody could have left without that thing clanging up a storm. Besides that, there were no fingerprints that didn't belong there on either side of the door."

That can't be right. "But Pete, I'm quite sure I heard a door open and close while I was up there."

"Remember? You *didn't* mention it when I first asked you about it." He was right about that. I hadn't remembered *any* sound at first. It was only when I'd closed my eyes and tried to put myself back there in that frightening place that I'd heard—*thought* I'd heard—a door.

"Oh, Pete. I'm sorry. Maybe I gave you some bad information. You know, between the visions and my being afraid of the stacks in the first place—and finding the dead man—I *could* have been wrong about the sound. It's actually a lot more likely that whoever killed him just walked down the stairs and out the door and the cameras somehow didn't capture that part."

I'd certainly prefer that explanation. Then I wouldn't be worrying about a killer thinking I'd seen him. I thought of something else. "What about the man little Pamela saw in the old kitchen?" I asked. "How did *he* get in the library in the first place?"

"Yeah. That's just one more reason we think the cameras may be faulty. It's an old system. Practically antique." I heard him sigh. "Gotta be something wrong with the cameras—or else the damned place is haunted!"

"I've never heard about any ghosts there," I said, laughing. "But let me see if I've got this straight. The old woman and the bearded man were wandering around there while Willie was upstairs in the stacks getting murdered. Then there's the gray-haired man in the old kitchen. Nobody but a frightened kid seems to have seen him."

"Seems that way."

"Must be the bearded man then," I said. "I doubt that an old woman would know karate and we're not actually sure the gray-haired man exists. Pamela could have imagined him—or made him up."

"Wait a minute. Karate? What made you think of that?"

"Rhonda guessed it as soon as they announced about injury to the upper vertebrae near the brain stem. She used to date a karate master."

"Chances are she's right. A quiet, effective way to kill somebody. He probably never knew what hit him."

"Do you think Willie found the book they were looking for? You think maybe the man killed him and the woman got away with the book?"

"No, Nancy." Patient cop voice. "No, I don't think anything like that. First, I think the library needs new, up-to-date cameras and a new monitor screen. Then I think a person or persons unknown gained access to the stacks and killed Willie."

"Anyway, I'll ask Aunt Ibby about the cameras first thing in the morning, but you know up until this happened, there probably hadn't been any reason to check them. There are buzzer alarms on the exit doors that ring if someone takes a book that hasn't been checked out properly. That—and Dave—is about all the security they've needed."

"You're probably right. But how does that buzzer thing work?"

"Aunt Ibby says it's just a simple radio frequency technology," I said. "A piece of special tape—we call it 'tattle tape'—is stuck inside the book cover. There's a gadget at the circulation desk that desensitizes it when you check your book out. Simple."

"Thanks. Always wondered about that. We'll send one of our tech guys over in the morning to check all the cameras. That needs to be done anyway. Well, babe, I should let you go to sleep. Getting late."

"O'Ryan's already gone to bed. I'm about ready to join him."

"Good night. I love you."

"Love you too. Bye." I picked up the pen and the three index cards and put them on the counter, squirted some glass cleaner onto the table and wiped it. I looked at Kit-Cat. The late news would still be on. Maybe I'd catch my pumpkin-ride segment. I turned on the TV and turned down the volume so it wouldn't disturb the sleeping cat.

One of Francine's beautiful nighttime shots of the library loomed on the screen while Buck Covington's smooth, professional voice narrated. "People in Salem have been paying a lot of attention to this fine old building lately," he said. "In the midst of the annual Halloween Happenings, where adults and kids alike enjoy being scared by witches and goblins, there's been a real murder right here in the public library." Close-up of library window where a cardboard jack-o'-lantern smiled. *Nice touch, Marty.*

Buck continued the voice-over. "The Salem police department has asked WICH-TV viewers to help with the investigation. I have two pictures to show you that were captured by security cameras in the library. These people are 'persons of interest.' They are not considered to be suspects. The authorities would like to talk with this man and this woman because they may have heard or seen something on the day that William Wallace lost his life in the stacks in the Salem main public library."

The person Pete called "the old woman" appeared on the screen first. This was a much better picture than the one they'd shown earlier. Better detail. Close up. She wore a navy blue hat with a little dotted veil covering the top half of her face. I'd seen similar hats on Sundays at Tabernacle Church. There were perfectly round spots of rouge on her lined cheeks. I'd seen that method of makeup on elderly ladies before too. I leaned toward the screen, trying to get a closer look, but she'd disappeared, replaced by a male face—one with a neatly trimmed beard and shaggy brows. He wore blue-tinted glasses.

"If you recognize either of these folks, call the number at the bottom of your screen," Buck advised.

"He looks like a college professor," I muttered, "and she looks like every cartoon little old lady I've ever seen." I picked up the remaining blank index card and scribbled, "What can be in an old book that's worth killing a man for?"

I turned off the TV, picked up my cards—which held questions and no answers—carried them into the bedroom, and joined the cat on the bed.

Chapter 32

I woke to the sound of the alarm. There was no smell of coffee. No country music. I stretched, sighed, and sat up, realizing that not only was I alone, but I'd forgotten to prepare Mr. Coffee for the morning pot. Never mind. It was good to know that just downstairs there'd be coffee, a variety of flavored creamers, and undoubtedly something nutritious and yummy to eat. *I'm so darned lucky—and almost as spoiled as the cat.*

O'Ryan was missing from the foot of the bed. I hadn't heard either of his cat doors swing open—but then, maybe hearing doors wasn't one of my strong points. I felt under the bed for my slippers and after a quick look around the apartment for the cat, stopped at the bathroom to brush my teeth and headed down the back stairs. I knocked at my aunt's kitchen door. "It's me, Aunt Ibby," I called. *I know. Who else would it be? But she raised me to be polite.*

"Come on in, dear," came her reply. "It's not locked. O'Ryan is already here."

"Pete says we need to be more careful about locking

doors," I scolded while at the same time wondering if I'd locked mine.

"I know. I unlocked it when I went out to get the newspaper off the back steps." She held up the *Boston Globe*. "I figured you'd be along shortly since O'Ryan had already arrived, begging for his breakfast. Coffee's on. Cinnamon buns in the warming oven. Help yourself."

"I'm so spoiled," I said, helping myself. O'Ryan looked up from his red bowl, which I could tell contained those crunchy things with salmon-flavored middles that he loves but I hardly ever buy because you have to go to one of those boutique pet stores to get them. "O'Ryan is too."

"I know. You're both worth it. What's on your agenda for this fine day?"

"First of all," I said, "Pete wants me to ask you if there's any problem that you know of with the security cameras in the library."

"Not an actual problem." She opened her paper to the arts and entertainment section. "There's a little thirty-second lag on the side door camera, so the time stamp is perpetually out of sync with the others, but we're used to it. It doesn't really matter." She looked up. "Does it?"

"I don't know," I admitted. "But I guess they'll have their tech people take a look at it. There's some confusion about who went up into the stacks and who came down."

"Really? How strange."

"I know. It is." I gave a synopsized version of the old woman and the bearded man, and their various journeys in and out, to and from. "Pete says it's got to be something with the cameras. Nothing else makes sense."

"I expect he's right. It's a very old system. Have a cinnamon bun, dear." She waved a hand toward the warming oven. "What do you have planned for the day?"

"I'm finally going to interview Agnes Hooper—Katie the Clown. I'm really looking forward to meeting her."

"I can imagine." She gave me her "wise old owl" look. "Of course you'll be concentrating on the anniversary show while working on the Wee Willie connection at the same time."

"You know me too well," I said. "I can't help wanting to know exactly what her relationship with him was."

"Of course they worked together."

"Yes, but did she stay in contact with him after the TV careers ended? I'll be surprised if there isn't a connection there somehow to Larry Laraby and his collectibles shows. By the way, I just found out that young Howard Templeton's daddy is a major collector of sports memorabilia."

"For goodness sake! That might explain why Wallace Williams' name is on the Templeton's party list."

"Exactly. It's entirely possible, even likely that Wee Willie was still in the collectibles business."

"Are you thinking that whatever he was looking for up in the stacks was something particularly collectible?"

"That's what I'm thinking." I transferred a warm, fragrant bun to an ivy-patterned Franciscan Ware plate, filled my ironstone mug, and joined her at the table. "Rhonda says Templeton Senior paid two thousand dollars recently for a Pete Rose rookie card."

She did the "tsk-tsk" thing. "Who knew that little pieces of cardboard that kids collected would bring thousands of dollars one day?"

"I know. Like that card Larry Laraby used to keep in the locked case. If it's really a Honus Wagner it's worth a couple of million now, according to Marty."

"I suppose his widow inherited that when Larry died." My aunt looked thoughtful. "I imagine she must have sold it. I'm sure I would have. I understand she lived very nicely in Palm Beach, Florida."

"I'm glad she did. It must have been terrible for her, finding her husband's body the way she did." *Finding a perfect stranger's body is bad enough. Finding a loved one must be beyond horrible.*

"Strange, isn't it? About those books. The ones around Larry Laraby's body and then the ones you saw around Wee Willie."

"Everything about this is strange. And everything seems to be connected to him. To Wee Willie Wallace or Wally Williams." I shook my head. "I've almost given up on my flowchart idea. It's becoming overwhelming as more and more people get added to the list."

"Including Howard Templeton now," she said. "Is there any further research I can do for you? I'm leaving for the library in a little while."

"I'd like to know a lot more about the high-end sports collectible market," I told her. "Maybe you could dig around a little and see what comes up."

"I'll do that," she promised. "And you need to get along and see what Agnes-Katie has to offer. It'll be fun for you to meet one of your childhood favorites in person."

"I'm looking forward to it—on several levels. I'll tell you all about it tonight."

"Is Francine going with you?"

"No. This'll just be an informal meeting between Agnes and me. I need to see how she feels about doing the anniversary show of course—and not so incidentally, I want to hear what she has to say about her co-workers at WICH-TV from the old days. All of her co-workers." I stood up to leave. "Thanks for the coffee and cinnamon bun."

"You're welcome. I'm going to carry the rest of them to the library to share in the break room." Sly smile. "Dave especially likes my cinnamon buns." *So Marty*

McCarthy isn't the only one who finds the security guard attractive!

"Thank you," I said, not commenting on Dave's taste in buns. "See you this evening. Have a good day."

"You too." She returned to her paper and O'Ryan continued to concentrate on the contents of his red bowl. She'd given me several things to think about. Does a thirty-second delay on the library's side-door camera mean anything? And how involved in sports collectibles was Willie/Wally and how does Howard Templeton Senior fit into this puzzle?

Before long I was dressed and ready for my meeting with Agnes/Katie. The weather was October-crisp, cool, and bright. Siri had figured out the best way for me to avoid the Halloween Happenings traffic. There was no humidity to speak of, so my hair looked pretty good and I'd taken special pains with my makeup. I wore new jeans with a matching denim jacket, white silk blouse, and cordovan booties. As the Corvette approached Highland Avenue I felt as though I was a peculiar cross between a skilled and competent field reporter and an excited little girl.

Agnes's house was what realtors call "mid-century modern," the kind of home that was popular with families in the 1950s. This was a nice one—white with green trim, carefully landscaped, with a handsome big maple tree in the front yard, red-gold leaves shimmering in the morning sunshine. I parked in the driveway in front of a carport where a bright red VW Bug looked like the perfect car for Katie the Clown. There was a narrow porch with a row of smiling pumpkins lined up on the railing. A straw-stuffed scarecrow-man wearing striped pants, black frockcoat, and top hat sat in a wooden rocking chair. I approached the porch and spotted a real black cat peering at me from the large picture window often featured in these houses.

Agnes Hooper opened her front door well before I'd had a chance to knock or ring the bell. "Lee Barrett!" she shouted. "I'd recognize that beautiful red hair anywhere! I watch you on TV all the time. I even remember when you were Crystal Moon! Come in. Come in."

I wouldn't have recognized her, of course, since she wasn't wearing a Katie the Clown costume, or Princess Waterfall Raindrop's face painting, but I would have known that joyous, happy voice anywhere. She enveloped me in a big hug, which I retuned. It felt right. The black cat was named Percival and as soon as I was seated in a vintage Danish lounge chair with its distinctive sculptured oak frame and gray upholstery, he curled up at my feet.

"Percival likes you," she said approvingly. "Do you have a cat?"

I told her about O'Ryan and how he'd once belonged to Ariel Constellation, the one-time WICH-TV call-in psychic, my immediate predecessor on *Nightshades*.

She clapped her hands together in a decidedly Katie-like move. "Orion! I've often wondered what had happened to him after Ariel's sad passing. I'm so glad he found a good home."

I explained how we'd changed the cat's name from "Orion" to "O'Ryan," which seemed to us to suit his personality better. She agreed that it did. Agnes was easy to talk to. I told her about Mr. Doan's plans for a November celebration of the station's seventieth anniversary, and how we planned to assemble as many as we could find of those folks who, like her, had helped to build WICH-TV into one of New England's leading independent stations.

"I suppose you've located Rob Oberlin," she said. "I understand he's still over in Rockport with his beloved horses."

"He is," I told her. "He seems to be doing well. He's planning to join us for the anniversary celebration. We hope you will too."

"Wouldn't miss it for the world," she said with a broad smile. "Shall I dig out the old clown suit? Big red nose and all?"

"I know the audience would love that. Would you do it?"

"Sure. I can still fit into it too. Fortunately it's pretty baggy."

"I remember it perfectly," I said. "The clown shoes too. Remember when you and Officer Tom went outside and taught us how to cross a street safely? Between the white lines? Only when the light said 'walk'? You looked so cute in those big shoes trying to follow him with his long legs all the way across Derby Street."

"Rob looked good in that cop suit, didn't he?" She had a faraway look in her eyes. "We used to sneak it out of the studio sometimes so he could wear it at a collectibles show, playing a security guard." She laughed a silvery Katie the Clown laugh. "Eventually he outgrew the suit though. That was the end of the Officer Tom character. I heard they hired another guy to wear it at those shows."

A young Dave Benson?

"Jerry Mercury hasn't changed a lot since those old shows," I told her. "I would have recognized him. His hair is a little bit gray, but his face hasn't changed very much."

"Humph. He always worked out. Proud of his body, you know? I bet he had plastic surgery on the face though. He's older than me." *Oops. Where has happy voice gone?*

"Could be," I agreed, and promptly changed the subject. "Did you know Wee Willie well? I've learned that he played a lot of different characters."

"He did. A good little actor. He would have been a good mime." She made robot-like motions with her arms. "Athletic, you know? Good muscle control. Too bad he turned out to be such a weasel."

"You're right. My aunt says some people are just self-destructive."

"She's right. Wise woman, your aunt. Back when the little man was playing Cactus, he and Rob were great pals. That's how Rob got the security guard gig at those collectibles shows." She tilted her head to one side—another Katie-like move. "Rob and I dated for a while, even after the shows ended. I remember when he learned about the horses. The beautiful horses that little snake had harmed. Poisoned. Killed one, you know?" She made a "tsk-tsk" sound almost like Aunt Ibby's. "Rob was so angry. Angry enough to . . ." She didn't finish the sentence. "But where are my manners? Would you like some tea?"

Chapter 33

It was still fairly early in the day when Agnes Hooper and I finished our visit. I'd enjoyed the time we spent together and I knew that Bruce Doan would be pleased to know that she was truly enthusiastically looking forward to the anniversary celebration. She'd even offered—without being asked—to shoot some promotional teasers in full Katie the Clown costume. "Maybe you can get Rob and Mercury to do the same," she'd said, "though I guess Rob might have to get a new outfit. Those skinny little jeans of his won't fit anymore!" She laughed, but not in a mean way. "You say Mercury looks the same, huh?"

"Pretty much," I agreed, bending to pat the black cat, who was busily rubbing the corners of his mouth along the edge of my booties, marking me as a friend, I presumed—or maybe sending a coded message to O'Ryan. Who understands the language of cats? "Goodbye, Percival," I said. "I hope we'll meet again soon."

"We surely will," Agnes said, giving me a hug. "It'll be fun working with you, Lee, and all the people at WICH-TV. Thanks for inviting me."

As I pulled away from the driveway I waved to the

woman and the cat who stood on the porch behind the row of smiling pumpkins. I decided to go to the library and fit in a few volunteer hours before heading for the station. I didn't want to look as though I was trying to interfere with young Howie's on-air face time. Anyway, I was anxious to see if my aunt had learned anything yet about the high-stakes sports collectibles market.

Siri managed to lead me to the library with a minimum of stop-and-go through Salem's near-Halloween streets. (If you've never visited my fair city during October—think a combination of Mardi Gras and *Dia de los Muertos*.) Rolling the Vette into a white-lined space next to Aunt Ibby's Buick, I looked up at the familiar façade of the brick and brownstone building—once the home of a prosperous ship's captain, now a place of learning and growing for an entire community. I smiled, spotting the jack-o'-lantern I'd seen in Buck's report, grinning from a tall window in the kids' media section. That warm and friendly space had been my home-away-from-home throughout childhood. The row of windows above that gave a glimpse of study alcoves on the mezzanine, my favorite place during high school and college years for uninterrupted concentration on homework, or a quiet getaway for pleasure reading.

The much smaller windows at the top of the building admitted limited light into the stacks—a place that had inspired fear for virtually all of my life, now more than ever. I locked the car and took a deep breath. My volunteer status here would, without question, require that I climb those stairs, move between those narrow, claustrophobic aisles, past those dark spaces beneath the shelves where imagined horrors might lurk.

I squared my shoulders and walked to the library's side entrance, taking a quick glance toward the camera. The door to the old kitchen bore a new "no admittance" sign—in contrast to the "welcome" mat on the floor just ahead. I went directly to the research desk, where I was pretty sure I'd find my aunt. I was right. She looked up from a bank of computer screens, her face brightening when she saw me. "Maralee, what a nice surprise."

"I have a little time before I need to be at the station." I gave a mock salute. "Volunteer Barrett, reporting for duty."

"Good," she said. "We can use the help, and look, Maralee. Your official volunteer badge arrived." She handed me the plastic-coated pin-backed card with my name— Maralee Barrett—in bold letters. "Wear it proudly." She pointed to two wire carts overflowing with books. "Our return carts runneth over. The library corps kids emptied both of the book drops yesterday afternoon and there hasn't been time to put all of these away." She dropped her voice below regular acceptable library level. "We've seen a lot more patrons than usual since the recent—um— unpleasantness. I think a lot of it was due to curiosity, but there's been a nice increase in requests for library cards."

"Hopefully, some of them will stay with us," I said. "I'll just put my jacket in the break room and get busy with those returns."

The library break room is similar in purpose to the one at WICH-TV, but is much different in décor. The station room is stark, windowless, and utilitarian, with Formica countertops—replete with cigarette burns—odds and ends of chairs, mostly of the cast-off office variety, along with an avocado green refrigerator. The one in the library has brightly patterned draperies and two comfortable love seats and a recliner. A butcherblock table is surrounded by pine ladderback chairs and the refrigerator is of the ice maker, water dispenser, clean white variety.

I wasn't surprised to see Aunt Ibby's cinnamon buns displayed in the center of the table in a clear-plastic-covered cake dish beside the Keurig coffee maker. I wasn't surprised either to see Dave Benson sitting at the table enjoying both.

"Good morning, Dave," I said. "You're here early too."

He stood up. "Morning, Ms. Barrett," he said. "Yep. The library board gave me some extra hours." Modest shrug. "They think a 'uniformed presence' during the day is a good idea for a while—at least until they catch the guy who killed old Willie."

I waved an indication that he should sit down, and hung my jacket in the open closet and tucked my purse into one of the cubbies marked "Volunteer." I faced Dave. "Wow. You can't work all day and work all night too, can you?"

He smiled his nice smile. "Nope. I'm drawing the day duty for a change. They got another guy for the night shift." He looked down at a shiny security badge. "I guess the board thinks the uniform makes people feel safer."

"I believe it does," I said truthfully. "Speaking of uniforms, I saw a picture of you wearing one at a Larry Laraby collectibles show. How'd that come about?"

"Boy! That must have been an old picture. Yeah. I was just a kid. Laraby had a gimmick at his shows where he put a real expensive baseball card in a locked glass case and he had an armed guard stand next to it."

"Was it a Honus Wagner card?"

"Sure. Most expensive baseball card in the world. Back then, anyway."

"And the armed guard was you?"

"Not at first. He had a guy who already had the suit. An old TV actor who used to play a traffic cop on some kids' show. Anyway," Dave continued, "the guy started putting on weight so Laraby bought the suit and looked around for somebody tall and thin to wear it. He hired me."

"I'll bet the locked case and armed guard worked well for him. That was a clever promotional gimmick."

"Sure did. Got my picture in newspapers all over the country posing with the world's most expensive baseball card."

"Was it real? The card?"

"Laraby always swore it was. I believed it."

"Interesting," I said. "Well, I have to get to work. Nice talking with you, Dave. By the way, Marty McCarthy sends her regards."

Again the nice smile. "Marty McCarthy. You know, when I worked on the electronics at WICH-TV back in the eighties, I had a wicked crush on her."

"You worked at WICH-TV?" That was a surprise.

"Sure. That's how I met Willie. He used to work there too."

"Interesting," I said again. "Well, I guess I'll be seeing you here daytimes."

"At least until they catch that killer," he said, no longer smiling.

I walked back to the reference desk, rolled up the sleeves of my white blouse, and grasped the handle of the first cart. I could tell at a glance that although the library corps team had made a good-faith attempt to organize the returns so that they could be shelved in some sort of logical order, they hadn't been completely successful. There were mysteries mixed in with travel, antiques alongside juvenile board books, even a couple of CDs in the mix.

There seemed to be more adult fiction titles than anything else, so I began there. The fiction books are generally shelved alphabetically by the author's last name. After about twenty minutes I had cart number one about half empty and moved on to the random selection remaining. There were a few YA fiction books, one copy of *Winnie-the-Pooh*. The rest were nonfiction books belonging in various sections, but at least the cart was lighter and I moved quickly from antiques to biography to hobbies to World War I. I finished up in the children's section, helped myself to a mini Snickers bar from the trick or treat bowl, returned the empty cart to its proper place, and grasped the handle of cart number two.

By this time I'd found my rhythm. Sorting as I moved along, placing books on the shelves according to category and number, I felt as though I was on automatic pilot. Resisting the persistent urge to hum as I worked—after all this was a library—I gathered speed. Finishing cart number two was a piece of cake—until I found a book destined for the stacks. Oh well, I knew sooner or later I'd have to do it. I just wished it could have been later. Would it be so awful if I asked Dave to come up there with me? I answered my own question. Yes. It would be awful. I parked the cart, picked up the book and walked toward the stairway, eyes straight ahead. I glanced at the spine where the number, the author's last name, and the title would be. I'd find the shelf, shove the book into its place, and zoom right back down those stairs.

"Number seven-ninety," I said to myself as I began climbing the stairs "Sports. Author's name—Kahn." I knew in an instant what I held in my hand. The third step was as far as I got. I turned around.

Chapter 34

Wordlessly, I laid the book on my aunt's desk. She gasped, then frowned. "*The Boys of Summer*," she said. "The missing book. Where did you get it?" I pointed to the abandoned cart at the foot of the stairs leading up to the stacks.

"There," I whispered. "It was in the returns cart."

"How can that be? Someone returned it?"

I knew her questions were rhetorical. Which was good, because I had no answers. I just stood there and stared at the book. She did the same. A woman with a small girl in tow approached the desk and my aunt looked up with her usual welcoming smile, at the same time placing a yellow flyer advertising the Monday morning writers' group meeting on top of *The Boys of Summer*. "May I help you?"

"I'm looking for a book on how to make Halloween costumes." The woman nodded toward the child. "Lilly wants to be an astronaut." She patted Lilly's blonde curls. "I mean she *really* wants to be one."

"There's a special display on costumes just inside the entrance to the children's area." Aunt Ibby pointed the way, then, placing her hand over the yellow paper, turned to me. "Shall I call the police or do you want to call Pete?" she whispered.

"I'll call Pete," I said. "Shouldn't we put it into a plastic bag or something? Fingerprints."

"There are probably hundreds of prints on it by now. I'll just slide it into the drawer here." With the paper tucked around the edges of the book, she pushed it into the top desk drawer. "Run out to the break room, will you dear? Get the key ring from my purse in my cubby. I think I'd better lock this away."

I did as she asked and returned to the empty break room. I pulled Aunt Ibby's practical brown Etienne Aigner bag from the cubby marked with her name, and noticed that a brightly printed Vera Bradley was in Tyler Dickson's space. Dave had left the room and I realized that Tyler must have arrived while I was shelving books. I pulled the keyring from my aunt's bag.

Anybody on the staff can walk in here anytime and take things from our handbags. The thought was disturbing. It had never occurred to me before. *We've always trusted each other. We've trusted our security cameras. We've trusted our emergency exit and no admittance and staff only signs.* Had Wee Willie Wallace somehow changed everything?

I replaced the bag, left the room, and called Pete.

Funny. He asked the same question Aunt Ibby had. "Somebody returned it?"

"Looks that way. The library corps kids emptied both book drops sometime yesterday. Apparently, it was in one of them."

"When were they emptied last? Don't they usually do it every day?"

"Yes, usually. But in all the commotion over the weekend, nobody thought to empty the outdoor drops."

"Okay. Where is the book now?"

"It's in the top drawer of Aunt Ibby's desk. She's just about to lock it up."

"I'll be right along to get it. I guess there aren't any cameras on the book drops?"

"Sorry, no," I said. "But wait a minute. There was a picture on the news showing that old woman standing on the wheelchair ramp near the side door. That's where the drop is. I thought at the time it must have been taken from another building."

"You're right. We obtained some footage from that big house next door. Private residence."

"Gee, they probably film everybody who uses that door," I said, walking toward the reference desk, realizing how little privacy there is in the world these days.

"I'm on my way," he said. "Keep that drawer locked."

I handed my aunt her key ring. "Pete's on his way."

She locked the drawer, then handed the keys to me. "Do you mind putting them back? I feel as though I should stay right here with the book."

"No problem," I said, then paused. "Did it ever occur to you that practically anybody can walk into the break room and riffle through our purses?"

She arched one eyebrow. "We've never had any such problem."

We've never found a dead man in the stacks before either.

The break room was still empty when I put the keys back into her purse. When I returned Pete was already at the desk, speaking in low-toned cop voice with my aunt and Tyler Dickson. I joined them. Pete acknowledged me with a nod and continued. "We'll be checking the book for prints and DNA but since it's passed through a lot of hands before Lee recognized it, it may not tell us much." He pulled a pair of latex gloves from his pocket and placed what I'd come to recognize as an evidence bag on the desk. "Now Ms. Russell, if you'll open the drawer, then step away, I'll come around to your side and remove the book."

Aunt Ibby followed his directions and stood between Tyler and me while Pete slipped on the gloves, frowned slightly when he saw the yellow paper, then moved it aside. The book was face-up, a plain-looking volume with a black front and red spine. In one quick motion he lifted the book, slipped it into the open evidence bag, and sealed it. "Maybe this'll tell us something," he said.

"If a book is worth killing someone over, why would anyone toss it into a book drop?" I asked, thinking out loud.

Tyler spoke up. "Maybe it *wasn't* worth it," she said. "Maybe it was the wrong book!"

"Maybe it wasn't the book at all." My aunt, with wise-old-owl face in place, spoke quietly. "Maybe there was something important *in* the book. I remember reading about a conservation technician at Brown University who found an original engraving by Paul Revere in an old book on medicine!"

"I believe it," Tyler said. "People use the darndest things for bookmarks. I once found a strip of bacon in a library book."

We all laughed at that, but the idea that the book might have contained something valuable made a lot of sense. It might explain the opened books on the floor in the stacks, It could explain the books on the floor around poor dead Larry Laraby too.

Pete tucked the evidence bag under his arm. "Thank you, ladies, for calling this to our attention. It could be important. Is there any way to figure out which book drop it came from?"

"Maybe," Tyler said. "I divided the library corps kids into two teams. Three kids per team. They each emptied one of the drops. They each filled a book cart."

"There're still some books in the second cart," I said. "That's where *The Boys of Summer* was. If anybody remembers any of the titles that are still in the cart, that person would know which drop they emptied."

"I'm on it," Tyler said. "I'll text all six of the kids and tell them to get back to me right away."

"I'll give you a list of those books," I said. "So long, Pete. Talk to you later."

"Later," he said and started for the front door. He stopped short when the buzzer shrieked, indicating that some culprit was sneaking off with an unchecked-out book. The look on his face was the same as everyone else's when the tattler sounds off, in a library or a department store. Confused, guilty, and embarrassed. My aunt smilingly waved him ahead. He waved back, and hurried outside. Tyler went back to the main desk and got busy texting while I pulled the remaining dozen or so books from the wire basket, writing down the names on the back of one of the yellow sheets. Aunt Ibby stayed at her desk, concentrating on the computer there, fingers flying over the keys.

Tyler was the first of us to come up with an answer to Pete's question. The books in the second cart had come from the side door drop. No doubt about it. The first girl Tyler had texted remembered seeing two of the titles I'd listed. *18 Things* by Jamie Ayres, and *Chainbreaker* by Tara Sim, both teen favorites. I called Pete right away.

"Thanks, babe," he said. "That was fast."

"Of course," I said. "You want to know anything about books, ask a librarian."

"I'll remember that. We'll be taking a closer look at those videos from the building next door too. Are you going to try to make it through the Halloween crowd to the TV station later today, or are you going to stay put? I had to use the siren to get through 'em to get back here."

"It's pretty crazy out there, isn't it? But everybody seems to be having a good time. I'll call Rhonda and see if they need me, otherwise I can work from here."

"Good idea. Probably won't see you tonight," he said. "Chief wants us on call in case of the bad kind of Halloween craziness."

"Be careful out there," I said. "I love you."

"Love you too."

I returned my attention to my aunt, still focused on the computer's screen. "Aunt Ibby," I whispered. "Are you thinking what I'm thinking?"

She looked up. "I am if you're thinking about what extremely valuable item Larry Laraby might have had that would fit between the pages of a hardcover book."

"That's what I thought." I leaned over her shoulder, peering at the screen. "Looking for Honus Wagner cards?"

"Yes I am. What if Laraby's widow *didn't* inherit it? What if it's been stuck in a book all these years?"

"Dave told me he believed it was real," I said. "I wonder if Rob Oberlin thought so too."

"If it *is* real—wherever it is—it can be worth more than a million dollars," my aunt said. She shut down her computer and stood up. "Is Dave still in the building?"

"He's on day duty. The library board thinks seeing the uniform makes people feel safer." I glanced around the room. "There he is. Right by the front door."

"I'll see if Dave knows where Larry Laraby kept that card when he was between collectibles shows. You call Rob Oberlin and see what he says about it." I could tell she was excited. "Let's look for a copy of that picture Sharon Stewart is missing too. What do you bet the book in her father's hand was *The Boys of Summer*?" She hurried toward where Dave stood, his expression serious as he held the door open for the departing future astronaut Lilly and her mom.

I called the station and told Rhonda that I could work from the library instead of braving the traffic unless they needed me. "No problem," she said. "Howie's here." *Good. The more face time Howie gets, the quicker I'll get my job back.*

I tapped "Double R Riding Stable" into my phone and pulled up Rob's number. I recognized the hearty "Ranger Rob" voice when he answered. "Hello, Mr. Oberlin," I said. "Lee Barrett here." I paused, adding, "from WICH-TV."

"Oh, yes. Ms. Barrett. Do you have any dates set yet for the anniversary shows? I'm looking forward to it. Talked to Agnes about it too."

"I'm sure we'll have the details nailed down soon." I promised. "Just now I'm gathering information on another WICH-TV alum—Larry Laraby. About the collectibles shows he did. I'm fascinated with that clever display of the world's most expensive baseball card."

"Yep. With the armed guard standing next to it." His laugh was genuine. "He was quite a showman, Larry was."

"Do you think the card was the real thing? A real Honus Wagner?" I waited for his response.

"You know, I went back and forth on that for a long time," he said. "It was in one of those plastic cases they use to keep the cards flat and clean. Then it was on a little plastic stand inside the glass case with a spotlight on it. It looked real important, you know? He always swore that it was the real McCoy. But, like I said, he was a showman—and a salesman. Didn't always tell the truth."

"I talked to Dave Benson." I told him. "He was the guard after you left. He says he thinks it was real."

"I thought it might be at first, but then when we were

packing up after closing down a show one night, I saw
what he did with it when it was out of the glass case."

"What was that? What did he do with it?"

He laughed again. "He just took it and shoved it into a
book he was reading. He used the darned thing for a
bookmark. Nope. It wasn't real."

Chapter 35

I could hardly wait to report to my aunt—and to hear what Dave had to say about the bookmark idea. I thanked Rob, promised once again to stay in touch about the anniversary show arrangements, and looked across the long room to where the two were still in conversation. I thought about the photo albums, which I'd last seen in Aunt Ibby's kitchen. We'd only studied the first one and hadn't examined the second one at all. My first instinct was to jump into my car and rush home to get them—to see if I could find a duplicate to the stolen snapshot— then I remembered the Halloween traffic and quickly dismissed that idea.

Aunt Ibby walked back to the desk and Dave resumed his erect posture and solemn expression. She sat beside me. "Well?" We spoke in unison, then laughed. (Softly, of course.)

"You go first," she said. "What did Rob say about the card? Real or fake?"

"Fake," I said.

"I'm surprised." She frowned. "Dave is sure it was real. What's Rob's reasoning?"

I repeated what Rob had said about Larry Laraby using the so-called "most expensive baseball card in the
world" as a bookmark.

This brought another soft laugh. "Same reason," she
said. "Entirely different conclusion. Dave says that Larry
told him that the safest way to transport the card was to
treat it as if it was just a common cigarette-package pre-
mium. That way, he figured, no one would try to steal it."

"Makes a certain amount of sense, I suppose."

"Dave agrees with Rob's story about the card being
used as a bookmark though," she said. "He thinks that
was part of Larry's plan to make it look unimportant. So
it may very well have been stuck there within the pages
of the book for all these years."

"I think we're right," I said. "I wish we had those albums here. I'm dying to get a good close look at every
picture to see if there are any more of Larry Laraby holding the Kahn book."

"Do you think we should tell Pete what we think about
the bookmark?" she asked.

"No. Not yet," I said. "Let's investigate a little more.
Pete always needs *real* evidence, not just what we *think*
might have happened or what a couple of security guards
think about what might or might not have been in an old
collectibles show display case. Anyway," I added, "the
important part is who else thinks it's real and who—besides Wee Willie—figured out where it was."

"About those photo albums, Maralee. We know there's
at least one picture of Laraby with the book we found
today. If we can find another, or if the one Sharon Stewart
claims is missing turns up, that would indicate that he
very likely used that particular book to hide the Wagner
card, don't you agree?"

I nodded agreement, but my attention was on the man
entering the front door. I tapped my aunt's shoulder.
"Look," I whispered. "It's him."

"Who?" she said, following my stare.

"It's Professor Mercury."

I watched as Dave pointed to where we sat and, smiling, Jerry Mercury moved toward us with long strides, right hand outstretched. "Ms. Barrett," he said, not using his library voice. "They said I might find you here."

There were a few annoyed "shushes" from nearby readers and browsers. Aunt Ibby raised a displeased eyebrow, which is usually sufficient to quiet loud-voiced offenders. It didn't deter the oncoming professor. "Jerry Mercury," he boomed. "Remember me?"

Automatically, I put one index finger to my lips in the universal sign for "hush." He glanced around in apparent embarrassment and approached the desk where we sat. "Oops. Sorry," he whispered. "I guess I'm more accustomed to being on stage than in a library."

"It's okay," I said. "What can we do for you?"

"I called the television station looking for you," he said, "and the young woman said you might be here." He gestured toward my aunt. "I beg your pardon," he said, giving a little bow in her direction. "I've been rude. I'm Jerry Mercury, and you are . . . ?"

"I'm Isobel Russell," she said. "Maralee's aunt. I'm happy to meet you."

"My pleasure." Again, the little bow. He turned toward me, blue eyes focused on mine. *Kind, friendly blue eyes. Why had I thought they were creepy?* I looked away, concentrating on his words. "I've talked with Agnes and Rob today," he said, "and of course they both say they're thrilled with the idea of getting together for the station's anniversary."

Yes. I know that. I talked to them too. "Good. We're very pleased about it."

"There may be a problem and I wanted to tell you about it right up front, before too many plans are made."

This didn't sound good. "Yes. Go ahead."

"It's about Rob." He'd found his library voice. I had to lean forward to catch what he was saying. Aunt Ibby leaned forward too.

"About Rob Oberlin?" I whispered.

The blue eyes looked down toward the floor. "We think he might have done something—something very bad."

"We?" I asked. "You mean you and Agnes?"

He looked up. "Yes. Of course. Agnes and I agree." *Had the voice become a little testy?*

My aunt tipped her head to one side. "Exactly what do you and Agnes think he's done?"

"We could be wrong," he said. "We certainly don't want to accuse anyone—especially an old friend—" His voice trailed off.

"If it's something that affects the station I think you need to tell me what it is. We have considerable time and resources invested in the anniversary project," I fibbed. *Just my time so far, and no money at all yet.* "Mr. Doan doesn't like surprises," I added, and that part was completely true.

"It has to do with what happened at the library—to Willie." Eyes downcast again.

"Perhaps we should discuss this in the break room," my aunt suggested. "I'll ask Tyler to take over here. Maralee, show the professor the way."

I stood and motioned for Jerry Mercury to follow me to the closed door marked "Library Staff only." The room was still empty, the coffee maker and the cinnamon buns still on the table. "Coffee?" I asked. He shook his head no. We waited in silence for my aunt.

We didn't have to wait long. "Well then," she whirled into the room, closing the door behind her with a firm click. She stood at the head of the table. "What's all this about Rob Oberlin being mixed up in the death of that man in the stacks?" I could tell that so far, she didn't like the direction this conversation was taking one bit. "Speak up," she commanded.

It was apparent that Jerry Mercury wasn't used to being told what to do. But he was on her turf, and there's always something pretty intimidating about a head librarian no matter how old you are, or how important you *think* you are.

"It was about the old woman they showed on television," he began. He stood facing her from the opposite end of the table. "I was at Agnes's house to talk about the anniversary show. Her television was on and they were showing pictures of some people the police are calling 'persons of interest.'"

"Did you recognize the old woman?" I asked, excited by the idea that we might at last have an ID. Since neither of them had taken a seat, I remained on my feet too.

"Maybe." A half smile. *An irritating half smile.* "We didn't actually remember *her.* We remember who is pretending to be her."

"Who's that?" I pressed for more information. "Do you know who the woman is or not?"

"We believe the woman is actually Rob Oberlin. And Rob is dressed up as old Mrs. Blatherflab."

"Of course," Aunt Ibby exclaimed. "I should have recognized that big purse with the cat on it she always carried. Remember, Maralee?"

"I think so. Vaguely," I agreed. "She wasn't a regular."

"When Rob gained weight and got too fat to be the cowboy or the cop, they cancelled his show and put together the old lady costume, so he could work out his contract with appearances on Agnes's show. He hated being Mrs. Blatherflab." Jerry Mercury spoke slowly, as though we were too dense to follow his story. "Agnes fixed it up with the station. She and Rob used to be lovers."

"And now you believe Rob put on that dress and killed Willie?" I wasn't buying it. "Why?"

He held up two fingers. "Two reasons. One, because Willie had something Rob wanted, and two—and most importantly—he hated Willie because of the things Willie had done to those racehorses."

I didn't comment on that. I knew Rob had good reason to be furious about the horses. And he surely knew all about the Honus Wagner card. He used to guard it. But he'd told me he thought it was a fake. Was that some kind of a cover-up? I didn't want to think that Rob (who I still thought of as Ranger Rob—childhood idol) would harm anyone, let alone kill somebody—even if the somebody was a true low-life creepy villain who had a card worth a million dollars.

My aunt, however, didn't hesitate to comment "Nonsense. Absolute nonsense, sir. You haven't the slightest idea what you're talking about." Her expression proved that she wasn't kidding.

Jerry Mercury seemed surprised, at least momentarily. He took a small step back from the table. It looked to me as though he wasn't used to having anyone disagree with him, and it also looked as though he didn't like it one bit when someone did. "You might want to have a little talk with Agnes, then, Ms. Russell." The smirky smile was back in place. "She'll tell you that the Mrs. Blatherflab outfit has gone missing."

I found my voice. "Missing from where?"

"Oh, didn't Agnes tell you? She wound up with all of the old costumes. Actually, she was the only one who had room for them. Of course she made it clear that we could help ourselves to them anytime. Especially at Halloween." A nonchalant shrug and another smirk. "I certainly didn't want any of them and I've always provided my own magician gear." He paused. "And Rob was too fat to fit into most of them." Snarky laugh.

This conversation had begun to wipe away all my fond memories of the wise professor who'd taught me to love science, who'd fostered much of my curiosity of how things worked, who'd used a cute beeping robot as a valuable teaching aid. Another disturbing thought intruded. If I'd been wrong about brilliant and entertaining Professor Mercury, could I have been wrong about the brave, handsome ranger who'd taught mc and thousands of other kids about honesty and justice and loyalty, and who'd used a cute little guy in a sombrero to underline those basic truths?

Aunt Ibby wasn't out of questions. "Have you gone to the police with your suspicions, Mr. Mercury?"

"Not yet," he said. "I thought I'd run it by you two first." He looked at me, the blue eyes still kind and friendly. "I've heard that you might have seen the killer up there in the stacks, Ms. Barrett. Did you?"

"No!" I blurted. "I didn't see anyone. Who told you that? Agnes? Rob?"

"Rob doesn't confide in me. He told Agnes you two were over at his place. Asking questions about the old days. About the costumes."

"And Agnes wound up with all those old costumes?" my aunt asked.

"Sure. They're all stuffed in an old trunk in a little utility room in her carport. She showed me. It's not even locked."

"I think you'd better report your suspicions to the police," Aunt Ibby said, pulling her phone from a pocket. "Shall I dial them for you?"

"No thanks." He smiled. "I'll take care of it." He backed away from the table. "I'll be going along. I'm

firming up plans for a magic show at the Doans' Halloween party. I expect I'll see you there, Ms. Barrett?" He
walked toward the door. "Shall I let myself out?"

Neither of us answered. He pulled the door open and
walked away, not looking back.

Chapter 36

"What in the world . . . ?" Aunt Ibby didn't have to finish the question.

I had no answer. What *was* that? Was Jerry Mercury seriously accusing Rob Oberlin of murder? Would he take my aunt's suggestion and call the police? This was no time for Nancy Drew. I called Pete and told him what had just happened—what Mercury had said.

"He sounded serious, Pete," I told him. "I don't know whether he'll call you or not, but do you think the idea that Rob has something to do with Willie's murder is even possible?"

"Mercury hasn't contacted the department, Lee," he said, "but we're looking into all the possibilities. And yes, we're aware of the old lady costume Oberlin wore on that TV show. Actually, Chief Whaley's mother recognized it. Oberlin has voluntarily agreed to come in for questioning."

"What about Agnes—Katie the Clown? Don't tell me she's a suspect too."

"All the possibilities, babe. All of them—including Mercury. Gotta go. Call you later."

I followed my aunt back to the main desk, where Tyler Dickson waited, wide-eyed, holding a long-stemmed red paper rose. "Who is that guy? Some kind of magician? He made this flower appear right in front of me!"

I had to smile at her reaction. "Yes," I said, "he really is a magician. When I was a kid he had his own TV show. He called himself Professor Mercury back then."

"He seems nice," she said, "and he has such pretty eyes."

My aunt and I looked at each other and didn't comment on Jerry Mercury's niceness. "Thanks for holding down the fort, Tyler," Aunt Ibby said. "Anything interesting happen while I was away?"

"No. Pretty quiet. The genealogy group is meeting in one of the study rooms and Dave is still standing over there like a wooden Indian." She gestured toward the front door with her rose. "Looks like a real cop, doesn't he?"

He does. The right costume is important. If it wasn't for her voice, I never would have recognized Agnes as Katie the Clown. I'm positive I wouldn't have recognized Rob Oberlin as Mrs. Blatherflab. I was sure that the many faithful fans of *Tarot Time with River North* wouldn't identify the glamorous night show star when she wasn't made up and costumed. "Dave is one of those men who looks good in uniform, no doubt," I told her. "He was a security guard when he was a young man, then served in the military for almost thirty years—Special Forces, I understand—then came back to security work. Uniforms all the way. In fact," I added, "I've never seen him out of uniform!"

"He still looks good," she said. "I'll get back to checking out books." Carrying her rose, she returned to her desk.

Checking out books! "Aunt Ibby!" I spoke a little too loudly and drew a raised eyebrow from my aunt and a "shush" from a nearby patron. I dropped my voice to a more acceptable pitch. "Pete didn't check that book out and the buzzer went off. How did whoever took it from the stacks get out of the building without tipping off the tattle?"

"You're absolutely right. It should have sounded. Unless . . ."

"Unless they got out without passing the sensor," I finished the thought.

"I don't think you could jump over it like a subway turnstile," she said, "and I know it doesn't work to kick a book through on the floor. That's been tried."

"So we still have no clue as to how they did it," I said, almost talking to myself. "Up and down stairs, in and out of doors, back and forth, forward and back. Now, according to Jerry Mercury, we can add 'in and out of costume.'"

"I could tell that you didn't like it when he suggested that Rob could be a killer," she said. "I didn't like it either. What did Pete say about it?"

"Pete says they're considering all options. They already knew about the old lady costume and Rob has agreed to come in for questioning. They haven't discounted Agnes or Mercury either."

"I thought they'd have it solved by now," she said. "I didn't like it when Mercury suggested that you might have seen the killer." A quick "tsk-tsk." "And now that old lady costume is missing."

"I'm going to ask Agnes about it," I said, "but first I think I'll go up to the mezzanine and do a little WICH-TV anniversary show work rather than trying to fight the traffic between here and Derby Street."

"Wise choice," she said. "I'm right here if you need me."

"You always have been," I said, and headed for the short flight of stairs and somewhat steep wheelchair ramp that led to my favorite space for studying and thinking. I would have liked to spend the afternoon in the *Saturday*

Business Hour set. There were still personnel folders in the file cabinet I hadn't examined. *They've been there for over forty years. They'll still be there tomorrow.*

I ducked into one of the small study alcoves overlooking the parking lot—and the house next door. I pulled a handful of clean index cards from my purse, spread them fanlike on the blonde wood desk. I decided that our visit in the break room with Jerry Mercury counted as anniversary show research. After all, the information he offered was about his fellow WICH-TV kid show actors. On the first card I wrote, "J. Mercury says that he thinks Rob Oberlin, wearing a costume from Agnes's show (Mrs. Blatherflab) killed Willie." On the second I jotted down, "All the costumes from the old shows are in a trunk in an unlocked utility room at Agnes's house." I stared at the card for a moment, then added, "O'Ryan on a trunk in my vision. Important?" That comment sent me off onto another train of thought. I made a note on a card about the missing tattle tape, and on another I wrote, "Does Agnes really believe Rob is guilty or is Mercury lying? Mercury says Agnes and Rob once were lovers."

I stopped writing then and looked out the window. I could see the telltale black circle on the side of the house next door that marked their security camera. *It must be the one that captured the picture of the old lady.* It must record everyone who uses the book drop too, I thought. It must have picked up an image of whoever returned *The Boys of Summer.* Does Pete have that image? Time to stop writing and start phoning.

I called Pete and told him about the tape that didn't tattle and asked about the security cameras next door. "Could you tell who returned the book to the book drop?"

"We think so. Looks like it was the old lady. She came out the side door and dropped the book."

"But she wasn't in the stacks. And nobody even saw her come into the building in the first place."

Pete sighed. "I know."

"The backpack guy had plenty of time up there."

"I know, babe. Maybe the cameras are screwed up. Maybe we are. Maybe backpack man and the old lady are working together somehow. But don't worry, we'll figure it out. Want me to bring something over to your place for dinner tonight? Have siren, will travel."

"That would be great," I said. "I have some more note taking to do here, then I'm going to try to see Agnes before I go home. I'd like to get a look at those costumes."

"That's on my list too, but chief says we can't spare anyone right now. Halloween craziness everywhere. Fingerprints at Agnes's won't mean much. All the prime suspects have been there recently and the room is apparently left unlocked."

"I guess Agnes doesn't have a security camera," I said.

"Nope. See you tonight. Love you."

"Love you too. Bye." I picked up a card and wrote, "The old woman may have put the book into the drop," then returned to staring out the window. Thinking.

I called Agnes and asked if I could come by for a few minutes. She said she'd be thrilled to see me. "I don't have a lot of company these days." She didn't say it in a sad way. Just matter of fact.

"I'll be along as soon as I can," I told her. "Lots of traffic all over." I looked out the window again. *Costumes. One costume anyway. The old lady.* I didn't like the idea that Ranger Rob could be a killer. And wouldn't he be smart enough to wear a different costume—one that hadn't been made especially for him? After all, Agnes had a whole trunkful of them. If Agnes wanted to do something terrible, she surely wouldn't do it in Katie the Clown's costume. And Jerry Mercury wouldn't wear his magician's cape and top hat to commit murder. All of the WICH-TV's alums had a variety of looks to choose from.

Except Dave. I remembered how I'd just told Tyler that I'd never seen Dave out of uniform.

Dave, who had access to all of the library. Dave, who had a set of keys to every door, every room—including the door to the old kitchen, including the emergency door to and from the stacks. Dave, who knew Willie, who'd worked for Larry Laraby, who'd even guarded the Honus Wagner card.

I hated the thought. But, reluctantly, I selected another blank card and wrote one word. *Dave.*

Chapter 37

I pulled the new cards into a pile and added them to the rubber-banded stack in my purse. I looked out the window for a few moments longer, gathering my thoughts—trying to get things straight in my mind. I looked at my watch. Well past noon. I wasn't hungry yet and Pete would bring dinner later. It would be a good idea to get started for Agnes's house right away. It would take a while to get to Highland Ave, I was sure, what with bands of roving witches and goblins and assorted princesses all over town. I'd trust Siri to find a circuitous route to get me there.

I said so long to Aunt Ibby and Tyler, grabbed my jacket from the break room closet. There were still a few cinnamon buns in the covered cake dish. It would be a while before dinner. I wrapped a bun tightly in a paper napkin, slipped it into my jacket pocket, and left the library via the side door. It only took about half an hour to get to Highland Avenue. Siri led me almost to Peabody, down Concord Street, through a couple of streets I could swear I'd never seen before, and somehow I found myself in front of Agnes's cute house. I parked behind the VW Bug in the carport and walked up the path to the pumpkin-lined porch. Percival peered from the window the same way O'Ryan likes to do from our front hall. Agnes threw the door open as soon as I reached for the doorbell.

"Come in, Lee," she said, reaching for my hand. "I told Percy you were coming and he's been waiting here at the window ever so patiently." I patted the black cat and followed Agnes to her kitchen. The room was done in pink and gray—even the refrigerator and wall oven were pink. The kitchen table had a gray Formica top and chrome chairs were padded in pink fabric with a boomerang-pattern design. A wonderful Marc Bellaire vase held fresh pink gerbera daisies. It was the perfect 1950s kitchen.

"This is wonderful," I said. "Suits the house."

"Suits me," she replied with a big smile. "Now what can I do for you? I'm guessing you have some more questions for me."

"I do," I said. "Mostly it's about the costumes. Jerry Mercury told me that the Mrs. Blatherflab outfit is missing."

"It is," she said. "The dress and gray wig and the purse with the cat on it and that darling veiled hat and the gray gloves. Even her little black boots." She laughed. "They weren't actually little of course. Rob had size thirteen feet."

"Jerry told me that Rob hated wearing it," I said.

"Oh, he did. The poor man. Just imagine—going from being handsome Ranger Rob and strong, brave Officer Tom and then having to play a silly old fat lady." She shook her head. "But he needed the job. Needed to fulfill his contract. He was saving his money to buy that stable over in Rockport."

"He seems happy there," I told her. "It's a very nice

place and he does love his horses."*Do I dare to bring up the possibility that Rob may have taken the costume from her utility room?*

I didn't have to. She brought it up first.

"You know, Lee, when I first saw that tape of the old woman on TV, the first thing I thought of was Rob. Naturally I recognized Mrs. Blatherflab right away. I'm sure plenty of others did too. At least those of us of a certain age."

"The police chief's mother spotted it," I said. "Do I understand correctly that the old woman costume has been in your utility room all these years?"

"It is. I mean it was." She gave a clownlike jazz hands motion. "Not there anymore. Gone."

I pressed a little more. "Is it possible that Rob could have—borrowed it?"

"Oh, darlin'," she protested. "*Anybody* could have borrowed it. I've loaned all those silly rigs out God knows how many times. Anybody who needs a costume is welcome to use one. All I ask is that they wash it and return it when they're through."

"So it's true that the utility room door is unlocked?"

"It's true. Most of my friends and quite a few of the neighbors know that. Who told you?"

"Jerry Mercury."

"Oh, yes. Jerry. He has no use for the old outfits." She gave a little sigh. "He's kind of stuck up, don't you think? That's his Abraham Lincoln costume on the straw man out front, by the way." I remembered the striped pants, frock coat, and top hat on the scarecrow guy. *So even the professor had played more than one role.*

"Would you let me look at the collection?" I asked.

"Of course. Come on outside. Come along, Percival." The cat fell into step beside her and we all walked together onto the porch, past the pumpkins and the well-dressed straw man, over to the door at the end of the carport. She pulled it open with a quick motion. The black cat took one leap and landed directly on top of a large black trunk. There were a few other items in there. A rake, a shovel, some hedge clippers. But it was the vision of O'Ryan, poised on the old trunk that used to be in our attic, that actually registered with me and suddenly made sense. This was a black cat on a larger, somewhat newer trunk, but the message was the same. The trunk, or what's in it, is important—somehow.

"Now, there may be a few things missing," she warned. "It's Halloween in Salem you know. Costume parties all over the place and the neighborhood folks know I have a pretty good assortment here for free."

"And people always return them? All washed?"

"They do. Sometimes I might have to rewash one—to get wine stains out. But generally speaking, people take good care of them." She shooed the cat aside and opened the lid. "The costumes are all professional quality, you know. WICH-TV didn't stint on wardrobe." She pulled a silvery metallic jumpsuit from the pile. "Look. This was Marvel the Robot's little suit. His helmet is here too. See? And there's a small bulb sewn into the glove part of the sleeve that makes the beep-beep. I'm surprised one of the neighborhood kids hasn't grabbed this one already. Listen." I remembered the sound and couldn't help smiling.

"It's a little harder to keep track of the accessories," she continued. "Like the shoes and the hats and the wigs and the eyeglasses and the mustaches and beards and the elf ears and fake noses." She pointed to a large round hatbox on the floor beside the trunk. "I try to keep all that stuff separate." She removed the cover of the box and pulled out a black wig with two long braids. It made me think of River's hair. "This was mine," she said, with a note of nostalgia in her voice, "when I was Princess Waterfall Raindrop."

"It looks like it's in very good condition," I said.

"Of course. Real human hair. I told you. They didn't stint. I try to take good care of the wigs. You know, shampoo them and style them once in a while." She touched her own gray hair. "I even set Mrs. Blatherflab's wig in those tight old-lady pin curls every so often."

Gray hair and pin curls. Pamela had reported seeing a man with curly gray hair. "Agnes," I said. "Did you say that all of the accessories to Mrs. Blatherflab's costume are missing? The wig?"

"Everything. Even the padded bra."

"Thanks for showing this to me, Agnes," I said, "maybe when we do the anniversary show we can put a few of these costumes on mannequins. Would that be all right with you?"

"Sure thing. Look, are you going to any Halloween parties? You're welcome to help yourself to whatever you like."

"I hadn't really thought about it," I admitted.

"Well, if you decide to, just come on by. The door is open. Take your pick. Just wash it when you bring it back." She put the trunk lid down and replaced the cover on the hatbox. "Come on Percy." The cat and I followed her and we both waited in front of the VW while she closed the utility room door.

"I think it's quite possible that the police will want to check out the room," I said. "They may ask you to lock it up after all."

"Really? Well, I guess they can check it if they want to, but there've been so many people in and out of it I don't think they'll find any clues."

She said "clues." I wonder if she read Nancy Drew too.

Chapter 38

After my interview with Agnes I decided to take the regular route home. It would take longer, but I needed some thinking time. I called Rhonda and asked her to run my idea on displaying the old costumes on mannequins by Mr. Doan, and told her I was heading for home to select some publicity pictures of Larry Laraby. True enough, and all relating to the anniversary show.

I could hardly wait to get into that photo album. Pete would bring dinner, but I was going to be the one who'd bring new facts to the table! I'd already decided not to call him yet. It would be more fun to tell him in person about the curly gray wig, the open-door policy on the costume trunk, and my disturbing recent thoughts about Dave. I might even mention the cat-on-the-trunk thing. Maybe not. Finding more Laraby pictures relating to the book in question—and I was confident there'd be some—would just be icing on the proverbial cake. *Cake. I'd better stop somewhere and pick up dessert for tonight. Pete likes sweets.*

Recalling that Jim Litka had said Agnes walked to Market Basket every Monday, I knew it must be nearby. I found it, parked, and headed for the bakery department. I settled on an ice cream cake—covering the best of both worlds—added a package of English muffins and a dozen eggs in case Pete stayed for breakfast, and returned to my car. Since that man had stared at me the other day, I couldn't help but check my surroundings in supermarket parking lots. Couldn't help it. That damned green Subaru still haunted me. Subarus are popular in New England. Unlike my beautiful Corvette, they're good snow cars. There were several in the lot—none of them green.

The ride home was slow, as I'd anticipated. Salem's streets, which many people believe were originally cow paths, wind, curve, and dead-end in strange ways. Add too many tour buses jockeying for position, costumed and celebratory pedestrians, and the normal congestion of people like me trying to get from point A to point B and you have near-gridlock at every corner. Slow going, but it did allow for some thinking time. (Hopefully, I'd get to Winter Street before the ice cream cake began to thaw.)

The Dave question wouldn't go away. I didn't *want* to believe anything bad about him. He represented safety and protection. Everybody liked him, especially women of a certain age—like my aunt. The library board surely trusted him—easy to get along with, worked any hours they asked him to. But Dave was part of that early WICH-TV assemblage, with connections to *all* of the major players involved. He was tall enough to wear the old lady suit—probably could even wear size thirteen shoes. He had keys to everything in his capacity as security guard, undoubtedly including the emergency door. He was big and strong and ex-military. Did he know karate? Could very well be. He claimed the Honus Wagner card was real. He'd seen it close up, maybe even touched it. He knew it was used as a bookmark too. No reason in the world he wouldn't have known which book to look for. I didn't like those thoughts.

After a brief verbal altercation with a tour bus driver who had the rear end of his bus blocking my way onto Oliver Street, I coasted up to our yard and hit the garage door opener. I coasted into the garage, picked up the grocery bag, peeked inside to be sure the ice cream cake was intact. O'Ryan waited for me on the back steps, then dashed inside through his cat door while I fished for my keys. Aunt Ibby wasn't home yet, but I had a key to her kitchen door on the same key chain. I'd just duck in there, grab the albums from the cookbook shelf, and get to work. Just before pushing the door open, I sneaked a peek back toward the street. That green Subaru still had me spooked. Of course, it wasn't there.

Once inside I put my purse and the bags containing the ice cream cake, muffins, and eggs on the stairway leading up to my place, and opened the door to my aunt's kitchen. O'Ryan was already inside. He was in one of the captain's chairs, back toward me, stretching upward, his paws on the back of the chair, his eyes nearly level with the cookbook shelf. Reaching out with a big yellow paw, he tapped one of the albums. "Okay, smarty-pants," I said. "This time I'm way ahead of you. That's exactly what I came for. Come on. We'll take them upstairs."

O'Ryan gave me one of his snooty superior looks—the kind Aunt Ibby calls "catitude." He stalked toward the cat door with his tail erect, which I'm pretty sure is the cat version of flipping me off. I locked the kitchen door, picked up purse, albums, and cake, and followed him up the twisty staircase to the third floor. By the time I got inside he was already curled up in the zebra-print wing chair, pretending to be asleep. "Oh, come off it," I told him. "Once in while I can think of something before you do. Come on out to the kitchen. You can help me look at pictures." His whiskers twitched and the golden eyes opened the tiniest bit. "Suit yourself. I'm going to put this cake in the freezer and then get to work solving a mystery."

I attended to the ice cream cake first, stowed the eggs and muffins, then put the albums on the kitchen table, dug the big magnifying glass out of the junk drawer, hung jacket and purse on a chair back, and turned on the overhead light. Although we'd already looked through that first album pretty thoroughly earlier, I decided that a second look wouldn't hurt. Even if I didn't find another shot of Laraby with the book, maybe something else interesting would turn up. I'd just opened the padded cover to the first page when O'Ryan decided to join me. He jumped up onto the windowsill and sat up straight, giving him a clear view over my shoulder. He said, "Merrrow" in a purry sort of way, so I assumed I'd been forgiven for the "smarty-pants" remark. That, or else he was so curious he couldn't stand being left out.

I took my time, examining each page with the glass. The only sound was the tick-tick of Kit-Cat's tail, marking the seconds. I was about halfway through album one, about to turn a page that held several pictures of vendors' tables displaying their sports-related wares, when O'Ryan made a sudden leap from sill to tabletop. He planted one of those big paws firmly on the open album.

"Nothing interesting there, big boy," I told him. "They're just pictures of the tables the different dealers set up for the collectibles show. These were probably taken before the doors even opened. See?" I pointed to one of the pictures. "No people. Just cards and balls and bats and programs and jerseys and that kind of stuff." He moved closer to the page, head down, as though he was sniffing each photo. Then, once again, the decisive planting of the paw on one of them.

Might as well humor him or he'll keep this silly game going all night. I picked up the magnifying glass and pushed his paw aside. "All right. Let's take a look and see what's so all-fired important about some old-time sports collectibles dealer's idea of what might sell at a Laraby show."

It took a minute for me to see what he saw. I scanned the picture inch by inch. Neatly packaged baseball cards, signed hockey pucks, autographed baseballs in plastic globes, colorful plastic action figures, nicely framed game jerseys. I finally spotted it. A small white oblong on the lower left hand edge of the display table. It was the dealer's identification card.

TABLE #43—H. TEMPLETON

So Howie Templeton's daddy had been a dealer at Laraby's sports collectibles shows—at least one of them. That's where the connection to Wee Willie must have come from. "Good cat!" I offered O'Ryan a high five. He looked puzzled, gave my palm a lick, and returned to his windowsill perch. I marked the page with a "Support Your Local Bookmobile" bookmark. There were a few more pages of dealer setups, but I didn't find another with Templeton's name on it.

I'd have several new things to share with Pete when he arrived. Feeling quite proud of myself, I returned to my examination of the first album. There were a couple of pages of photos of athletes signing autographs. Each one sat at a table with his or her name on a large banner. I recognized some of the names, few of the faces. The photos showed long lines of autograph hunters. Larry Laraby sure knew how to attract crowds to his shows—and his long association with Wee Willie had undoubtedly helped him in attracting big-name athletes to sit at those tables.

I used the magnifying glass extra carefully after nearly missing that H. Templeton ID card. I moved the glass slowly across each picture, not knowing exactly what I was looking for but hoping I'd recognize it when I found it. There were a few more shots of a smiling Larry standing behind his own dealer table. Behind him I could see part of the glass case. It made perfect sense that he'd keep it close, especially if that card was the real thing. I marked that page with a bookmark too. I could hardly wait for Pete to arrive, mostly because I was anxious to share what I'd learned, but also because I was getting hungry.

I'd just reached the end of album number one when O'Ryan left the windowsill and scooted out of the kitchen and into the short hall leading to the living room. That could only mean that Pete had arrived. The cat disappeared through his cat door and I stopped beside the bay window, peeking out into the darkness. Pete's car was already parked in the driveway and I saw him start up the flagstone path. He carried a large paper bag with one arm and a long narrow one in the other. *Chinese or Italian and a bottle of wine. Yum.* O'Ryan met him on the path, did a quick ankle rub, then trotted beside him toward the house. I hurried into the hall and down the stairs. Music coming from Aunt Ibby's kitchen told me that she'd come home. By the time I'd reached the first floor, a little out of breath, Pete had already used his key and come inside. He handed me the wine, gave me a hug, and said, "I brought Chinese. Hope that's okay."

"Perfect," I said. "I'm sort of starving."

He tilted his head toward my aunt's door. "Want to ask Ms. Russell to join us? I brought a little extra, in case."

"Good idea." I knocked. "Aunt Ibby? It's me."

She pulled the door open almost immediately. "Come in, dear. Hello, Pete. I thought I heard you drive up."

"Pete brought dinner," I said. "Want to join us?"

"I'd like that," she said. "I've done a little digging around at the library and I may have learned a few things I can hardly wait to share with the two of you."

"Me too," I said. "Come on up as soon as you're ready."

Pete and I have learned to work pretty well together in my kitchen. I cleared the albums off the table, gave it a squirt of cleaner, wiped it down, and arranged three place settings of Fiestaware, while Pete transferred the wonderful-smelling contents of the distinctively shaped cartons into serving dishes. "Crab Rangoon, vegetable spring rolls, white rice, shrimp fried rice, beef chow mein, fried noodles," he recited, "and some egg rolls and other stuff. I guess I was hungry."

I put three wineglasses on the table. "I think we can handle it. Plus the ice cream cake I bought for dessert. Aunt Ibby says she has something to tell us and I've found a few things too. It might be a long dinner."

"I have a one or two items to contribute too."

"Give me a hint."

"Chief got a court order to open that Wallace Williams post office box number you gave us."

"And . . . ?"

"I'll tell you when your aunt gets here."

Chapter 39

I begged a little, even whined a bit, but Pete wouldn't budge on sharing whatever it was he'd found out about Wallace Williams. It was okay, though. I wanted to wait for her myself, visualizing a kind of snoop sisters tag team, the two of us bombarding him with fact after fact, clue after clue, photo after photo. It was a delicious thought.

O'Ryan dashed for the kitchen cat door and bolted out into the upstairs hall seconds before my aunt tapped and called, "Hello, Maralee, it's me."

Pete let cat and aunt in, receiving a hug and an ankle rub simultaneously. "Perfect timing, Ms. Russell," he said. "I hope you're hungry."

She put a manila folder on the counter and took her usual seat at the table. "I am. It smells wonderful and looks so pretty."

I uncorked the wine—a nice Pinot Grigio—and glanced over at the folder. "That the results of the library digging you mentioned?"

"It is," she said. "I can hardly wait to show it to you."

"Pete has something to share too, don't you Pete?"

"Egg roll, Ms. Russell?" He passed the platter. "Lee's been pestering me to tell her, but I wanted to wait for you."

"Thank you, Pete. I appreciate that. I know how persuasive Maralee can be when she wants something. I think I'll have one of those wings, too."

"I've found out a few new things." I poured wine into the three glasses and sat in the chair in front of the window. O'Ryan positioned himself beside Aunt Ibby, knowing she'd undoubtedly sneak him a shrimp or a bit of crabmeat. "Shall we do 'show-and-tell' during dinner," I asked, "or wait until after dessert?"

"Mine will keep," Pete said, reaching for the chow mein. "How about yours, Lee?"

"Mine involves pictures," I said, "and I wouldn't want anyone to spill duck sauce on them. Aunt Ibby?"

"Papers. Transcripts. Unfounded rumors. Let's wait until after-dinner coffee." Wise old owl face. "Of course, that doesn't preclude anyone dropping a hint here and there during the entrée."

And so it went. It was almost as if we'd invented a new game, making up the rules as we went along. Pete started by telling us that as soon as I'd given him the Wallace Williams post office box number, he'd passed it on to Chief Whaley and the chief actually woke up a judge to get a court order.

"No kidding. It was that important?"

Pete didn't elaborate, but instead deferred to Aunt Ibby, as he passed the crab Rangoon in her direction. It's her favorite. "Did the library yield any secrets today, Ms. Russell?"

"Thank you. Yes. Larry Laraby produced collectibles shows in cities all over the country and dealers paid several hundred dollars for a single six-foot display table. Maralee? Your turn."

"Hitchhiking on your hint, Aunt Ibby, I found that one

of those tables at one show at least was used by Howard Templeton Senior. Pete?"

"Good work, Lee," he said. "There were several pieces of mail in Wallace Williams's post office box, and one of them was from Howard Templeton Senior. I think we're getting somewhere! What have you got, Ms. Russell?"

"Do the hints have to be in any particular order?" she asked.

Pete and I each assured her that they didn't. "Just toss in any hint you've got," he said.

"Okay. Tyler found this one. William Wallace applied for a library card on the day he got killed."

"Wow. Good one, Aunt Ibby. He must have been planning to check out a book. On sports. Now I've lost track," I said. "Whose turn is it?"

"Your turn, babe," Pete said.

"Okay. Katie the Clown, I mean Agnes Hooper, has a trunk full of costumes from the old days at WICH-TV. They're in an outdoor utility room and the door is never locked." I helped myself to a spring roll. "Looks like anybody could have grabbed the old lady costume."

"Including the gloves," Pete said. "We 're thinking along those lines too. No fingerprints."

I spoke out of turn. "Mrs. Blatherflab's wig is made of high-quality human hair. Human *gray* hair. Agnes says she washes it frequently and"—I paused for effect—"she regularly sets it with 'old lady pin curls.'"

Pete caught on right away. "Curly gray hair. Young Pamela saw a man with curly gray hair."

"For heaven's sake," my aunt said. "Here I've been thinking the old woman and the bearded man were in cahoots. What if they're both the same person?"

"And Pamela caught that person in the middle of transforming from one to the other. From bearded man to old woman!" I was excited. "He'd already put on the curly gray wig. What do you think, Pete?"

Serious cop voice. "It makes a certain amount of sense. He—or she—could have been a bearded man who left the stacks through the emergency exit—then on the way down the stairs, into the old kitchen, and out the side door, changed costumes and became an old woman. What young Pamela saw was a person who'd removed the beard and put on the wig." He nodded. "Yes. You ladies may have something there."

"Now we just have to figure out who's under the wig and behind the beard," my aunt said. "Ideas, Maralee?"

"I hate to say it," I admitted, "but lately I've been having some suspicions about Dave."

"Dave?" My aunt's eyebrows went up. "Certainly not Dave. Why would you say that?"

"Well, he'd fit into the old lady outfit for one thing. He knows where the costumes are kept, has keys to everything in the library, knew all about the Honus Wagner card, and he's big and strong enough to have killed Willie."

"Pete?" Aunt Ibby clearly didn't like my reasoning. "The police don't suspect Dave, do they?"

He sighed. "This is one of those situations where no one is a suspect, so everybody is a suspect, Ms. Russell. We've checked Benson's background. So far, he looks clean."

"Thought so," she said. "Is Rob Oberlin on your list too?"

"He is, but he won't fit into your one-person-playing-both-parts scenario. He'd fit into the old lady suit, but he's too heavy to be the bearded guy we have on video."

"How about the others from the old shows? Agnes and Jerry Mercury?" I wondered.

"Agnes is too small and too old to have killed Willie by herself," he said. "Mercury is a possibility, but as you've said, virtually everybody in town has access to those costumes and a lot of people had reason to hate Willie."

"Is there anything in Mercury's background?" I pressed for more information.

"Can't discuss the background checks," he said. "Confidential, you know. Got any more hints?"

I'd almost forgotten about our game. "Jerry Mercury told me he thinks Rob killed Willie," I said, "because Rob hated the way Willie had abused horses."

"I've got something new about Willie and horses," Aunt Ibby said. "I found a little article in the *Palm Beach Post* dated a couple of years ago, mentioning a William Wallace, a rodeo clown, who rescued a young boy who'd fallen from the stands. No picture or further description though, so maybe it wasn't our William Wallace."

"A rodeo clown, hmmm? Palm Beach, Florida, you said?" Pete pulled out his notebook for the first time that evening. Apparently, Pete found that small bit of information particularly interesting—which made it particularly interesting to me, too.

Chapter 40

We played the hint game for a little while longer, Aunt Ibby giving some statistics on the waning popularity of collectibles shows nationally, and a list of the top ten collectible sports items. I tossed in the fact that the straw man on Agnes's porch wore Jerry Mercury's Abraham Lincoln costume. Pete reported that the people next door to the library had turned over their videotapes for the past two weeks, but that he hadn't personally viewed them yet. Even with all the conversation going on, we'd managed to dispose of virtually every bit of our bounty.

I cleared the table and set out dessert plates, ice cream cake, and three fortune cookies, while Pete loaded the dishwasher and started a pot of coffee. O'Ryan, having enjoyed both shrimp and crab tidbits, had already retired to the bedroom. Repeated glances in the direction of the large book on the counter revealed that all three of us were clearly anxious to get into that second photo album.

"If we put three chairs in a row on one side of the table, we can all see the photos at the same time," my aunt suggested. "Do you have three magnifying glasses,

Maralee?" I admitted to having only two. "There's a nice big one on my office desk," she said. "I'll attend to these dishes when we're through if you'll run down and get it."

I pushed my chair back. "I think I've had enough cake," I said. "I'll open my fortune cookie when I come back."

"I already opened mine," Pete said. "It says, 'Smile more often and think positive thoughts.'"

"Good advice for everybody," my aunt said, opening hers. She glanced at it then laughed. "It says, 'The fortune you seek is in another cookie.'"

I was still smiling about that one as I hurried down the front stairs, across the foyer, through the living room, and into her office. I clicked on the overhead light. The magnifying glass, as she'd said, was in a Chinese vase along with assorted pens, pencils, and a ruler on her neat cherrywood desk.

Carrying the glass, I returned to the darkened foyer. I paused by the front door and as I often do, peeked out onto Winter Street through one of the tall side windows. There's not usually a lot of traffic on our street at that time of night, so the slow-moving car caught my attention. The silhouette of the compact car with its distinctive lines stood out against a streetlamp's glow. A Subaru, no doubt, dark colored. Was it green? I didn't know. I looked away and told myself once again that it's a popular make and model and that there were undoubtedly hundreds of them in Salem. *This is not even worth mentioning to Pete or Aunt Ibby.* I climbed the stairs, trying to think about something else.

Back in my own kitchen, the table had been cleared, the chairs lined up as my aunt had suggested, the album opened to the first page. Our coffee cups and my fortune cookie were neatly arranged just above the album and my two magnifying glasses awaited us. I put Aunt Ibby's beside her cup, and took my seat beside Pete. "Are we ready?" I asked.

"Open your cookie," Pete said, "and we're all good to go."

I did, and read aloud. "'Your dearest wish will come true.'" I shrugged, rolled it into a little ball and picked up my magnifying glass. "I didn't know I even *had* a dearest wish."

Other than occasionally bumping elbows as we examined the pages, we worked pretty well together. We must have been an odd-looking group though, with the three of us on one side of the table, all trying to study the same photos, none of us sure exactly what we were looking for in the first place. Many of the pages were similar to the one where O'Ryan had found the Templeton table, showing a variety of display tables at various venues around the country. I glanced occasionally at the open bedroom door, wondering if the cat might join us, but he'd apparently lost interest in the project.

After we were more than halfway through the album it appeared that O'Ryan was right. Nothing of particular interest had shown up at all. I even found myself stifling a yawn here and there.

"I need to stand up and stretch for a minute," my aunt declared. "These old bones are starting to protest."

"Me too," Pete said. "How about a short break? More coffee, babe?"

"Okay," I said, moving a little closer to the open album when Pete left his chair. The photos on these pages showed crowds of show-goers. "That Laraby was quite a promotor. He had to be drawing hundreds of people to every show. Maybe thousands."

"He advertised a lot," my aunt offered. "Our newspaper microfiche showed full-page ads at every city on that schedule you showed me. Plenty of news coverage too. All with pictures of the glass case and the security guard."

"Yes. Dave told me he got his picture taken a lot at those shows." I put my magnifying glass down and accepted the coffee cup. "Are you two through with this page? I don't see anything unusual here. Mind if I turn to the next one?"

They each voiced agreement and I turned the page.

"Holy cow!" I breathed softly. "Look at this." It was a two-page spread of those old-time, deckle-edged, five-inch-square snapshots. "Pete, are these pictures like the one Sharon Stewart is missing?"

"Exactly," Pete said, returning to his chair and picking up his own magnifying glass. He lifted the corner of the page and peeked at the next one. "There are more." He riffled the edges of the remaining pages. "They go all the way to the end. He must have used professional photographers to record the events most of the time, then used his own camera for these."

By then Aunt Ibby had joined us, and newly energized, we returned to our examination of each photo. These weren't as sharply focused as the professional shots, but they weren't bad. Laraby had taken some close-up shots of various individual items, and had printed a few words of description under most of them in black marker, sometimes—but not always—including a price. Many of the prices noted were in the thousands of dollars.

"I think these were things he offered for sale to special customers, probably by mail," Pete said, "since they didn't have eBay or Craigslist in those days."

"And those were nineteen-seventies or nineteen-eighties prices," my aunt said. "Think of what they'd bring in today's dollars. Did you know Muhammad Ali's boxing gloves from the Floyd Patterson fight brought one point one million?"

"It's so handy, having a research librarian for an aunt," I said. "You're a wonder."

"It seems that Wee Willie may have been doing about the same thing Larry Laraby did." Pete spoke slowly, cop voice engaged. "Some of the contents of that P.O. box appear to be bids."

"Do you know what they were bidding on?" I asked.

"Yeah. A baseball card. And the bids were high."

"Can we assume that Willie was accepting bids on the Honus Wagner?" My aunt lifted the corner of the next page. "Maybe even before he had it?"

Pete shrugged. "That might be a reasonable assumption, I guess."

"Maybe Howard Templeton Senior made a bid on that card," I said, almost thinking out loud. "And maybe that won Wally Williams an invitation to the Halloween party."

"The invitation was in the post office box too, Lee," Pete said. "And I may take you up on that offer to escort you to the party after all. Chief thinks it would be a good idea for me to be there. I'll be undercover security of course, so I can't promise to be with you all the time."

"That's okay. Thought about a costume at all?"

"I guess I can't go as a cop, huh?"

"You'll both need to decide on something pretty soon," my aunt said. "If the Witches' Ball is tomorrow, Buffy's party is the day after that. So you have only a couple of days to throw something together."

"I don't want to make a big fuss over it," I said. "Something simple and comfortable. No high heels or sequins. He hasn't said anything yet, but I'll bet Mr. Doan is expecting me to treat this more like an assignment than a party. I bet he'll send Francine or Marty with camera and mics."

"You're probably right," Aunt Ibby said. "Why don't you dress as a fictional cowgirl? One of the Bad Girls, maybe. Cody Zamora or Lilly Laronette."

"Bad Girls?" I asked.

"Sure. *Bad Girls.*1994. Twentieth Century Fox. Andie MacDowell was in it. Drew Barrymore too. You looked so cute in your boots and jeans and checked shirt when we went to visit Rob Oberlin. Add your old hat and a neckerchief and you're good to go."

I'd never argue about old movies with Aunt Ibby. "Good idea," I said. "Pete, want to be a cowboy?"

"Not especially. I guess I'll just rent something from Chris Rich's store."

My aunt and I had put down our magnifying glasses during the costume conversation, but Pete hadn't. He'd continued inspecting each square photo on the page slowly and carefully. "Mind if I turn the page, ladies?" he said—as he turned the page.

We hastily—and a little guiltily—picked up our magnifying glasses and leaned toward the album. The next few pages were similar to the first ones we'd noticed. Individual sports-related things, some marked with prices—mostly in the one- to five-thousand-dollar range—some with brief descriptions, and many showing the same item from varied angles.

There were only a few more pages left to view in that second album when the photo we'd been looking for appeared. We all spotted it at once. We all pointed at once—yelled at once. We even woke O'Ryan, who appeared, stretching, in the bedroom doorway.

It was just as Sharon Laraby Stewart had described it to Pete. Laraby, with a cigar clenched in his teeth, held a book in his right hand. The title of the book was plainly legible: *The Boys of Summer.* Like some of the photos of expensive collectibles, there were several photos of Laraby in this pose, taken from slightly different angles.

"I understand why he took several photos of things he had for sale. Must have sent them around to likely buyers," I said. "But why all the pictures of himself?"

Pete tilted his head from side to side, studying the snapshots, and didn't answer.

"I think these were intended as a clue for those he wanted to know that the book was special," Aunt Ibby offered. "He must have given one to his daughter. I'll bet Mrs. Laraby had one too."

"If it's all right with you, Lee," Pete said, "I'd like to give one of these to Sharon Stewart—to replace the one that was stolen."

"I'll have to ask Mr. Doan," I said, "but I'm sure it'll be okay." O'Ryan, after a few puzzled looks around the room, had retreated to the bedroom once again. I stifled a yawn. Bed seemed like a good option. "Since we've found what we were looking for, can we put the albums away? I'm beat."

"Me too," Pete said. "Chief's got everybody working extra hours. It's this way every October. The Witches' Ball tomorrow night is the height of the craziness. Media from all over the world will be here clogging up the streets even worse than they are now."

"That's hard to imagine," I said. "But this is one time I'm glad young Howie is on hand to cover a big story instead of me. He's going to love being part of it and it just holds terrible memories for me."

"I remember." Pete covered my hand with his. "I remember." The room grew still then, for about three ticks of Kit-Cat's tail.

My aunt stood, breaking the awkward silence. "I guess I'll toddle on downstairs," she said. "Thanks for dinner,

Pete, and thanks to both of you for letting me help with this investigation. I do love snooping!"

"I'll walk you home," Pete said, standing and offering his arm. (He often escorts my aunt downstairs. Especially if we've had wine!) They exited onto the third-floor landing. I looked toward the bedroom again, but the cat had apparently decided to spend the night with us. I grabbed my navy blue satin pj's and headed down the hall to the bathroom.

Chapter 41

I tidied up the kitchen while I waited for Pete to come back upstairs. Carrying the albums into the living room, I put them on the coffee table, planning to return them to the station in the morning.

"I'm back," Pete called from the kitchen. "Aunt delivered safe and sound."

"Thanks," I said, hurrying back down the hall. "Not everybody gets a police escort home after dinner. She really appreciates you."

"My pleasure," he said. "I appreciate her too. You two snoop sisters make a good investigative team."

The comment pleased me. "I think we all did a good job with the albums tonight, didn't we? I'm going to return them to the station tomorrow so if you need them for evidence or anything, you'll have to deal with Mr. Doan."

"That'll work. We'd both better get an early start. With the Witches' Ball going on tomorrow night it'll be crazy wild out there all day."

"I know," I agreed. "I'm just glad I don't have to cover it. That's one assignment I'm glad to turn over to young Howie."

Pete pulled me close. "I know the Witches' Ball holds bad memories. You were terrified that night."

"I was," I said. "And you were there for me."

"I hope I can always be there for you whenever you're frightened."

I smiled at that. "Can you come with me every time I have to return a book to the stacks? That place still scares me."

"Because of finding Wee Willie?"

"Not entirely. It goes back to when I was six and got lost up there in the dark. Never got over it."

"I'd do it if I could." He ruffled my hair. "Childhood terrors can be the worst of all."

"They are," I said. "The vision I saw in my patent leather shoes when I was five still haunts me."

"Your parents' plane crash."

"Yes." I shook the terrible image away and changed the subject. "Shall I set the alarm for six-thirty? Traffic might not be too awful then."

"Right. I'll go grab a shower." He looked at the clock. "Time for the late news. Want to see what Covington has to say?"

"Sure." I reached for the remote. "Hurry back. You might get to see me with cute puppies and kitties in Halloween costumes."

"Be right back," he said. And he was, wearing the Arizona Diamondback pajama bottoms and smelling deliciously of Nautica Voyage. Buck Covington had just read (flawlessly) the first commercial and had announced that several high-profile entertainers were in town for the Witches' Ball. There was a report from Howard Templeton on a haunted house display in South Salem that had drawn so many people that they'd had to block off the street.

"Chief had to call off-duty guys for that one," Pete said. "I'm glad Halloween only comes once a year."

"Amen," I said. "Look. Here's the pet shop segment." I lowered my voice. "I was tempted to bring home that black kitten dressed up as Batman."

"Shh," he said, with a glance toward the darkened bedroom. "Don't let you-know-who hear that."

"I've already apologized for the thought," I said. "He knows I wouldn't do it."

"That cat knows a lot of things, doesn't he?"

I didn't answer, just watched as the spot played out. We'd done a good job on it and the animals had all been photogenically adorable. "I don't know yet whether Mr. Doan expects Marty and Francine and me to put together some kind of field report from Buffy's party," I said. "He hasn't mentioned it but since we'll all be there, I'll bet he does."

"Wouldn't be surprised." Pete stifled a yawn. "You're cuter than those puppies, by the way. Want to watch the rest from bed?"

"Good idea." I turned off the set. "You go ahead. I'll fix the coffee for morning and set the alarm." I did as I'd promised, then joined boyfriend and cat—both sound asleep—on my big bed. I turned off that TV too.

Pete was up before the alarm sounded and O'Ryan had already left for greener pastures downstairs before I followed the smell of fresh coffee and made my sleepy way into the kitchen. "I found English muffins and eggs," Pete said. "That what you had in mind?"

"Yep," I said. "There's some orange marmalade in the fridge too." Pete toasted and buttered the muffins while I scrambled half a dozen of the eggs and poured the coffee. We were both dressed, fed, and ready to leave before Kit-Cat showed seven a.m. We work well together.

We left the house, Pete backing the Crown Vic onto Oliver Street, me—glad I didn't have to drive—on foot, wearing sensible shoes and with one of Larry Laraby's albums under each arm, heading for Hawthorne Boulevard.

I had to pass the Hawthorne Hotel, where the big Witch festivities would take place later that night. Several trucks were parked, more or less illegally, in front of the building, while workman-types carried boards and panels, boxes and cases, lighting and sound paraphernalia inside. *Buffy's party will be in the same ballroom as the Witches' Ball. I wonder if it will need as much stuff.*

I'd just passed the Nathaniel Hawthorne statue when I saw three familiar figures. The laughing trio of Marty, Rhonda, and Wanda descended the steps of one of Salem's fashionable new time-share condos. *This must be Wanda's boyfriend's place. Nice.* Marty spotted me first. "Hi, Moon," she called. "Fancy meeting you here."

"Good morning," I said. "You all look cheerful."

"Having a ball," Rhonda said. "You should join us. We have the place 'til the end of the month. There's plenty of room. Francine's coming over tonight after she covers the Witches' Ball with Howie."

"I'd love to," I said. "But I have aunt and cat to consider. Hey, Doan's going to be amazed. All of us showing up early to work!"

"That might make up for us taking a long lunch hour later," Wanda said. "We need to check out the boutiques on Pickering Wharf."

"Completing our costumes for Buffy's party," Marty explained. "We need one more thing."

"Four more things," Wanda corrected. "One apiece."

"One *pair* apiece," Rhonda said. "Or would that make eight?"

The three dissolved into giggles. "As long as they're all green," Marty said, to more laughter.

I'm sure I looked confused and felt just a little left out of all this girly chatter. "Sounds intriguing," I said.

"Oh, Lee, I'm sorry," Rhonda said. "We're being awful.

But there's a prize for best costumed group. We've been working hard on ours. They'll be four of us, including Francine. I think everyone's going to be surprised."

"I understand," I said, and I did. It was good to see them having fun together. "I can hardly wait to see what you've come up with." The albums were growing heavy. I switched each one to the opposite side, trying for better balance. "Gotta go put my homework away."

"I'll carry one." Wanda reached for one of the albums. "These for the anniversary show?"

"Yes," I said, gratefully handing it over. "Thank you. It's taking more research than I thought it was going to, but it's all pretty interesting."

Conversation about Buffy's party continued on the way to Derby Street without further reference to group costumes. We all agreed that it didn't seem right that River and Buck, Old Eddie and Scott all had to work on Halloween eve and miss Buffy's party, but as Mr. Doan had said, "Somebody has to watch the store." Howie and Francine had drawn late-night duty for the Witches' Ball so they had the night before Halloween off. River and Buck had their regular live shows to do. Old Eddie and Scott would cover production and videography and if it happened late-breaking news.

We all clocked in and Rhonda wrote my name on the white board for "anniversary show prep on site." I walked down the center aisle of the darkened studio to the *Saturday Business Hour* set, still feeling a little guilty about never actually watching the program, turned on the desk lamp, and put the albums on the desk for one last look at the contents.

I realized that I hadn't brought along a magnifying glass and pulled open the narrow center desk drawer. *That's where I'd keep one, if this was really my desk.* Bingo! There was one in there along with a small stapler, a WICH-TV ballpoint pen, three paper clips, and a couple of rubber bands. It wasn't much of a glass—small with a black plastic rim and a two-inch-diameter surface. *Oh well, better than nothing.* I pulled a tissue from my purse, polished the glass surface, then held it up to inspect for spots. Big mistake. The swirling colors began right away.

It only took a few seconds for the image to register. Silver colored with round black eyes, the robot moved with typical jerky motions, arms bent at the elbows, head turning left and right. The visions are always silent but I knew that if this one did have sound, I'd hear Professor Mercury's sidekick Marvel's happy "beep-beep." The robot stopped moving and faced me as though it was looking into a camera. Then his head began to turn away, turning ever so slowly to the left—and didn't stop turning. That silver head turned all the way around. I remembered Rhonda's words when she'd heard the M.E.'s report on Wee Willie.

"Someone must have twisted his head around like a corkscrew."

I put the magnifying glass back where I'd found it and shoved the albums—rather unceremoniously—back into the bottom file cabinet drawer. I opened the top drawer, pulled the file containing the names of those old sponsors, and immediately headed upstairs to get the key to the well-lighted, cozy, familiar dataport.

I knew that examining the files, separating the information on the businesses that were still doing business in Salem from those long gone was what Aunt Ibby calls "busy work." It was an excuse for me to get away from the vision, from thinking about the way Wee Willie had died. I read yellowed pages of advertising copy, looked at the attached photos and artwork, put aside the items I thought might be useful to the sales department. So far I'd found more than a dozen places still doing business in Salem.

I realized that my motions had become almost as robotic as Marvel's—mechanical and unthinking. Using the old ads to generate new business for WICH-TV was a damn good idea and I wasn't doing it justice. I picked up a sheet dated August 1987. A thirty-second spot for Dube's Seafood restaurant read just as well today as it had three decades ago. I imagined how it would sound if Buck Covington read it, or River North or even Scott Palmer. There was an old photo of the restaurant on Jefferson Avenue too. It was one of Pete's and my favorite places. I turned on the desktop computer and began to write a proposal for Mr. Doan on updating the wealth of historic material in the files, blending it with new features, and pitching those faithful advertisers on a new program of television advertising to coordinate with the WICH-TV anniversary shows.

He has to love it! Time flew by and my enthusiasm for the project grew. The files were each neatly cross-referenced with dated tapes, which, I devoutly hoped, were still on the premises. I was really getting into this research project, with its exciting promotional possibilities. There was a gentle tap-tap on the glass-windowed door behind me. "Just a minute," I called, holding up one hand, just a tad annoyed by the interruption.

I spun around in my chair and faced Francine and Howard Templeton peering in at me. I stood and opened the door. "What's up, you two?"

"Sorry to bother you while you're working, Lee," Francine said, "but I hope you can do us a favor."

"I'll try," I said. "What do you need?"

"I really need your expertise," Howard said. "I'm kinda new at this."

Yeah. We've all noticed.

"Here it is, Lee," Francine said. "Doan wants Howard and me to go over to the Hawthorne Hotel while they're arranging the ballroom for the Witches' Ball. Buffy's party is the next night and Doan thinks Howard needs to know how the setup should be done."

"Makes sense," I said.

"The thing is," Francine continued, "he wants us to do it at noon. On our lunch hour. And I have other plans."

"I heard," I said. "The group costume shopping trip. Sure, I'll do it. Give me a few minutes to get all this organized, Howard." I waved at the mess of papers on the desk. "I'll meet you in Rhonda's office at twelve o'clock."

"That'll be super," Howard said. "Aunt Buffy made a sketch for us of the way her party has to be set up, so we can make sure it will work the way she wants it to."

It had just better work. Aunt Buffy doesn't take no for an answer.

The two left and I bundled up the various files as neatly as I could. I printed out what I'd done on the proposal for Mr. Doan so far, took a deep breath, and headed back downstairs to the studio. Separating the papers I'd been working on from those remaining, I replaced them in the top drawer, took a quick look around making sure I'd left everything as I'd found it, grabbed my jacket, and hurried up to Rhonda's office.

Francine and Marty stood in the hall next to the elevator and Rhonda looked ready to bolt from behind her desk any second. "Wanda's already over at Pickering Wharf checking out the boutiques," she explained, slinging her purse over her shoulder and moving toward the door. "There's a recording on the phone to take calls. We've got a lot of shopping to do in just an hour. Thanks a lot, Lee. You're a real friend. Have fun, Howie. See ya!"

Young Howard, looking slightly confused by the sudden whirlwind of female shopping activity, but at the same time willing to proceed with the task at hand, gestured toward the station manager's office. "Do you think I should tell Uncle Bruce we're going now?"

"I'm sure Rhonda's already told him," I said. "But go ahead. I'll wait for you by the elevator." While he knocked on his uncle's door, I stepped out into the hall. That vintage elevator, slow and noisy, is to many people one of the most attractive features of the old building. The intricately patterned brass doors have become a matter of pride for Mr. Doan. They are polished regularly and I've even seen him pull a handkerchief from his breast pocket to wipe away an imagined fingerprint from the gleaming surface.

Gleaming surfaces are not a good thing for me. I'd only been there for a few seconds, waiting for Howard Templeton to report his plans to his uncle when the flashing lights and swirling colors appeared. The silver robot was back. This time he reached toward me with both arms, his round robot eyes blank, his little robot hands full of money, green bills falling around him.

Howard's voice came from behind me. "Ready to get out of here?"

I certainly was. "Let's take the stairs instead of Old Clunky," I said. "It's way faster."

Chapter 42

I enjoyed our walk to the hotel. It gave me a chance to spend some overdue one-on-one time with my part-time replacement. He asked good questions and made intelligent comments about WICH-TV, the broadcasting business in general, and about Salem. He turned out to have a quirky sense of humor and by the time we'd reached the corner of Essex Street any earlier awkwardness between us had dissolved. Laughing and chatting easily together, we entered the spacious and elegant Hawthorne lobby. Here Howard took the gentlemanly lead, explaining our mission to the manager and politely asking permission to check out the ballroom in preparation for the upcoming party.

The Hawthorne ballroom is often the venue of choice for wedding receptions, debutante presentations, big-bash birthday parties, meetings, and conferences, and of course, the world-famous Witches' Ball. Howard and I were immediately escorted to the elegant room by the event manager, a tall blonde named Willow. "There's a lot going on in here right now," she said, "what with the carpenters, the decorators, the caterers, the floral designers . . ." she waved an inclusive hand. "It looks a little chaotic I know, but believe me, we know what we're doing. Everything will be in place in a couple of hours." She consulted a clipboard. "I have your aunt's proposed layout here. It's pretty similar to what they're doing now." She pointed to a corner of the room where a stage was under construction. "Your stage will be a little smaller than this one with lower elevation. They come in various sizes—all prefabricated, quick to assemble. Come on. I'll show you." We followed, carefully threading our way between a row of cauldrons filled with fresh flowers and several long tables piled high with boxes overflowing with orange and black decorations. "Your party will have more tables and chairs than this one does. Mrs. Doan has arranged for a wonderful buffet meal. And wait 'til you see the cake! She designed it herself. The witch people prefer nibbling on appetizers, drinking, dancing, moving around in the room."

We'd reached the stage area, where workmen assembled prefitted dark-stained wooden panels, some with carved details. I could see how the finished product would look as though it had always been there. "Your stage will be about half the size of this one," Willow explained, "but it's just as pretty. You just have the one stage act. Jerry knows the layout."

I was surprised. "You know Jerry Mercury?"

"Sure. He's worked this room before. Corporate meetings, bar mitzvahs, kids' birthdays. Nothing recently though. It'll be good to see him." She led us around a pile of Styrofoam tombstones. "Come on. There's a little dressing room just behind the stage. Used to be a cloakroom back when the hotel had a hatcheck girl."

"Hatcheck girl?" Howard smiled that winning smile.

"Yep. That was then. Now we have coat racks with numbered hangers out in the lobby near the magazine stand. Nice matronly lady runs the stand and keeps track of the coats," Willow explained. "More efficient that way."

"I guess so." Howard's smile faded a bit. "We don't have a band either, huh?"

"Mrs. Doan has hired a wonderful organist. The organ will be to one side of the stage. You'll see. He makes that thing sound like an entire orchestra." We followed Willow into the cloakroom/dressing room. A faded sign read YOUR TIPS ARE APPRECIATED. Howard's smile was back and I guessed he was imagining a beautiful, scantily dressed hatcheck girl.

Willow opened a door at the end of the narrow room. "You see, it opens onto the lobby. Not an ideal setup if there's a play with a large cast or, God forbid, a kid's ballet recital, but for most events it's just fine." She pulled the door closed and we returned to the ballroom.

"I think this beautiful room with the little tables with fresh flower centerpieces and the Halloween decorations and the organ music is going to be just what Buffy—Mrs. Doan—has in mind," I said. "Do you agree, Howard?"

"I do," he said. "It looks as if you have everything under control, Willow. Thank you." He put a guiding hand under my elbow. "I think we have time for lunch at Nathaniel's, Lee," he said, steering me out into the lobby and toward the entrance to the hotel's popular restaurant. "My treat."

"I have something I've been dying to tell you," he said when we were seated and had ordered sandwiches and sodas. "I haven't even told Uncle Bruce or my parents yet. Can you keep a secret?"

I made a little cross on my lips with one finger. "Promise," I said.

"I've been sending all my tapes up to a little station in Maine. They've offered me a job."

"Oh, Howard. That's wonderful. I'm so happy for you!" *And for me too.* "Have you accepted?"

"I think I'm going to. It's not much more than an internship to start, but I'll get a little salary. Most of all, they don't have to hire me like Uncle Bruce did—because I'm a relative. They really want me."

"I hope you'll accept it, Howard. When can you start?"

"As soon as I can get there."

I think my fortune cookie dearest wish just came true. I'm going to get my job back! "I'll bet your parents will be pleased," I said.

"I'm not sure. My dad doesn't think being on TV is a *real* job. You know, like being a dentist or a stockbroker or something."

"You might not get rich," I said. "But doing what you love is important. Besides, some TV people do actually get rich. What does your dad do, by the way? I'm looking forward to meeting him."

"He used to be a lawyer. He's retired now. Spends most of his time on his collection."

"Oh yes. Rhonda told me. Sports memorabilia, isn't it?"

He smiled. "That Rhonda! She knows everything, doesn't she? Yes. Dad's really into collecting. He probably has one of the best collections of sports-related stuff in the country. Baseball especially."

I pushed a little. "Rhonda says he bought a Pete Rose rookie card recently."

"He was thrilled to get that. Expensive, but to him—it was worth it. I don't get it myself. You collect anything?"

"I have a little collection of NASCAR stuff," I said.

"No kidding? You like the car races? Me too." His eyes widened. "Wait a minute. Barrett. Johnny Barrett? You . . . ?"

"Right. Johnny was my husband."

"Oh, wow. My dad will be thrilled to meet you. He'll probably try to buy your collection."

"Not for sale," I said. "I understand your dad knew

Larry Laraby—one of the station's old-time sports announcers. Larry used to run collectibles shows all over the country."

"I wouldn't be surprised. Dad used to love those shows. Most of it is online now, though. You bid from home. Probably not as much fun as going to a show, I'll bet."

"I think you're right. Buying online is okay but I like to see what I'm buying, especially if it's expensive."

Howard looked around the restaurant and lowered his voice. "It's a good idea to know who you're buying from too. Dad had a chance not too long ago to buy a baseball card he's always wanted but he had to turn it down." He shook his head. "Dad called it 'the holy grail of baseball cards.'"

"A Honus Wagner, I'm guessing," I said. "Right?"

"Right. How'd you know?"

"I'm older than you," I said. "I know a little bit about a lot of things. How come he didn't buy it?" *Tell me it's the same card everybody is looking for.*

"The seller seemed kind of shady. Wanted cash and he didn't seem to plan on telling the IRS about it, if you know what I mean."

Sounds a lot like Wee Willie Wallace—with those greedy little robot hands reaching for money.

Chapter 43

Howard and I made it back to the station before our costume-shopping friends did, but only by a few minutes. We were still in the reception area when the four women, all smiles and giggles, tumbled from the elevator and joined us, each one laden down with bags and boxes.

"Did you find your four pairs of green whatevers?" I asked.

"Tights," Marty said. "Took us three stores but we got 'em."

Green tights? Are they going to be elves? Martians? No point in asking, I knew. I'd have to wait for the party.

Rhonda headed straight for her desk, piled her packages on one of the chrome chairs, and turned off the recorded greeting. "Doan isn't back from lunch yet, is he?" she whispered. "He likes the phones answered live." The phone in question rang immediately.

"WICH-TV," Rhonda said, "where Halloween is happening. Rhonda speaking. How may I direct your call?" There was a short pause. "Oh wow. Listen, you guys. Old Eddie and Scott are stuck in traffic over at Bertram Field and there's a truckload of pumpkins spilled all over the road blocking traffic both ways on Federal Street. We're the closest. You guys have to cover it. Francine? Howie? Lee? Marty? Somebody?"

"I've got it," Howard spoke first. "Come on, Francine. Let's grab a camera and the golf cart and get over there."

I looked at the sunburst clock. "It's after one," I said. "My shift." But I was speaking to three retreating backs as Francine, Howie, and Marty ran for the exit leading to the newsroom. Rhonda and Wanda looked at one another, then at me.

"I have to get changed for the afternoon weather spot." Wanda, still burdened with packages, beat a quick retreat back to the elevator.

Rhonda smiled, shrugged, and turned on the TV over her desk. "Oh well, if you snooze, you lose, Lee."

So much for the Kumbaya moments young Howie and I had shared in the morning. We were competitors in the field reporter business once again. I could only hope his coverage of the great smashed pumpkin saga would enhance his resumé for that Maine TV station.

I held out one hand to Rhonda. "Key to the dataport, please?" I figured I might as well get back to work on my old-time ads project. She dropped the key into my palm. "Don't worry," she said. "I heard he had an offer from some station up in Vermont."

"Maine," I said. "I'm pretty sure he's going to take it."

I hurried down to the studio, retrieved the files and printouts I'd left in the file cabinet, and climbed the stairs to the little sanctuary where I could pout in private—and hopefully, get some work done that would enhance *my* resumé. I was pretty sure that Mr. Doan, the sales department, and the ad clients would like my proposal. I decided to call it "Project: Yesterday." Subtitle: "Everything Old Is New Again."

It took almost all of the rest of the day, but by five o'clock I had a complete, illustrated, annotated, cost-projected advertising campaign proposal—complete with sample ad copy for each client, spiral binding, and plastic cover. My college advertising and promotion class professor would have been proud of me.

Tomorrow morning I will knock Bruce Doan's proverbial socks off with this.

It was with that positive attitude that I set off down Derby Street on my way home. On Hawthorne Boulevard, fantastically costumed people—fairies, elves, sprites, mermaids—were already lined up in front of the hotel in anticipation of the ball. Christopher Rich must have enjoyed excellent sales in his costume department. I decided to take the shortcut across the common, where speakers housed in the old bandstand blared spooky haunted house sound effects and a drum circle surrounding the structure kept time. What a noisy, crazy, colorful place my city is in October. *I wouldn't want to be anywhere else.*

My mind was busy as I walked past the playground swings, where costumed toddlers were being pushed by smiling moms and patient older siblings. I waved absently to Stasia, the pigeon lady, who wore jack-o'-lantern deely boppers over newly dyed pink hair. *I'll need a verbal pitch to go along with my presentation,* I thought. *I'll practice it on Aunt Ibby.* I would have liked Pete to hear it too, but I knew he'd be working overtime. I wanted to tell them both about Howard Senior's near miss at buying a Honus Wagner too.

I entered home through the Winter Street door, where O'Ryan—as usual—greeted me with delighted rubs and happy cat sounds. "Aunt Ibby," I called from the foyer, "I'm home. I have something to show you. Got a minute?"

"I'm in the kitchen," she answered. "Come on back. I'm watching something funny on TV."

"We're coming." I followed the cat across the living

room and into the bright, cheerful, and always good-smelling kitchen. My aunt sat at the round table, eyes focused on the TV.

"Look at this, Maralee," she said. "Did you ever see such a thing? The tailgate of that big truck popped open and about a thousand pumpkins rolled out onto Federal Street. Oh my goodness, what a squishy mess. Here. Sit down." She patted the back of the chair beside her. "The Templeton lad is so funny. Talking about making a world's record pumpkin pie with them or inviting the high school soccer team to kick them out of the way. He's really doing well, don't you think so?"

"Yes," I tried hard to sound enthusiastic. "Getting better all the time. He's been offered a job at a good station in Maine."

"I'll bet he's thrilled about that."

"He is," I said. "He told me all about it when he took me to lunch at Nathaniel's today."

"I'm glad to hear that, Maralee. I thought for a while you were a bit resentful about his taking on some of your responsibilities."

Who me? Resentful?

"Not at all," I lied. "It's given me a chance to develop some of the skills I haven't used lately. Like selling. I used to do a home shopping show in Miami, remember?"

"I do. You have many talents. I'm sure Bruce Doan recognizes that."

"I think he will tomorrow." I put my presentation folder on the table. "Ready to hear about my new idea for the station's anniversary?"

It took about an hour for her to see my work and to listen to the plan of action I had in mind. She closed the cover on the last page and leaned back in her chair. "It's perfectly wonderful, Maralee," she said, "and I'm not just saying that because I'm your aunt and I love you. But be careful. You know how Mr. Doan is. If you don't watch it, he'll probably want you to work in sales—along with being both field reporter and investigative reporter."

As usual, of course, she was absolutely right.

I was in bed that night by eleven, cozily tucked in with a warm cat curled up beside me, the TV tuned to the late news, listening to Buck Covington's soothing voice while a searchlight from the roof of the Hawthorne Hotel shone intermittent patterns on my kitchen windows and music from the bandstand on the common accompanied Buck's reading of the headlines. There were shots of beautifully costumed people at the ball and some more pictures of the pumpkin truck disaster. Buck said that Federal Street was such a mess that the city had changed the route of tomorrow night's scheduled Horribles Parade. Pete called to wish me a good night, and while the rest of Salem celebrated, I slept like the proverbial baby.

Chapter 44

On Wednesday morning I was only halfway through my verbal pitch when Mr. Doan sent Rhonda to Staples to make copies of the presentation for all of the station's sales staff. "How come you never told me you could do this stuff, Ms. Barrett?" he blustered, not waiting for an answer. "I'm asking all of the salespeople to join us. You do that pitch you gave me. Don't leave out the part where Katie the Clown has offered to do guest appearances. Get the other two to do commercials too, Ms. Barrett. The cowboy and the magician. I'm sure you can convince them."

And *voilà!* Like magic, my third WICH-TV hat was bestowed upon me. I wasn't required to actually make sales calls, but I was to be "invited" to attend weekly sales meetings. I was sure the "suggestion" that I get Ranger Rob and Jerry Mercury to cut commercials was meant seriously. Since I knew where to find Rob Oberlin and still had no idea where the professor hung his top hat (or his crown) I called the number for the Double R Riding Stables. Rob Oberlin answered the phone in that rich baritone voice I remembered from childhood. It occurred to me that even though his television career hadn't gone as planned, he could easily have transitioned into radio if he'd wanted to.

"Hello Ranger Rob—I mean, Mr. Oberlin. This is Lee Barrett."

"Of course. The pretty lady from WICH-TV. Are you ready to take me up on my offer to ride Prince Valiant?"

"Not quite yet, thank you," I said. "But I haven't forgotten about it. I'm calling about the anniversary celebration here at the station. Agnes has offered to cut some promotional commercials as Katie the Clown and Mr. Doan sees a tie-in with some of our long-time sponsors. I wonder if you'd be open to doing something similar. There'd be extra pay involved, naturally."

There was a pause. "I'll do it if I can wear my regular Western riding clothes I'm not dressing up like Mrs. Blatherflab, no matter what Doan wants to pay me." His voice became harsh. "Especially after what she did."

"What she did?"

"Mrs. Blatherflab. She killed somebody, you know. At least somebody wearing my costume did."

"I'm sure your regular clothes will be perfect. All of your old fans—like me—would know you anywhere. Don't worry about costumes at all."

"You'd recognize me? Really?"

"Of course," I said.

"Agnes thinks Jerry Mercury looks the same as ever," he said. "Jerry never drank or smoked like the rest of us. Worked out all the time. Biking, running, swimming, karate, body building. Thinks a lot of himself. Agnes thinks he had a face lift."

Karate? Does Pete know about that?

"I wouldn't know." I dodged the cosmetic surgery topic. "But speaking of Mr. Mercury, did you ever find that business card you said you had? I still don't have his telephone number."

"Wait a sec. I think I stuck it under my desk calendar." Pause. Sound of papers shuffling. "Yep. Here it is. He wrote a phone number on the back. Ready?"

Pen poised, I said, "Ready. Shoot." He recited a number with a local area code. "Thanks, Mr. Oberlin. Our audience is going to love seeing you again."

"Thanks for inviting me. And you come on over for that ride, hear?" I promised that I would and said goodbye, anxious to use that elusive number.

I was disappointed, but not surprised, when my call was answered with a recorded message. "Hello. You've reached the Magic King—Professor Jerry Mercury. Mystify your friends and business associates! The Magic King, master illusionist, is available for children's parties, trade shows, corporate events. A touch of magic makes any gathering more fun. Leave your name and number and the professor will return your call promptly."

I followed the instructions and left my cell number, hoping the reply would be prompt as promised. If I could offer all three of the station's long-ago top kid show performers delivering commercials for those loyal advertisers, I might add "sales promotion" to *my* resumé. I'd see the professor later at the party anyway, but he'd be up on stage and I'd just be one of the crowd. I hoped he'd call.

I checked Rhonda's white board to see if there was anything there for me. This close to Halloween there are so many citywide events going on, there's no way the station could cover all of them, along with the regular news, the traffic and weather spots, and the all-important commercials, but Rhonda had posted a list of "Halloween happenings."

"You can pretty much take your pick of those," Rhonda said. "Howie's been recruited to help his aunt with last-minute details for the party. Doan says we only need one from the list but you should stick around anyway in case of breaking news."

"No kidding?" I moved in for a closer look at the list. "How about this one? Last-minute costumes at Christopher's Castle. Francine and I could walk over to his shop."

"Good choice. He's an advertiser. Takes all the free publicity he can get."

"I know. Is Francine in yet?"

"She'll be along in a few minutes. She's back at the apartment sewing initials on head scarfs."

"I guess I'm not allowed to ask what that means, am I?"

"Nope. I'll ask Marty to get her shopping cart ready to carry the camera and sound gear over to Chris's shop."

"Good idea. I'll call Chris and tell him we're coming," I said, "but if anything more interesting shows up, let us know."

Nothing more interesting *did*—no overturned pumpkin trucks or police department press conferences—so within half an hour Marty, Francine, and I were trundling the official WICH TV decorated shopping cart along the Essex Street pedestrian mall toward Christopher's Castle. The weather was pleasant, and we were met with the smiles we generally encountered whenever we used the unusual but efficient mode of transporting our gear when driving was out of the question.

I tried without success to get the two to tell me what the green tights and initialed head scarves indicated and admitted willingly that my costume required little imagination. "A cowgirl," I said. "From some movie called *Bad Girls*."

"Is Pete going as a cowboy?" Francine asked.

"No. He's going to rent something."

Chris, naturally, was delighted to see us. "Business has been fabulous!" he gushed. "Between the regular Halloween costumes—you know, like Spiderman and Wonder Woman and Princess Ariel—and the beautiful high-end fantasy outfits like everyone wore last night at the Witches' Ball, well I couldn't ask for more! And now another big party coming tomorrow night. Life is sweet."

The shoot went smoothly. Chris had rounded up a few regular customers to serve as models and did most of his own narration. I introduced him, asked a few questions as women and teens paraded back and forth in front of the David Copperfield photo dressed as witches and fairies, princesses and vampires. I thanked Chris for sharing his beautiful costumes with the viewers and did the usual sign-off. While Francine disconnected Chris's mic, I began putting equipment into the cart. "By the way, Lee," Chris said, "thanks for sending Pete Mondello in. He stopped by earlier and picked out his costume for the Doans' party. With that dark hair and brown eyes he makes a *fabulous* Lawrence of Arabia."

Quick mental picture. *I'll just bet he does!*

Chapter 45

Once back at the station I checked the white board again. Nothing had changed. I asked Rhonda for the dataport key again. I planned to call Pete about Jerry Mercury possibly knowing karate. I liked the privacy of the dataport for phone calls.

"Rob Oberlin told me that Jerry Mercury knows karate," I told him. "I don't know if he's a black belt or anything like that but I thought I'd better tell you."

"Thanks, babe. It's good that you keep your eyes and ears open around there. But be careful. Remember, none of the people you deal with every day are officially murder suspects, but both the TV station and the library have 'persons of interest' wandering around freely."

"I'm always careful," I said, "but I'm glad you worry about me. Makes me feel safe."

"I feel as though I should be there to protect you all the time."

"My own personal Lawrence of Arabia," I said.

"Chris told you!"

"Of course he did! We did a little costume fashion

shoot there this morning. You know Chris. Not much for keeping secrets."

"I'm going over to my sister Marie's before I pick you up so she can help me get into it," he said. "Miles of white cloth and a fancy headpiece with sides that drop down and a fake dagger stuck in a waist sash thing."

"I can hardly wait to see you in it. Chris says you look *fabulous!*" (That comment brought the expected snort of denial.) "My costume is easy. Jeans, boots, plaid shirt, and a cowgirl hat. What time should I be ready?"

"Around eight, I guess. I've got a friend right around the corner from the hotel who says we can park in his yard, so we won't have a parking problem."

"Good deal. I'll be getting out of here by five. See you soon."

There wasn't a great deal of productive work getting done at WICH-TV. It was like being in school on the afternoon of prom night. Mr. Doan left right after lunch. Howie hadn't been in at all. Wanda taped all of her forecasts for the whole day, changing outfits in between each one. Marty, as usual, stayed busy and Rhonda answered the phone whenever it rang, but there was a general feeling of "let's get out of here!"

At four thirty, with nothing new on the white board, Rhonda suggested that I might as well go home, since I had to walk all the way to Winter Street. She and Marty and Wanda and Francine just had to go to nearby Hawthorne Boulevard and Mr. Doan had said they could use the golf cart for transportation to and from the party.

Aunt Ibby wasn't at home when I got there. I let myself in through the back door, accepted and returned O'Ryan's loving greetings, and climbed the twisty stairs to my quiet apartment. I'd already hung faded jeans, plaid shirt, and red neckerchief on my bedroom closet door. Newly polished boots were next to my bed and my trusty old cowgirl hat was on top of the bureau. Wardrobe ready,

I had plenty of time to fool around with hair and makeup. I even treated myself to a long, luxurious bubble bath. By seven, with hair washed, curls tamed, eyes and lips carefully made up, I was ready to don my Bad Girl Western outfit.

What did those cowgirls do that was so bad? I must ask Aunt Ibby.

I dressed, pulled on the boots, and placed the hat at just the right angle, then stood in front of the long oval mirror in my bedroom to check out the effect. Quite Western, I decided, giving the red neckerchief a tweak. I transferred wallet, phone, comb, and lip gloss into a tiny tooled leather handbag, tossed a denim jacket over my shoulders, and went downstairs to get Aunt Ibby's approval.

"It's just perfect, Maralee," she said. "All you need is a horse. You know you really should take Rob Oberlin up on his offer of Prince Valiant."

"I intend to," I said, "and just wait until you see Pete's costume. He could use a horse too."

"Oh, a cowboy?"

"Nope. Far more literary. You'll see."

O'Ryan announced Pete's arrival by ducking through the cat door into the back hall. I pulled the kitchen door open so Pete would know I was at Aunt Ibby's instead of upstairs. When Pete stepped inside, O'Ryan stopped short, sat, and stared at the man. Chris was right.

Fabulous.

"Wow," I said.

"Let me get my camera," Aunt Ibby said.

"I feel like a damned fool," Pete said, but he agreed to pose with me for a few pictures. By then, O'Ryan had overcome his initial surprise at seeing this stranger in white robes, and joined us at the foot of the front stairs, which has always been my aunt's favorite spot for photos.

Photo session over, Aunt Ibby and O'Ryan escorted us

to the back door and stood in the doorway together. "Have a wonderful time," my aunt said. "You both look great."

"Oh, Aunt Ibby," I said. "Exactly what did the bad girls *do* to earn the name, in case anyone asks?"

"They were—um—ladies of the evening. Have fun, you two!" She closed the door.

"Maybe you'd better claim to be Dale Evans or Annie Oakley," Pete said, managing a straight face. We climbed into the Crown Vic, taking the long way around Washington Square, arriving at Pete's friend's place with remarkably little trouble, and proceeded on foot toward the hotel.

A uniformed doorman admitted guests, checking names against a list. There were several people ahead of us, sporting a colorful a variety of costumes. But it wasn't difficult to identify my four co-workers, Francine, Wanda, Marty, and Rhonda. From green tights to green-painted faces, they were unquestionably the Teenage Mutant Ninja Turtles.

"Lee! Pete!" The turtle with the purple headband extended green-gloved hands and executed a 360-degree turn, displaying a nicely detailed oval shell. "What d'ya think?"

"Amazing," I said. "If you guys don't win the prize, there's just no justice."

"You're Donatello, right Marty?" Pete said. "The smart turtle."

"Right," she said. The other three, Wanda with an orange headband, Francine with blue, and Rhonda with red, gathered around us, all talking and laughing at once.

Pete pointed to the three, one at a time. "Michelangelo, Leonardo, Raphael."

"How do you know?" I asked, seriously impressed.

"Two nephews," he said. "You can tell the turtles apart

by the headbands. I've seen all the movies, read all the comic books."

The line moved forward. Our names were duly checked off the list and we, along with our turtle friends, joined the festivities. Organ music soared. Willow had been right. It sounded like a whole orchestra. The buffet table was almost embarrassingly sumptuous. People danced, glasses clinked. The undercurrent of conversation and muted laughter was at a perfect level—pleasant, unobtrusive. This had all the makings of a truly great party.

"Excuse me, babe," Pete said. "I need to take a walk around the room every once in a while. Just checking things out. I'll be back in a few minutes."

"No problem," I said. "I'm not going anywhere." I gave him a smile and a little wave.

When Professor Mercury made his entrance into the hall, it was pretty spectacular. A drum roll sounded, loud enough to silence conversation and turn heads toward the stage. There was a crackling noise, a flash of brilliant light, a puff of sulfurous smoke, then the shimmering glitter of what looked like a thousand Fourth of July sparklers. From the center of this circle of manufactured fire and brimstone strode the professor, looking very much like the cartoon magician pictured on Jerry Mercury's business card—tuxedo, cape, white gloves, even the gold crown instead of a top hat. He carried a magic wand too. Spontaneous applause rose from the audience and many of the guests left their tables and moved toward the stage.

When the silver curtains behind the magician parted and the organist began to play some appropriate background music, I found myself standing in the front row. In tweed, with tousled hair and tragic expression, Christopher Rich as Heathcliff stood on one side of me with my four turtle friends in a bright green row on the other.

"See the tall black box behind him?" Chris whispered, a little more loudly than necessary. "He bought it from me. Absolutely top quality. It's for the disappearing woman trick. Same one Criss Angel uses."

"Expensive, huh?" Marty whispered back.

"Oh, yes indeed." Chris was obviously proud of his connection to the star of Buffy Doan's show. "Nothing but the best for Jerry Mercury these days."

On stage, Jerry Mercury produced a long-stemmed rose—seemingly from thin air—and with his other hand pointed the wand off stage. With a nod to the audience, and amidst another burst of applause, Buffy Doan, as Cinderella, magnificent in purple chiffon and clear plastic pumps, walked toward him. With a broad gesture, he held the rose toward her and, as we all watched, the single rose became a full bouquet. Amazing! I could smell the roses. They were clearly real, not the crepe paper kind he'd produced for Tyler in the library.

"For our lovely and gracious hostess," he declared, handing her the flowers. Buffy, blushing, accepted the bouquet, and with a smile, and amidst more applause, left the stage and joined her husband and the Templetons. The magician crossed the stage, passing just in front of us, and gestured toward the table where the Doans and Templetons sat, and once again pointed the wand. "Howard Templeton Jr. is our guest of honor this hallowed evening," he said. "Come on up and join me, young man. Howard is a rising star in the television industry," Mercury announced, as Howie, dressed as Robin Hood, hurried toward the stage.

"Rising star, my butt," I heard Rhonda, aka Raphael, mutter. "The kid's still wet behind the ears."

"Professor Mercury hasn't lost his touch," I said. "In fact I think he's even better than he was back when he was on TV. More professional."

Chris nodded agreement. "He doesn't just do kid shows, you know. He gets plenty of corporate meetings, private parties like this one."

"I don't like him." Wanda-Michelangelo spoke softly, but firmly. "Don't like him one bit."

"Who?" Marty-Donatello asked. "Howie or Mercury?"

"Mercury, of course. Howie is sweet. Mercury is bad news." Wanda sounded positive.

"You know Jerry?" Chris Rich asked.

The "M" on Wanda's orange head scarf wobbled back and forth as she shook her head. "Nope."

"She doesn't *have* to know him," Rhonda put in. "Wanda knows *men*!"

Marty agreed. "Meteorology and men. Wanda knows 'em."

On stage, with Howard Jr. as his willing assistant, Jerry Mercury proceeded to dazzle Buffy's grown-up party guests with a barrage of astonishing card tricks and sleight-of-hand magic. I remembered how those long-ago TV shows had mesmerized me, along with the rest of Professor Mercury's vast audience of children, as he and his robot, Marvel, had used magic tricks to open to us the world of science. Pete managed to blend his cop-at-a-party obligation with his escort-of-a-bad-cowgirl duties, appearing at my side every so often with the occasional glass of punch or whispered "I love you."

The magician handed Howie a dollar bill, had him write his name on it and put it into an envelope, then put the envelope onto a chair and sit on it. Then, with a flourish, he pulled what appeared to be an egg from behind Howie's ear, tapped it with the wand. He handed the sitting man a bowl. "Crack the egg, Howard," he instructed. "Be careful not to get any on that nice costume." Howard did as he was told and—of course—the egg contained the signed dollar bill and the envelope on the chair seat was empty. For nearly an hour, Jerry Mercury performed trick after trick. Howard Junior's face reflected the happy wonder of a six-year-old. Probably all of our faces did. The professor hadn't lost his touch.

"For my final illusion of the evening," he announced, "I'm going to attempt something I've never tried before." With the wand, he gestured toward a tall black box. "I recently purchased this most amazing and miraculous item from my friend Christopher Rich. Chris, as you may know, is purveyor of all things magical, a personal friend of the great David Copperfield."

Chris, publicity lover that he is, dropped his sad Heathcliff face, beamed, turned to face the crowd, and lifted both arms in the air. "He's going to do the disappearing woman act," he said. "You just watch."

"I know how it works." Wanda shrugged, managing to make the motion look graceful even under her green turtle shell. "I moonlighted as a magician's assistant for a while when I was in college. I was really skinny then. Got to wear some super cute tiny little outfits. There's a false bottom in the thing. I don't think I could fit in it now though. I'm sure Howie can't. Just watch. He'll ask for a volunteer. There's probably a ringer in the crowd. You watch."

"A ringer?" I asked.

"A shill. A setup. Somebody he's rehearsed," she said. "You'll see."

I watched—and was not prepared for what happened next. The magician pointed that magic wand at me. Those piercing blue eyes focused on mine. "Yes. You. The cute little cowgirl. Come on up and join me, young lady."

I handed my purse to the closest turtle and felt myself walking toward the stage, climbing the two steps up, reaching for Professor Mercury's extended hand. He continued to hold my hand, pulling me across the stage until we stood together in front of the black box. "What's your name?" he asked.

"Maralee," I heard myself say. "Maralee Kowalski."

From that moment on, the night of Buffy's Halloween party was like an out-of-body experience. I was aware of what I was doing. I walked and talked, responded to the professor. Although my thought process was that of thirty-three-year-old Lee Barrett, my responses, my voice, my actions were that of six-year-old Maralee—and little Maralee was thrilled beyond belief to be one of the kids on Professor Mercury's TV show.

"Ready to go on a magical trip, Maralee?" Jerry Mercury asked.

"Oh, yes," Maralee answered, clapping her hands together. *My hands. But I can't control them. What's going on?*

Maralee's gaze was fixed on the professor's face. His eyes. *I don't want to see his eyes. I can't look away.*

Howard Templeton Jr. stood beside the professor. Maralee didn't recognize him and tried to hide behind Jerry Mercury. "This is my friend Howard," Jerry Mercury pulled me forward, keeping those eyes fixed on mine. Naturally Howard looked confused. *I know perfectly well who Howard is and he knows me.*

"Okay," said Maralee.

No. This is not okay. Make it stop.

I saw the door to the black box swing open. "Step right in here, young lady," he said.

No! I don't want to!

"Okay," said Maralee. She smiled with my lips. Stepped into the box with my feet. My legs.

"Don't worry," the professor said. "I'm coming with you."

No! Let me out!

"Okay." Maralee reached for his hand.

He pushed me to one side and crowded in beside me. "Howard," he said. "I want you to close the door of the box. Turn it around once. Go to the front of the stage and close the silver curtains behind you. Then you and the audience must count slowly to thirty. Got it?"

Howard said, "Yes."

"At the count of thirty, you tell them this pretty little cowgirl and I will reappear in an amazing way. Then open the curtain, give the box one more spin, and open it. If I do this correctly, the box will be empty and the reveal will be worthy of Houdini!"

A turtle wearing an orange headband started toward the stage. "No, Lee!" the turtle shouted.

"Hello turtle!" Maralee called in delight. Howard closed the door to the box and the professor put his hand over Maralee's mouth. *My mouth*. The box began to turn. The audience sounded far away. I heard them begin a slow count. "One . . . Two . . . Three . . ."

The professor opened the black box door and climbed out, pulling the child with him into the offstage dressing room. "Shhh, Maralee." He put a finger up to his lips. "We're going to play a good trick on them. Come along and be quiet."

She followed the man through another door and straight into the hotel lobby. Far away, she heard the count. "Nine . . . Ten . . . Eleven . . ."

"Put your jacket on, Maralee," the professor ordered. "It's getting cold outside."

"Okay," Maralee held her arms—*my arms*—out awkwardly. The man lifted the jacket from her shoulders and put her arms into the sleeves, one at a time.

A bell man greeted us. "Show over already, Mr. Mercury?"

"Not yet," Jerry Mercury said. "Intermission. We're just sneaking outside for a smoke."

"I understand. Need any help with anything?"

"No thanks. We've got it."

I need help! Please!

"We've got it," Maralee repeated.

"Too early to bring the cake in, I guess." The bell man pointed to a huge gingerbread house on a wheeled trolley. "See? It's the evil witch's house from Hansel and Gretel. Perfect for a storybook Halloween party, huh? Mrs. Doan designed it herself."

"Perfect." The professor grasped the man's arm, looking into his eyes. "Forget that you saw us. I'm not supposed to be smoking. Come on, Maralee." But she lagged behind, fascinated by the cake. He tugged at her hand, a little roughly. *Maralee doesn't like being pulled away from the wonderful cake.* She shoves her free hand into her jacket pocket. *My hand. My jacket pocket.*

The stale cinnamon bun was still in that pocket. I'd meant to throw it away. But little Maralee, with childlike imagination, had a better idea. "Come on, Maralee," the man said. "We have to run. The car is just across the street."

Hansel and Gretel had dropped bread crumbs in the forest so that they could find their way home. Maralee began to crumble the bun.

Chapter 46

Maralee concentrated on dropping crumbs. Three steps across the hotel lobby's plush carpet and a crumb. Three more steps and another crumb. And another and another. Once outside, she dropped crumbs on the front steps. The sidewalk. The man pulled her along as they crossed Essex Street to a darkened parking lot. Maralee hesitated. *She's afraid of the dark.* The man pulled her hand harder. Her other hand was busy crumbling the stale bun as she counted—one, two, three.

Will the birds come and eat the crumbs? Maralee thought.

No. The birds are all asleep in their nests. I thought. *Keep dropping the crumbs.*

Okay. Maralee thought. *But my crumbs are almost all gone.*

"Here we are. Get in." The man opened the passenger door of the green Subaru. "Come on. Hurry." He pushed her into the seat, reached across and buckled the seat belt. "We're going for a nice ride." He leaned over, those strange eyes focused on Maralee's. "When I let you out of the car you will not remember this ride. You will not remember me being here with you. Same as before. You will not remember me this time either. You understand?"

"Okay." Maralee scattered the remaining crumbs onto the ground an instant before he closed the car door.

Before? I will not remember him this time? The same as before?

I felt the child begin to relax against the seat. She was sleepy. If child-me fell asleep would she lose contact with adult-me? I decided to try the thought-contact again, just in case I was about to lose her. *What happened the other time?* I thought.

He told the lady, she thought. *Not me. The lady in the bad book place. He told her but I was listening. I always listen when the lady is scared.* She yawned and closed her eyes. My eyes. *Good night,* she thought.

I forced her eyes—my eyes—open. Jerry Mercury was in the driver's seat and the Subaru's engine had growled to life. He eased the car out of the lot and onto the street. I couldn't feel Maralee in my mind any more. Had Jerry Mercury told *me* to forget something that had happened in the stacks? The murder of Wee Willie Wallace? I *must* have seen him up there.

I don't remember. I don't remember it at all.

The professor looked left, then right. Lighted floats, costumed kids pulling costumed younger siblings in decorated wagons, a bagpiper, a Spiderman on horseback, a drum and bugle band—crowded lower Essex Street. "What the hell is going on here?" he blew the horn, signaled for a turn onto the boulevard.

It's the rerouted Horribles Parade, I thought, but couldn't speak

I decided I'd better not let him know that Maralee had figuratively left the building. Since her conversations with him so far had been pretty much limited to "Okay," I was quite sure I could maintain the child persona if I had to. I closed my eyes, avoiding his, and tried to figure out why he'd chosen to hypnotize the child in the first place.

Maralee! It was the name on the temporary volunteer nametag. He must have used it and the frightened child in the stacks had responded. So where were we going? And why did he want me to go with him wherever it was he was headed?

It occurred to me then that if he thought I had witnessed what had happened that day in the stacks, I was a danger to him. If he'd somehow hypnotized the adult me along with the child, how could he be sure I wouldn't someday remember it all?

There was, I realized, only one way he'd be absolutely sure of that. I would have to disappear along with him. I stirred and rubbed my eyes.

Even with my eyes closed I could tell that we were making very slow progress. The windows of the Subaru were closed but the sound of Halloween eve revelers on the streets of the Witch City told me it would take a while for Jerry Mercury to make his "getaway" if that's what this was supposed to be. Didn't he *know* he was in the middle of the annual Horribles Parade?

He doesn't watch the news! He said so. He doesn't know about the squashed pumpkins, the rerouted parade.

Back at the hotel Howard would have opened the doors of the black box by now. As far as the audience was concerned, the cowgirl and the magician had disappeared and Howard would have informed them that they should watch for the two to appear in an amazing way. They'd be expecting a Phantom of the Opera appearance of the two of us swinging over their heads from a chandelier or maybe they'd think that we'd pop out of the damned gingerbread cake. Meanwhile we'd be winding our way through the crowded streets in the most ubiquitous of cars. By the time

Pete and the others figured it out Mercury could be long gone. And me along with him.

"Lee Barrett." The magician spoke suddenly. "Can you hear me?"

"Yes," I said.

"Look at me."

No. I don't want to. But I turned toward him anyway and looked directly into those awful eyes.

"You are relaxed, Lee. You feel comfortable here with me. I am a wealthy, attractive man and you are pleased that we are taking a trip together."

In my mind, Maralee began to sing. "Old MacDonald had a farm . . ." I lost my focus on what Jerry was saying—concentrating instead on Maralee's song.

"Why are we moving so slowly?" I heard my words, slightly slurred. Maralee sang "with a moo-moo here and a moo-moo there . . ."

The professor frowned. "Traffic. We'll be out of it in just a minute. You are happy that we're taking a trip." He tapped the horn, losing eye contact for a brief instant.

"Ring around the rosy, a pocket full of posies . . ." Maralee's singing in my mind grew louder.

"It wasn't hard at all for me to do it—and to arrange all this," he said, and reached for my hand.

Don't touch me. I couldn't pull my hand away. "This old man, he played one . . ." Maralee sang.

"I'm sure no ordinary man could have pulled it off." His smile was nearly as chilling as those eyes. "You're proud of me, aren't you?"

"Proud of you," I repeated. *Keep singing, Maralee. Don't stop. You're keeping me from falling into his terrible eyes.*

"Want to know how I did it?"

"Proud of you," I said again, still unable to form words of my own that made sense. "Jesus loves me, this I know . . ." Maralee's voice was strong and joyous.

"Of course you're proud of me." He patted his breast pocket. "You'll be even prouder when I collect one and a half million tax-free dollars for this."

"For the card?" The words were mine, still slurred, as though I was drunk.

"You saw me take it away from him, didn't you? Doesn't matter now. Nobody believed the card was real in the first place." He leaned on the horn. "Get out of my way, you morons!" he shouted, then lowered his voice again. "I know it's worth more than a million and a half, but Willie's contact isn't exactly a solid citizen. Big drug kingpin. Anyway, Willie'd already made the deal. The customer is paying cash. It'll fit in a suitcase." He shook his head. "Imagine that. A million and a half dollars in a suitcase. All I had to do was follow him into the library and take the card away from him. At first he didn't want to give it to me."

He laughed then. A terrible, crazy, high-pitched giggle. "Poor Willie. He used to let me practice my hypnosis on him back when he was Marvel the Robot. Willie did all the work on finding the card for me, you know. After he messed up and killed Laraby for nothing, the little runt even went down to Palm Beach to see if Larry's wife still had the books." Another giggle. "Told her he was a book collector but she didn't have them anymore. Said she was leaving them all to her daughter." He frowned then, an angry grimace. "Stupid bastard broke into the daughter's house," he growled. "Got nothing." He pounded on the horn again, and Maralee sang, "The wheels on the bus go round and round . . ."

"Willie was such an easy subject to hypnotize." Mercury's voice returned to its normal pitch. "He really thought this was all his own idea. He thought that he'd find the card and sell it and be rich. I walked up to him in the library, said the magic words, and he just handed over Larry's book and told me where to deliver the card. Then

I had to kill him." He sounded pleased with himself. "I haven't lost my touch," he bragged. "The only thing that could have screwed it up was a witness remembering what happened to Willie." He smiled that chilling smile. "I was pretty sure you recognized me up there in the stacks. Then when you saw me again, when I followed you to the grocery store and you took off like a scared rabbit, I was sure of it. Problem solved. I have the card—and the witness. Couldn't take the chance that you'd remember what happened that night. You won't remember any of this conversation either. Too bad. Anyway, there's a private jet waiting at the Beverly airport. We'll be on our way out of the country while they're all still back there anticipating a big reveal!" He patted my knee. "Want to know how I disabled the alarm system?"

I really did want to know that. "Okay," I said.

"It was brilliant, wasn't it?" He didn't wait for an answer. "You said you were a fan of my TV show. Don't you remember the many magnet experiments I taught you? The alarm system on the emergency door operates on a simple magnetic principle." He sounded exactly as he had on those long-ago science shows. Friendly and kind. "Whenever the magnetic connection is broken by opening the door, the alarm is triggered. All I had to do was bypass the alarm sensor. And how, my little student, did I do that? Hmmmm?" He fixed those eyes on mine.

"I don't know," I mumbled. "How?"

"You disappoint me." He pinched my leg. A hard pinch. "A simple strip of foil—a candy wrapper from the bowl of Halloween treats someone thoughtfully placed in the children's media center—a strip of foil pressed in exactly the right spot, between the magnetic connectors basically does the same job that the connectors do. As long as the foil contacts the right spot the alarm will not be triggered."

"But then . . . ?"

"So. You remember my lesson. Good." He patted my knee again. "You're wondering if the alarm would sound if I released pressure on the foil. Of course it would. But what if I reached down with my free hand and simply removed the ordinary battery which powers the sound? So brilliant!" He laughed again. "I closed the door, replaced the battery, changed into Mrs. Blatherflab, and walked right out." His smirk was self-satisfied and evil at the same time. Like the wicked queen when she hands Snow White that apple.

What about me? Are you going to have to kill me eventually too?

By then Maralee was fairly shouting the *SpongeBob SquarePants* theme song. She'd turned her head—my head—away from Jerry Mercury. I looked out the window. Moving at what was surely less than twenty miles an hour, we passed scores of people, mostly in costume, dozens of floats, mostly lighted, crowding the street, overflowing onto the sidewalk. "The side-view mirror gave me a partial view of the vehicle directly behind us.

Oh my god! Am I seeing what I think I'm seeing? Or is this one of those maddening mirror-visions?

It wasn't a vision. It was real. In any other time, in any other place, what I saw in that mirror would have attracted plenty of attention. But in Salem, Massachusetts, on the night before Halloween, in the Horribles Parade, four Ninja Turtles and Lawrence of Arabia riding in a pink-and-white golf cart drew barely a passing glance.

The golf cart picked up speed until it was almost beside the Subaru. "Hello, Turtles," I called, tapping on the closed window. Jerry Mercury hit the horn again.

"What the hell is going on?" he demanded. He rolled down the window. "Get out of my way, you fools!"

The golf cart kept coming, crowding the Subaru against the curb. Mercury leaned on the horn. Somebody pounded on the trunk. "Slow down, you jerk!"

"What's going on here?" He looked at me.

"Parade," I said in my own voice.

Mercury brought the car to a stop. "We'll have to wait until it passes by. Shouldn't take long."

The turtle in the driver's seat pulled the golf cart ahead, blocking the Subaru's way. The four turtles scattered.

Lawrence of Arabia flashed a badge and a gun.

Jerry Mercury shut off the engine, turned and glared at me. "You won't remember," he said and got out of the car, his hands above his head.

Maralee sang "Row, row, row your boat . . ."

Epilogue

If I ever have grandkids, this'll be for sure a story to tell them—about the time one Halloween eve in Salem, Massachusetts, when Grandma was saved from a mad magician by the four Ninja Turtles and Lawrence of Arabia.

After Pete arrested Jerry Mercury, and a patrol car took the magician away in handcuffs, I sat alone in the passenger seat of the Subaru, confused and unsure of exactly what had just gone down. Wanda was the first person to reach me. She pulled the door open.

"Are you okay, Lee? Jesus. What was he trying to do?" Eyes wide in her green face, with a green gloved hand she gently released my seat belt. "I yelled at you. Tried to stop you. I knew the trick was going wrong." She hugged me. "But we followed your bread crumbs. Called Pete."

"You called Pete," I said in my own voice.

Pete, minus his Arabian desert headgear, reached across Wanda's shell. "Let's get you out of here, babe," he said, taking both of my hands in his and pulling me to my feet. The turtles gathered around, shielding me from the curious stares of a costumed crowd gone suddenly silent.

Next was a ride in a police car, sirens screaming, through the darkened streets of Salem. Pete stayed with me while I gave my statement to the police stenographer. I hoped the things I said made sense. It turned out that what I remembered, along with what Jerry Mercury confessed to, was enough to solve our locked room mystery after all.

First, let me admit that I do not remember seeing Jerry Mercury in the stacks that day, although, according to him, I did see him, and recognized him too. Perhaps somewhere, deep in my subconscious, six-year-old Maralee remembers. Maybe someday I will too.

According to Mercury, it was Willie's idea to steal the Honus Wagner card from Larry Laraby. He knew Larry kept the thing in a book about baseball. Willie had some pretty unsavory friends and one of them had offered Willie a lot of money if he could get it. So Willie pretended to have a signed Mark McGwire homerun ball, and went to the Laraby house to make the sale, then threatened Larry with a gun. When Laraby laughed at him, called him a no-talent little runt, Willie got angry and killed him with a single blow to the back of his head. Willie searched among the baseball books, looking for the card, but gave up and ducked out the back door when he heard Larry's wife coming. Everyone was convinced that Larry had fallen from his library ladder. So the no-talent little runt got away with murder. That's Mercury's story anyway.

After that, the professor got interested in having that card, and selling it for big bucks himself. He "programmed" Willie to keep trying and gave him a secret telephone number to call as soon as he found it. Willie became totally obsessed with getting that card. He even followed Mrs. Laraby to Florida, pretending to be a book collector.

When Willie found out that Larry's books were still in Massachusetts he came home to try again. Another fouled-up attempt, but because of a small square picture of Larry, he was pretty sure he'd figured out which book he should be looking for. He already had some practice in pretending to be a book collector. He simply knocked on Sharon's door one day and asked if she had any sports books to sell. "Oh no," she said. "I gave them all to the library." Easy-peasy. He made that phone call to the professor.

Mercury sneaked into Agnes's utility room and grabbed the old lady outfit along with Abe Lincoln's beard. He stuffed dress, hat, satchel, and all into his backpack and followed Willie to the library. I was able to fill the police in on what Mercury had told me about how the whole upstairs-downstairs change of characters thing worked.

Wanda had spotted trouble with the disappearing woman trick right away and had hurried backstage trying to find me. Everybody thought the idea of dropping crumbs to let the people know where I'd gone was brilliant. I couldn't figure out how to tell them that leaving the crumbs was Maralee's idea—that it never would have occurred to me in a million years. I haven't told anyone about her singing either.

The plans for the WICH-TV anniversary celebration are continuing on schedule. Agnes and Rob have been rehearsing together and it looks as though they may be an item again. Young Howard has taken the offer from that station in Maine and my regular hours will resume shortly. My investigative report on the murder in the stacks has drawn some national attention and a couple of job offers for me too. I've decided to stay where I am. "Bloom where you're planted," as Aunt Ibby says.

I never did make that flowchart. In the first place, I didn't have a big enough white board to fit all the names and anyway I wasn't quite sure about which name should be at the top.

There was some controversy over what to do with the Honus Wagner card. Sharon Laraby Stewart settled the question. She said that she'd given that copy of *The Boys of Summer* to the library and as far as she was concerned, that included whatever was in it. (I guess that explains the "unexpected inheritance" River saw in my reading.) The card will be auctioned soon and Aunt Ibby is pretty sure the proceeds will pay for someone to do all that pesky copying and filing of old paperwork, and might just buy the library another much-needed bookmobile.

RECIPE

Aunt Ibby's Chicken à la King

1 cup sliced mushrooms (or one 4.5-ounce can
    mushrooms)
½ cup chopped green pepper
6 tbsp. butter
6 tbsp. flour
1 tsp. salt
⅛ tsp. pepper
1½ cups well-seasoned chicken broth (Aunt Ibby uses
    Progresso Tuscany Chicken Broth)
1 cup light cream
sherry (optional)
1 cup cut-up cooked chicken
¼ cup chopped pimento

Cook and stir mushrooms and green pepper in butter over medium heat for five minutes. Remove from heat. Blend in flour, salt, and pepper. Cook over low heat, stirring constantly until mixture is bubbly.

Remove from heat. Stir in chicken broth and cream. (Sometimes Aunt Ibby also adds a splash of sherry.) Heat to boiling, stirring constantly. Boil and stir for about a minute. Stir in chicken and pimento. Heat through.

Serve hot in patty shells, or over biscuits or toast points.

Acknowledgments

I want to acknowledge special people from my past who nurtured and influenced my writing journey far more than any of them ever knew. Those mentioned here have passed on. River North might say they've gone to the Summerland.

First, the teachers. Seventh and eighth grade at the Pickering Grammar School in Salem gave me virtually all of the basic tools I'd need to be a writer. I'm forever grateful for those years of memorizing grammar rules and diagramming sentences under the tutelage of English teacher Anne Berry, and the extraordinary introduction to fine literature, poetry, and classical music given by Claire Davis. At Salem High School Valentina Glebow deftly, lovingly presented me with Shakespeare and Joe Lyons made me work extremely hard to eke out an A in his English class, teaching me much needed discipline. Librarian Dorothy Annable recognized and encouraged the budding writer.

My first job was as a thirteen-year-old docent at the Ropes Mansion in Salem. Director Nellie Messer gave me real appreciation for Salem's rich history and fostered a lifelong love of antiques. Mary Mason hired me for my second job in the Old Salem Bookstore. I worked there all through high school and what a fabulous environment it was for a voracious young reader. After my freshman year at Boston University, Florence Gilmore, advertising manager for the Pickering Fuel Company in Salem, took a leap of faith and hired nineteen-year-old me as her assistant and taught me the economy of words it takes to write ad copy. Later, Bill Brown, CEO of Brown's of Gloucester, hired me as advertising and sales promotion manager of that grand old department store, where I worked and learned for more than a decade. When we moved to Madeira Beach, Florida, I applied for work at Aden Advertising, a small agency located right on the beach. Ray Aden hired me. I learned to write and design restaurant menus and motel brochures. Ray taught me how to call on the client and actually sell the idea. For the first time I learned to do the face-to-face sales pitch—a good thing to know when meeting agents and editors at writers' conferences.

Instructor of my first writing/critique group was professor Larry Holcomb in Rockport, Massachusetts, where I studied with some wonderfully talented authors, and later, when I moved to Florida I joined another writing group headed by Martha Monigle, who became teacher, friend, and mentor, guiding me to my first published magazine articles and the sales of my first books.

My aunt Carrie Russell and my ex-mother-in-law, Isobel "Ibby" Hill—two strong and beautiful red-haired women—became the models for Lee's Aunt Ibby in the Witch City Mysteries.

Don't miss the next adventure of
Lee Barrett and Co.
Coming soon
And be sure to read
All the books in the Witch City series
Available now from
Carol J. Perry
and
Kensington Books

Connect with Us

Visit us online at
KensingtonBooks.com
to read more from your favorite authors, see books
by series, view reading group guides, and more.

for sneak peeks, chances to win books and prize packs,
and to share your thoughts with other readers.

facebook.com/kensingtonpublishing
twitter.com/kensingtonbooks

Tell us what you think!

To share your thoughts, submit a review,
or sign up for our eNewsletters, please visit:
KensingtonBooks.com/TellUs.